# Before The Brightest Dawn

# The Half-Bloods Trilogy Book 3

# Jana Petken

ISBN: 9781072655701

Before The Brightest Dawn is a work of fiction and bears
no factual resemblance to the fictional characters or what
happens to them in the story.
Cover design by Adriana Hanganu

**Synopsis: Before The brightest Dawn**

**Jana Petken's extraordinary historical epic, The German Half-Bloods Trilogy, reaches its sweeping, heart-wrenching conclusion.**

In *The German Half-Bloods* and *The Vogels,* Jana Petken followed the turbulent lives of an Anglo-German family as they forged their paths through the Second World War. Now, the conflict intensifies in the Soviet States, the boiling Western Desert of North Africa, and the growing resistance movement in Poland.

Will Max, Paul, and Wilmot Vogel survive the most ruthless phase of the war to date?

Max takes a path to momentous events in North Africa where he balances undercover games of espionage in decadent Cairo with dangerous missions behind the German Afrika Korps' lines.

Paul's loyalty to the Third Reich continues to wane as Germany's extermination programmes in Poland expand, and he is stalked by the new Kriminalinspektor, Manfred Krüger. Can he stay one step ahead of a man who has been ordered to destroy him?

Wilmot faces new challenges in the Afrika Korps, but is he mentally and physically prepared to lead his men into Libya's fiery desert and against the British 8th Army?

Before The Brightest Dawn, the long-awaited Book 3 of the Half-Bloods Trilogy, concludes the story of the inextricably entangled fates of three brothers … through a war that becomes increasingly brutal and cruel.

## Other titles available from Jana Petken:

Multi Award Winning #1Bestseller, **The Guardian of Secrets**
Screenplay, **The Guardian of Secrets**
#1 Bestselling Series: **The Mercy Carver Series:**
Award-Winning Bestseller **Dark Shadows**
Award-Winning Bestseller **Blood Moon**
Multi-Award-Winning #1Bestseller, **The Errant Flock**
Award-Winning Bestseller, **The Scattered Flock**
Award Winning, **Flock, The Gathering of The Damned**
Multi-Award-Winning #1Bestseller, **Swearing Allegiance**
Multi Award Winning, #1 Bestseller, **The German Half-Bloods**
**#1Bestseller The Vogels: On All Fronts**
**Before The Brightest Dawn**

## Audio Books

**The Guardian of Secrets,** in association with Tantor Media
**Swearing Allegiance, The Mercy Carver Series, The Flock Trilogy.**
**The German Half-Bloods.**
in association with Cherry-Hill Audio Publishing
In production: **The Vogels: On all Fronts**

## Acknowledgements

Many thanks to my dear readers.
Thanks to my editor, Patricia Rose
Proofreading and historical fact checker, Caro Powney
Adriana Hanganu, Graphics and cover design

## Author's Note

This book is written in UK English and all spellings, punctuations, and grammar adhere to UK English, World English, and the Oxford English Dictionary
Hope you enjoy, ***Before The Brightest Dawn!***

# Part One

*"If such a thing as sympathy existed in war, no one would die, and soldiers would shake hands with the enemy and march homewards without a drop of blood being spilt. Empathy, thoughtfulness, even conscience are luxuries we can ill afford. There is only duty – that is everything."*

*Manfred Krüger, Kriminalinspektor Gestapo.*
*Łódź, Poland, 1942*

*Jana Petken*

# *Chapter One*

## Max Vogel

*Cairo, Egypt*
*29 June 1942*

Max sauntered through the streets of Cairo's commercial centre, situated between Miden Ismail Pasha and Ezbekieh Gardens. Everyone ambled at a slow, easy pace; Cairo was as hot as hell, sucking the life and energy out of the people living there during summertime. This district was a cauldron. Broad streets were lined with office buildings, apartment blocks, the odd department store, banks, cinemas, cafés, and nightclubs. The taller buildings blocked the hot and uncomfortable afternoon breezes from flowing freely while affording welcome shade; he didn't know what was worse, a stinging breeze or no air.

He marvelled at the architectural styles of the structures: Viennese, Italian, Art Nouveau, and flamboyant Neo-Arabic with intricate engravings. Cairo had many faces, Max had discovered on his orientational trips around the vast city, and he knew most of them.

For British troops in the desert, the capital meant fleshpots and military brass hats, a boiling version of square-bashing, field exercises, and nightly battles with bedbugs. It held the promise of barrels of cold beer, exotic Egyptian women with piercings in bare bellies that rippled like gentle waves when in dance, and European escorts, more than willing to open their legs for a price to tired, lonely soldiers.

For well-connected officers, the city signified polo matches or rounds of golf at the Gezira Club, cocktails on the Shepheard Hotel's terrace, and swanky dinners requiring black-tie formalwear at the Turf Club; an establishment favoured by the Egyptian royals. This Cairene scene suited many British business and military men, who lived a life far beyond what their wallets could have afforded back in Britain. It was easy-going, trivial, elegant, and hedonistic.

When Max arrived at The Shepheard Hotel, a Cairo landmark some said was second only to the great pyramids, he headed towards the Moorish Hall. It lay beyond the terrace where wicker chairs and tables commanded a lofty, yet shaded, view of the city. As he weaved his way through the crowded area, he overheard two British men lamenting that they'd pinned all their hopes and money on a country that was now in danger of being overrun by Rommel's Afrika Korps or an enormous influx of British soldiers who would undoubtedly tarnish Cairo's sophisticated, well-mannered character.

"I don't know which would be worse … seeing a Nazi general sitting here drinking a schnapps or watching a troop of His Majesty's soldiers vomiting beer on Cairo's streets," one of the men complained.

The other whined, "Let's face it, Cairo's not been the same since those lower-class refugees from the Balkans descended on us. I fear life as we know it has gone forever, old chap."

Max moved on, leaving the mishmash of resentful, bitter voices on the terrace and entering the Moorish Hall. People flocked there during the hottest time of the day to hide from the brilliance and heat of the midday sun. It was deliciously cool and dimly lit by the coloured-glass dome ceiling that sat high above small diagonal tables and stumpy-legged stools being occupied by men with sour, worried frowns.

With his eyes becoming accustomed to the dimness, Max searched the faces of men in the dining room area sitting in small groups on padded, dining-room chairs positioned around small circular and rectangular linen-covered tables. The place gave an air of intimacy, and more importantly, discretion, which was precisely why it had been chosen for the forthcoming meeting.

Finally, Max spotted British Intelligence officer, Captain Theobald Kelsey, and his Egyptian MI6 counterpart, Gaidar Shalhoub. Both men stood at the entrance, as Max had done, their eyes sweeping the room and blinking away any residual flashes of sunlight on their retinas.

Max raised his hand in a subtle wave while guarding the only available table, which, as luck would have it, was in a corner position and had only four chairs around it.

The three men shook hands in a businesslike fashion. "It's a hot one today," Theobald Kelsey, known as Theo, said.

"It's hot every day," Gaidar Shalhoub scoffed. "You English make me smile. You complain about the heat you expertly avoid, whilst we Arabs toil in the fields without complaint or respite. You should both try it one day." Gaidar took a seat. He was exceptionally tall and spare for an Arab; as tall as Max's height of six-foot-three. Coal-black hair framed an unusual face; instead of the typical hooked Arab nose, his was straight, short, and tilted upwards at its tip. He was endowed, however, with large, almost black almond-shaped eyes, framed with eyelashes that any woman would envy. And to top off that feminine feature, he also had full pouting lips above a hairless chin. His mother, he'd informed

Max, was Egyptian, his father an English diplomat who had died years earlier. He held both Egyptian and British passports.

Max took his seat. "I'm glad you could keep our appointment," he said, his voice laced with a heavy German accent. "Everyone is in a bit of a flap today."

"Yes, we're all a bit nervy, what with Rommel being so close to Alexandria. The world is going to hell, but we still need to know the time, eh?" Theo smiled.

Max gestured to his briefcase. "*Ja* … I have plenty of watches with me. Let's order drinks before we get down to business. You're looking decidedly sunburnt and freckled, Captain Kelsey."

"Cairo will do that to a peely-wally Englishman, Herr Fischer."

Max rested his briefcase against the leg of the table. Full of genuine Swiss timepieces, pricelists, and an array of interchangeable straps, it had become increasingly heavy on his walk. He gestured to a waiter and slipped into his Swiss-watch salesman's cover.

"Whisky? Theo?"

"Sounds good. Water on the side for me," Theo replied.

"Tea for me," Gaidar said, directing his request to the arriving waiter.

After ordering, Max sat back in his chair and sighed with relief as his hot skin cooled. "I love this place," he said.

"It has been around forever, or so it seems. The British are proud of it. In the last century, it was home base for travellers on some of the earliest expeditions organised by Thomas Cook," Gaidar explained. "My grandfather told me stories of archaeologists of great note who stayed here when taking a break or trying to garner more funds for their digs from wealthy patrons. We are in more sinister times, I'm sorry to say. Nowadays, it is the perfect haunt to do business and find out the latest news on the war and the order of battles to come. Not quite the romantic picture of old, eh?"

"How's business?" Theo asked Max.

"Couldn't be better." Max lifted his case, put it on the table, and then opened it to reveal a selection of watches.

Theo casually glanced around the room. The young freckled-faced man was of medium height and build with a mop of sandy hair, worn straight from the pages of a 1920s magazine. He plastered it to his head with a deep side parting, using English Lavender Brilliantine to keep it in place. His nose was birdlike; hooked, and thin and pointy at the end. His most noticeable feature, however, was his limp. He'd been wounded the previous year in the Tobruk siege and had almost lost his foot. He wouldn't see action again but being kept on in Cairo made him feel useful, he'd told Max at their first meeting.

Disapproving patrons ogled Max from their tables. He wasn't popular in this city. If the British clientele had their way, they would get him kicked out of their social haunts. If it weren't for Theo and Gaidar, both MI6 officers, keeping him out of trouble, he would probably be in a British prison with some bogus charge to his name. He had come close. The British in Egypt hated his German accent and the fact that he was from neutral Switzerland, a country that still did business with Axis countries as well as the Allies. Max had heard men grumble that the Swiss government had no morals, no shame. It would sell to the devil for profit.

Max ignored the British *down-the-nose* glares while laying out a display of fobs and wristwatches. "Take your time," he grinned at Gaidar, "and excuse the pun."

The waiter appeared with the men's drinks. Max, giving Theo and Gaidar a moment to study each watch, sipped his whisky whilst keeping his hooded eyes on the men at the table closest to him. He felt vulnerable, naked, *out in the cold.* His previous missions had always been conducted in enemy territory in a foreign country, but Egypt was like an extension of Britain, with more snobbery and backbiting to deal with, and he was having a hard time adjusting to his Swiss character. This time, he was not afraid of being arrested by the Gestapo but by British authorities who might see him as a spy. He was treading a hazardous path in Egypt, and although necessary, he was uncomfortable using the exaggerated German accent.

With another swallow of his scotch, he brushed aside his concerns. His cover was solid. He had gone to great lengths to consolidate it with bad behaviour in the most public places. Twice he had instigated a brawl in a Cairo nightclub with two British army officers, and on another occasion, he'd bad-mouthed Winston Churchill, saying he blew more smoke out his arse than out of his cigar-loving mouth. No, Rolf Fischer wasn't popular, but infamy had been his objective.

He lived and breathed Rolf. He conducted secret meetings in various public venues, deserted buildings, and in the desert itself under the stars. Cairo was a hotbed for spies – he didn't know how many British or German agents were operating in the North Africa arena, but he surmised that MI6 and the Abwehr didn't either. Everyone, including petted wives of important diplomats, wanted to shroud themselves in suspicion and intrigue. They craved a piece of the Cairo notoriety and mystique that their peers perpetually talked about; holding onto tantalising rumours that might give them currency and make them stand out in a crowd.

"Are you selling many watches on this trip?" Gaidar asked Max.

"Yes, I'm pleased to say I am," Max replied. "Despite the Allies establishing a blacklist of Swiss firms who trade with Germany and Italy, I'm doing more business with the British than ever. Every officer I meet wants to wear a new wristwatch." He smiled to cover his lie; he had sold a grand total of six watches since his arrival in the country six weeks earlier. "I am selling my products at good prices to the English, but they don't appreciate how small my profit margin is. You fellows are not easy to barter with, especially northerners."

"Don't you mean the Scots?" Theo said, himself being from Manchester.

"No, the Scots are my best customers, and they always throw a whisky or two into the deal."

The discussion turned more serious. Being in the corner afforded the three men a view of the entire room, and after sitting there for a while, they could now gauge who might be close enough to hear their conversation and monitor people who were arriving and leaving. This setup reminded Max of the lunch he'd had almost three months earlier with Judith in London. She had wanted … no, needed, to speak German to express herself, just as he needed to have a candid conversation with Theo and Gaidar Shalhoub about the case they were working on together.

"How is your friend, Anubis? Any problems with him?" Theo finally got to the grain of the meeting.

Max pondered the question of his asset. To the world at large, Anubis El-Masri was a well-to-do Egyptian translator working for the British Consulate in Alexandria. The man behind the façade, however, had been born into poverty on the banks of the River Nile at Luxor and had spent his formative years pickpocketing tourists. Innovative, and with a brilliant mind, he had made the British blacklist as a racketeer. Life could have ended badly for him, but British Intelligence had seen something in the unassuming-looking Arab. He'd been exactly what they'd been looking for: wily, a great liar, a flatterer, and an entertaining storyteller.

From nothing, Anubis had set up his racket using organised gangs of British army deserters to rob Ordnance Corp and NAAFI stores, and he was so successful that SOE had ordered he be handed over to them when captured. Tough luck for SOE that MI6 had got to him first, offering the man a choice between life as a British spy or being taken out to the desert and shot in the head along with the deserters he'd trained.

"Let's say if it were not for our soldiers holding his family hostage, I wouldn't trust the man as far as I could spit. Having said that, he's sticking to our bargain. I think he's finally made a breakthrough. We're getting close."

"To a suspect?" Theo's face lit up.

"Yes. Anubis thinks so. He's befriended a Sudanese driver at the consular offices … a bit of a loner, originally from Cairo, with a wife and five children. He'd be uninteresting were it not for a rather revealing conversation he had with our man."

"Oh?"

Max nodded. "This man – Abu Hanifa is his name – wanted to know if Anubis studied his Koran, and if he did, how often he devoted his time to it. He said he knew scholars who could give instruction and open Anubis' eyes to the evil of British occupation."

Max paused to glance around the immediate area, then leant in to take a handful of peanuts from the glass bowl on the table. "When Anubis feigned interest, Abu let slip he was a member of the Muslim Brotherhood."

"Could he be our murderer? Our way into the Islamist group?" Gaidar asked.

"I don't know, but this initial contact is a step in the right direction."

"Does Anubis know everything about the operation?"

"No, not yet. He knows he's part of a murder investigation, and there is a connection between the two murdered men and the Muslim Brotherhood. I told him that Farid, the Arab employee, was stabbed nine times in what was an angry, personally motivated attack. Anubis then asked why John Bryant, the MI6 agent, was strangled in an alleyway in Cairo when he worked in Alexandria's consular offices. He suspects Bryant was a spy."

Gaidar's eyes widened in surprise. "That's not good."

"Anubis is a thinker, Gaidar. He analyses everything I say. He's not stupid, and I won't keep him in the dark for much longer. The way I see it, the more I tell him, the more he'll trust me."

For show, Max handed Theo a watch. The latter turned it over in his fingers and studied the face and back of it. "Go on."

"I admitted to Anubis that Bryant *was* a British intelligence agent who'd been investigating the Muslim Brotherhood's false propaganda operations against the British. He asked about Farid, the dead Egyptian boy, and his connection to Bryant. I explained that according to the consulate's records, Farid accompanied John Bryant on trips to Cairo. He was at John's beck and call and could've known about Bryant's operation to infiltrate the Brotherhood's gunrunning operations."

Max popped a few nuts into his mouth and crunched. "That's all he knows, and all he will know until I'm ready for phase two."

Theo nodded his agreement. "One step at a time. Well played, sir."

Max sipped his drink, set the glass on the table and asked Gaidar, "Why haven't the Egyptian Army made more Muslim Brotherhood arrests? You must have an idea of where they hold their meetings, or at least an inkling of where their leaders live?"

Gaidar tried a watch on for size. "We do know where they held their last meeting, but because of my government's success in suppressing the group's militant activities, their Supreme Guide, Hassan el Banna, has agreed to halt *all* violence until the war in this region ends. It's a tacit agreement, but an accord, nonetheless. I suppose they don't want to upset the status quo."

Gaidar spooned sugar into his tea and continued, "You must understand, the Muslim Brotherhood extends all the way to our Egyptian military academy and into our universities. I believe it also has supporters in the palace. We have uncovered a secret officer's association within our army and air force, and we know the ring extends the palace's protection to certain young officers in return for their devoted obedience to the group. We do not want to chop off the arms of the group; we want its head, and that will not be easy to obtain when the leadership is behaving itself, both politically and militarily."

Theo, on a completely different tack, said, "They can smell a rat a mile off, as John Bryant sadly found out for himself…"

Max gasped as a familiar figure sauntered into the Moorish Hall.

"Are you all right?" Gaidar looked concerned.

Max recovered, but his heart still raced. "Yes. Sorry, I thought I knew someone … ach, I think I've had too many whiskies and too much Egyptian sun. Where were we?"

Gaidar handed Max a roll of English pounds, concealing a piece of paper containing a message from Heller in London. Then he put the watch he'd just purchased on again. "Please remember, it will take some time to get you a meeting with the Brotherhood Council … months, perhaps. First step: your asset, Anubis, must be accepted by the group."

Max agreed. "Which is why being *pally* with the Sudanese man is important."

Gaidar concurred and continued, "Step two. If he can get in with the group, he must focus on the military wing."

"You mean the Secret Apparatus?"

Gaidar nodded. "They're the ones who will be interested in buying weapons. Step three. Once he tells the Brotherhood about your devotion to Adolf Hitler and interest in selling guns to the Nazis for use against the British, they will begin to follow you everywhere you go. They will dissect every aspect of your life, both in Cairo and in Alexandria, and only when they have decided you are genuine and not a threat, will they allow you within ten feet of the Secret Apparatus leader – one sniff of you being undercover for the British, and they will take your head, no explanation given – yes, Theo, like John Bryant."

Max knew how dedicated members of the Muslim Brotherhood were. In April of the previous year, Rommel had been advancing on Egypt. The British had pulled back the Arab units at the front to stop the gunrunning operations which were going on in these far-flung outposts between Egyptian soldiers and the radical Islamists. Disloyalty and deceit were everywhere, which was probably the reason his MI6 colleague, John Bryant, had got himself killed.

Gaidar's face creased with a frown. "Make no mistake, Herr Fischer, we have tried this approach several times, and we have failed."

"Ah, but you have not tried it with me," Max grinned.

The Egyptian's scowl increased until his eyebrows met in the middle with anger. "You think this is a joke? It is deadly serious…"

"We'd better get back to the office. Yes … it's late," Theo stuttered. "It's been good doing business with you, Herr Fischer."

Theo stood, abruptly ending the meeting and stopping Gaidar from saying anything else for the moment.

After Theo had said his goodbyes, Gaidar reluctantly shook Max's hand. "You become cocky, as you English say, and you are a dead man on a street in Cairo," he muttered in Max's ear.

# *Chapter Two*

Alone, Max ordered another whisky while willing his brother-in-law to turn in his chair and spot him. Had Max not already been sitting, he would have fallen over when he saw Frank Middleton stroll into the place. This day had just got better.

Feigning a relaxed pose, Max opened his briefcase displaying his watches. He held his newspaper below face level so that Frank could see him if he turned, and he had his empty whisky glass by his side. His cover was secure. He wasn't going anywhere until he'd spoken to his best friend.

A while later, Max's head shot up from his newspaper at the sound of Frank's booming voice.

"Ah, there's the Swiss watch bloke. I think I'll treat myself. My damn watch keeps losing time," Frank said to the men he was preparing to leave with.

After Frank's company had mumbled their disapproval to him, they left.

Frank sat next to Max and beamed. "Well, sink me in the bloody Med. You're the last person I thought I'd see here."

"I'm glad you remembered my Swiss cover. Nicely done, Frank."

Satisfied they were being largely ignored and that the people at the nearest table were on their feet about to leave as well, Max asked, "Any news from home?"

"Yes, at last," Frank replied when the people had left the hall. "I got a letter from Hannah. She's moved in with your parents, and she's much happier. I hated that she was living in Kent with the baby and having to travel to see your mum and dad every week. At least they're all together now, and far enough away from London for me not to worry too much about the damn air raids hitting the capital."

"Did she mention the situation between Judith and me?" Max asked.

"Situation? That's a bit on the formal side for what you two have done," Frank laughed. "Yes, of course she did. Judith is spending a lot of time in London, working with Heller. Hannah told me your fiancée is happy. Worried about you, but also excited about the wedding. Your sister also said you're planning on getting married as soon as you get back to England. Is that true?"

"Yes, the sooner, the better."

Frank lit a cigarette while holding Max's eyes. "I don't mind telling you, I was shocked when I read about you and Judith getting together. I didn't even know you'd been seeing her." Frank hesitated, as though considering his words. "Are you sure about your feelings, Max? Don't get me wrong. I like Judith, but you hardly know the girl. Has this anything to do with you trying to get over Klara Gabula? Damn shame about her death. Dying on a jump is a bloody awful way to go."

"No. How I feel about Judith has nothing to do with Klara." Max shook off his hatred of Florent Duguay. Frank apparently didn't know the real story of Klara's death, and he was not going to share classified material, not even with his sister's husband. "I saw a lot of Judith when I was in England, Frank," he said, returning to a more pleasant subject. "We spent enough time together for me to know. I've never felt this way before … not with anyone."

Frank nodded, satisfied with Max's answer. "And here's me thinking I'd be your best man if you ever got hitched.

Thought I might even have to fight Paul for the job. It's not right … you, tying the knot without your brothers and me by your side … especially Paul, given his association with Judith."

"I know. I don't suppose you've got news of Paul and Wilmot?"

"No. Sorry, mate."

Disappointed and with a heavy heart, Max's eyes swept the area again. He'd like nothing more than to talk all day about Judith and his two brothers – who were still missing as far as their family were concerned – but he and Frank had little time before someone would get suspicious. Frank could only take so long to choose a watch or converse with a stranger from Switzerland.

"It's a mess over here." Frank's expression grew serious as he fingered a watch.

For the first time, Max noted the dark, unhealthy rings under Frank's eyes. "What *are* you doing in Egypt?"

"Various things, but not what I was sent out to do … that was a bloody nonstarter." Frank continued to handle a watch, turning it over in his fingers, peering closely at the quality inscription on the back of it. "I was originally sent here to turn Italian fascists being held in prisons on the Delta to our side. We thought they might already be disillusioned with Mussolini; we could train them, then send them back to work on the downfall of *Il Duce's* regime. Hard to believe, but so far, we've not found one recruit. Our failure is probably the reason I got shifted into a commando group a month after I got here."

Frank drew on his cigarette. "Our defences have fallen like skittles, Max. We had what looked like an impregnable line

17

from Gazala to Bir-Hakeim. It was well-constructed with a series of fortified barbed wire areas and minefields. We had rough-made dugouts big enough to house a brigade with field artillery, armoured car units, and camouflaged tanks to boot.

"Our battalions dug in for the long-term with underground bunkers with reinforced ceilings to resist air raids. We had plenty of food, medicine, and ammunition, and we'd planted over a million mines in the desert between the keeps and dugouts. We thought we were set. Then Rommel's Panzers smashed into our armour and dug into the middle of the British positions. At one point, they were behind our lines!" Frank rolled his eyes. "In their wisdom, the British commanders thought they'd keep the krauts busy in an area known as the Cauldron, called that for obvious reasons – did you know you could fry an egg on the ground in that place?"

"Really? And who'd want to eat a dirty egg?" Max grinned. "Sorry, carry on."

Frank chuckled then grew serious again. "That was another mess. It was all over when Rommel took out one of our dugouts and almost two thousand men with it."

"Jesus, I heard it was bad," Max said, having heard a more palatable version from Theo days earlier.

"It was a lot worse than bad. The Free-French Forces at Bir-Hakeim also surrendered," Frank continued. "There are hundreds of miles of road going around the North African coastline. Airfields lying behind the highway are full of stores, ammunition, gasoline dumps, and military vehicles. We managed to get into a couple of Rommel's depots and do significant damage to his supplies. That slowed him down, but to be honest, I don't know how we're going to stop him –

Christ, he's sixty fucking miles from Alexandria. Who'd have thought it?"

Given they were in a public place, Max was loath to ask too many questions or prolong the conversation, but no one was paying them the slightest attention. He knew about the latest British defeat; everyone in Cairo had heard about the fall of Tobruk and Rommel's superhuman advances. What he didn't know was why Frank was still in Egypt.

Whilst looking at watches, Frank pre-empted Max's question. "I've been attached to a team who are carrying out commando-style raids in the desert in the effort to damage Rommel's supply lines. I can't say any more than that, Max."

Max surmised that the teams were operating in secret, unknown even to each other. Heller had spoken about a new unit called Special Air Services, or SAS, being set up in North Africa.

"How the hell did we let Rommel take Tobruk?" Max hissed. Not having military contacts in Cairo, he had depended on Theo Kelsey's intelligence to know on what was going on in the desert. According to him, the British Commander-in-Chief of the Middle East theatre, General Claude Auchinleck, had insisted Tobruk be held at all costs.

'Easy to say, when he's on Shepheard Hotel's terrace sipping mint-juleps and kissing the hands of refugee royals like the ex-Prince Regent of Yugoslavia, Prince Paul, and his wife, Princess Olga,' Theo had spat during that conversation. Then he had added that Auchinleck was a mediocre general, who was overconfident and overly optimistic about his chances of defeating Rommel. 'He's a man who believes in perpetual British Empire glory but ignores the messy parts that go into achieving and maintaining it.'

"Rommel's forces broke through the Eighth Army lines to Tobruk's town and harbour," Frank finally answered Max's question. "I saw how hard our soldiers fought. If you ask me, they hung on for as long as they did because of their courage, and despite the mismanagement and military incompetence at the top. Command headquarters looked like a bloody harassed committee with the left arm not knowing what the right one was doing. Supplies and reinforcements were juggled about and cobbled together as the moment dictated – total chaos in careless hands."

"The BBC should be shot and dragged through the coals for its broadcasts," Max said, veering from the topic of battle. "Saying Tobruk might be lost, but it wasn't that important anyway must have demoralised the shit out of our troops fighting for their lives inside that town."

"I'd shoot the announcer myself if I could get my hands on the idiot. To be honest, Max, we had no answer for the Germans' bombardments of the harbour. They sent wave after wave of Stukas, plus we were expecting the assault to come from the south-western sector, but the sly bastards came in from the south-east. The South Africans held the harbour for a while after the Eighth Army retreated, and when they were eventually pushed out, they burnt all our petrol and pierced every water tanker they could find. Tell you what, if I hear any bluffer making excuses about this loss, I'll belt him in the mouth."

Frank handed the watch back to Max, regret crossing his face. "I need to go. It's been great seeing you, Max, but we won't be meeting again, at least not here. I'm being shipped to Jerusalem tomorrow. SOE's Cairo branch has established a commando and parachute training school near Haifa. I suppose I'll be teaching there for quite some time."

The men grew silent. Max was also disheartened. He'd cheered up no end when he'd thought there was a chance of seeing Frank around the city.

"Short but sweet, eh, Frank?" Max said, shaking Frank's hand.

"At least, you know where I'll be," Frank said, apparently gauging Max's mood. "When you get home, tell Hannah I love her."

Max smiled as he replaced the watch in its case. "Here, take this as a gift. Heller's office paid for them."

# *Chapter Three*

*Alexandria, Egypt*
*30 June 1942*

After an hour and a half spent travelling on an almost-empty train from Cairo, Max arrived in the coastal city of Alexandria. A week earlier, the same train had been full of people, desperate to escape the capital's oppressive heat and to have a pleasant summer by the sea. Today, however, Alexandria was synonymous with fear; it was going to fall to Rommel, and the British were preparing their messy exit in full view of the Egyptian residents.

"We're getting out before the Germans get in. We're going to South Africa. It's the safest place left to us," Max overheard one man saying to another on the crowded platform.

Max, although understanding why he was witnessing the most substantial exodus from Egypt since Moses and the Jews, was still confident the British could hold the Germans and their Afrika Korps back. Yes, they had seemed unstoppable; striking deep into Egypt and threatening the vital Allied supply line across the Suez Canal. They'd pursued the chaotic British Eighth Army like adults chasing short-legged children, but the situation had changed. Rommel now had overextended supply lines and a lack of reinforcements. His troops were desert-weary and physically exhausted, and though he might yet surge forward before the Allies built up their defences, Max thought it unlikely. Even the *Great*

*Rommel,* thus named by treacherous Arabs, would have to regain his strength. He was not invincible, and neither were his men.

Taxis, most of them mule or horse-driven, arrived at the station's drop-off point then drove off again to look for new passengers trying to get to the trains. Max decided to walk to his destination to get a better sense of the city's mood and to see the bomb damage from a recent heavy air raid.

Egypt's two major towns painted a stark contrast to one another, Max thought. Cairo, an Islamic centre looking to the East, was embroiled in politics and royal court scandals. Alexandria, Greek-Levantine, faced the Mediterranean, thrived on summer tourism, and had a strong expatriate presence, dominated by Greeks. It was a playground, and unlike Cairo, it catered to the poor as well as the rich.

The city centre was almost deserted and eerily quiet. Max heard no noisy street vendors and saw no Arabic men chatting or debating outside cafés while puffing away on their shisha pipes. He looked at his watch; it was prayer time, when the world stopped.

A few foreign women were doing their rounds of the shops – *things must be dire.* On the Corniche, where entire families usually ate outside cafés under straw shadings, tables and chairs were empty. Instead of the cacophony of city noises, telephones rang intermittently in empty houses whilst outside their residents packed up cars with belongings, and strapped mattresses onto their vehicle roofs as a precaution against falling debris from explosions. Meanwhile, the Egyptians looked on, some amused, others terrified by their British colonials' public withdrawal.

Max halted mid-step, his jaw tightening with indignation. In this commercial street, a shopkeeper was decorating his windows with signs of welcome, written in German, proclaiming: '*Long Live Adolf Hitler.*' Next door, a handwritten placard outside a ladies' dressmaking store said in German and Italian, '*Get out your party dresses – we're on our way!*'

His temper flaring, Max pulled the placard from the window and kicked it halfway along the street, cursing the shopkeeper who ran after him. Perhaps the man was expecting *Il Duce* to ride in on his white stallion claiming victory – Mussolini saw himself as a Caesar in the throes of building a new Roman Empire stretching across the Middle East. The man was as corrupt as Hitler, if not quite as ruthless.

Max had learnt that the Egyptians curried favour with those who held the balance of power and purse strings, but they were not against the idea of transferring their allegiance. Foreigners fuelled the economy, and there was no place for sentiment or loyalty. The British were there today, but the Germans could walk in tomorrow, and the Arabs were prepared to switch portraits of Churchill and King George VI for Hitler and Mussolini at a moment's notice.

Max scoffed at the British incompetence as he strode through the district where the British Consulate and military offices stood. The city couldn't be more inviting to the enemy if it tried. He'd made detailed maps of Alexandria and its harbour and airfield to the west. Each drawing was accompanied by warnings to the Intelligence services in London about the danger of clustering innumerable tanks of crude oil and benzine together in small areas and surrounding them with timber yards, warehouses, and a highly populous

25

native quarter. Generalleutnant Rommel was now at a railway
halt in a town called El Alamein, sixty miles from this
stunning, ancient city. It didn't take a genius to presume he
had numerous spotters in Alexandria, reporting that a booty of
supplies and gasoline was lying around like a whore with her
legs invitingly open.

When he got to the financial district, Max saw quite a
different sight. These streets were not empty; queues stretched
along the pavements and spilled into the road as people waited
impatiently to withdraw all their money from the banks. He
stopped walking to listen to a heated argument between two
British men, pompously colonial in appearance but cursing
like London dockyard labourers while pushing each other for
a spot further up the line. Tempers were frayed, especially
amongst the Europeans, who were unaccustomed to waiting in
line for anything.

Max backtracked and arrived at an apartment located a
stone's throw from the consular offices. Anubis, his MI6
asset, opened the door.

"You're back, then."

Without waiting for a response, the Egyptian, who came
up to Max's shoulders, walked down the hallway to a room
that was both bedroom and living room.

Max went straight to the shade at the French doors and let
the cool air hit his burning face; his head was a little cooler
since he'd worn his fedora.

Anubis el Masri was a trim, fastidious man, well-groomed
and well-scented. He dabbed on his jasmine-based cologne
numerous times a day, he'd informed Max, after the latter had
remarked that the apartment smelt like a brothel. *I like spices,*
Anubis had explained, but his favourite, harissa chilli-paste

from Tunisia, didn't care much for him. Its smell seeped through his pores along with his sweat and shot out his arse like bullets. *But,* he'd boasted, *I've never been constipated.*

MI6's Egyptian mission, known as Operation Lanner Falcon, was concealed behind two other British operations: one, a double murder investigation; the other, an assignment to identify the gunrunners in the Muslim Brotherhood. As tragic as the death of John Bryant, an MI6 agent, had been, the crime had allowed Max to pursue Heller's primary objective, which Max and one other person in Egypt knew about. That operation had not yet begun.

The murdered men, John Bryant and an Arab boy called Farid, had worked together at the Alexandria consular offices. Anubis, whom MI6 had placed in the same office, was being tasked with finding possible suspects to the murders and integrating himself into the Muslim Brotherhood. He was Max's key to opening that elusive door, but like many other informants he'd had, Anubis was not an enthusiastic participant in Max's game.

"Have you seen the panic out there?" Anubis asked, spreading his arms in horror. "Two-thirds of the British Navy ships have gone. We are defenceless. The BBC bulletins talk of Rommel's successes being due to his superior tactics and weaponry. They are calling the fighting around El Alamein the battle for Egypt – *battle for Egypt!*"

"Calm down. Don't believe everything you hear." Max slumped into a chair, removed his shoes and asked Anubis to bring him water. His face was crimson with heat, and his shirt, damp with sweat, stuck to his skin.

"I should have taken a damn taxi," he muttered, studying Anubis who was filling both a glass and an Arabic coffee pot with water. The pot had so many names, Max couldn't keep up with them all: *dallah, cezve, rikwah* or *kanaka,* depending on which coffee house one went into. He hated the stuff.

"… you want *Qahwah arabiyya* – Arabic coffee?" Anubis asked Max as an afterthought.

Anubis was sullen, either by nature or as a result of his subjugation. He had not volunteered his services; military police were holding his wife and children hostage.
Max, frustrated by the Egyptian's lethargic attitude, had made it clear they would be killed if Anubis betrayed the British. Of course, that was a lie and a cheap tactic, Max admitted, but an effective method of keeping the Egyptian in line. Max appreciated the irony of threatening the man's family; the British were doing to Anubis what the Abwehr had done to Romek when they'd coerced him into working for them. Holding hostages over people's heads was the order of the day in this war.

Anubis, in his late thirties but with skin the colour and texture of a dried prune, had complained to the British authorities upon his arrest the previous summer that the vanity of women was to blame for his downfall. Apparently, European blondes in Alexandria were having a hard time finding peroxide. Anubis, using two small Greek boats, crossed with his band of British deserters and thieves to Malta under a sky of angry Stukas and found a stash of the chemical. Not satisfied with merely that, he and his men then went on to Tunis to stock up on other contraband, such as silk stockings, condoms, spaghetti, cheeses, and medical supplies. He was captured upon his return to Alexandria after one of his buyers had been *encouraged* by the British to give him up. His men were shot by firing squad.

"I won't be going back to the office today," Anubis dourly informed Max. "The consular officers are burning their files. Rumours are spreading that British forces are going to burn everything in Alexandria as they withdraw. It is *haram* – forbidden! This is not their country to burn."

Anubis continued to curse the British, and Max's anger simmered. He hated the rumourmongers. They were causing the mass evacuations and fomenting panic with their over-exaggerated talk of destroying nearby villages. The British contingency plans were, in fact, limited to blowing up the power stations, excluding those harnessed to sewage and irrigation systems.

Despite Anubis' furious glare, Max lit a cheroot and relaxed. It was like staring at another Romek, he thought. The man's eyes were full of condemnation, and he had an ugly downturned curl at the edges of his lips. *Look how well my relationship with Romek turned out.* Max had learnt his lesson on that score; he would not befriend or fully trust Anubis.

The Egyptian handed Max the coffee mug and watched Max lob three sugars into the cup. The former's disapproval was etched in the deep lines between his eyebrows and the way he clicked his tongue, but when he next spoke, it was not about Max's sweet tooth.

"You asked me to spy on my Arab colleagues in the consulate. You told me to look for the Muslim Brotherhood's connection to the people who work there, but you did not say what you were going to do with my information. If you are putting my life in danger, you *will* tell me what your plans are."

Max drew on his thin cigar, and Anubis' eyes narrowed further.

"Why do the British authorities need me to help them solve two murders?" Anubis demanded. "Tell me, Rolf Fischer from Switzerland, whom you are probably not, why are the British military police not in charge of this investigation? And if you are fixated on the people at the consular office, why are you not working there instead of me? You talk like an Englishman, yet you say you are a Swiss businessman whose native tongue is German. I do not know if you are a British intelligence officer or a German spy pretending to be Swiss, but I do know you are a liar. Ever since I met you, I am blind beggar fumbling in the darkness. It is time you gave me answers."

Anubis took a breath, then went to the French doors where the sun was now entering. He closed them, then bleated, "I might be a poor *fellah* to you, but even *fellahin* peasants have the right to ask questions and receive answers when it concerns their safety. They also have a responsibility to keep their families safe, but you have taken that most sacred duty from me. May Allah forgive you for what you are doing to my poor wife and children!"

"Don't be so damn melodramatic," Max grunted.

Anubis, furious now, waved his finger in Max's face. "I know who you are. I can smell the deceit … your dirty tricks." He reopened the French door and spat over the balcony. "That is what I think of you and your English Empire!"

"That would be *British* Empire," Max corrected him, unperturbed by the insults. Had Anubis been more cooperative with the British, they wouldn't have threatened to kill his family, would they?

Anubis returned to his chair and slurped his coffee from a small tubular glass. Eyes blazing, he slammed it into the grooves of its decorative saucer, smashing it into three pieces. He grunted, wiped his mouth, and clearly not finished with Max, hissed, "See what you made me do. What is your real name, eh?"

*Which question should I answer first?* Max pondered, staring at the broken saucer. *The one about why the British military police are not investigating the murders or the question of my identity?*

"If you do not answer my questions, I will go no further with you," Anubis threatened before Max could speak. "I swear to you – whoever you are – I will not. My family will be martyrs!"

Max leant forward in his chair to stub out his cheroot in the ashtray. "Cut it out, Anubis. It is thanks to the British authorities you're not being executed for your crimes, and you know it. You're a free man for as long as you're useful to me, but if you cross me you will get a bullet in your head. Do you understand?"

Anubis gave a reluctant nod.

"Good."

"Am I allowed to ask any questions at all?" Anubis asked in a chastened tone.

"You may, but you will not *demand* answers."

"Very well. Why are you here? Are your military police not clever enough to find a murderer? It has taken me six weeks to befriend the Arabs in the consular office and to uncover the Sudanese driver's allegiance to the Muslim Brotherhood. All that I have done, you could have achieved in a week under interrogations. I know how much the British like to torture people – yes, yes, I know you are British and not a *Herr* this or that or anything."

"The British are efficient, but there's more at stake here than capturing a murderer," Max replied, neither denying nor confirming Anubis' nationality assessment. "Yes, I could have worked at the consulate instead of you, but I wouldn't have got the information you did. Only an Arab can weed out secrets from another Arab. You know that better than I do."

Max swallowed the last of thick powdery coffee laced with cardamom seeds and grimaced at the unpleasant texture and taste on his tongue. "More importantly, had I spoken directly to the Muslims working at the consular offices, I wouldn't now be able to get close to the Brotherhood, who are at the heart of my enquiry."

Anubis' eyes widened in surprise.

Max measured his next words. Give too much away, and he risked being vulnerable. Tell Anubis too little, and he risked losing the man's cooperation. "I am Rolf Fischer, a successful watch salesman and Swiss national. I am most certainly not a German spy. That is all you need to know about me, and what everyone else in Egypt must believe."

Max moved on to more pressing matters. He was tired and could do without this annoying budgie chirping in his ear. "Here's what I can confirm. The murdered men were connected to the Muslim Brotherhood, but perhaps in different ways and for different reasons…"

"I already know that."

"And knowing that, do you think your Sudanese friend was capable of committing these two murders?"

"No. You joke. Abu Hanifa is a small, skinny man with bones almost visible under his skin. He wouldn't be able to punch his way to the bottom of a bucket full of water. How could he strangle the British man, a much bigger and stronger fellow? How would he get to Cairo and back in a matter of hours with the little money the British pay him?"

Max raised a suspicious eyebrow. "How do you know the size of the British man?"

"Everyone at the office is whispering about John Bryant. The Arabs are afraid. They believe they will be blamed for his death. We get the blame for everything."

Max ignored the petty complaint and continued, "Before Bryant died, he'd been investigating the Muslim Brotherhood's propaganda in support of Germany. Unfortunately, his intelligence is sketchy, mostly second-hand and without any eyewitness accounts of where the Islamist group gathers to plan their subversive activities. I know they recruit young men from the Egyptian military academy and universities, but Bryant wasn't successful getting anywhere near the group, which means he was either lax in his job, some of his findings were stolen from other sources, or someone was always one step ahead of him."

Max had never met John Bryant, his fallen MI6 colleague. His records showed him to be a family man, not one to blur lines of conduct or stray from orders. An uninventive but decent agent in his early forties, he'd had years of experience in Egypt and North Africa. He had married an Egyptian woman from a wealthy Cairo family, had three children, and had never been keen to return to Britain. In other words, he had not been hungry for a win.

Max had cooled down, but his skin was still moist, and his hair plastered to his head was itching. He pushed his fingers through it, saying, "According to John Bryant's records, the dead Egyptian, Farid, accompanied him on trips to Cairo. He might have been using the boy to find out more about the

Muslim Brotherhood, as you are doing with your Sudanese friend … maybe Farid knew too much?"

"It is possible, I suppose, that Farid used the opportunity to spy for the Islamist group. It's no secret that young people like the Brotherhood's doctrine," Anubis said, a glimmer of thoughtful optimism in his expression.

"Perhaps. But it's also possible the Islamists found out he was working for British intelligence if, indeed, he was. This is all conjecture … all I have. And now you know what I know."

"I have something for you." Anubis looked pleased with himself. "I have discovered the location of the next Muslim Brotherhood meeting. It will take place in a village outside Alexandria."

"When?" Max shot up in his chair.

"Tomorrow, when the sun goes down. I believe their Supreme Guide, Hasan el Banna, will speak, or someone will deliver texts written in his hand – and I have more for you … my Sudanese friend has asked me to go with him. I will not, of course, but it shows he is beginning to trust me, as we wanted."

Max digested the news with a mixture of excitement and apprehension. This was exactly what he'd been hoping for. Anubis had come through for him, albeit without knowing what he was getting himself into.

"You should go," he said, the cogs in his mind turning. "Ingratiate yourself with the leaders. Find out what they're planning, if they're carrying weapons. Eventually, I want you to get close to the paramilitary branch, the Secret Apparatus, as they're called. Remember names, find out where people work and live, make yourself popular…"

"No. You are a crazy man! The leadership of the *Nizam al-khass* – the Secret Apparatus –is reserved for the elite members of the Muslim Brotherhood, many of whom are influential members of the Guidance Council. This is not an insignificant off-shoot. It is the future. The Supreme Guide is impressed by the fascist youth groups in Italy and Germany, and he wants to establish an Islamic equivalent. He began the Secret Apparatus after compromising with the more radical conservatives who demanded that Islamic tradition and sharia be implemented through force if necessary –"

"You know a lot about them for a man who knew nothing four weeks ago," Max interrupted. "Have you been lying to me? Have you dabbled with this group in the past?"

"I have not. I am interested in enterprise not religion."

Max studied the man's steady gaze. He was probably telling the truth. There were two kinds of Arabs; religious fanatics, or those who craved wealth and power. Anubis was the latter.

"I have taught myself many things over the years," Anubis said matter-of-factly. "Reading material on the Muslim Brotherhood is widely available if a person is looking for it, as are its members, who are more than willing to spread al Banna's doctrine to any Arab who is willing to listen."

When Max said nothing, Anubis stormed from the room, returning moments later waving a sheaf of papers.

"Abu Hanifa told me to study these teachings." he said, leafing through the pages until he found what he was looking for. "Listen to this one: *Allah is our objective, the Qur'an is our constitution, the Prophet is our leader, jihad is our path, and death in the name of Allah is our goal.* I will not get myself killed for British Imperialists. If the Brotherhood find out what I am doing, they will cut my head from my neck and feed it to their dogs. Even if they don't find out I'm working for you, I will never be able to turn my back on them. Once they know my face, they will never un-know it."

Anubis ran nervous fingers through his wiry goatee. "You do not know what these fanatics are capable of … *Allahu akbar,* save me from this!"

Max's eyes were pools of grey ice as he retorted, "Allah can't save you, Anubis. *I* am what stands between you and a firing squad. You will attend this meeting and the one after that, and another and another until you get me an introduction. And you will share everything you hear and see with me – everything."

"You are mad with the Egyptian sun! These people will never agree to seeing a foreigner."

"I think they will – oh, it might take you a month or two to arrange a meeting, but they will see me when the time is right."

Anubis sneered. "Why should they? What can you offer them?"

"They need weapons, money, maybe a way to help Herr Hitler. I can deliver all of those things."

Max yawned, feigning boredom, but inwardly, his pulse was racing with excitement. This was a real breakthrough. Theo had been candid the previous day about Max's limited chance of success. British intelligence had a lousy record for infiltrating the Muslim Brotherhood's meetings for good reason, he'd said. British authorities had arrested members of the group and other Arabs who were too vocal with anti-British rhetoric, but the prisoners had always been released at the request of the Egyptian government, without having cooperated. MI6 had given money to young Arabs to spy on students in Cairo University, that being one of the Brotherhood's recruitment centres, but every one of their embedded men had betrayed the British and sworn loyalty to the Islamists.

"I'm a patient man, Anubis. If your Sudanese friend is the killer we're looking for, he will confess to you. It might take him a week or a month, but eventually, you'll gain his trust and he'll tell you. If he isn't the murderer, he will lead you to the person who is. In the meantime, let him take you to the meetings. It's time for you to do what you do best..."

"And what is that?"

"Lie."

Anubis shot Max a thunderous look.

Max stood, stretched his muscles, and then changed his antagonistic tone to one that was almost friendly. "C'mon, Anubis, you're a charmer. You managed to recruit British deserters into your little racketeering business, so I'm certain you can walk through the Muslim Brotherhood's door. You must do it; if not for yourself, for your family. You don't really want them to be martyrs, do you?"

Anubis flinched. "I will do as you ask," he muttered.

# *Chapter Four*

## Wilmot Vogel

*Berlin, Germany*
*2 July 1942*

Wilmot got off the train at Berlin's *Anhalter Bahnhof* station, situated five hundred metres southeast of Potsdamer Platz. Outside, soldiers he'd been on the train with were fighting to clamber onto the only tram in sight. In the busy streets around the station, he saw a handful of cars and buses, but hundreds of people walking. The Reich was short of fuel. Romania and Hungary supplied a large percentage of Germany's needs, but it was not enough to satisfy the appetite of the Wehrmacht's gas-guzzling tanks and fighter planes. He'd seen for himself how much fuel was used on the push into the Soviet Union – *stop it, Willie. You're on leave. Forget about the war for five minutes and enjoy yourself.*

He had no hope of finding a taxi, nor any desire to make his way to his parents' house by tram. No one would be there to greet him anyway, unless Paul were back. What a marvellous coincidence that would be.

After giving himself a good talking to about forgetting the war for a while, Wilmot crossed the road to the street leading to Potsdamer Platz. Happiness surged through him as he sauntered along with his army sack slung over his shoulder, his greatcoat doubled over its strap, and his army boots thumping the pavement as he tried to balance the weight. He was home; seeing, hearing, smelling, touching his Berlin in every brick, street, and tree he passed. Swastika banners fluttered on lampposts, pictures of Herr Hitler adorned shop windows. *I've met him, spoken to him;* an unbelievable event that he replayed every day in his mind's eye. He wanted to share that memory with the people walking on the pavement with him, to confide in them his faith, that der Führer would lead Germany to victory and into a brighter, better future.

Wilmot drank a beer and smoked a cigarette in a Potsdamer bar he used to frequent as an adolescent, although he'd not been old enough to drink schnapps then or be out after midnight. Come to think of it, he'd not been the best of sons, he acknowledged, savouring every mouthful of German ale. Max and Paul had been the studious ones in the family, the good, obedient boys who were happy doing as they were told. But not Willie; he was the youngest, the sometimes-forgotten brother who was left to his own devices most of the time because his parents were far too busy, and his brothers were much older than he and barely acknowledged his existence.

In the Biergarten, he sat at a table alone, breathing in the aroma of German hops and malt; real beer, not like that piss-water in Finland. *Ach, I've made it home. The army has been good to me.*

The journey had been perfect; he'd been extremely lucky to get on a supply plane from Viipuri, with a smooth flight to Brand-Briesen Airfield at Brandenburg.

When it landed on the single thousand-metre airfield, a truck had been waiting to take him and fellow soldiers, also on leave, to the Brandenburg train station. There, he'd had a fifteen-minute wait in the sunshine and a great conversation with other military men who were genuinely interested in how he'd come to receive his Iron Cross.

After three beers, Wilmot walked back through the bar towards the exit. In the hallway, a public telephone hung on the wall. He searched his pocket, pulled out a handful of pfennigs, and put them on the narrow counter. Then he searched his wallet for a small, folded piece of paper. The beer had made him sentimental. He was becoming gloomy at the thought of going home to an empty house. He'd kill to see his mother and brothers, to hug Hannah, even to have a decent conversation with Frank; he wasn't such a bad man.

A terrible thought struck him. *Is my parents' house still standing? Had Berlin suffered air raids?* He hadn't seen much bomb damage on his way into the capital; a few damaged buildings but nothing to write home about. And here in the centre, everything looked the same as it had on the day he'd left for Poland, three years earlier. The shelves in the shops were bare in places; the butcher's shop his mother liked was closed, and apart from a few ladies' dress shops displaying tired-looking costumes, window displays seemed to be a thing of the past. He wasn't worried; the allies couldn't hit Berlin. His house was safe, and he was working himself into a morbid state of mind when he should be celebrating his homecoming.

He dialled the telephone number on the piece of paper and after three rings, Kriminaldirektor Fredrich Biermann answered. "*Ja...?*"

"Hello, Herr Kriminaldirektor Biermann, sir. It's Wilmot Vogel, here. I'm home ... well, I got off the train in Berlin an hour ago." He tensed at the long silence on the other end. "Hello, sir ... are you there?"

"Wilmot – *ja,* Wilmot, it's good to hear from you. Are you on leave?"

"Yes, sir. It came right out of the blue. I was told last night. They said not to leave anything behind, so I'm half expecting to be posted somewhere else when my two-week holiday is over."

Another long pause.

"I was wondering if I could see you, sir … perhaps meet for a beer … or a spot of lunch, maybe? I'll see my aunt and uncle while I'm here, of course, but it would be nice to thank you in person for your kindness to me when my father died."

A strange clicking sound and static that grew and dimmed in volume continued for a full minute, then Biermann's faint voice came back. "Of course, Wilmot. I'll send a car to your parents' house this evening at seven. My wife and daughter, and Paul's daughter as well, will be delighted to see you."

Wilmot's eyes filled with tears, the beer making him emotional. "I have a niece … Paul's? *Göttergestalt* … my God, how wonderful!"

When he hung up, Wilmot sniffed and wiped his eyes. *Silly sod.* He'd survived Russia. He was probably one of a handful of men who had escaped Russian capture, and here he was, weeping like a girl. He was an uncle. Paul was a father! Christ, who'd have thought it?

*Now I will take a tram home,* he thought, crossing the road. He had something to look forward to that evening, and he needed a good sleep beforehand.

He walked back towards the station, acknowledging that he might be seeing double in places – Jesus, German beer was stronger than he'd remembered. He was going to put his dress uniform on and wear his Iron Cross for dinner. Kriminaldirektor Biermann might be proud of him.

Wilmot got the correct tram and paid the conductor, and during the journey his thoughts wandered to his own family. Did his mother, Hannah, and Max know about Paul's baby? Probably not; they were living with the enemy. He didn't like considering the British Germany's enemy. He felt disloyal to the Fatherland for not thinking it, but when he did, he felt he was betraying his mother and extended English family. It was a strange situation to be in; not one he'd talk about, not even to the Kriminaldirektor. Maybe Paul had informed their mother and Hannah in a letter, sent via the Red Cross Association? Perhaps *he* could also write to his family in Kent, now that he was in Berlin and could personally arrange such a thing with the Red Cross. He'd talk to the Kriminaldirektor about that.

He alighted from the tram, walked along a few blocks and crossed over the road until he stood in his parents' garden staring at each window in the house's upstairs before sliding his eyes to the downstairs living room, kitchen, dining room, and his father's office. He drank in the sight and drowned in the melancholic nostalgia that came with it. Everything looked the same, except for the drawn curtains. Winter or summer, they had always been open

The garden was overgrown. In the month of July, his mother's roses were usually blooming, and shrubs and plants burst into beautiful shades of greens and purple. He thought of himself as a man's man, a bit of a tough nut, but he'd always enjoyed helping his mother prune and cut and shape her garden. He liked the beauty of nature, the marvellous scents in early morning and the hum of insects late at night.

The kitchen's wooden shutters were closed, but the *Willkommen* mat was still on the front porch.

Before opening the door, he went to the garage and looked up at the apartment above it. "Kurt – Kurt, are you home?" When there was no answer, he walked back to the house. *Kurt must be away; otherwise, he would have at least tidied the front lawn*, Wilmot thought.

He saw the damage inside as soon as he stepped into the reception hall. A lamp was on the floor, its porcelain stand, broken. The telephone table was lying on its side. The phone was missing, and the address book his mother had used to keep her important phone numbers was ripped apart. The carpet and some floorboards underneath it had been lifted, and the door to the cubby hole under the stairs was wide open. He peeked his head into the dark space where his mother used to keep brooms and dustpans, her cleaning materials, and sewing machine. The items were still there, but they had been knocked about.

The kitchen had also been vandalised, and the person or persons who'd broken in had apparently been angry. They hadn't taken anything from the shelves or cupboards, as far as he could tell, but for the sake of meanness alone, they had smashed every glass, plate, cup and saucer.

He strode from room to room, his anger growing at the devastation and clear signs of malice that met him: bed clothes tossed in piles on the floor, ornaments smashed, couch cushions slit open, feather stuffing pulled out of pillows, looking like snow covering the bedrooms' floors. *God damn the people who did this to hell!*

Finally, he went to his father's office and found its door ajar. Even knowing his *vati* was dead, Wilmot hesitated before going in; never in his life had he stepped inside this forbidden room. To his knowledge, no one, not even his mother, had ever broken that house rule.

The contents of the desk drawers were strewn across the carpet. Most of the papers were blank, apart from a few bills and work-related documents. A couple of fountain pens and envelopes were lying on top of a messy pile of books probably pulled from the shelves that lined the wall behind his father's desk. It looked as though someone had pulled each book out individually and then tossed them on the floor for spite.

Wilmot stared at the strange break in shelving directly behind the desk chair. A wooden panel had been pulled out by rough hands to reveal a cavity.

A torch was on the floor. Willie picked it up and tried it; he was surprised the battery still worked. When the light hit the wall inside the black aperture, he popped his head in and looked right and left; it revealed nothing but empty space and a lot of dust.

For a while, he sat stiffly on the office room's carpeted floor. *Did Kurt do this?* Of course not, why would he? He was family. *Was this a random robbery?* No, the lock on the front door was intact, as was the one on the kitchen door. Someone with a spare key had done this. The office door, however, had been kicked in with brute force. The lock and handle and part of the wooden frame were broken.

The residual aroma of his father's cigar tobacco filled Wilmot's nostrils, and he began to cry. What a miserable homecoming. How he missed his father, and everything that went with *the old days.*

*Who had keys to the house now?* he wondered. Family members, of course. Kurt. Possibly his aunt and uncle. *Maybe*

*Mother asked those two to keep an eye on the place?*

"Whoever did this is a rotten, filthy bastard," he muttered.

They'd certainly taken the word *Willkommen,* written on the front door mat, seriously.

# *Chapter Five*

## Wilmot and the Biermanns

Freddie Biermann opened the door to Wilmot. "Ach, young Vogel! Wilmot, it is good to have you home. Come in, come in."

In the hallway, Biermann shook Wilmot's hand and prolonged his grip. "Look at you. The last time I saw you, you were a boy. You've had a hard war ... *nein?* Never mind. Follow me. Frau Biermann and Valentina are looking forward to seeing you."

Biermann was thin and frail. He had a greyish tinge to his skin and walked slower than he considered masculine because breathlessness constricted his chest to the point of pain whenever he exerted himself. Damned heart. The pervasive, often-terrifying glare he used on prisoners had dulled; his sharp, green eyes were now cloudy and red-rimmed, and they tired quickly. Even his booming, guttural bellow reserved for the Jews in Łódź was now a slow murmur that wouldn't intimidate a cat. Hearing from the youngest Vogel had got his heart racing with hope, but it had also made him anxious, and being anxious was not good for his ailing health.

Olga and Valentina stood in front of the couch. Baby Erika was in a crib. She was awake and stared contentedly up at the lights on the ceiling. Wilmot stood at the door like a shy, awkward boy until Olga rushed to him and gave him a kiss on each cheek.

"Oh, Wilmot, you have no idea how happy I was when Freddie told me you were in Berlin." Her eyes shot to the medal. "And you have the Iron Cross! Your father would have been proud of you. Yes, indeed he would have..." she croaked to an awkward stop.

As her mother's words tapered off, Valentina stepped forward, her eyes scrutinising Wilmot's face. "You don't look anything like Paul," she said, momentarily disappointed. "You take after Frau Vogel. You're her image." Then her face lit with a proud smile. "Let me introduce you to your niece. You're the first Vogel to meet her." She picked the baby from the crib and stepped closer to Wilmot.

Wilmot stared at the baby. He said nothing, but emotion filled his eyes when her tiny, raised hand wrapped around his index finger. "She's beautiful," he eventually murmured. "She definitely takes after her mother."

"Dinner will be ready in about fifteen minutes, dear," Olga informed her husband. "Why don't you have a nice chat with Wilmot while Valentina and I are in the kitchen?"

Biermann poured Wilmot a whisky and himself a glass of water from a porcelain jug then led his guest to his study and invited him to sit in a comfortable chair facing the bay window. It was still light outside, with a sky streaked with red bands. The branches of a Linden tree swayed in the breeze, and underneath them, purple Knapweed Kornblume crowded a flowerbed that sat next to bushy mounds of the slender, threadlike bright green leaves of Love in a Mist. The smell of freshly cut grass wafted in through the open window and mingled with the perfumed long-stem roses sitting in a vase on the ledge.

This was the peaceful vista that Biermann craved now; his days at the Reich Main Security Office were coming to an end, as was his life, he feared.

He waited until Wilmot had taken his first sip of whisky. *The boy must need a stiff drink after seeing the state of Dieter's house.*

Biermann finally broke the silence. "You must be delighted to be home, Wilmot. I was worried about you for a long time. I got the notification you were missing in action, and I admit, I wasn't hopeful you'd be found alive. I'm afraid *missing in action* means *dead* in most cases nowadays, especially in Russia. Anyway, I got the letter from a Major von Kühn a few weeks ago. He confirmed you were well and serving again after sustaining an injury. I hope it wasn't too serious."

"I lost two toes. It could have been a lot worse," Wilmot said, sitting proudly upright.

Biermann watched Wilmot gulp the whisky. He hoped the boy would talk about the mess in his house now, and not wait until they were at the dining table with Olga and Valentina. He'd rather not have that conversation with the women present. He hated lying to Olga; she had never lied to him.

"Is everything all right, Willie? You look worried about something," Biermann said, prompting the boy.

"The last time I had a whisky, I was with my father ... it was not long before I went to Russia," Wilmot said, looking tearful. He drew himself up even straighter. "To be honest, sir, I'm glad I have these few minutes alone with you. Something dreadful has happened at home. I wasn't sure whether to go to the police or tell you first ... it was all a bit of a shock, you see. Christ, I still can't get over it..."

"Whatever it is, you can tell me, Willie. This conversation won't go any further," Biermann assured him.

Wilmot nodded. "After speaking with you on the telephone, sir, I went home and found my house trashed. Everything breakable was destroyed. Someone, or maybe a group of people by the amount of damage I saw, had gone into every room to make a mess. The door to my father's study was broken – you know it was the first time I'd ever set foot in there? Anyway, apart from the curtains, they turned over everything they got their hands on. The place is in a terrible state."

"Dear God … *scheisse* … that is dreadful, Son. Was anything taken?"

"I don't think so, but I honestly don't know what my parents had in the way of valuables. My father's paintings weren't on the walls, but it's possible my mother or Kurt put them into storage when she left for England. They're worth a fortune, so I can't believe my mother would have left them hanging in there when she knew the house would be empty for months … or years. I'll ask Kurt when he returns from wherever he is." Wilmot's voice hardened in annoyance. "And I'll ask him why he hasn't tidied the place up!"

"Can you think of somewhere your mother might have taken the paintings to?" Biermann ignored the remark about Kurt and focused on the only detail that interested him.

Wilmot considered. "The factory? No, she wouldn't have taken them there. If we get bombed, the factory will be the first place to go up in flames. The garden bunker, maybe?"

Biermann's damaged heart thudded, skipped a beat, then resumed its normal rhythm. He fought to keep his voice mildly curious. "There's a bunker?"

"Sort of." Wilmot rolled his eyes. "My father dug it out for my mother shortly after the war began, but she said she'd never go underground, she'd rather go under the stairs. She's claustrophobic, you see. I suppose it's grassed over by now – ach, I don't know. I never even thought to look out the kitchen window to the back garden – I don't think my father would have shoved his valuable paintings into a dirt hole."

"So, it's in the garden?"

"Yes. At the bottom of the back lawn beside the tool shed."

Biermann nodded. The night had become a glorious success. How had he missed that bunker? As soon as he'd got back to Berlin, he'd gone through the Vogels' house with a magnifying glass looking for the paintings. The mess he and his men had made was for show. He hadn't been stupid enough to think he'd find the framed art under beds or in wardrobes, but he'd thought Dieter might have left a clue or an unexplained address for his wife and children to find. Dieter had always been a sly bastard; probably why he'd done well for himself.

The office: now that had given him surprising insight into his old friend, Dieter's character. In it was incontrovertible confirmation that Vogel was a traitor to the Third Reich. The discovery of a movable panel behind the desk might have been overlooked by other men, but not by his well-trained subordinates. They had missed nothing … except a damned bunker.

A Kriminalassistent had tapped the walls in Vogel's office, finding a cavity behind a panel; it had been empty, apart from a solitary book covered in dust on the concrete floor. Pages of the novel, *Green Hills of Africa* by Ernest Hemmingway, had been marked in places: words, sentences, complete lines, and notes written in pencil on the margins. It didn't take a genius to work out that it was a code book used for transmitting messages; in this case, to the enemy. Even without the presence of a radio, he'd reported the find as proof of wrongdoing … treason. Dieter had been careless in that instance.

In his conversation with Paul, when he'd accused Paul's father and Kurt Sommer of being spies, Biermann had not truly believed his dearest friend could commit such heinous crimes. Well, Vogel had perpetrated his treachery time and again, judging by the tattered, well-scribbled-upon book concealed in a secret place.

Biermann shot a sideways glance at Wilmot who was still looking distraught. *Your father is a traitor. The crafty devil is in England with your mother and two siblings. They're safe from the Gestapo, SS, and the might of German justice, but you're not!*

Ach, maybe he wouldn't punish this Vogel. The boy had been awarded the Iron Cross, was loyal to the Reich, and was going to be much more manageable than Paul had ever been. He might even sit Wilmot down and tell him all about his father's treachery; that would be punishment enough for the boy, and perhaps, Dieter as well. If Wilmot got out of the war alive, he'd never speak to his father again.

Biermann looked at the wall clock. Olga was going to call them for dinner any minute and he still had a lot to get through with Wilmot. The last thing he wanted was Valentina or Olga shooting their mouths off about Kurt Sommer being a Jew and living and dying in the Łódź ghetto. That information had to come from him. He'd say it in his own way at the right time.

"I promise you, Wilmot, I will have my men investigate this crime, although it appears more like the hateful acts of jealous men than a robbery. You know how people are … always wanting what others have. It's a damned disgrace, having to come home to find your house in that state. Thank God, your mother wasn't there."

"Thank you, sir. I hate the thought of the bastards getting away with it. After I see my aunt and uncle, I'll go to Dresden for a few days. I don't want to live in that house the way it is. I don't even want to clean up the mess."

Biermann cleared his throat; he'd ransacked the Dresden house as well and had found nothing. "About Kurt, Wilmot … he won't be coming back to Berlin." He paused, partly to give the boy a moment to absorb his words, but more for effect. "This is going to come as a terrible shock to you, but you have the right to know. Your driver was a British spy. We caught him transmitting messages to the enemy – he confessed to treason and signed his confession in front of my own eyes."

"My God." Wilmot's face turned purple, and his eyes widened in shock as he stared at Biermann's grave expression. "Our Kurt … a spy?" He let out a nervous chuckle. "This is a joke, right?"

With an exaggerated shake of his head, Biermann said, "I wish it were. He was arrested and detained in Spandau prison. I questioned him myself … oh, he denied it at first, as all spies do, but eventually, he admitted to me that he'd been a British agent for years.

"There's something else." Biermann played the silence for a long time, the expression of sorrow and pity on his face worthy of recognition as *künstlerisch wertvoll* by the *Deutsche Filmvertriebs*, the German cinema industry. "Willie … Karl was a Jew. That was his real name, although you knew him as Kurt."

Wilmot's face drained of colour. His stomach heaved, then he let out another high-pitched, nervous giggle.

"I was lenient with him," Biermann continued. "I could have had him executed at the prison, but because he was in your father's employ for years … and I knew you were all fond of him, I spared his life. He was sent to the Łódź ghetto in Poland as a Jew, not a traitor … that crime that would have seen him hanged. My intention was to interrogate him further to find out who else was involved in his treachery, but unfortunately, he died of typhus before I could obtain that information."

Biermann could almost hear Wilmot's thoughts: *Not Kurt. Impossible!* The blood had returned to the lad's face, tears were sprouting from his eyes, his lips were quivering, and questions, lots of questions, were on the tip of his tongue.

Freddie sipped his water, allowing Wilmot the time he needed to take in the news. The boy wouldn't get answers, not from the Gestapo nor his brother in Poland. Before leaving Łódź, Biermann, as Kriminaldirektor, had taken steps to block Paul's outgoing mail. He could receive letters from Wilmot, should the boy choose to write, but in them, he would hear glowing reports about what a generous, supportive fellow Kriminaldirektor Biermann was. Paul, however much he might want to disparage the Biermann family, would not be able to send letters to anyone, including Valentina or his family in England, should he try to slip a letter through the Red Cross. He was *incommunicado.*

"I'm sorry, Wilmot. Karl … Kurt, whatever you want to call him, was given the best treatment available, but Paul's

Jewish doctors couldn't save him. I suppose he got justice from God in the end, if not from the Third Reich."

Wilmot's eyes widened in surprise. "Paul is in Poland...?" he began as the door opened, and Valentina popped her head in.

"Dinner's on the table," she announced gaily. "Let's eat before Erika demands her next feeding. She's such a good baby, Wilmot, but she is always hungry."

# *Chapter Six*

During dinner, Wilmot tried to keep the company entertained with his experiences in Russia and Finland. Numerous times, however, his voice broke with emotion and he was unable to speak about the events leading up to and during his time as a prisoner of war. He couldn't focus on what was being said or answer the questions Frau Biermann and Valentina were throwing at him. His mind was full of Kurt, treason and deceit, death, his house being trashed, and the brother in occupied Poland who couldn't be bothered to write a letter to find out if his youngest sibling were still alive.

He was heartbroken and bitter. He had meant to ask about Paul's situation the minute he arrived at the Biermanns' – Paul had been foremost in his mind on the drive over – but Herr Biermann had been kind and supportive and easy to talk to, and he, Wilmot, had instead plunged into the emotional conversation about the break-in at home as soon as he'd got there. He should have left that nasty subject until the end of the night after he'd enjoyed his evening with his new, extended family, now related through baby Erika.

"More carrots, Wilmot, dear?" Frau Biermann asked.

"Yes, please. This is delicious, Frau Biermann. German chickens are the best."

Wilmot didn't even feel like boasting about meeting Adolf Hitler in Finland. He wanted to go home. He needed to be alone, not sitting here with a false smile planted on his lips while fighting to keep his tears at bay. Kurt was dead, and Paul was ignoring him. It was too much to take in.

"… and of course, I said to my Freddie that you couldn't be dead. I always knew you'd be found safe and well, as Paul was."

Wilmot raised his head. *How long had he been staring at his plate?* "Was Paul missing, too?" he asked Olga.

Valentina answered, "Why, yes. He was in France, and those criminals – those terrible people who call themselves the *Resistance* – kidnapped him. He was brave to escape the way he did."

Wilmot finally concentrated on the conversation, "And he's in Łódź, you said?"

"Yes. He's the supervising doctor at a hospital," Valentina said, a touch of scorn in her voice. "The downside is the place treats Jews from the Łódź ghetto, and he's not allowed to touch that filthy, diseased lot. He's not getting any surgical experience. That place! All he does is order his Jewish staff about all day."

"Paul was frustrated because he wasn't allowed to personally treat the Jews," Olga explained further, "but I do agree with that law. There are plenty of Jewish doctors in that city. Let them get their hands dirty."

Valentina then remarked, "Your brother can be moody at times, Wilmot. He's never been the same since his ordeal in France." She rolled her eyes. "He's become attached to his Jews. I'm convinced he likes them as much as he does real people. I don't know what's come over him."

"The question we should ask ourselves is why would he *want* to treat Jews?" Olga said. "They're contaminated with sicknesses that spread like the lice on their heads. I suppose they're born with some ancient plague in their blood … they *all* carry nasty germs from birth, you know."

Wilmot's night was being ruined. He didn't like the conversation or the tone the ladies had taken. It was a shame they felt this way, for he had long since rejected that overused assessment of the Jewish race.

Valentina patted Wilmot's arm. "I was sorry to hear that your poor papa's driver, Kurt, died in Poland. Paul was upset about it all."

Olga shovelled more mashed potatoes onto Wilmot's plate, then noisily tapped the serving spoon against the bowl's lip. "Who'd have believed he was a Jew? I thought he was such a nice man when I met him."

"Will Paul be coming home soon?" Wilmot asked, wishing his brother were with him right now.

"No, it's unlikely. Leave is a luxury few soldiers get, Wilmot. You're lucky indeed." Biermann finally joined the conversation.

*Haupt's dead eyes, blood running from his wrists and down a floor drain.* The memory hit Wilmot like a punch to the face, pushing him to his limit for the evening. "Me, lucky? Lucky, you say. I don't think so, unless you consider being a starving prisoner of war – or rather, a bag of bones on legs – to be fortunate. Yes, I'm luckier than some. I'm alive when every day I watched my fellow soldiers being executed for no reason at all. Once, I was standing in line, and a Russian guard shot the prisoner next to me – funnily enough, his name was also Wilmot. I closed my eyes, waiting for my own death, wondering what it would feel like … was it going to hurt? Would I linger between life and death, or would the blackness be instant?

"I prayed for forgiveness. I worried I might not have time to confess all the terrible things I had done to innocent people

… yes, including Jews. I asked myself if I was satisfied with what I'd achieved in my short life and the answer came back, *no*. Every night, I wondered, is tomorrow the day I die? When will a bullet come to me? I was convinced it would, eventually."

Wilmot's eyes shone, and like an out-of-control train, his words sped on. "When prisoners collapsed with exhaustion, the Russians didn't pick them up or even allow us to carry them. They shot them where they lay and walked on – *bang* – *snap!* Those were the sounds that accompanied us on our long treks. *Bang!* Another one of us gone … lost and forgotten, I'd say to myself."

Tears slipped from his eyes. "There were days I craved the oblivion of death. The peacefulness of it appealed to me – is that the way fortunate men think, Kriminaldirektor?"

Wilmot sipped his water, wishing he had something stronger. The Biermanns had lost their appetites. Valentina's fork remained in the air as though frozen. Olga swallowed uncomfortably, and Herr Biermann stared at his plate of uneaten food with the bones under his gaunt jaws dancing with anger.

Wilmot couldn't stop himself, even as he sensed their growing resentment. They didn't want to hear the truth about a war they'd never experienced; not the way he had. No civilian would ever understand the nightmares that encroached on his waking hours. They didn't want to. *Well … too bloody bad for them!*

"Before I was captured, I spent months at the Leningrad Front, fighting against Russians who kept coming and coming … now, *they* were like the head lice you mentioned earlier, Frau Biermann. We'd kill one Russkie, and five more would appear in his place. We had Leningrad in the palm of our hands, yet they ordered us to wait and wait until, finally, the Russians dared to push us back."

Wilmot continued, not giving a damn about the Biermanns' horrified expressions begging him to shut up. "I dreamt of marching victoriously through those city streets to the sound of our drums and our swastika banners fluttering above us. Instead, we, the aspiring conquerors, were marched like a herd of nanny goats while being battered with sticks and bomb-damaged rubble by Russian civilians who didn't look the least bit defeated." Then Wilmot, winding down, laughed, "Maybe more soldiers like me should get leave, by law. It might stop them from ranting on like me, eh?"

Genuine sympathy swept Olga's tearstained face. Valentina's eyes were also wet, but Biermann's expression was as sour as vinegar on his sick-looking face.

"Please forgive me," Wilmot muttered.

"There's nothing to forgive, Willie, although I don't like seeing my Olga and Valentina upset. There are some things women don't need to know about, don't you think … hmm?"

Biermann's words were a gentler rebuke than Wilmot would have expected.

"I know how dreadful it is over there," Biermann went further. "We at the Reich Main Security Offices are worried about this new Stalingrad development. I believe we're about to see the start of a terrible battle that could make or break the war…"

"Oh, Freddie, how could you say such a thing?" Olga cried through her tears. "Nothing will break Germany. We're going to win despite all the setbacks we have and might still face. To say otherwise would be an insult to all the young men who have died … like the friends Wilmot lost … those poor prisoners, forced to march for days and weeks with hardly enough food to keep them alive." Olga sniffed. "It breaks my heart to think of the mothers waiting for news of sons who will never come home from that awful country. Oh, why did we have to go to Russia?"

Biermann took Olga's hand. "Forgive me, *mein Schatz,* neither Wilmot nor I should be talking about battles at the table. I know how much war-talk upsets you."

"You can't keep the war from her, Father," Valentina said. "We should all know what's going on at the Eastern Front, and on any other front for that matter. It's our duty to support our troops, not hide in Berlin and pretend they're not suffering. Mother, don't you agree? After all, wouldn't it be an even greater shock to you if you found out we'd lost thousands of our men, and you knew nothing about the battle they'd died in? I told you, you should be like me and join one of the ladies' clubs … you know you want to." Valentina's eyes shot to Wilmot. "We gather warm clothes and food parcels from donors to send to our troops. I know it's not winter, but by the looks of things, we might still be fighting in the Soviet Union for another year…"

"Longer than that," Biermann piped in.

"Yes, well, that might be true, Papa. Even more reason to pray for Stalingrad – not for the Russians that live there, of course, but for our men who are trying to take it."

Wilmot had calmed and was now slightly embarrassed. His outburst had come from nowhere, an eruption of emotion over which he had little control. That was the reason he deliberately avoided talking about his time as a prisoner. Flood gates opened, and a torrent of hellish memories gushed from his mouth without his permission. He was, he thought, responsible for the dinner conversation becoming morbid. "I thought I might find a letter from Paul waiting for me at home," he said, changing the subject. "I can't understand why he hasn't written to me."

"I'm his wife, and he hasn't written to me either, not even to ask how his daughter is," Valentina grumbled. "It's impossible to get him on the telephone nowadays. I gave up trying." She gestured to her father. "I know Paul is all right, though, Willie. Papa is in touch with Manfred Krüger, his Kriminalinspektor in Łódź. He took over from Papa when we left Poland, and he sees Paul from time to time. You needn't worry."

"I'm afraid Paul was a bit of a disappointment to us." Biermann set his water glass down with a thud. "He's not the easiest man to work with, Wilmot."

"He's always been stubborn if that's what you mean," Wilmot said with a wry smile.

"Yes, that, too. But I'm talking about more than him having a bad attitude and a problem with taking orders. He openly disagrees with our Jewish policies in Łódź. I'm with the ladies … he has an unhealthy sympathy for them. Ach, he'd have been better off remaining a civilian doctor in one of the Berlin hospitals. He sees things differently to most of us. It'll get him into trouble, eventually."

"He did save your life, dear," Olga reminded her husband.

"Oh?" Wilmot said.

"It's nothing. I had a heart attack, but I'm feeling better now."

"Nothing, you say. You almost died!" Olga snapped at her husband. "Wilmot, my Freddie is retiring at the end of this month. He can't manage the tremendous workload his superiors are giving him." Olga sniffed, dabbing her eyes with her napkin, and stared adoringly at her husband. "I'm sorry, I can't help it, but … well, I'll be glad to see you out of it and have you home with me."

Wilmot, surprised to hear that Paul was not being viewed as the perfect son-in-law or husband, now worried about where *this* conversation was going. "I don't think Paul would do anything to jeopardise his career. It means too much to him."

"He did jeopardise it," Valentina retorted. "He was smuggling food out of the hospital and giving it to Jews in the ghetto. He was fortunate my father was in charge at the time. He'll never be a good Party member or a good husband, I'm sorry to say."

The atmosphere had soured, and at this point, nothing would sweeten it. Valentina appeared bitter; not at all as a young mother and wife should be feeling about her husband.

Wilmot frowned with confusion. "You mentioned you were in Poland, Valentina?"

"Yes, but I wanted to come home to have the baby and see to Papa's recovery."

"Oh, right. Paul must have been disappointed when you left him…"

"Let's talk about you, Wilmot, shall we?" Olga interrupted. "Where do you want to be posted?"

Wilmot flicked his eyes from a sullen Valentina to Frau Biermann. There was more to Paul's story than they were letting on, but it wasn't his place to ask for details. Paul was in their bad books, and he deserved to be; not writing to his wife was inexcusable.

"I suppose if I were fortunate enough to have a choice, I'd ask for somewhere warmer than Russia. I'd love to go to Paris, or anywhere in Europe that's not to the East." In a last attempt to steer the evening back on course, Wilmot smiled with wry humour. "I've already lost two toes to the cold; I'd like to keep the rest."

Valentina gasped, horrified. The joke had fallen flat … again.

Olga's hand shot to her throat. "How awful – two toes! You didn't tell me that, Freddie," she admonished Biermann.

"I found out five minutes ago, dear." Biermann lay down his fork, narrowed his eyes in thought, and tapped the table with his fingers. "Hmm, you know, Willie, I might just be able to steer you away from Russia and towards Central or Western Europe. I have friends in the Wehrmacht who owe me favours. Leave it with me. I'll get onto it first thing tomorrow." Biermann cocked his head. "Tell you what, why don't you stay with us tonight?"

"That's a lovely idea, darling," Olga said.

Wilmot wanted nothing more than to be in his own bed, in his own bedroom, in his own house … but every mattress in his house had been ripped open and gutted. He couldn't face the house, not tonight. "Thank you, sir. I admit I didn't relish the thought of going home."

"Really? Why ever not?" Valentina asked.

"The Vogels have had even more bad luck, dear," Biermann said, then he told his daughter and wife about the break-in.

# *Chapter Seven*

## Freddie Biermann

Biermann sat on a wrought-iron chair in the Vogels' back garden, watching his men uncover what had been Dieter's insipid attempt at making a bomb shelter. Dawn had yet to break, and the men worked under portable gas lights, but he had been determined to get a head start on young Vogel, who would wake up this morning, eat one of Olga's most elaborate breakfasts, and then come home to find that the hole had been disturbed. *What if he did?* Dieter was a boaster. He didn't hide his art collection, and one of a hundred people could have broken into his house and messed up the hole in the garden looking for the paintings. The boy wasn't stupid. He knew the value of each piece, just as his father had.

Next month, life was going to become difficult for the Biermann family, Freddie thought, staring up at the Vogels' numerous bedroom windows. The letter forcing him to retire had arrived when he'd least expected it. Granted, he looked frail, and often took days off because he couldn't get his body to function in the mornings without pain or needing oxygen, but he was still useful to the Gestapo and commanded respect from his men. He'd given everything to the Führer, the Third Reich, and the Fatherland, and they were tossing him aside like an old shoe.

He'd lose his men upon retirement – a disaster – being able to command them was his true source of power. A *nobody;* he'd drown in bitterness and his need for revenge. He already felt the resentment building like a mountain of bile in his stomach. Göring, his mentor, and Himmler, the sycophant who wanted to control everything and everyone, wouldn't give him a second glance once he cleared out his desk. They'd forget his years of service, his excellent police work, the sacrifices and steadfast loyalty. No one would thank Kriminaldirektor Fredrich Biermann. He'd be like the thousands of old soldiers who went cap in hand every week for their measly pensions. *No. Not me. Why should I? I deserve more, much more.*

"Hurry up and get the damn hatch open. Blow it off if you have to!" he shouted at two Kriminalassistents trying to prise the steel panel on the ground off its hinges with crowbars. Blowing the hatch open was not an option, of course. "Just hurry up, will you."

When the hatch was finally removed, Biermann got off his chair and peered into the hole. Its dirt floor and walls had not been reinforced, but the hollow was intact and dry. "Get down there," he ordered one of his assistants.

Biermann's heart was thumping as he waited for the good news. The hunched over Kriminalassistent disappeared, meaning the hole was quite deep and longer than the hatch. Freddie slumped in his chair again as his heart began to race. If he had one of his scary episodes, where he couldn't breathe and got dizzy, he would have to lie down, and he no time to waste on health matters.

"It's about two metres in length and width, sir," the dirt-blackened assistant said, as his head peeked over the lip of the hole.

"Well, what did you see?"

The other two Kriminalassistents helped pull the man up. He brushed his fingers through his soil-matted hair and said, "Nothing, Herr Kriminaldirektor. There's nothing but dirt and worms down there."

Biermann stared at the man, willing him to retract what he'd just said. "Nothing? No floor covering of any sort?"

"No, sir, just soil that hasn't been dug out yet."

"Damn you. Damn you to hell, Vogel!"

\*\*\*\*\*\*

Biermann got into the back seat of his Gestapo staff car, furious and exhausted. Two weeks earlier, he'd searched Dieter's Dresden factory and house and had found nothing. The previous week, he'd shut down Dieter's Berlin premises for a morning under the pretext of some security issue. His Gestapo had searched the manufacturing plant from top to bottom, but they also had found nothing. Dieter's brother-in-law, Hermann Bergmann, a dour-faced man with zero personality, had reported him. He had been reprimanded by Herr Himmler's office for halting the production of ammunition shells for four hours – a Kriminaldirektor of the Gestapo reported by a low-class factory labourer! That was how far he'd fallen.

He'd run out of time and places to look, he admitted bitterly. Without Gestapo resources to command, he would flounder. Dieter had won. He was a hero, remembered for his magnanimous donations to the Nazi Party and his partnership with the SS in the fledgling Zyklon-B gas programme. He was victorious and probably laughing his head off in London or wherever he'd fled to. No one would listen to the truth.

When Biermann arrived at the Reich's headquarters, he went straight to his office and placed a call to the offices of the Wehrmacht Chief of Operations Staff, under *Generaloberst* Alfred Jodl.

Biermann's contact at Operations was Major Karl Hess, a regular at the Einstein Club, which had recently been renamed the *Der Siegerklub – The Victory Club.* The man was a dog. It was well known he loved all women, skinny, fat, short or tall … except for his wife.

Hess answered with a terse, "Good morning. Kriminaldirektor, what can I do for you?"

Biermann explained why he was calling with a slew of untruths about Wilmot. "… I realise this is none of my business, Karl, but I promised Dieter Vogel – you remember Herr Vogel?"

"No, at least not personally … a good man, by all accounts."

"Yes, he was. That's why I feel responsible for his son. Ach, Wilmot is a bit of a troublemaker, always has been. He spent time in Dachau for trying to kill a fellow SS Schütze and was thrown out of the SS. To tell you the truth, he didn't perform well in Russia, either. I'm afraid he's going to get himself into serious trouble …"

"Yes, Herr Direktor, this is all very interesting, but why are you telling me?"

Biermann scowled at the mouthpiece. "I want you to give the boy a posting where he will finally learn some discipline. I was thinking North Africa, under General Rommel. I know they're desperate for reinforcements. I spoke to someone last week who said men are being pulled from other postings across Europe to shore up the Afrika Korps. If any commanding officer can put the fear of God into young Wilmot Vogel, it's Rommel."

"Just a moment, Herr Direktor."

Biermann waited for the response. He would get what he wanted; he always did. What he wanted was Wilmot Vogel to suffer the fires of the desert. He wouldn't forgive the lad's outburst at the dinner table in front of Olga and Valentina – the patronising, little *scheisse* – he was proving to be as rotten as his older brothers after all.

"I shouldn't get involved in military personnel postings, Freddie," Hess said when he came back on the line. "This sort of thing is done two floors down. It might seem as though I have a personal stake in this…"

"I'll make it worth your while, Karl," Biermann cut the man off. "I have a fine bottle of Scotch sitting in my office drawer with your name on it,"

"You do know what's happening in North Africa?"

"I hear the news, Karl. I know Rommel's men are getting ready for something big, and I've also heard you're shipping reinforcements out to Libya this week – do this for me?"

Another silence, then Biermann heard disappointing news.

"I'm sorry, Freddie, I can't help you. As you pointed out, reinforcements for the North Africa campaign are shipping out in a couple of days. I won't be able to get the paperwork done in time. I will have to locate him … his commanding officer, find Vogel's military records…"

"Rubbish. You're taking men at short notice from everywhere without desert training. Wilmot Vogel is in Berlin on leave. You can get him out to Afrika whenever you want. He's rested – look, Karl, this is important to me, so don't let me down … the way you let your wife down with every prostitute you sleep with. I'd hate her to find out about your weekly extramarital liaisons."

Silence on the other end, then Hess said, "Send over Vogel's contact details immediately. I'll make sure he's on the list for Libya – anything for you, Freddie. Have a good day."

Biermann sighed with satisfaction as he hung up the telephone. He sat back in his chair and folded his arms. Wilmot Vogel wanted somewhere warmer than Russia; well, he couldn't get anywhere hotter than the Western Desert in July. Good riddance. The smarmy bastard probably wouldn't make it out of there alive.

To celebrate that small victory, Biermann asked his secretary to bring coffee. Olga didn't allow him to drink it at home. It wasn't healthy for him, she repeatedly told him; neither were most things in life, according to her.

Whilst waiting for the coffee to come, he made another telephone call; this one to ask a favour of Friedrich-Wilhelm Krüger, subordinate to Rudolf Höss, the Commandant of the Auschwitz concentration camp in Poland. The Gestapo had dirt on him as well.

*Paul Vogel will like it there,* he thought, waiting to be connected.

# *Chapter Eight*

## Paul Vogel

*Łódź-Lidmannstadt, Poland*
*1 September 1942*

Łódź was in blackout, but a birthday party hosted by the Gestapo was in full swing in the *Gęsi Puch* nightclub, situated on Dworska Street near the Łódź *House of Culture* and a few blocks from the ghetto. The joint eatery and cabaret club was within easy walking distance of the German military barracks. It rarely had the food items posted on its modest menu, but the men who went there were looking for alcohol and a good time; a place to blow off steam and celebrate special occasions away from the stifling confines of the officers' mess hall.

During the initial occupation, prominent Jewish restaurants had been boarded up by order of the Gestapo. Later, Christian Polish businessmen saw a marvellous opportunity to make money by reopening them as clubs or bars that specifically targeted the German occupiers' wallets. Cabaret girls were brought over from Germany to entertain the men and were accompanied on stage by well-known musical talents straight from the heart of Berlin. Gęsi Puch, by far the most popular and easily accessible restaurant in the vast city, also hosted the highly sought-after Emilia Fischer, the *Golden Goddess of Dresden,* as German men called her.

Manfred Krüger, the party's host, had invited Paul. The latter had tried twice to slip away unnoticed from the gathering but had been hauled back inside by two inebriated

Gestapo Kriminalassistents bent on keeping him there. No other Wehrmacht officer was present, but four SS officers, including Gert Wolfe, had reluctantly accepted Krüger's invitation.

Krüger was even more unpopular than Biermann had been during his tenure. The former was respected, but not liked by his SS and Wehrmacht colleagues or his raw recruits, who feared his violent temper. Like Biermann, Krüger had a loose, self-aggrandising tongue. Brimming with self-importance, he couldn't stop himself from verbalising his strategies, which evoked dutiful compliments from his subordinates and the more obsequious of the arse-licking SS junior officers. He liked to shock people with his sadistic brilliance.

In conjunction with the SS, the Gestapo had tightened security in the ghetto by closing its hospitals' mortuaries and ordering regular curfews, more searches for contraband, and twice daily roll calls of the population. He had also directly damaged Paul's ability to function by diverting the hospitals' supplies and pharmacy contents to the German military hospital in Warsaw. He'd alienated German soldiers by conducting inspections of their barracks without giving prior warnings to the ranks on watch rotations. Rumour had it, the *Ornungspolizei,* the Orpo, was looking for Jewish contraband being sold on the black market.

Paul peeked at his wristwatch; the one Max had given him when he'd come secretly to Berlin in 1940. It was 2300, and his hospital shift began at 0700. He sat at the end of a long table, set up with a collection of small square tables joined together and covered with a red and white squared tablecloth that irritated one's eyes after a while.

Every man in the place was German, except for the waiters, kitchen staff, barmen, and coat check hostesses, who also served as waitresses at the tables when required. Polish customers had been refused entry by order of the Gestapo, but even if they were permitted entry to the Gęsi Puch, now frequented by the occupation army they detested, why would they want to go there?

Krüger looked relaxed, holding court, lounging in his chair with his small bottle of beer in one hand and a cigarette in the other. His jacket hung over the back of his chair, his collar was undone, and a circular red wine stain spoilt his otherwise pristine white shirt and the edge of his trouser braces. Paul, ordered to attend by a note left under his billet's door, wasn't fooled by Krüger's laidback façade. Like all Gestapo, the man watched, listened, and held information over others like nooses around their necks.

Paul gulped his wine, banging the glass on the table when it was empty. He detested Krüger. Because of him, the hospital wards were now nothing more than rooms with beds where the only treatments were the doctors' voices giving encouragement to their patients. Under dire circumstances, and in the face of isolation, helplessness, and hopelessness, *they* had become the medicine.

Krüger had also removed the hospital's only X-ray machine. It had been based in Medical Centre Number 4 but shared with the other three hospitals. No bandages, linens, or disinfectants had been delivered since June. The pharmacy's shelves housed little more than a few hidden boxes of aspirin, some gauze, and a crate of potatoes; the hospital had started months earlier to give potato peelings to patients on prescription for they were found to contain some essential vitamins, minerals, and fibre content. Paul, desperate for any type of medicine, had given the skins to the Jews to treat burns, warts, stings, infections, heartburn, stomach pain, and indigestion; however, he'd freely admitted to fellow doctors that the specifics and quantities of this *potato treatment* were pure conjecture. That was how bad things had become.

Anatol and Hubert had also been dismissed from Hospital Number 4. Both men had transferred to the Lodz Christian hospital after Krüger had hardened the Gestapo's stance against Christian civilian doctors treating Jews. One week later, the Christian hospital shut down and the two men were out of work.

As his comrades sang yet another song about the Fatherland with drooling, discordant voices, Paul slid his favourite photograph from his wallet sleeve. It was tattered at the edges and smudged in the centre where his fingers continually brushed the image. He held it between his index finger and thumb, a whimsical smile playing on his lips…

"Is she yours, Paul?" The man sitting next to him at the table jolted Paul from his thoughts as he tapped the photograph with his finger.

"Yes," Paul smiled at the Gestapo assistant. "She's my daughter, Erika. I can't believe she's almost three months old. You'll have to excuse me … I never get tired of gazing at her."

"She's beautiful. She must resemble her mother, *ja?*" the man laughed.

"I also got a letter from your father-in-law today, Paul," Krüger shouted from two chairs away, just as the singing died in the middle of the third verse. "His health continues to improve, and he's even taking on more work. Aren't you due leave? You must be eager to meet your daughter in person?"

Paul caught Gert out of the corner of his eye. He looked drunk, swaying on his feet at the bar as though he were in a rowing boat in rough seas.

"Herr Oberarzt, are you bored with our company that you have to sit there looking at photographs of home?" Gert slurred. "Are we not entertaining enough to hold your attention?"

"I could look at my daughter all day, Untersturmführer. It's better than looking at these drunken louts," Paul retorted with a laugh.

"All you … medical types are far too serious for your own good," a man shouted down the length of the table. "C'mon, Herr Doctor, get another drink down you!"

"You never know, it might give you back the good humour you lost somewhere between Germany and Poland," Krüger goaded, and everyone else at the table laughed or hooted their agreement.

Gert staggered towards Paul, knocking into an empty chair on the way. Of the four SS officers who had attended, he was the last of them to leave. "I'm going to my bed. I could do with a helping hand. How about you, Doctor? Like the Kriminalinspektor said … you're as boring as Methuselah's farts…"

Krüger butted in, "I didn't say that. I said he was … ach, who cares!"

As the laughter continued, Paul replaced the precious photograph in his wallet and then stood up with an exaggerated yawn. "*Ja.* I think you might need help getting home, Untersturmführer. I'll take you," he told Gert, as he buttoned his jacket.

When the two men reached the door, Paul turned to face the long table. Chuckling, he wagged his index finger at the partygoers and shouted, "Don't any of you here think you can come to me tomorrow for hangover remedies. Thanks to the Inspektor, who's as drunk as a fly in a wine vat, I have no medicines to give you." He refused to thank Krüger for the invitation since he had hated every minute of his bloody party.

Next to the exit, Gert was fumbling in his pockets while the young hostess looked bored. "Damn coat check ticket … here somewhere."

"You don't have a coat. Come on, Gert. Let's get you back to barracks," Paul said, finally leading Gert outside as he put his cap on.

When the two men cleared the street, they took a quiet road that led to the city's park. It was a shortcut to the barracks, which was situated approximately halfway between the club and ghetto. They reached a clump of trees where Gert halted. He swept the deserted area, then dropped his drunken charade.

"We don't have much time before the others catch up to us," Gert said, looking behind himself again.

"What's going on?"

"In about six hours, the Gestapo and SS will close the remaining ghetto hospitals. Everything in them is being tossed out. Your patients are being deported to Chelmno. I'm sorry, Paul."

Paul felt the sting of bitterness hit him. "Damn them. No one has said a word about this to me. Are you sure about this, Gert?"

Gert nodded. "I've already received my orders. We're going in at 0500 to round up every patient. Whatever equipment and medicines remain are being transferred to the Gestapo's offices in Alexanderhoffstrasse."

"This is insane."

"You had to know it was coming?"

"Of course, I did, but I thought the Gestapo would do me the courtesy of telling me beforehand."

"When have they ever been courteous?"

Paul shoved his hands into his pockets. "I should have guessed. One of Krüger's men asked me tonight why I didn't give up on my job. The bastard said, 'Do you now sing your patients better?' He got a good laugh, as though it were a standing joke."

Paul's eyes smarted. He'd always known this day might come, but now that it had, he found it inconceivable. "It's all been for nothing. My job *is* a joke. All my patients are going to die."

Gert started walking. "We'd better get back."

"I should go to the hospital," Paul said, hesitating.

"There's no point going there. You won't be allowed inside the building unless the Gestapo or SS order you to go in. Paul, there's nothing you can do to stop this or slow it down. You must not interfere on the Jews' behalf. I can't stress this enough to you."

Paul checked his wristwatch; it was just after 2330. His throat closed as he imagined his sick, terrified Jews being dragged from their beds. Incensed, he croaked, "There are one hundred and seventy doctors, nurses, and hospital staff in those four hospitals. Almost all of them are Jews. Are *they* safe?"

Gert cast his eyes around the area. "C'mon, Paul, we can't stand here discussing this. Those drunks we left at the party will be coming this way any minute."

Paul reluctantly obeyed, striding at a good pace beside Gert. "Tell me, Gert, are my staff on the deportation lists?"

"Yes, but I don't know their names or how many are being expelled."

"Dear God." Paul angrily pulled the peak of his cap down. "Fuck them ... fuck the Gestapo and SS. I'm going to my office now before they start blocking the entrances. They can't keep me out if I'm already inside, can they?"

Gert's eyes widened. He staggered and slurred, "Ach, I do ... I miss my Germany ... had enough of this bloody country."

Caught off guard, Paul glanced behind himself then called out, "Help me get him to his bed, will you?"

Three genuinely drunk Gestapo officers staggered towards Paul and Gert. "What are you two up to?" one of the men slurred.

"I can't manage the heavy lump alone. I've picked him up off the ground twice already," Paul explained when the men had reached him. "Do me a favour, will you? I need to pick something up at the medical centre, and it can't wait until morning. Will you take him the rest of the way?"

Paul left the three men to deal with Gert and hurried across the park towards the hospital. He had no idea what he was going to do when he got there, or what he'd say to his nightshift staff. *This is it,* he thought. This was going to be the last time he'd treat patients in Łódź. He'd be transferred before the end of September; a failure as a doctor and human being. His redemption now would be for him to serve on a battlefield. Saving the lives of German soldiers thrown into battle alongside him would make him feel human again.

Another ghetto posting would finish him off.

*Jana Petken*

# *Chapter Nine*

Paul went through the floors, wards, and offices, praying his Jewish doctors had heard about the deportations and had already gone into hiding. In the staffroom, he tried to telephone Leszek Lewandowski, the hospital administrator, to warn him not to come in. Lewandowski often arrived early to sleep on the staffroom couch, which was, according to him, more comfortable than the bed he shared with three other people in his ghetto tenement apartment. Paul had no fondness for the man but didn't want to see him murdered at the hands of the SS.

"Damn it!"

Paul threw the telephone across the staffroom and watched it smash against the wall. No operator had come on; the lines had already been cut.

He sat for a moment, his mind reeling with dismay. Ninety patients were in the wards. Most were expected to die, and soon, but they should pass away with the comforting presence of a doctor or nurse by their bedside, not while being tossed into a truck, train, and gas van in their final hours.

Paul wept; his tears ran down his cheeks, and squeaky sobs escaped his tight lips even as he opened the door to the corridor.

In the pharmacy, he pushed aside his emotions and set to work. He emptied the boxes of aspirin that had been hidden and put the pills into brown paper bags. He removed his jacket and shirt, then taped the bags to his chest using ribbon gauze bandages. After re-dressing, he filled his trouser and jacket pockets with leftover pills until they bulged. He wanted to take the last of the syringes, petroleum jelly ointment, and suture kits, too, but if he tried to conceal too much on his person, he'd appear oddly shaped.

Krüger and the higher ranks of the SS and Gestapo had deliberately kept the details of this operation to themselves. Had it not been for Gert warning him, Paul would have reported for duty two hours after the deportations had begun. Both he and Gert made a point of not being seen together except when in the company of a larger group of men. Krüger had spies everywhere. They followed Paul every time he left the ghetto, and he was certain they were watching him in the officers' barracks as well, which was why he hadn't been able to speak to Gert for over a week.

Whether he was in the hospital now would not change the lethal outcome for his patients, he acknowledged, as he continued searching for anything that might be useful in the future. But he could try to guide his staff to safety and calm the situation.

The staff nurse was at her desk in the centre of the third-floor ward. Paul's first instinct was to ask her to hide the Jewish patients or tell them to run for their lives, but he reconsidered. *If they could run, they wouldn't be in the damn hospital in the first place, would they?*

Twenty patients were either sleeping, weeping, or groaning; the familiar, pitiful sounds that filtered through every ward during the night when everything was bleaker. Their legs, affected as they were by peripheral oedema, were unable to support their skeletal frames. Jaundiced, with bellies swollen from starvation, each patient was moments or days from death; there would be no miracle of modern technology that could save even one of them.

Paul halted at the bedside of a young woman who had suffered a miscarriage due to malnutrition. Since he'd been in Poland, he had recorded four live births. He had concluded during his first weeks in Poland that the Jewish women in the ghetto were too unhealthy to conceive or carry babies to term.

The woman smiled at Paul.

"Hello, Doctor."

Paul held her hand. "How are you tonight, Margarit?" he murmured.

"I feel better. Can I go home soon? My little boy misses me terribly."

Paul's grim expression mirrored his thoughts. One wrong word or move and he'd be charged with aiding and abetting Jews. No word or move and his soul would be damned.

The staff nurse looked up from her paperwork. "Doctor, can I help you?" she asked, a worried frown creasing her young forehead. No more than twenty-five years old, she was skinny, and her once-pretty face was gaunt. Like most of the staff, she appeared to have aged ten years in the last few months.

"Why are you here, Doctor Vogel?" she asked again.

"Come with me, Nurse Wiśniewski," Paul said quietly.

In the corridor, Paul explained the situation. "At five o'clock, the Gestapo and SS will come here to remove everyone in this building. The hospitals are being closed, and patients and staff are being deported." He paused to swallow the hard ball of cowardice at the back of his throat. "I can't stop this, Zusanna," he said using her first name. "I must follow orders, and you must help yourselves."

Her chalk-white face crumpled. "What can we do? What shall I tell the patients? You've heard the rumours, Doctor. You know what people are saying. They're going to kill us!"

Paul, inadequately equipped to deal with the weeping woman, shook her by the shoulders until she gasped for breath. "Look at me – look at me," he ordered.

She stared at Paul as though he were her executioner. "I'm sorry. I'm scared."

"No ... no, I'm sorry." He let her go, ashamed of his overly harsh response. He should be giving her hope, not shaking the life out of her.

"What do you want me to do?" Zusanna asked.

"When the Gestapo and SS come through these doors, they will order everyone downstairs. Give them your full cooperation. See that every patient who can walk gets out of their beds and makes their way to the ground floor."

Zusanna's teeth were chattering as she nodded her understanding.

Paul had not denied the rumours of the death camp, which had been circulating for weeks in the ghetto, nor had he alleviated her fears of being killed once in German custody. His Jewish staff had finally begun to respect him. To lie would be to break the trust he had built over the past year and a half.

He swallowed painfully again. "Zusanna, if you, your colleagues, and your patients attempt to leave the hospital before the Gestapo and SS get here at 0500, I will not stop you. I will not stop Margarit over there, nor the woman in the next bed, nor any of the sick in the wards."

The nurse, still hoping for answers, appeared confused as she stared up at Paul. "What do you mean?"

"Listen carefully," Paul snapped in a deliberately hard tone. "I am going now to the mortuary, to open its exit doors to the street. When I arrived, the area at the back of the building was still clear, so if anyone were going to, for example, take a walk, they should do it now … *now,* before it's too late. Do you understand?"

"Yes, I understand, Doctor. I know what to do." She looked into the ward from the corridor, her eyes shining with tears. "I will give my patients the choice to go or stay. If I don't see you again … goodbye. I wish you well."

Paul's resolve to remain neutral dissolved somewhere between Zusanna's ward and the stairwell. Before making his way to the mortuary, he went through every floor and ward again, this time to explain to his staff about what was coming for them. To hell with the Gestapo. He and his hospital workers had made private covenants with the sick, to support them and not to abandon them under any circumstances. In the weeks since Krüger's thugs ransacked the hospital, Paul had witnessed heroics and acts of innovation more common on battlefields.

He wasn't sure how many of the staff would leave their patients, but a young nurse put her reason for running away into perspective. "If the medical staff are taken, the weakest Jews in the ghetto will suffer even more than they do now. I have to hide because I will be needed to care for the sick tomorrow and the day after, and for however long we can survive the Germans." She'd given Paul hope that other staff members would follow her example and try to escape.

Paul hung his head as he walked down the last few stairs to the basement. This heralded the end of the shabby, but still semi-functioning, treatment centre. Understanding and compassion were all that remained, but insubstantial as those things were, Paul was convinced they gave the human spirit hope, and that was a vital commodity when healing the sick.

"You're doing the right thing. You're *not* cowards," Paul told his staff when they began to leave their posts. *No, they weren't cowards; he was the spineless shit amongst many brave people.* Krüger was going to arrive cloaked in self-importance, and he, Paul, would bow his head, nod when appropriate, and follow orders like a good little Hitler youth boy.

The abandoned mortuary stunk of rotting flesh. For months, it had been used as a storage room for the dead. It had ceased to be a place of learning or for performing medical procedures and autopsies after the Gestapo sent a letter stating they weren't interested in causes of death, only that a Jew had died. Strict records were kept in the ghetto of every death and birth, of which there were, respectively, many and few.

Paul studied the four corpses lying naked on the floor. According to the register, they had died between 2000 hours and 2200 hours. He recognised the youngest male. The boy, about fifteen, had been admitted the previous morning, too far gone to be saved. He'd literally starved to death. "You're lucky. You've found peace," Paul muttered.

A foot scuffed, the mortuary door opened, and four staff members, their faces tinged blue in the torchlight, entered the room.

Startled, Paul put his finger to his lips, opened the locked exit door to the street with his key, and went outside to check if the area was still deserted.

Satisfied it was, he went back inside to face the three men and one woman. "If you know the locations of the bunkers in the ghetto, hide in them."

The men looked shocked.

"It's a long story. Suffice to say, I know they exist," Paul said, "and I've never said a word to anyone about them."

"Will they hunt us down if we are on the lists?" one of the men asked.

"Yes. But the authorities will be too busy to search for missing people today."

"And tomorrow?" the same man asked.

"Tomorrow, they'll go door to door in every tenement block in every street – go now, and wherever you find to hide, don't come out until the deportations are over."

*He'd incriminated himself after all,* he thought, closing the door behind the last person to leave. If the runaways were caught and gave his name, he'd lie through his teeth and feign outrage at the Jews' filthy, deceitful mouths. Whether the Gestapo believed him would be a different matter, of course.

He climbed back up the stairs, his feet dragging and thumping hard against every concrete tread. Had the remaining staff members informed the patients they were being deported? Had any of the patients fled yet? Had Zusanna left? He'd not seen her in the mortuary. It was 0230; two and a half hours to go until chaos and death descended on this place of supposed healing.

# Chapter Ten

At precisely 0500, the hospital's main doors opened to admit the Gestapo, SS, and *Schutzpolizei* – Schupo. The ghetto Jewish police were ordered to wait outside to help with the loading, but a further detachment of SS also entered the back of the building through the mortuary.

Paul observed the start of the deportations from the entrance to a first-floor ward. He was silent and being largely ignored, apart from the odd *Heil Hitler* received from overzealous SS soldiers who loved to snap their heels and arms every chance they got. He was asked twice to assist with the sicker patients, and twice he refused. "My job is to heal, not to drag ill people out of their beds," he snapped at an SS Schütze.

Within minutes, the shooting began. Paul jumped every time a pistol shot rang through the ward and patients screamed. It was still dark, and the guns flashed blue when fired, or was he seeing something that wasn't there?

Pyjama-clad patients began to file out of the ward in a single line at gunpoint, and as they passed Paul, they pleaded with him to help. To his disgust, he could hardly bring himself to look at their frightened faces, much less meet their eyes.

When the last of the walking patients had left under guard, Paul went into the ward. He halted, his eyes darting from one occupied bed to another. In the first one was an elderly woman, her withered hands gripping the apron of a female nurse who had evidently decided to stay behind.

In the other bed, another female nurse had got on top of the covers, partially concealing a male patient. She looked up, saw Paul, and screamed, "Doctor! Don't let them do it. Please, tell them to go away!"

Paul opened his mouth, then snapped it shut as two shots were fired from a rifle at close range. He turned sharply to the other bed, his ears ringing and heart pounding furiously. The old lady was dead, shot through her eye socket. Blood and brain matter slid down the wall to the left of the bed, and on the floor below the stains, the nurse who had stood at the elderly patient's bedside had also been killed with a shot to her temple.

The two SS soldiers approached Paul, who was shielding his nurse at the man's bedside. Amelia Bartek was one of his favourites, a quirky, good-humoured girl, who often carried on working long after her shifts ended. Rage burned inside him. *He'd be damned if he let the soldiers harm her!*

"Put your guns away!" Paul yelled at the two men.

"With respect Herr Oberarzt, we have our orders. All those who cannot walk must be disposed of here. Tell the nurse not to resist."

Nurse Bartek and her patient clung to each other, defiance sparking in their eyes. Paul was veering close to disobedience, and the soldiers knew it.

"This patient can walk," he said, trying to calm the situation. "I'll get him downstairs. The nurse will help me."

"Very well, Herr Doctor. We'll watch you get him out of bed and see for ourselves if he can stay on his feet," one of the soldiers said, his expression just short of derisive insubordination.

Paul hardened his voice. He rarely used his rank, because he wasn't certain how much additional authority the SS and Gestapo had over other branches of the military. "I said, I'll deal with this patient. You two can go." It was apparent that the patient couldn't stand, never mind walk; nonetheless, Paul drew back the covers and began to pull one of the man's bony legs over the side of the bed.

Paul glanced at Amelia who was still holding onto the patient for dear life. He leant towards her, aware of the SS standing their ground behind him. "Help me," he mouthed.

"No. You're not taking him," the nurse whimpered back.

The patient's eyes were sunk deep into their sockets, and his mouth looked oddly enlarged on his skeletal face. Narrow shoulders supported a fragile neck where translucent skin was stretched over two jutting collarbones and an enormous-looking Adam's apple. His breath rattled, coming and going in quick, shallow pants. Unequivocally, he was at death's door.

Paul straightened and turned to the soldiers who were smirking at his failure to move the man. "You could help," he hissed.

"No, no, you said you could do it," one of the men tittered. "You have two minutes, Herr Doctor. We have no more time than that to waste on this bag of bones."

Trying to sound officious, Paul shouted, "If you don't want me to report you to your commanding officer, you will leave – *now!*"

"What's going on here?"

Paul spun around to the ward's entrance and saw Gert, pistol in his hand, approaching the bed.

"Herr Oberarzt, do you need assistance?" Gert asked.

"No, on the contrary. I ordered your men to leave this patient to me, but they either don't understand my instruction or are being deliberately insubordinate."

"They're doing their jobs, Herr Doctor," Gert retorted.

"They can have him once he's on the truck, but whilst he's still in this bed, he is my responsibility. They could stand to be disciplined, Untersturmführer."

Gert's eyes drifted to the dead nurse on the floor, the old lady in the bed, and the blood splatter on the wall behind her. With a stony expression, he told his men, "You two, come with me. Let the doctor deal with his patient."

"Yes, sir," the soldiers said, clicking their heels together.

When the soldiers had stepped into the hall ahead of him, Gert said, "Doctor, make sure this patient reports to the reception area – in the meantime, you won't be disturbed like this again."

Alone in the ward with Nurse Bartek and the man in the bed, Paul said, "I don't know this patient. Who are you to each other?"

"This is my husband, Ari," Amelia sobbed. "I brought him here at ten o'clock last night. I shouldn't have, but…"

Paul cut the nurse off and led her to the corridor. There, he spoke to her in whispers. "He's critically ill. You must know this, Amelia. If I take him, he'll be loaded onto a truck and then taken to the train station. If he makes it that far, they'll put him into a cramped train wagon with no room to sit or lie down, and eventually, he will arrive at a camp where they will execute him."

Her ashen face was sleek with sweat. She shook her head as though trying to rid herself of the images he had placed in her mind. "No … no, they can't…"

"They can, and they will." Paul had already said too much but continued regardless of the terrible effect his information was having on her. "Amelia, if he goes, he'll suffer terribly in his final hours. He might not even make it through the journey. I can save him from a bullet, but he *will* die today."

Amelia's dark eyes overflowed. She drew herself up, sniffed, wiped her puffy eyes, then said, "I know he's dying, and he knows it, too. Help him, Doctor. Please give him dignity in his last moments – take away his pain – please."

Paul looked down the length of the corridor. As he'd predicted, the Gestapo and SS had started on the lower floors and were making their way upstairs. This floor looked deserted. Gert had taken the last of his men away, and he wouldn't return with them, at least for a while.

"Do you want to say goodbye to him, Amelia?"

She nodded.

Paul stood at the ward's entrance. The sounds of shouting, screaming, and gunshots coming from the floor above him pierced the cracked ceiling. He wanted to give the nurse and her husband more time, but the sound of thumping feet coming down the stairs was growing louder. Gert and his SS squad might not return, but he had no idea where the Gestapo and other SS officers were.

He returned to the bedside and asked the man," Are you sure you want me to do this, Ari?"

"Yes. Thank you, Doctor … let me go now … God bless and keep you," the dying man rasped, his eyes then turning to Amelia.

Paul searched Amelia's face.

"I'm not leaving him."

"Very well."

As Paul took the man's pillow from under his head, he said, "It will be uncomfortable for a moment or two, then you'll go to sleep."

"Like going to sleep," the man repeated, a wan smile on his face as he looked at his wife.

Paul got onto the bed, straddled the patient, and then pressed the pillow into the face staring up at him. For a few seconds, Ari's arms flailed, scratching at Paul's downturned face. The human instinct to survive was kicking in but he was too weak to put up a real fight and his struggle ended within a minute.

Paul lifted the pillow, threw it on the floor, and then got off the bed. He would think about what he had done later, not now. He checked Ari's pulse at the neck and wrist and found nothing. He used his stethoscope to listen for a heartbeat. Nothing.

Amelia kissed her dead husband's forehead. Ari looked like a corpse who had been in the mortuary for days; his lips were already blue, his mouth wide open, his eyes semi-closed, and his waxy skin already beginning to cool without his life's blood circulating.

"I'm sorry Ari had to die like this, Amelia," Paul finally said.

Amelia walked around the bed to Paul. "You did him a kindness, Doctor. It was all so quick … as though he just let go." She lifted Paul's hand and kissed it. "Thank you … God thanks you. He's not covered in blood like that poor woman over there, and he won't suffer like those other poor patients being taken away. He's clean." She sighed. "Should I report to the SS now?"

"No. No, Ari wouldn't want that." Paul pictured hiding places that might be overlooked. It was possible the SS would do a final sweep of this floor. The dead Jews in this ward would have to be disposed of at some point. His eyes widened as he had a thought. The pharmacy was at the end of the corridor. It had been the first place the SS ransacked, although they'd found nothing but empty aspirin boxes. That victory was his. Without thinking it through, he said, "Amelia, Ari is at peace now. Come with me."

She hesitated.

"If you want to get out of this mess alive, you must do as I say," he said more severely.

She cried, kissed her husband one final time, and then followed Paul into the corridor.

A cacophony of sounds permeated the area, but it was difficult to know where they were all coming from. Noise seeped through the old brick walls, down the stairwells, and through the ceiling. The SS officers' booming voices were, at times, overwhelmed by snapping gunfire and high-pitched screams, and now the sound of breaking glass was adding to the mayhem.

The Germans were like a pack of feral dogs devouring a defenceless prey. It was easy for Nazis to kill Jews, Paul had long since concluded. They did it for Hitler and the Fatherland and were so devout in their beliefs, they found no wrong in their murderous rampages.

Paul hid Amelia inside the pharmacy storeroom behind some shelves that had been tipped over. Filing cabinets lay on their sides, their drawers ripped out and thrown in a pile on the floor. Empty intravenous bottles had also been thrown across the floor and smashed for no other reason than the soldiers' perverse enjoyment of the destruction.

"Stay here. I'll try to come back for you after dark," he told her.

"What if they lock the doors?"

"Leave getting back in up to me. If you're not on the list, I'll escort you back to your apartment…"

"And if I am on the list?"

"We'll tackle that problem if it arises."

She looked terrified as she lay down behind a cabinet and drew her legs up to her chest.

"I know you're scared, but you must be strong. It may take some hours until I can make it back to you. Promise me, you won't make a sound or move until I return – say it."

"I promise, Doctor."

Paul left, leaving the pharmacy door ajar. He made his way to the stairwell at the end of the corridor, took a quick glance over his shoulder, saw no one, and took to the stairs.

\*\*\*\*\*\*

Paul gaped at the scenes in the street below as he watched from a window in a now-empty ward on the top floor. Dozens of ghetto residents were running towards the hospital, screaming patients' names and fighting with Jewish and German policemen to get closer to the building. Shots rang out, and some people fell to the bullets whilst others stumbled over the dead bodies, undeterred by the weapons. News travelled fast in the ghetto, and people were coming for their loved ones.

The hospital building was surrounded by a cordon of German Order Service and SS. They were being backed up by numerous Gestapo, some wearing their familiar black coats, hats and deadpan expressions.

Military trucks with their flaps up were full of patients. One pulled away from the kerb and straight into the crowd of screaming ghetto residents trying to see if their family members were on it.

Paul staggered backwards, shocked, as a patient flew vertically past the window from the flat roof above him. He went back to the window, just as another patient was plummeting to the ground, then another, and three more people after that, to the screams of the people in the street. Cautiously, he stuck his head out and glanced up, then down. The kerb, strewn with dead bodies, was a river of blood.

Rifle fire echoed further along the street. Paul had a limited line of sight, but he saw the two remaining trucks in the street below, the dead bodies, the Germans manning the perimeter, and the crowd gathering close to the building. He tentatively stuck his head and shoulders out of the open window again; craning his head upwards to the flat rooftop. To get a better sense of what was happening at the other end of the building, he gripped the window ledge and pushed himself out further until his whole torso was twisting left and right to view the length of the road.

Two pyjama-clad women were being mown down by machine-gun fire as they scrambled off the second truck pulling away. One was Margarit, the woman who'd had the miscarriage, and who hadn't been strong enough to lift her head. He looked at her crimson nightclothes, riddled with bullet holes, and unable to watch the scene unfolding, he turned from the window.

"Ach, there you are, Oberarzt Vogel," a familiar voice called.

Paul took in Manfred Krüger's satisfied smirk. He looked like a man who was thoroughly enjoying his job; standing with his chest puffed out and four of his ghouls behind him.

"Kriminalinspektor Krüger, I was wondering when you'd show up."

Krüger sauntered past the rows of beds, a roll of papers in his hand, and a smile through gritted teeth. He gave the impression that spreading his lips was a chore, for he never managed to hold the pose for long. He was one of the most sour-faced Gestapo pigs Paul had ever encountered.

"I was told you got here hours ago. Why did you report for duty straight after my party and under the influence of alcohol?" Krüger asked when he came nose to nose with Paul.

Paul fought his panic. *Who had told Krüger?* "As supervisor, I often come in early to do paperwork or stocktake, not that there's much of anything to count nowadays," he said, mirroring Krüger's contemptuous tone. "Why wasn't I informed yesterday of this operation? A courtesy call would have been nice, don't you think?"

Annoyance sparked in Krüger's eyes as he looked Paul up and down as if inspecting his uniform, then he joined him at the window. "The decision to begin this operation was taken at our headquarters in Alexanderhoffstrasse at 2300 last night. I believe a list of deportees and the schedule was sent to your billet around 0130. That is the time the SS and Gestapo agreed to begin the deportation of Jews to Chelmno from the hospitals, before beginning with the ghetto residents, and that is the time the SS notified me."

Krüger was almost as tall as Paul, but he had grown painfully thin with a permanently malicious expression. His new look had nothing to do with a shortage of food – the Gestapo never went without anything. It was, Paul believed, the stress of the job or maybe illness that was shrinking the Inspektor. Although he hated the man, he could see the strain in his eyes. *It must be exhausting killing Jews day after day,* Paul thought.

"We are beginning the *Gehsperrle Aktion* – the deportations will continue for ten days," Krüger said, unrolling the papers and thrusting them at Paul. "Go through these lists. You'll find the names of today's deportees on them. Sign and stamp their death certificates. I'll be back in an hour to collect them."

Krüger was lying, Paul knew, taking the lists. Birthday or no birthday, a man this obsessed with his job would not have missed an important meeting about the timing for such a large operation. He was a key voice in all ghetto decisions, yet he'd been in a club socialising all evening, which meant the operation had been sanctioned much earlier than he'd stated. Did any of the other party guests, apart from Gert, know about the expulsions beforehand, or had they been kept in the dark too?

Paul scanned the lists. Most of the names on them belonged to patients with typical Jewish surnames ending in *berg, shon, blat,* or *blum,* making it difficult for him to picture the people in his mind. When he reached the bottom of the second page, however, he found titles before the names: doctor, nurse, sister, and after them, other staff: orderlies, ambulance men, cleaners. He was losing two Jewish doctors, one being the indolent hospital administrator, Doctor Lewandowski, who'd always maintained that he was indispensable to the Germans and not at all like all the other Jews in the ghetto. Tragic, but also ironic, that he was going to his death with the people he'd consistently failed to care for or about.

Paul's gut twisted. Sick with disgust, he saw Sister Zusanna Wiśniewski's name right at the bottom, scribbled in as though she'd been an afterthought. Had she got out in time, or was she on one of the trucks? He hadn't seen her since her goodbye to him hours earlier.

Above Zusanna's name was Tomaz's, the ambulance orderly whom Paul had guided through the mortuary exit hours before the culling began. That might be one victory he could claim.

Amelia, whose husband he'd smothered an hour earlier, was not on the list. Inadvertently, he sighed with relief. He'd go back for her and then escort her to her tenement as soon as he could.

"They're not dead yet," Paul said with a strangely casual tone. "I won't sign a certificate stating a patient has died if they haven't. That goes against my Hippocratic Oath and everything I believe in as a doctor. I refuse to do as you ask."

As his eyes continued to glide over the names, Paul recalled a Jew he'd secretly treated days earlier. The man's name was Isaac. He'd snuck out of the ghetto to steal cement with which to build a bunker to hide his family and neighbours. The plan, he'd explained openly to a nurse, was to put the bunkers under the ghetto's stinking septic system to throw off the bloodhounds the Germans used to hunt Jews. He was shot in the leg by a German patrol while sneaking back into the ghetto carrying a forty-five-kilo bag of cement. After being hit, he'd left a bloody trail, but he'd somehow managed to evade the Schupo, to get to the hospital.

Paul hadn't had any surgical instruments left, but he'd sterilised a coat hanger as best he could and using that, along with a knife, dug out the bullet from Isaac's leg. With his leg bound tightly to stop the bleeding, Isaac had made it back in time for morning rollcall, but Paul had heard via another orderly that Isaac had been shot later that day by a member of the German patrol who'd been searching for him. The man who told him about Isaac's death was also on today's deportation list.

Paul waved the lists in Krüger's face, his rage making him breathless. "No. I won't do as you ask." Then he almost stomach punched Krüger as he thrust the papers at him. "It's all been a waste of time, hasn't it? Everything we have achieved … the people we have saved … the heroic attempts of my staff to help dying patients or those in agony when they had no medicine to give them. It's all been for nothing. You're going to kill my patients, Kriminalinspektor, but I won't sign their death certificates until it is confirmed that they are *dead,* so you can take these lists and give them to a doctor in Chelmno, or you can stick them up your bumptious arse hole. Am I clear?"

Knowing he was in the right, Paul marched out of the ward without a backwards glance. As he reached the stairs, however, his bravado shrank. Shaking, he clung to the bannister and made his way downstairs to the pharmacy. He had never felt so alone, bereft, or scared in his life.

# *Chapter Eleven*

## Anubis el Masri

*Alexandria*
*3 September 1942*

Anubis el Masri set the ten-minute timer on the explosives that were hidden in a dustbin behind a Cairo police station. As he was leaving, his eyes swept the area, taking in the building's windows as well as those of nearby houses. A dog was barking behind a gated property, disturbing a roosting cockerel that then crowed from the rooftop, but he didn't hear a single human voice; as anticipated, everyone was at evening prayers.

He walked towards a café a block away. When the bomb went off, the damage would be minimal: probably cause a fire, shatter window glass, and scatter terrified people in the area. It shouldn't hurt anyone, at least he hoped not. Murder was not part of the plan.

When Anubis reached the café, he took a seat outside with a view of the street and ordered mint tea. As he waited, he counted down the minutes, then seconds, until the blast disintegrated all thought and he ran through the streets, along with everyone else in the vicinity. He'd done it. He had achieved his objective and gained the trust of the Muslim Brotherhood's Secret Apparatus members. *More than that. I have reached the top of the ladder without having to climb the bottom rungs.*

Anubis managed to say late prayers in the Al-Hussein Mosque before heading to the *Hookah* store to buy tobacco. People had calmed down. No one was scrambling to get away or yelling about terrible carnage, and he hadn't seen any British military police nor Egyptian policemen in the streets marshalling the population to safety. He stopped a man and woman who were walking from the direction of the blast, and asked, "What was that loud bang? Was anyone hurt?"

"No. *Al-ḥamdu lil-lāh* – thank God!" the man replied. "The police said it was a fire in a dustbin. It must have ignited something highly inflammable to make that noise – scared the life out of my poor wife."

"It sounded like a bomb to me. I thought the Germans were coming. *Allahu akbar* – Allah be praised," his wife said.

Anubis strolled at a leisurely pace towards the café where he was to meet his Sudanese friend and two members of the Brotherhood. He was fifteen minutes early; the men were coming from prayers at a mosque some distance away, and he didn't want to be the first to arrive.

He found benches with wrought-iron arms lining one side of a street. He sat and began to roll a cigarette with the tobacco he'd purchased whilst observing the busy thoroughfare crammed with people who appeared to have forgotten they'd been running for their lives less than an hour earlier.

Rolf Fischer's mission was going well, Anubis admitted. He didn't like the Englishman's character; the way he hid behind his false name and secrets and wielded God-like power over him. But Fischer had a steady hand. He knew exactly what he wanted, and more importantly, how to achieve his aims. Never in his life had he, Anubis the thief, the trickster, followed another man's orders without making personal financial gain his priority. This was a first for him and his skin crawled with resentment.

A little boy giggled as he kicked a loose stone on the pavement. Anubis, observing the child, missed his wife, his children, and his freedom, but he'd continue to toe the line with Fischer, do as he was told, put his life in danger. The mess he was in would be tidied when the operation was deemed successful, and he was pardoned and allowed to go home. When that day came, he'd tell *Ya Ibn el Sharmouta* – the son of a bitch – exactly what he thought of him and his countrymen.

Since being in the Muslim Brotherhood, Anubis had attended numerous meetings and taken part in violent acts that went against the wishes of the Society's Supreme Guide, Hasan al Banna. The leader had been imprisoned twice, albeit released within weeks. He advocated for peaceful political reform and had, after the Egyptian government suppressed the Brotherhood's journals, banned its meetings, and forbidden all reference to the group in newspapers, adopted a low profile.

Anubis learnt that the main arm of the Muslim Brotherhood, known as the *Society*, was organised into small groups called *battalions*. They rarely met in the same place twice, and it was uncommon to learn other members' names since the title *Brother* was generally used.

He found out at his inaugural meeting that some of the most active cadres had left the Society to form a rival organisation called *Muhammad's Youth*. As a result of this conflict, the Brotherhood created their own military wing called the Secret Apparatus, the group Herr Fischer was so determined to subvert. When Anubis infiltrated it, he had expected to find fanatical fools dreaming well beyond realistic expectations, but instead, he had come to support the Society's principal goal of an independent Egypt and a cleansing of Western debauchery.

Down but not beaten, the Brotherhood was managing to maintain and expand its base and extend its social welfare programmes, which included humanitarian assistance to the victims of Axis bombings of Egyptian cities. The Brotherhood's leadership was determined to avoid confrontations that could give the government a pretext to suppress the Society altogether, but not all members agreed with the cautious approach. Anubis had already learnt that the members of the Secret Apparatus were intent on actively undermining the government, but they had achieved very little; tonight's display had been their first attack in weeks, and it was being called an accidental fire by the police. It certainly wasn't worth raising the Brotherhood's victory flag for a brief pop and bang in the street.

Apart from weapons training, Anubis found the meetings boring and long. Consisting of sanctimonious rhetoric, rigorous Koranic studies, and physical exercises, they usually ended with a call to violence. A sane man might say that calling for violence after preaching the religion of peace was a somewhat hypocritical way to end the gatherings, but Anubis was under no illusion; defeating the British, and even ousting King Farouk's government, was high on the agenda for members.

Anubis looked at his watch, a shoddy timepiece that had once belonged to his much older, now-dead sibling, Abdullah. Of Anubis' six brothers, Abdullah had been the wealthiest and most law-abiding. He'd rented a shell of a building and had learnt how to repair motorcars. He'd found out where to buy the parts needed to keep a vehicle running and had taught other men as well as himself how to be good, reliable mechanics. Abdullah had been clever, guiding his business away from old motorbikes and Volkswagens and towards the bigger, better class of cars driven by British diplomats and high-ranking military men. He'd given Anubis his watch on his deathbed, telling him it would be the most expensive thing he would ever own – he'd been wrong.

Cobblestones dug into the soles of Anubis' lattice sandals as he strolled to the meeting place; a café called *Naguib Mahfouz,* situated on a narrow street not far from the mosque. He entered, pausing at the door for a moment to scan the sea of men in their long white thawbs within the semi-darkened room, already blue with misty clouds of smoke from hubbly bubbly pipes. Breathing in a mixture of tobacco, fruits, jasmine, and strong Turkish coffee, he listened to the booming Arabic voices resonating in the cramped space until his ears caught the Sudanese man, Abu Hanifa's squeaky tone.

Abu sat with two men at a round copper table on a wooden quadripod stand in the centre of the room. He waved, his young, animated face beaming when he saw Anubis.

Anubis raised his arm in greeting then joined the three men. Clutching his fat, amber *misbaha* prayer beads in his fingers, he sat on the remaining stool before greeting Abu's companions.

This would be no ordinary meeting, Anubis thought, nerves turning his stomach to mush. For the first time, he was going to wet his feet in the mysterious world of espionage and plunge himself and his family into even greater danger. He didn't like the way the two strangers were staring at him, but it wasn't uncommon to meet suspicion every time he attended a gathering and met someone new. Members were distrustful by nature.

"*Salām 'alaykum. Fursa sa'ida* – hello, pleased to meet you," Anubis finally said, shaking each man's hand.

The elder of the two strangers eyeballed Anubis without a hint of welcome in his black eyes, barely visible under hooded lids framed with long lashes. "*Ahlan wa sahlan* – welcome, pleased to meet you," he said, dropping his unfriendly gaze.

"*Allahu akbar* – God is great," the other stranger said, more curious than wary. "We are pleased with you. You did well, Brother. Your request deserves to be heard."

"You saw the explosion?" Anubis puffed his chest out with pride. "I told Abu I would go through with it when I volunteered. I want a return to a pure Islamic society, free of corrupt Western influences. I will commit any sabotage the *Secret Apparatus* orders if it furthers our cause."

Anubis sounded believable even to his own ears, so he relaxed, as much as one could on the hard, unyielding wooden stool that left part of his left buttock hanging over the edge.

"Do you swear to this, Brother Anubis?" the elderly man asked.

"*Allahu akbar,* I do swear. I want to contribute in a meaningful way."

Abu poured mint tea from a silver teapot into tubular glasses while the two men continued to study Anubis.

When the teas were served, the elder of the two strangers took a sip of the steaming, pale green-coloured water; then surprised Anubis with his question, "What is the greatest lesson you have learnt since becoming a member of the Muslim Brotherhood?"

"That the Brotherhood symbolises the promise of an Egypt without red-faced British soldiers swarming our cities and sacred desert." Anubis' solemn tone earned him satisfied nods. "I believe that Adolf Hitler's personal achievement gives us all a profound message of hope. That a former corporal in a defeated army could defy the rest of Europe to make his army and country great again proves that we can also defy the British and French who are the enemies of Egypt and Islam. The liars promised us our independence, but they went back on their word." He leant in closer to the men, his confidence growing as their stares became friendly and attentive. "They carved up the Levant between them and tried to stifle our religion, our sacred laws and culture, but with the help of Allah, Adolf Hitler, and his German army, we can defeat them and finally take back what belongs to the Egyptian people."

"You may call me Brother Sarraf," the older man said, honouring Anubis. Then he gestured to Abu. "Brother Abu has spoken to us about your German associate. Tell us about him."

Anubis threw Abu a filthy look. The boy was useless; he couldn't even get his facts straight. The fool was out of his depth in this important meeting. He'd not uttered a word, nor was he expected to, judging by the way his two influential companions were ignoring him. Abu was exactly what he was in the Alexandria consular offices; a tea boy, a messenger, and certainly not the murderer Rolf Fischer was looking for.

"Abu has made a mistake," Anubis apologised. "The man I spoke of is from Switzerland but lives near to the German border; however, he *does* speak German and supports the Führer." Anubis paused, then, as though he were thinking about it, added, "From what I know of the man, I believe he must be a more ardent supporter of the Third Reich than the average German. I haven't told him I am meeting with you tonight, but should you agree to hear what he has to say … what he can offer you, you will not be disappointed."

Brother Sarraf conferred with his younger companion with a simple look, then asked, "And what *does* he have to offer us?"

Anubis sipped his tea slowly, savouring its sweetness on his dry tongue. He set the glass in its saucer, and his eyes flicked to the main part of the room. "He has guns and money – lots of money."

"You trust him?" the younger man asked.

"Yes. I know hatred when I see it, and this man hates the British. He hasn't agreed to a meeting yet. He worries about British intelligence agents being in your ranks. But should you and he decide to deal, he will give you what you need for a good price."

Brother Sarraf threw Anubis a scathing look. "Hah, he thinks *we* might be infiltrated by British agents? No, no. It is the British who are careless. I assure you … their *spies* have already been dealt with in the strongest possible way."

Butterflies swarming in Anubis' stomach took flight. *Had he just heard a confession to murder? Was Sarraf referring to John Bryant and Farid?* If so, Fischer was one step closer to ending the investigation. "I hope you cut off their heads to send a message. Violence is what the British understand."

Brother Sarraf gave Anubis a blank stare and silence ensued until the younger man asked, "What type of guns can this Swiss man offer us? How and where does he acquire them?"

"He has stocks of infantry weapons: British Lee-Enfield No. 4 MK I rifles, American Colt 1911 handguns, Sten guns, and Bren light machine guns … and of course, he can also supply ammunition and grenades."

Anubis surged on, despite the reticence that met his pause. If they didn't believe him, his head would leave his shoulders before he'd reached the corner of the street. "As to how does he acquire them … well, he's a wealthy but frustrated man who is against his country's neutrality. He travels undercover as a common salesman but has already been successful in trafficking arms to Libyan and Iraqi anti-government factions. He partners with dissident groups who steal the weapons from supply depots and dead soldiers in the desert. He buys his merchandise cheaply and sells at lower than average prices. He does not tell me everything, of course. You will have to ask him yourselves for details."

"Where did you meet him?" Brother Sarraf stroked his thick whitish beard.

"I was doing business in Tunis. Herr Fischer was smuggling weapons out of that country and offered to pay me British pounds for the use of my boat. I obliged, and we struck up an ongoing partnership – if you are thinking of following him, to test his sincerity, don't bother. He comes and goes like a ghost, has a man working for him who delivers messages to me by hand but … you should know … I have my own suspicions about the Swiss…"

"Oh?"

Anubis waved his hand. "Not about his intentions to trade weapons. No, I think he might be a spy for the German army." Anubis took an exaggerated long breath. "I thought you should know. I am your servant and will keep nothing from you."

Anubis let the men digest all that he had said. His words had been rehearsed. Fischer had given him a written text and had warned him not to deviate from it. "Speak word for word without embellishments. You are an actor saying your lines; that is all. You do not think for yourself or make up stories because you like the sound of your own voice. You are my mouthpiece, nothing more." Fischer had drummed into him. Mentioning that he thought Fischer might be a German spy seemed counterproductive, but … *what do I care if Fischer gets himself killed? Good riddance.*

The two men had their heads together now, leaving Anubis and Abu out of the discussion. The café was packed with men who had come there after prayers. Music on the *Sintir* and *Buzuq* was playing in the background. Smoke from shisha pipes was becoming denser and settling on food dishes and Arabic sweetmeats, and conversations were becoming more robust.

Anubis, unable to hear a word, waited for his companions' responses to his request that they meet with Rolf Fischer. It had been over a week since he had taken the plunge and asked Abu to set up this meeting. The two men present were well known within the Muslim Brotherhood as being advocates for a more aggressive policy. That he'd even reached the men's ears was a great achievement, and it deserved a British pardon, he thought, struggling to keep his face placid while his anger simmered.

"We are agreed. We will meet with your Swiss weapons trader next week in Cairo, at a place of our choosing," Brother

Sarraf finally said. "Abu will tell you when and where nearer the time."

Anubis' body shook with anticipation as he stood to shake the men's hands, "*Ila likaa* – until we meet again."

*Jana Petken*

# *Chapter Twelve*

## Max Vogel

*Cairo, Egypt,*
*8 September 1942*

Max's Cairo apartment consisted of two rooms. Views of
Cairo's best and worst sights stretched beyond the main
room's French doors that led to a foot's width of balcony
enclosed by railings. Located near the Nile Delta, the area was
a mishmash of buildings, from the tired, old, and ancient, to
the amateurishly built modern constructions blasting constant
noise.

Standing on a chair and looking straight ahead, Max could
just about see the pyramids and the beginnings of the Sahara
Desert. With his feet on the ground, however, the view was
infinitely less impressive: an ugly concrete jungle of grey,
cement block apartments that no one had ever bothered to
paint, standing shoulder-to-shoulder on narrow, garbage-
littered streets stinking of domestic animal shit.

On their flat-roofed buildings, people grew vegetables,
kept poultry and pigeon coops, and erected ubiquitous
washing lines with crude wooden poles that were cemented
into hollow bricks. A perpetual skyline of white, cloudy
*thwabs* and *ghutra* head coverings billowed eerily in the wind
like an army of ghosts. They stood testament to Arabic wives
who tried to keep their men's robes white despite the
billowing sand that stuck to the wet garments. Max didn't hate
the area: a man could disappear into its maze of closely-knit

streets; no one asked questions, and the British military police deemed it uninteresting. It was as discreet as one could get in the Egyptian capital.

A single bed, set of drawers, wardrobe, and a rather luxurious bathroom were crammed into the other room. Max thought having the bathtub, sink, and toilet seat inside the bedroom a strange notion, but as off-putting as it was to shit next to where one slept, he was also grateful that the Egypt-based chief of MI2, the British Military Intelligence Section 2, had placed him in this modern middle-class apartment. He could have shoved Max into cheaper lodgings where he would have had a bucket of water to wash with and a walk to the communal toilet in the muddy back yard whenever he needed to have a piss or shit.

Max was close to confirming to Heller in London that John Bryant and the Egyptian boy, Farid, had been killed by members of the Muslim Brotherhood. Anubis' meeting four days earlier with the militant arm of the group had surpassed his expectations. He'd not got a confession, but he was confident that a man called Brother Sarraf had been referring to Bryant and Farid when he'd said they had *dealt severely* with suspected British agents.

Anubis had told Max, 'Sarraf was talking about *them* … I know it. It's taken me two months to get here, but I believe we'll never get closer to a full confession.'

When Max informed Jonathan Heller about the breakthrough, the latter had closed the case. 'These murders are not the reason you are in Egypt. Do not engage in the Bryant case further – adhere to political protocols with the Egyptian government.' Max had understood the message behind the writing, and he agreed with Heller. Only when one was *in* Egypt, could one understand the complexities of culture and laws and the political minefields surrounding religion. One of the Muslim Brotherhood members was guilty of murder, but Max could not march a troop of military police into the group's stronghold and make mass arrests. The Egyptian government was trying to suppress the Brotherhood in their own way and had demanded the British authorities stay away from all Islamic matters, even when it involved murder, apparently.

On paper, Heller would blame the Brotherhood for killing the British Intelligence Officer and claim he'd solved the crime. He'd put the closed file in a box on a shelf where it would collect dust and be ignored for decades or forever. Bryant was a casualty of war, who, as a spy, would probably remain incognito even in his grave.

For more than two months, Max had lived as Rolf Fischer, settling into the life of a watch salesman and allowing his reputation to grow in both Arabic and foreign communities in Alexandria and Cairo. He was known as a philanderer who liked to drink cocktails as he displayed his watches to tipsy foreigners. He attended dances and paid for the services of beautiful escorts to make him stand out. Loud and brash, he had come to the attention of British officers who continued to look but hardly ever buy from his stock of watches. Both men and women displayed their contempt for his German accent and neutrality status, but that was precisely the attitude he wanted to cultivate. He was confident that his reputation, albeit sordid, would hold fast for the most critical mission still to come.

In the late afternoon, Theo Kelsey arrived at Max's apartment. Ten minutes later, Captain Gaidar Shalhoub appeared. Max was looking forward to seeing the men, for apart from a sitrep sent by radio transmission to Gaidar three weeks earlier, he had not seen or spoken to either man.

Kelsey was talking about the Bryant murder. He was frustrated, utterly fed up with the whole thing, he told Max before any of them even sat down.

Max, expecting Kelsey's outburst, felt strings of guilt tugging at him. He was misleading Theo, who was involved in the murder case but unwittingly ignorant of the primary mission. He was a small player in a big game; not much more than a liaison officer between Max and British Intelligence, but he was dedicated – fervent, even – and that made it hard on Max's conscience to stonewall him.

"We've interviewed every person John Bryant was associated with in the Cairo consular offices, and I have nothing of substance, zilch," Theo said, as he handed Max his reports.

Max skimmed the papers. "That's disappointing."

"What about Anubis' Sudanese friend … you know, the boy who was going to lead your man into the Muslim Brotherhood camp to look for suspects?"

"Anubis has discounted the Sudanese, Abu Hanifa. According to him, the boy doesn't have the gumption or physique to be an assassin. He's a devoted Muslim Brotherhood follower and a pious Islamic scholar who is demanding independence for his country. He's a radical Islamist but has the body of a ten-year-old. He's not our killer."

"What about the British employees at the consular offices in Alexandria?" Theo now asked, becoming more irritated.

"What about them?" Max shrugged. "Half of them left Egypt at the end of the June when we thought Rommel was going to invade. Most of them haven't returned."

"Are you telling me that after months of tying ends together, we've got sod all! What are we supposed to tell John Bryant's wife?"

"We'll tell her that her husband died in service to his country, the same inane platitude we tell every dead intelligence officer's wife."

Max flicked his eyes to Gaidar Shalhoub, who leant against the wall with his arms crossed as though he were bored or uninterested.

"Look, no one likes to lose…"

"Are you saying it is over?" Shalhoub asked, finally airing his own exasperation.

"No, it's not over until I say it's over."

"We're punching bloody air now," Theo said. "This is not good enough, sir. You've had Gaidar and me twiddling our thumbs waiting for your instructions while you've been … bloody incommunicado … and with respect, here you are, finally, with nothing in the bag."

"Remember your place, Captain."

Kelsey's face reddened. "I was concerned for your safety, sir."

"I appreciate that, but there's no need." Max spoke dryly, rejecting Kelsey's pathetic attempt to backpedal. "I will tell both of you what you need to know, when I'm ready, not before, understood?"

Theo mumbled, "Yes, sir."

Gaidar let out an angry sigh and rolled his eyes at Max's banal attitude.

"Do you have something to say, Captain Shalhoub?" Max asked.

"Yes. I do," Gaidar grumbled. "We have no one left to question. This should be shut down. It's a waste of time. If Bryant's killer is connected to the Muslim Brotherhood, we'll be pissing up a wall forever and a day. May I speak freely?"

"You already are but carry on."

"With respect, sir, your asset is no closer to getting you a meeting with the Brotherhood than he was the day you picked him up from a British prison and offered him the deal. I don't believe you will succeed with him. You must agree?"

"Must I?"

Gaidar's eyes narrowed. "It would be easier for a fat camel to go through the eye of your proverbial needle than it would be to get you through a Muslim Brotherhood door. I have been against this operation from the outset. Even before you came to Egypt, I advised Captain Kelsey that it is against the Muslim Brotherhood's nature to allow outsiders into their camps. Two years ago, they acquired weapons, but they dealt with Muslim soldiers fighting at the *front,* not foreigners…"

"What is your point?"

"My point, sir, is that they probably killed your John Bryant and they will kill a Swiss, German-speaking, Rolf Fischer just as easily – they *will* kill you."

"Have you finished?" Max asked.

Gaidar leant against the wall again, arms folded in their guarded position across his broad chest and nodded.

"Good, then that will be all, gentlemen. Captain Kelsey, when I need you, I'll let you know." Max lit a cigarette, then poured cold coffee from the pot into his glass. He glanced at the clock on the wall; Anubis would arrive in less than an hour. "In the meantime, use the emergency protocol if you need to contact me – and stay away from this apartment, both of you."

"What are we supposed to do now?" Gaidar asked.

"Take a couple of days off."

"Very well, Major. Good evening."

Alone with Theo, Max said, "I understand your frustration, Theo, but you should have known better than to question me in front of another officer."

"I apologise, sir."

"Accepted. Goodnight, Theo. We'll regroup in two days."

******

Anubis drove the battered Volkswagen through the Cairo streets towards the Mokattam Hills, situated at the edge of the city's eastern suburbs. He was silent, his eyes fixated on narrow roads and dirt tracks littered with people who ignored the concept of looking left and right before crossing from one side of the street to another.

Max, glad of the silence between them, tried to anticipate any contingencies that might arise. It was an oxymoron, he admitted, to try to second-guess unpredictable events, but he was unarmed, making his most effective weapons, should he need them, his well-prepared, smooth-talking tongue and his gut feelings.

Anubis slowed down, stopped, and cut the engine on a narrow road behind a house. "We must leave the motorcar here. We will go the rest of the way on foot. I hope you have saved your strength. It will take us at least an hour to reach the top of the hill."

"I'll be fine. You just concentrate on finding the meeting place."

Max, dressed in a khaki shirt and shorts that reached his knees, felt his feet dragging as they arrived at the Mokattam's halfway point. He stopped to drink water from the leather flagon slung over his shoulder on a leather strap and marvelled at the views. An ancient-looking structure bathed in the red hue of dusk stood on a jutting ridge to his left, as if peering down on the capital's streets like an all-seeing father. "What is that building?"

After drinking, Anubis wiped his mouth with the back of his hand, then pushed the cork top into the flagon's opening. "The Coptic Church. Mokattam is well-known to the Christians. There's a story – probably untrue – that describes the day Coptic Pope Abraham of Alexandria performed a mass here. He wanted to prove to the Caliph that the Gospel was true. It is said that at the precise moment the Pope declared, 'If one has faith like a grain of mustard, one can move a mountain,' the hill did move up and down. The Coptics believe this is the reason Mokattam has many protruding plateaus. Who knows whether it happened or not – who cares, but the Christians?"

Max, still catching his breath, observed the stunning magenta and peach shades of the sun melting into the haze. Cairo's vast panorama served as a backdrop, stretching westward over a sea of jumbled rooftops and minarets across the shimmering Nile towards the dark points of pyramids jutting through the misty horizon.

"It is striking, is it not?" Anubis said, following Max's eyes. "During the day, this place is full of nature's wondrous sounds, as satisfying as a puff of apple shisha in the quiet desert."

To the left of the shallow incline, the dusty hills' six-hundred fifty-foot cliff face loomed like a second citadel over the valley. It was both imposing and wild, and Max felt the first quiver of fear. "Why the hell did they want to meet up here? I could think of a hundred places where we don't have to climb a damn hill."

"The Muslim Brotherhood conducts its weapons training in these hills. I'm sure if you were to tell your soldiers about that, they could also come up here and arrest dozens of brothers."

"Egyptian *and* British soldiers have ears, Anubis. They already know about weapons firing in the hills, and if they haven't arrested the culprits, it's because the Egyptian government has forbidden foreign intrusion into their business." That was all Anubis needed to know.

Anubis, seemingly disinterested, checked his watch. "It will be dark soon. We need to move."

Max's trek came to a halt at a beautiful setting on the most eastern section of the hills' plateaus: mimosa, jacaranda, and cypress trees stood in an almost perfect circle, as though a visionary gardener had planted them with an eye to their future growth. The oasis, in what was otherwise a stony, arid landscape, was a stunning reminder of Egypt's fertile land. Max had been in the country for months, but he was still in awe of the plants and trees that produced the most delicious fruit he'd ever tasted, the spices and herbs that grew wild, and the ubiquitous shadows of palm trees that gave comfort and sustenance to the poorest of people and shade to those who toiled in the fierce Egyptian sun. If not for the violence of men, it would be a Garden of Eden.

The black shadows of six men shuffling in single file approached the clearing within the circle of trees where Anubis and Max waited. Max hung back, daunted by the half dozen rifle-toting Arabs wearing black thawbs hiked up to their waists with black undergarments to their ankles billowing softly in the breeze. Anubis, however, looked relaxed as he greeted the man Max perceived to be the group's leader.

"Brother, this is Herr Rolf Fischer – Herr Fischer, this is our esteemed Brother who will negotiate with you," Anubis eventually said, when he escorted the man to Max.

Max stared into the *Brother's* eyes; their irises were so large and black that they almost consumed the surrounding sclera. Those eyes were all Max could see; the brother and his men had covered the bottom halves of their faces with the same black material as was used on the ghutrahs covering their heads. Max was strangely comforted by the men's caution; he would have been more afraid had they shown him their faces.

"*Marhabaan* – hello. Thank you for taking the time to meet with me," Max said in a respectful tone.

Max studied the man's reaction when Anubis translated what he'd said. One thing he had learnt about the Arabs of Egypt was that they responded well to the compliments of foreigners who were not part of the British Empire. To them, it was one in the eye of the English occupiers who displayed, at most, a modicum of respect to their Egyptian hosts.

"I understood what he said," the Brother responded with a sharp tone of voice.

Max's biggest hurdle would be the language barrier. He couldn't hope to be understood if he used German, and had, therefore, elected to speak flawed English, laced with a heavy German accent. The accent was important. Most educated Egyptians understood the King's English. It was the universal vernacular in the Middle East and North Africa, and the imposing Brother would detect a flawless London accent, which would blow Max's cover out of the water.

The Brother ushered Max and Anubis to three stools around a copper tray balanced on a wooden tripod. The immediate area was lit by fire torches that had been dug into the soft ground. In the secluded spot, a man was boiling water and already putting a handful of mint leaves into a copper teapot. Another was filling a bowl with crunchy yellow unripe dates while the rest of the men were facing outwards and focusing on their surroundings.

"This is a real home-from-home." Max smiled. "I can see why you chose this spot. *Ja, wunderschön* – beautiful."

"We must pray to Allah that it is not destroyed by the careless hands of the English and Germans. Slowly, they are demolishing everything else, even our precious desert," the Brother said.

It was evident by now that the man wasn't going to give his name. Anubis had told Max that the leader was a man called Sarraf, and Max presumed that was who he was talking to now. "Brother, I agree, but all this will change when Adolf Hitler is victorious."

Sarraf crunched into a date, then spat out the stone. "At the end of June and into much of July, we believed the Germans would be successful, but now we are not confident General

Rommel will make further advances. What do you know of the battles?"

"Not much. I hear gossip at the dining tables ... not secrets and all one-sided, of course. Sadly, I agree with you the Germans may have hit a *vorübergehend* ... a temporary stumbling block."

"The Royal Air Force has relentlessly attacked Rommel's supply lines, forcing him to draw back for want of petrol, but Rommel is not a man to retreat and give up," Sarraf said in impeccable English. "Some believe he will still find a way to break through the British defences."

Max accepted a small tubular glass of mint tea, then continued, "I am a selfish man, Brother. Merchants like me like conflict ... we make money in war. We see demand, and we supply. There are thousands of weapons lying around the desert, from Libya to El Alamein. The trick is to follow the battles from a safe distance, picking up what's been abandoned. Hot winds cover the dead, but with keen eyes one can spot jutting limbs and rifle butts – *ja,* one must be able to look – *so weit das Auge reicht* – as far as the eye can see, and with great patience. I have become quite the Bedouin in the last year."

Max glanced at Sarraf's German Mauser K98 rifle leaning against the table next to the teapot, and the pistol head just visible in the folds of his thawb; reminders that he was talking to a dangerous man and surrounded by men who would shoot him at their boss' nod. He smiled to break the uneasy silence. "Why am I telling you this? Well, I presume you know the desert better than I. I am just an ignorant Swiss man. To be honest, I am surprised you have not collected those abandoned weapons for yourselves."

Sarraf's pervasive eyes remained steady.

"Tell me, how many rifles do you need…?"

The deafening sound of a gunshot hit Max's left eardrum. His hands shot up to press against the pain and high-pitched ringing that was coursing through his head. Grimacing, he looked to his left and saw Anubis, face down on the ground with a bullet hole in the back of his head.

# *Chapter Thirteen*

Max lurched to his feet, knocking his stool over. He brought his arm up and stared stupidly at the red, warm fluid staining his left hand. He lifted it, swabbed the side of his face, also slick with Anubis' blood and brain matter, then righting the stool caught a glimpse of the man holding the offending pistol by his side. Terrified, he resumed his seat, faced forward, and like a torpid fool, flicked his eyes from Sarraf to the bodyguard standing behind him.

Although furious, Max couldn't halt the flood of terror rushing through him. He hid his trembling hands between his shaking knees, then finally found voice enough to rasp, "Why? Why did you kill Anubis?"

Sarraf shrugged, as though the answer were obvious. "I did not trust him. He was … how do I say in English? Ah, yes, too easily persuaded for my liking." Sarraf stared at the hole in Anubis' head. "I like William Shakespeare."

"Oh?"

"Ah, you think it strange that an Arab could enjoy such complicated use of language?"

"No. I'm not following what this has … I don't read Shakespeare," Max stuttered.

Sarraf spread his arms, a dramatic gesture to match his equally dramatic speech. "Ah, but you must! Hamlet is my favourite. 'The lady doth protest too much, methinks.' What a flowery way to call a person a liar." Sarraf leant in, his brows meeting in a frown. "Your friend Anubis … we saw through him as soon as he asked for this meeting. He was a big, fat liar." He spread his arms even further, then clicked his tongue. "We had to silence him."

Max, trying to contain the anxiety, which was beginning to push past his shock, stared at Anubis' body. "I didn't spot his lies. He seemed honest to me."

*I'm going to die,* Max thought. Like a character in a poorly written, predictable fiction novel without a plot twist in sight, he was going to follow John Bryant to the grave. Section MI6 was taking a bloody beating from scum like Sarraf, because men sitting behind their desks in London were repeating a flawed mission. A blind man could have seen this coming.

Sarraf got abruptly to his feet and stared down at Max. "Walk with me."

Max steeled himself for the end of his life, commanding his spine to straighten and his head not to bow by force of will alone as he followed the Arab into the thick treeline. *Would it be a bullet to his head, or would they torture him before throwing him off the cliff?* Behind him, the tall, broad-shouldered masked henchman tagged along, his rifle barrel grating against a shrub's branches.

Breaking through the trees, the three men arrived at a ridge overlooking the city. The moon was rising, surrounded by a blood-red haze.

"It is spectacular, is it not? The moon is a tempest. It makes men's blood boil and renders them mad. Did you know that?" Sarraf asked, as he sat on a large rock and stared up at the heavens.

"If you're going to kill me, do it. No need to make a *verdammt* – a damned meal out of it," Max retorted, refusing to take part in the man's theatrics. "You should have done your homework on me. You would have seen that I am who I say…"

"Ah, but we did." Sarraf spun around to Max. "You are Rolf Fischer, and you do indeed sell watches and steal guns. We know this."

Sarraf gestured with his head to his faceless ogre of a guard. "You see him? I trust this guard with my life, unlike your friend Anubis. I trust my man here with my children's lives. He has been following you for quite some time … even before your dead Anubis introduced you to us. He saw you weeks ago, Herr Fischer. He questioned friends of ours who work in the Shepheard Hotel and other places where foreigners go to enjoy life's many temptations and commit their sins against Allah. He believes you are sincere, and I believe in his judgement. Were that not the case, you would be lying dead on the ground beside Anubis, the big, fat liar."

With effort, Max kept the relief from his face. It appeared his hard-won cover story had stood the test of time. Anubis, however, had slipped up somewhere along the line, and it was important that Max find out how his asset's cover had been blown when his own had prevailed. Guilt flooded him, but with a stone-cold look, he said, "I'm glad to hear it. Now, can we talk about guns?"

"I do not want guns from you. They are not hard to come by, and I don't need to go to the graveyards in the desert to get them…"

Sarraf turned sharply as nearby leaves rustled. A man appeared. Dressed in western clothes, he had pale skin, fair-coloured hair, and a short, stubbed, piggy nose on a gaunt face. He walked laboriously to the group whilst cradling his stomach.

Max, standing unobtrusively behind the Egyptians, watched the new arrival stoop to kiss Sarraf's shoulder; a mark of respect usually reserved for royal persons and those in high governmental positions. It was evident by the black rings around the newcomer's eyes and the grey-tinged skin on his clean-shaven face that the man was ill, and this was made more apparent when he grimaced with pain as he straightened.

"Is this him?" the stranger asked Sarraf in clipped English laced with a heavy Italian accent.

"Yes." Sarraf pulled Max forward. "I believe he could be the man you are looking for. We should go back to the campsite. You are not well, my friend."

Max followed the men to the campfire and stools. Anubis' body had vanished, and all evidence, including his blood, had been wiped clean with a new sand covering.

Sarraf shouted in his harsh sounding Arabic to the four Muslim Brotherhood men who'd been waiting for his return. They disappeared into the trees. Max wondered if they were taking lookout positions or if they were not privy to the discussion that was about to begin. The mission, as outlandish as it was on paper, might be a *go* after all. It had certainly taken him long enough to get to this point.

The bodyguard threw logs onto the fire. Cairo was blazing hot even after the sun went down. The temperature, coupled with a cooking fire less than a metre from where they sat, caused sweat to trickle down the back of Max's neck.

As though feeling the same discomfort, Sarraf removed his face scarf and ghutrah, making a point of looking at Max as he coiled the strip of cotton around his hand.

Max was surprised by the man's advanced years. He was well into his sixties, with dark skin on a well-lined face and an almost white, thick bedraggled beard. His muscular arms, broad shoulders, and upright gait belied his age and suggested years of manual labour.

"I am Brother Sarraf, but you are not in our Society, therefore, I am no Brother to you, Herr Fischer. You may call me Sarraf."

"Fine. Sarraf, it is," Max said, with a respectful nod. Under any other circumstances, he would have initiated a polite conversation with the newcomer, but he had witnessed his asset being gunned down, execution-style, and was desperate to get this over with and leave with his head attached.

"If you don't want guns from me, what do you want?" he asked Sarraf.

Sarraf placed a hand on the newcomer's shoulder but kept his eyes on Max. "This is *Obelisk*. That is the only name you need to know. I want you to help him, Herr Fischer."

Obelisk studied Max again with a pensive tilt of his head, as though he had not yet decided whether to trust or kill the Swiss man. "I am an agent for the German Abwehr – have you heard of the Abwehr, Herr Fischer?"

"I know the name. It is a German military intelligence section, is it not?" Max said in stilted English.

"Correct," Obelisk replied.

Max, frowning with confusion, looked at Sarraf, then back to Obelisk. "You have me at a disadvantage. What is this about? Why are you telling me about the Abwehr? What does the Muslim Brotherhood have to do with them?"

"Listen with an open mind." Sarraf gave Max a patronising pat on the arm.

Max nodded, the skin on his arm crawling from Sarraf's touch.

135

Obelisk, again cradling his stomach, lifted his hand to silence Sarraf. "I will tell him." He focused on Max and began to speak in rapid German, perhaps testing Max's fluency in that language. "I was born in Genoa, Italy, but I was raised in Munich until my sixteenth birthday, after which I returned to Italy. I also have a British passport, which has been successfully active for two years. I have a small but efficient network of people in Cairo who help me maintain radio contact with the Germans on a twice-weekly basis, however, unlike you, I cannot conduct business with British officers.

He grimaced as though hit by a painful spasm. "My British passport has saved me from an internment camp, Herr Fischer, but being Italian forces me to keep a low profile in the city. I have been here for over a year, and thank God, I have not been suspected of any espionage activities, as far as I know."

The bodyguard offered Obelisk a cup, and the latter paused again to breathe in the fresh mint before sipping the tea. "Ach, it always smells good – *ja?*"

Max nodded absently. "*Ja* – go on."

Obelisk burped. "You must excuse me. It cannot be helped." After softly punching his own chest, he cleared his throat and continued, "I give my friends in the Abwehr information to help them make the best possible decisions on when and where to advance, when to hold, where to target their weapons at sea, and general insight into the Allies' strategies. The British, for all their arrogance in MI6, MI5, and their other intelligence apparatus, have not come close to detecting me, even though I average two transmissions a week to the Abwehr – I am the German's master spy in the Middle East."

Max, looking like a clueless idiot, scratched his stubbled chin. "I see. This is all very interesting, but what have spies to do with me? I'm a thief, a conman, a natural liar who makes friends easily. I know nothing of radios, or how to use a network, or anything about your murky world of espionage. Are you asking me to work for you?"

Evidently satisfied with Max's flawless German – with a Swiss accent to boot – Obelisk returned to English. "You came to the Muslim Brotherhood's attention because you *are* a conman and a thief, and despite being a Swiss national you have managed to stay out of British military police custody."

"Hmm … that's not quite true. I was taken in for questioning shortly after my arrival in Cairo. I learnt quickly after that to never as much as mumble in my own language," Max responded in German.

"Nonetheless, you have established yourself since then. That is good enough for me. You see, I have been looking for a replacement for almost two months. I know what you are thinking – and yes, the Abwehr did try to send someone, but the man wasn't right. He had no common sense, no initiative, and a terrible Bavarian accent. He'd have been arrested for spying within a week. I sent him back to the Germans with a note saying, *nutzloser Dummkopf* – useless fool."

Max chuckled.

Obelisk sipped more tea, then panted as though he'd run a marathon. "I am not a well man – I may be dying."

"I'm sorry to hear that."

"No, no. I don't want pity. I want you to take over from me. From all accounts, you're clever, efficient, and most importantly, someone who will be acceptable to the Abwehr … a reliable spy who will not be turned by British bribes or coercion if caught … a man I can introduce to the Abwehr as a dedicated and loyal supporter of Adolf Hitler and the Fatherland. I believe in him and in Rommel. I do not want to let the Germans down."

"What do you say, Herr Fischer?" Sarraf asked, wringing his hands and looking excited about the whole affair.

Max let out a heavy sigh as he mulled over his answer. Everything was going to plan, apart from Anubis getting his head blown off, but his response now would be pivotal; not his words as much as how he expressed them. "Correct me if I am wrong, please," he began. "You, Obelisk, are asking me to become an agent for the Abwehr in North Africa?"

"Yes."

"Even though, as I said, I have no experience –" Max cut his words short, straightening his back and widening his eyes as though he were struck by a thought. "Will I have to meet with the Germans in person?"

"It is highly unlikely. You will not even be expected to speak with my handler face to face in the desert. I have not met with a single contact in Egypt. The Allies have their backs to us, and the logistics of going through their lines to get to the Germans are unrealistic … of course, one never knows what might happen in the future."

Obelisk belched again, this time sounding like a growling dog. "*Ah … gut.* Where was I? *Ja …* Herr Fischer, no one has experience until they gain it in the field of battle. This is war, where each side makes new rules and breaks old ones. We are all learning how to kill, how to cheat and lie and trick our enemies to gain the upper hand. We search for situations to exploit, advantages to utilise. Being a spy is unlike any other profession. Every day is a test of skill and the broadening of one's intuition ... do you agree?" At last, Obelisk smiled.

"I believe I do." Max turned his attention to Sarraf. "I understand Obelisk's involvement with the Abwehr. I am not naïve ... I lie and cheat for a living ... but what is the Muslim Brotherhood's involvement, apart from brokering this meeting?"

"I am not directly involved in this war or in espionage," Sarraf answered. "The Muslim Brotherhood does not fight for the British or the Germans. They know nothing of my activities. I offer Obelisk transport and a safe house from where to send his transmissions, and I live in comfort away from Cairo's glaring eyes. That is all I am doing, and when the conflict ends, I will not even be a footnote in history."

That was the confirmation Max had been waiting for. The mission was a go, and he was in. Sarraf had verified he was on his own and did not have the Muslim Brotherhood's backing to assist Obelisk. For months, Max had pictured this moment, and the one soon to come where he told Heller his mission was on.

Obelisk stared at the mint leaf at the bottom of his empty cup and said, "Herr Fischer, you came to this meeting with a completely different objective in mind, but you were precisely the person I was looking for." Then he lifted his eyes to Max. "I apologise for your friend's untimely death. You must understand, we could not allow him to walk away from this meeting."

"Anubis wouldn't have told a soul," said Max, sounding naïve.

Sarraf swept his arm around the clearing. "Nonsense. Every man talks for a price, and your Anubis was a well-known thief. He could not be trusted. My men – look, you see they have disappeared, and we are alone, us four. Only *he* has remained." Sarraf pointed to his bodyguard who had been standing so still one could almost forget his presence. "We four know about Obelisk's mission … no one else. I will put to death any man who endangers his spy network or my association with it. I admit, your Anubis was probably *not* a liar, after all, but he *was* a liability."

"Well, will you give us your answer?" Obelisk asked.

*There is only one answer,* Max thought. A *no* and he'd be shot like a dog within seconds. "Yes. My answer is yes. I would rather see Germans in Egypt than British colonials." After a moment, he added, "I find Englishmen obnoxious."

*"Gut! Das ist sehr gut* – very good," Obelisk sighed.

"You will go with him," Sarraf told Max, pointing to the masked bodyguard. "He will take you to your home for your belongings. You will move to my safe house in the morning."

"We will begin your training then. I don't have much time," Obelisk got the last word.

Max was pleasantly surprised when the bodyguard escorted him to a waiting vehicle at the other side of the trees where two cars were parked. This was probably the route Obelisk and the Arabs had used, he thought, wondering why Anubis had made him climb the hill like a bloody mountain goat.

The Egyptian's death lay heavily on Max's conscience. He wouldn't be able to tell Anubis' wife he had died. She would never know what had happened to her husband. He will simply have disappeared, never be seen again.

In the passenger seat, Max studied the bodyguard as he whipped off the scarf around the bottom half of his face then removed his ghutra from his head.

"Did you know they were going to kill Anubis?" Max asked, eyes blazing as he glowered at Gaidar Shalhoub.

Gaidar retorted with equal heat. "Of course, I didn't. I was as shocked as you were. Sarraf doesn't tell me everything, Max. You heard him say he trusts me with his children's lives, but he's a devious bastard by nature. He keeps things to himself and then springs his plans on me at the last minute. I found out he'd killed John Bryant and the Egyptian boy because he needed me to give him an alibi should the military police come to his door." Gaidar sighed, and running his fingers through his dishevelled hair, warned, "Trust me, your biggest danger isn't the Abwehr finding out you're a British agent; it's Sarraf getting into trouble with the authorities and giving you and your operation up."

# *Chapter Fourteen*

Max and Gaidar, his face again covered, arrived at Sarraf's detached house on the morning after the meeting on the hill. It was shabbily constructed, as though cement boxes had been piled together at odd angles. Like most of the homes in Cairo's suburbs, it boasted unpainted grey walls that were interrupted by bare red bricks where frequent sandstorms had eroded the façade's exterior. Decorative, lattice shade panels protected the outside of the multiple narrow, arched windows, which were the construction's most attractive components, along with the intricate wood carvings on the door and the high wall that surrounded the property.

"It's opulent for an old cobbler, don't you think?" Max remarked to Gaidar.

"Wait until you see the inside. Sarraf has expensive tastes."

Sarraf opened the front door and escorted Max into the *majlis,* which Max learnt was the Arabic term for a sitting room or waiting room for guests. An extensive library of books housed in solid wood shelving stretched from one side of the wall to the other. At the far end of the spacious room, a semi-circular couch that could seat at least ten people was decorated with gold cushions. In front of the couch, inviting-looking silver bowls full of dates and boiled, honeyed candies sat on each of the five small octagonal tables. The thick cream brocade curtains with golden rope tiebacks and the cream Persian rug seemed out of place in this dusty, desert-like district at the edge of Cairo, as did the old Arab, Sarraf.

143

"As you can see, I am an educated man. I like my books and my solitude," Sarraf said, following Max's eyes to the bookshelves. "You are impressed with my home, are you not, Herr Fischer?"

Max's sickly-sweet smile hid his dislike for the man. "Who would not be impressed? You certainly like your home comforts," he said.

"And you will enjoy them as well. You'll see, you will never want to leave this house."

Obelisk appeared, looking even worse in the daylight than he had the previous night. His eyes were bright with pain, his skin grey and sleek with sweat. Max, genuinely concerned, said, "You should go to a hospital."

"Herr Fischer, glad you could make it," Obelisk replied in German. "We're going to have to shorten my handover, I'm afraid. I will return to Italy for treatment. I'm taking a flight out of Egypt tonight."

"Ah, Italy. I have always wanted to see the Colosseum in Rome," Sarraf said in German before popping a yellow, un-ripened date into his mouth.

"I'm sorry to hear that," Max said to Obelisk. He was also sorry to hear Sarraf speaking German, the sly old fox.

Gaidar spoke to Sarraf in Arabic while Obelisk sat on the couch and immediately closed his eyes.

Max, who'd been invited to tour the house alone, looked at the landscape through the lattice on an upper-floor window. The district was quiet, with no cars in sight apart from Gaidar's. From this top floor, Max saw the unstructured streets with a few houses surrounded by walls. The ground was coated with hard, sun-baked mud and a layer of sand from the desert that blew back and forth like gentle waves. Instead of people, he saw mules and carts, a couple of donkeys, bicycles, goats, and chicken and pigeon coops. He wouldn't have found Sarraf in a hundred years, had Gaidar not led him to the front door.

Max returned to the majlis, beaming with pleasure. "Wunderschön – nice place," he complimented Sarraf.

"You will be comfortable here," Sarraf said, the matter a foregone conclusion in his mind.

"Yes. It will do just fine. It's tidy. Do you have someone to clean it or to cook for you?"

"No!" Sarraf looked horrified. "We clean and cook for ourselves, do we not, my friend?" he said to Obelisk.

"Yes, and that is probably why my guts are on fire," Obelisk managed to joke.

Sarraf waved Obelisk away. "Ah, take no notice of him."

"How many people know about this house?" Max asked Sarraf.

"No one knows, apart from we four in this room. I told you last night, the Muslim Brotherhood and its Supreme Guide, Allah protect him, would not understand or condone my … how do I say … my love of life's indulgences? I have not even told my family about this place. It is my secret, and it will remain my secret. Also, while you are here, you will remove your shoes if you want to walk on my Persian rug."

Through Gaidar, Max already knew the answers to his questions, but he needed Sarraf to confirm the information he had, lest nasty surprises kick him in the backside later. "Where does your family think you are?"

"Living above my shop in Alexandria. My wife is not an easy woman to live with. She stays with her sister in Cairo, and my children are married. I do not see them often." His face lit up. "Ah, but when this war is over and I am a rich man, I will share my wealth with them. I despise seeing Egyptians bend to the British lash like brainless goats. It is better to have a goal that profits oneself, despite the dire circumstances in which one lives. I will not be an accepting victim of foreign tyranny and conflict … no, that is not who I am."

Sarraf was, as Gaidar had pointed out to Max on numerous occasions, *in it for the money* and probably didn't give a damn about what was going on under his nose for as long as he got paid. As with most hypocritical religious zealots, rewards and pleasures in this life were much more interesting than those being offered to the pious in the afterlife.

"I see … quite right," Max said absently, while glancing at Gaidar.

Sarraf, fond of his own voice, added, "When I am in Alexandria, Gaidar will come here each Saturday morning. You will pay him my rent money. I want English pounds, no Egyptian pounds or *piastres* – only British currency. Understand? And if you have any juicy gossip you can share with me … you know, about Britain's plans for Egypt, I will be most grateful to you."

Sarraf flicked his eyes to Obelisk who was still sitting on the couch and taking no part in the conversation. "You look tired, my friend. You have always paid me on time, and sometimes with a bonus attached – hmm, is that not so? Perhaps Herr Fischer will also be kind to me." His gaze slipped back to Max. "Tell me, Herr Fischer, do you enjoy a game of chess?"

Max crossed the room to Sarraf. Gaidar, still undercover as Sarraf's bodyguard, stood slightly behind his charge.

Max gave Sarraf a wry smile and said, "Yes, I like to play chess on occasion, but now I have work to do."

Like a striking cobra, Gaidar's right hand shot out and cupped Sarraf's mouth while his left arm locked around his victim's neck.

Sarraf's eyes bulged like a bullfrog being squeezed in a tight-fisted hand, his face reddening as his throat was constricted in the death grip. He struggled in Gaidar's grasp, but was incapable of reacting to Max, who was calmly playing with the dagger he'd been concealing in his trouser waistband.

Max plunged the serrated blade in centimetres below Sarraf's ribs. Releasing his anger at the man who had murdered the MI6 agent, John Bryant, his Arab boy, Farid, and Max's asset, Anubis, the previous night, he jerked the knife out, then stabbed his victim again, this time deliberately twisting the blade inside his gut.

Blood spurted from Sarraf's mouth and splattered Max's face. Cursing, Max pulled the blade out and grunted, "I won't be renting this house after all. Go to hell, *Brother.*"

Gaidar released his grip on the dying man's neck and stepped backwards as Sarraf fell to the floor like a felled tree and landed face first.

Max rolled Sarraf over. His thawb, stained red with blood, was stretched tight over his knees and the thin cotton garment tore open to display his open wounds, and below them, the strange sight of his manhood's erection at death.

"What was that for?" Obelisk gasped. "He was harmless – he was useful!"

"He might have been useful to you, but this is my operation now, and he is surplus to requirements," Max retorted, then added, "and you should never have involved him in the first place. Because of you, this handover is behind schedule, and your extraction was unnecessarily delayed. What the hell were you thinking?"

Gaidar, also angry, spat, "He murdered our MI6 colleague and Max's asset last night. Heller will not be happy about this situation."

Obelisk leant back on the couch, folded his arms and let rip in German. "You come here over a year after I have set this whole thing up, after I have tricked the Germans too many times to count and saved countless British lives. You dare tell me what I should and should not have done when I have had more success than you could dream of. How dare you! Did Jonathan Heller sanction this murder?"

"No," Max said, looking at the blade. "He didn't know Sarraf even existed. That's why you're going to get a bollocking when you get back to London." Max turned to Gaidar. "Check his pockets."

They were empty apart from a clean handkerchief which Gaidar handed to Max.

"We'll dump the body after dark tonight," Max said, using the handkerchief to clean the blood off his face and then his knife.

"I suggest we leave his corpse behind Opera Square. It'll be found quickly…"

"What if Sarraf is missed? What about his connection to the Muslim Brotherhood?" Obelisk pressed.

Max wiped the remaining blood off the knife whilst listening to Gaidar explain to Obelisk why killing Sarraf had been the proper action.

"... and he won't be missed. You heard him ... no one knows about this place, not even his family," Max joined the heated discussion.

"The Muslim Brotherhood won't be a problem, either," Gaidar now said. "There are eight men in Sarraf's group, and none of them liked the man. I was his number two. I'll take over as their leader until it's safe for me to withdraw."

Max said, "When the police discover the body tonight, they'll uncover Sarraf's unsavoury background. Gaidar has written a report about Sarraf's involvement with the Muslim Brotherhood and in the murders of John Bryant and Farid. The British will be happy to toss him into the Nile and forget about him."

"I will make sure of it," Gaidar confirmed. "What is your problem, Obelisk? He's one less radical for the authorities to worry about."

"I don't have a problem," Obelisk shrugged, "but this is still my operation, and you should have told me you were going to kill him. What happens to this house now?"

*Obelisk is right,* Max admitted to himself. He and Gaidar should have given the Italian the courtesy of a head's up before they had dispatched Sarraf.

Unwilling to apologise, Max said, "We will walk out of the house together and let the devil take it. As soon as I pack up the radio and all the other gear you've accumulated, we're out of here."

Max checked the time on his wristwatch. Four hours to go until dusk, and another hour after that for darkness to fall. Then he and Gaidar would have to wait until well after midnight before trying to dump the body unseen. Counting down, he had less than ten hours to get up to speed with Obelisk's operation.

"When is the next scheduled transmission to my operators in England?" Max asked Obelisk.

"In two hours."

"Good. Make tea while Gaidar and I get this murdering piece of shit out of our sight. We'll use his Persian rug to cover him, seeing as he was so fond of it."

# *Chapter Fifteen*

## Dieter Vogel

*London, England*
*September 1942*

Dieter Vogel and Jonathan Heller ate a light lunch in Heller's office. Their weekly luncheons at MI6 headquarters had begun after Dieter brushed off his earlier fears of being recognised by any remaining German spies milling around the capital. As in the previous year, the handful of German agents who had been captured had turned to British Intelligence and were now working for MI5 and MI6. The chances of being spotted by a German spy on British shores nowadays were slim to none; the Abwehr was losing the intelligence war against the British. Also, Dieter looked nothing like his old self since he'd stopped dying his hair blond months earlier and now had a mop of snow-white curls accompanied by a thick white beard.

During their lunches, the two men discussed everything from the weather to family matters, but they made a point of skirting all war-related conversations until after they had finished eating. On this day, Dieter had brought Laura to the capital. Before meeting Heller, he'd left her in a restaurant with her sister, Cathy. He loved it when his Laura got excited about something, for there was so little to get excited about these days.

After lunch, she was going to a shop in Piccadilly that sold handmade, embroidered baby clothes for their grandson. She still needed clothing coupons for the tiny garments like the rompers she wanted, she had warned Dieter. And the shop wouldn't take into consideration her donations – baby Jack was growing so fast that she and Hannah had given many of his tiniest garments away to various shops. Dieter was perplexed with his daughter, Hannah, who had refused to take an allowance from him. She could not afford to buy such luxuries regardless of whether she had enough coupons. Her pride would be her downfall, Dieter had warned her.

After Heller's secretary, Marjory, had removed the dinner plates, Heller and Dieter moved to the desk. Heller, now with his official face on, sat in his chair and uncoiled a piece of string that held a file closed, and then tapped the folder with his index finger.

"This is top secret. I thought it best we discuss it here because of its sensitive nature."

"Everything is sensitive nowadays."

Dieter always knew when Heller was going to say something a person might not want to hear. He watched now as the intelligence chief shuffled his large frame into his chair as though trying to nest in it and began with a ritual clearing of his throat, with two coughs at the end. A chill swept through Dieter, as his three sons came to mind. "Damn it, Jonathan, what is it?"

"I have in these pages Operation Lanner Falcon. It's being played out in North Africa and run by MI6 at Bletchley. I want you to come onboard."

"I see."

"You don't, not yet. When we concocted this operation, some thought it was at best audacious, and at worst, downright delusional, yet two years in, it is still operational and proving to be one of our most successful missions of the war, to date. Interested?"

Dieter nodded. "Go on."

Heller continued, "We have a double agent in Egypt, codenamed Obelisk. I should say *we had*. He's no longer in the field because of illness. We could run the whole operation from Bletchley in his absence, Dieter, feed the Germans a load of dribble as our agent Obelisk has been doing for over a year…"

"But?" Dieter prompted, raising an eyebrow.

"But we decided it would be better to have a replacement based in Cairo with up-to-date knowledge of what's going on in Egypt on a day-to-day basis. We flew Obelisk out of Egypt on one of our transport planes three days ago. He's in King's Cross Hospital, here in London, recovering from a major stomach operation."

"I presume someone has already stepped in for him?" Dieter was still confused.

"Yes. I'll get to him in a minute. Obelisk will hopefully return to Egypt at some point, but his recuperation in London could take some time. His benign tumour was the size of a melon … maybe a slight exaggeration, but still, it was a big bugger. It could take months to get him back to operational fitness. Dieter, this man has been crucial to our successes in North Africa, and when we found out in May that he would probably need surgery, we put together a mission to replace him with one of our own spies…"

Dieter leant in towards Heller. "I knew it. I bloody knew it. It's Max, isn't it? My son is in Egypt?"

Heller nodded. "Yes, it's Max. He partnered up with one of our Egyptian-based officers in May, and since then, they've been working together to achieve the right circumstances for Max to step into his role as Obelisk's temporary successor. Our delay has been because Obelisk took it upon himself to get an Arab involved, and not just any Egyptian, but a Muslim Brotherhood member – the silly sod could have blown the whole damn thing out of the water – and Max had to dispose of the man before taking over."

Dieter's fingers fumbled with his cigarette packet. He had no right to question Max's actions in the field or Heller's choice of agent or to make demands regarding his son. Max was doing his duty, and as such, even as a father, Dieter could not interfere or ask for more information than MI6 was willing to give. In this instance, however, Heller was offering direct access to Max if he'd read his earlier, *come onboard* correctly. "At least, I know where my son is. Thank you, Jonathan. I appreciate this. Tell me more about Obelisk."

"He's the son of an English father and an Italian socialite. She owns a string of hotels in Italy. He was raised in Germany – Munich – and he speaks four languages fluently. When you get to know him in this file, you'll find he's a cosmopolitan chap, flamboyant, loves to throw money around. He's also an imaginative storyteller … probably why he was able to invent such an intricate fictional spy ring around himself.

"Did he approach the British?" Dieter asked.

"Yes, he contacted us in '39 to report an approach by the Germans. We encouraged him to accept the Abwehr's offer, and he was eventually tasked by his German case officers to get to Cairo and report on Allied military intentions and capabilities. He got there via Istanbul under his Italian passport."

Heller finished the water in his glass, then continued, "He's had tremendous success slowing down Rommel's forces with misinformation. The man might have saved Cairo and the Suez Canal. He lost the Germans Tobruk by starving Rommel's Afrika Korps of fuel. Two months ago, he informed the Axis forces there were fourteen non-existent British divisions in North Africa. Rommel believed him and elected to postpone his offensive against the British until the end of last month, by which time our Montgomery had accumulated his Eighth Army forces."

"Have the Germans never questioned Obelisk's inaccuracies?"

"Yes. He claimed he didn't have adequate funds to recruit top-class informants. The Abwehr accepted his explanation … even went as far as making elaborate arrangements to pass him additional cash." Heller, evidently proud of his agent, continued, "Their plan resulted in another coup for us. Our warships sunk their submarine, and we captured the courier who was carrying the money to Obelisk. Once you get into the file, you'll understand why we couldn't let this operation die. What he's doing is too damned important. He's averaging two radio transmissions a week, Dieter. Think about that … two a week!"

"I can see why you want the operation to continue."

Heller got his box of cigars out and chose one. "It's a damn shame about Obelisk's illness. It couldn't have come at a worse time," he said as he cut the end of his cigar with a silver clipper.

"Is there ever a right time to be ill?"

Heller grinned. "I suppose not. There are complications in Egypt, which you'll read about in that file. I won't go into them now, but when you read up, you'll see the problems Max has, and will have, to face. It's ironic. Obelisk is not fond of the British. He told me without a hint of embarrassment that he likes the Germans but resents their treatment of Italian Jews – he's part Jew, you see."

Dieter's eyebrows rose in surprise. "Ah." Then he thought about Max again. "Is my son already undercover?"

"Yes. We got the confirmation four days ago. He lost his Egyptian asset in the process ... a long story ... another one you'll read about in this file."

Heller drew on his cigar then let out a tired sigh. "The whole thing has been rather complicated, to be honest." He finally handed Dieter the file. "I want you to run Operation Lanner Falcon from Bletchley, under our Ultra Programme. You'll be Max's primary controller. His code name is Mirror, as always. His job is to keep the Abwehr busy with distortions of the truth until Obelisk returns. I'll come to Bletchley tomorrow morning to go into more detail. In the meantime, pick your team, and familiarise yourself with the players here and in Egypt. You can start with Captain Theo Kelsey. He'll be debriefed downstairs in about an hour. He was in Cairo with Max but wasn't part of Operation Lanner Falcon. He'll give you the insight you'll need into the present conditions in Egypt, and more importantly, tell you how Max is doing. Observe only, Dieter, and don't mention your relationship to Max; at least, not yet."

"Has he been told why he was brought back?" Dieter asked.

"Yes, and he wasn't pleased with being kept in the dark. He's a good chap, injured at Tobruk last year. He'll be working for you on this phase of the operation. I'm sending him to you tonight. He can be in on my briefing at Bletchley in the morning."

Heller picked up the telephone, was silent for a couple of seconds, then said, "Marjory, bring me the Kelsey file, please."

Again, Heller shifted in his chair, but this time he grinned, and his face brightened. "I wanted to leave this news until we'd discussed our business. I didn't think you'd be able to concentrate if I told you when you walked in here. It concerns your Paul."

Dieter's eyes instantly began to water at the mention of his son. *News at last.* "Christ, Jonathan, you should have led with this. I've been here for over three hours – tell me he's all right. I can't – I won't give Laura bad news…"

"It's not bad. You asked me to badger Ernst Brandt for news of your boys … well, he finally came through for you. He picked up one of Goebbels' propaganda newspapers. It contained notices of medal recipients and the like, and the usual stories … you know, sentimental stuff about heroics and important families."

"If it's the newspaper I think you're talking about, it was one of Goebbels' pet projects." Dieter snorted. "It has only good news and praise for the Reich in it. Sorry, go on."

"Hmm, and as much as I hate Goebbels' propaganda machine, on this occasion, it has brought *you* good news. Oberarzt Paul Vogel, son of the late industrialist, Dieter Vogel, has become a father. He and his wife were mentioned in the birth section of the paper – a daughter, Erika Maria Vogel, Brandt said."

Dieter's head spun. All he could think about was getting out of the office and telling Laura and Hannah the wonderful news. "I'm a grandfather again – *ach du großer Gott* – my God! I can't wait to tell Laura." His misty eyes then widened with hope. "Did Ernst say where Paul was serving? Did he read anything in the newspaper about Wilmot?"

"No, on both counts, I'm afraid."

"I understand," Dieter sighed. "Still, it's better than Brandt reporting that he'd seen my boys' names on the obituary page. Please, thank Ernst for me."

Marjory brought in the file and left without a word being exchanged.

Dieter rose and shook Heller's hand while giving him a boyish grin. "I'm a grandfather twice over – baby Erika – wonderful. Thank you, Jonathan. You've made my day. I hope you'll stay for lunch tomorrow in Bletchley?"

"I wouldn't miss Laura's cooking for the world." Then Heller cocked his head to the side. "When are you going to trim that beard, Dieter? You look like a damn Santa Claus."

# *Chapter Sixteen*

## Wilmot Vogel

*1 September 1942*
*Alam el Halfa, the Western Desert*

Wilmot, with his fingers plugging his ears and eyes squeezed shut, hunkered behind a rock and braced for the engineers' explosive devices to ignite. When the blasts came, the ground beneath his feet vibrated: rocks, stones and hard clay shattered into small pieces that flew into the air like geysers, and a fine mist of sand covered his entire body.

The engineers collected their gear and went on to the next area. Wilmot then supervised his men as they began shovelling the recently blown up stones and gravel into piles. Afterwards, they would deepen the small craters that were to house the guns. The heavy weapons would lie horizontally over the lip of the trenches, be manned by one man, also dug in, and be practically invisible to the enemy using desert camouflage.

A scarf covered Wilmot's mouth and nose. Goggles shielded his eyes, and his cap kept the sun off his burnt head. He had been stupid enough to remove his headgear for a short while the previous day, but even with his mop of hair to protect him, the sun's brilliance had reddened and blistered his scalp.

"Obergefreiter, have you got water? No one's got any water. Can you believe that? This is shit. I'm going to die of thirst," a bare-chested man digging the hole nearest to Wilmot grumbled as he dug. "What are we doing this for? We'll be abandoning this place in a couple of hours and giving the gun holes to the enemy. Who comes up with these stupid ideas?"

Wilmot shook his head. Günter was one of those men who never stopped complaining. Wilmot had come over from Italy on the ship with the whiner, and no matter how hard he tried to keep away from him, Günter always managed to stick to him like a leech, nit-picking everything he saw and heard that didn't please him. He was a fresh recruit and had no idea what hardships men endured in the military. He must have been a spoilt brat as a child, Wilmot concluded.

"You'll get a drink when the tankers return," Wilmot gave Günter a curt answer.

"That could take hours, Obergefreiter. I heard they had to do almost three hundred kilometres round-trip to fetch fresh water. And what if they're blown up on the way back? Those English dive-bombers will be able to pick them off like skittles, now the sandstorm has died down."

*The man had a point,* Wilmot thought. Tankers often had to backtrack for hundreds of kilometres to fill up, and three full-to-the-brim water tankers had been destroyed on the first day of fighting.

"It's all right for you. You're standing there watching while we're drenched in our own fluids," Günter now complained.

"Well, when you have my experience and seniority, you'll be exempted from menial duties as well, but until then, dig the damn hole and shut up. And put your shirt on. You won't get off work details if you burn like a piece of toast."

Fed up with the man and feeling unwell, Wilmot left the line of diggers and found a bit of shade behind a lorry that

towed an 88mm anti-aircraft and anti-tank gun. He clutched
his stomach, groaning as diarrhoea dribbled out his arse then
down the length of his short trousers and onto his bare leg.
*Liquid gold,* the men called the shits. Steaming hot
*Frankfurter Würstchen sausage* was the name used to describe
a more solid variation which Wilmot had not yet been lucky
enough to experience. The cramps and shits came without
notice at times; they had turned farting into a dangerous game
of *wait and see,* for one never knew if a fart or shit would
come out.

He wiped his leg with his face scarf then cursed at his own
stupidity; without the scarf, he'd probably choke to death on
sand and dust. *Ach, never mind,* he thought, wiping as much
dung off his skin onto the sandy floor as he could while still
feeling sick at the thought of wrapping the stinking scarf
around his nose and mouth again. He'd take a scarf off one of
the enemy corpses lying about.

He slid to the ground and rested his head against the side
of the vehicle. He'd been in the desert for less than three
weeks and was experiencing acute gastric pains and fainting
fits that came at the most inopportune moments. On the
Russian front lines, he'd been used to a diet of bread and
potatoes, but when he'd got his first meal in North Africa,
he'd been shocked to see a plate of hard biscuits and beans.
Occasionally, the beans were enlivened by small amounts of
cheese and dehydrated vegetables. Sometimes they got tins of
Italian meat, the ancestry of which were always the cause of
much debate. He missed potatoes. He'd asked where they
were and had been told that bread and potatoes went mouldy
too quickly in the heat.

It was a monotonous diet and low in vitamins. Wilmot had found out that the British, on the other hand, luxuriated in tinned fruit and vegetables and something called bully beef. That gave the Axis troops the motivation to fight and capture allied supplies.

"Taking a break?" a voice asked.

Wilmot opened his eyes and looked up. His moment of contemplation on food and shits was over, and just as well, for he hated self-pity. "I'm having a bit of trouble with my bodily functions, Unteroffizier. I needed a few minutes to settle my problem," Wilmot said truthfully to the senior ranger.

The man stretched out his arm to shake Wilmot's hand, but then he saw the brown-stained scarf lying on the ground next to Wilmot and retracted it. "Ach, it happens to us all. You'll get used to it. I'm Uwe Schmidt."

"Willie Vogel." Wilmot perked up. It was comforting to see a genuinely friendly face, albeit one that was showing signs of stress from being in the desert for a long time. He had the strained look of Haupt, Wilmot's officer pal from Russia.

Uwe sat next to Wilmot and handed him his flask. "There's a mouthful of water left in there, but you can have it. It might be a while before the tankers get to us."

Wilmot guzzled the remains in the flask, inadvertently crunching on gritty sand that was lying in the bottom of it. "It's like nectar of the gods," he sighed nonetheless when he handed the flask back to Uwe.

"I knew this offensive was going to go to pot as soon as they told us we were attacking under a full moon. I blame the Italians," Wilmot said to the desert-hardened man sitting next to him.

"Generaleutnant Rommel agreed with the Italian Supreme Command," Uwe said, putting Wilmot in his place. "We're facing long supply lines and lacking reinforcements, and it was he, not the Italians, who decided to strike the Allies while their build-up was still incomplete. The plan was sound. We were supposed to break through the southern part of the front because it was held by weaker forces than the rest of the British line and afterwards advance by way of Alam el Halfa to Alexandria. Maybe if the first wave hadn't been bogged down in a minefield, our lot would have broken through. Who knows?"

Wilmot had joined the 90th Light Infantry upon his arrival in the Western desert. His division and the Afrika Korps had led the Italian XX Motorised Corps in the failed second wave. He still felt the adrenalin running through him after surging forwards against a barrage of enemy tank fire the previous day. "Yes, well, attacks always sound straight forward on paper, but they rarely go according to our commanders' plans."

The two men paused their miserable conversation to get out their packs of cigarettes.

Wilmot lit his, and still thinking about how he'd felt before the previous day's battle, reiterated, "I knew we were going to fail. I can't tell you why I was more nervous about this offensive than any other I've experienced in the war, or why I was pessimistic, but I had this strong feeling we weren't going to find a way through the British lines."

"Fear plays terrible tricks on a man's mind, Willie."

"That's the thing, Uwe; most people think I'm an optimist. If there's a silver lining to be found, I'll find it. Ach, maybe you're right. Maybe I was scared."

Uwe chuckled. "I wouldn't worry about it. I've been terrified since the day I landed in this desert." He drew on his cigarette and flicked an ant off his leg. "Did you hear about the commander of the 21st Panzer Division getting killed?"

"No, but I heard we lost the commanders of the Afrika Korps and our 90th Division."

Uwe nodded. "They're still alive but badly wounded. It was a bit of a shambles after they left the field."

"No one is infallible, eh?" Wilmot mused.

"The tanker we were expecting was torpedoed and sunk on its arrival in Tobruk. We were supposed to get four hundred tons of fuel yesterday, and we received a fraction of it because the transport planes had to use it themselves on the long trip."

"How do you know all this stuff?"

"I have my fingers in the supply chain and every other logistical chain. Got to know what's going on, so you can tell your men something. If we waited for news from the top, we'd never find out anything."

Wilmot wondered if the fuel shortage had caused the latest rumour that was picking up steam. Apparently, Rommel intended to break off the attack. "Do you think we should turn around?"

Uwe swept his eyes around the area before answering. "Yes. This is a no-go. We've got petrol shortages, and we lost materials and men yesterday … far more than anyone expected. If we try to move forward again, we'll get hammered by Allied Spitfires from the air." Uwe let out a tired sigh. "I hate the thought of retreat."

Wilmot's rank of senior lance corporal meant he was often given information that never reached the grunts in the lowest ranks. He enjoyed this privilege, but sometimes he wished he could go back to a simpler time when he was an ignorant Schütze blindly following orders and hoping for the best.

"You know, Uwe, before the ship docked in Libya, I pictured this place being full of vast swathes of sand dunes, camels, and the odd oasis with swaying palm trees. Not for a moment did I imagine this stony, barren desert. It's horrible. ... I've tried, but I can't say anything nice about it. This place must be pure hell for the men dealing with logistical support."

"It's a nightmare," Uwe said, trying to flick more ants off his arm. "Problem is, everything we need to fight and stay alive has to be transported from Italy. The crossing to Libya is about ninety kilometres, but the ships carrying our supplies have got to run the gauntlet past Malta. God knows how much stuff we lose on those cargo vessels that get hit by the Royal Air Force and British Navy. Then when the supplies land, the lorries have got to travel along the *Litoranea Balbo* – the *Via Balbia* road. The Italians built it. It extends through this filthy armpit of a country without a tree or shrub in sight for as far as the eye can see. It's the only main road in Libya."

"Christ. Imagine if we're waiting for cigarettes and they're on the last truck in the convoy leaving Tripoli…" Wilmot joked. "The war will probably be over by the time that truck gets to us. How far does the road stretch?"

"About eighteen hundred kilometres from Tripoli to El Alamein. It's rough. I've been here for eighteen months and I've spent as much time fixing vehicles as I have fighting. Tank tracks are always getting torn off and tyres split every five minutes. The sand blows up because of the constant movement of vehicles and trucks, and it blocks the tanks' air filters. Before they changed to the new desert filters, the walls of the engines were scoured to a standstill after eight hundred kilometres or so. I can't count the number of times breakdowns have delayed our advances. I'm having one more cigarette before I go back to work – join me?" Uwe sighed again, as though he had the weight of the world on him.

"I will. Have you been here from the beginning?" Wilmot asked.

"Yes. When we got here, there was no heavy artillery support. We were sent to Libya as a blocking force, because the Italians were losing ground to the British. They don't know how to fight, those Italians. They prefer singing opera."

"Is it true that General Rommel is under the Italian Supreme Command?"

"Yes, but he takes no notice of the pizza-lovers half the time." Uwe drew on his cigarette as though it were a straw in an empty glass.

Wilmot had come over from Italy with a brigade of German paratroopers and a division of Italian paratroopers. Apparently, thousands of men were rushed to North Africa at short notice to reinforce the gaps. "We didn't get any training when we arrived. All they gave us were a few lectures by experts in tropical medicine, plus a couple of chats with officers who've been here for a while. The lecturer told us what to expect from the effects of heat and sand and insects, but they didn't tell me I'd be shitting myself every five minutes."

"You got more information than we did when we arrived," Uwe grumbled. "Did they tell you about desert blindness?"

"No, they didn't." But Wilmot had come to know the phenomenon well. It was a strange phenomenon; between dawn and 0900 and between about 1600 and dusk, the reconnaissance patrols could identify enemy or friend from about eighteen hundred metres. However, when that shimmering mirage of full sun hit them, they couldn't see more than thirteen hundred metres.

"I suppose that's why we travel a lot at night and when there are raging sandstorms ... because they're good for the eyes, aren't they?" Wilmot chuckled at his own sarcasm.

"That's the main reason, but we also use that time to commandeer or blow up allied tanks that have been left on the battlefield. More than half our transport and tanks are gifts from the allies."

General Rommel had what Wilmot described as bouts of restless energy that were contagious. Unlike any officer Wilmot had previously served under, Rommel was hands-on and always wanted to know what was happening at the sharp end. When he was not at the helm of his command car, *Greif,* he was reconnoitring the ground and enemy positions from the cockpit of a tank. He sought to combine the infantry with the guns and tanks so that all weapons were on the battlefield together, fighting as an integrated whole. Rommel had spoken to Wilmot once. He'd said, *Good morning, Obergefreiter,* as he'd walked amongst his men.

"What do you think of Rommel?" Wilmot asked after a long but comfortable silence.

Uwe shrugged, noncommittedly. "The men like him, but some of the staff officers think he's reckless. I remember when we were trying to take Tobruk. He told my colonel to attack. My colonel answered back that he'd already lost fifty percent of his men. Rommel didn't care, and shouted, 'And is that any reason not to go forward? Attack!'

Uwe's eyes swept the area. "I was there, and I know what I heard. My colonel yelled back, 'My men will attack over my dead body!' I thought Rommel was going to shoot the man in the face and me along with him."

Not sure if he wanted to hear any more intimate details of conflicts between officers, Wilmot changed the subject with a rhetorical question. "Know what I like about this place? There are no Gestapo or SS sticking their noses in and causing trouble for us. For the first time since I've been in the military, I don't feel as though I'm being spied on or being asked to carry out duties I don't agree with. It's just fighting here – there's something pure and honourable about it…" Interrupted by a heaving, grumbling stomach, he then said, "Uwe, will you excuse me a minute? I need to see to something."

Wilmot's baggy shorts fell to his ankles. He squatted behind a decent size rock next to the gun trailer and sighed with relief. "Come on, come on, little buggers," he urged himself in a singsong, lilting tone. The noise of rumbling aircraft engines grew deafeningly loud, as did the accompanying sound of whistling shells dropping from an angry sky. He craned his neck, then leapt to his feet and was immediately blown off them, as a massive explosion erupted close to the 88 mm gun.

As he ran, head bowed into a torrent of fire that hit the German and Italian tanks and the men still digging in, Wilmot saw there was nowhere to hide, no Axis response to this latest attack, and no escape route whatsoever. He tripped, looked down his length and saw he had lost his shorts entirely and was butt-naked from the waist down.

Another blast took Wilmot's legs from under him, and he tumbled to the ground, his bum and manhood aired but forgotten in the turbulence. His ears were in excruciating pain, and he was deaf, dizzy, and feeling as though he were underwater where everything he saw rippled or swam towards him. The whirling sand, stones bouncing on the ground, and swaying bodies of men who were being blown to ribbons swam together in his vision with the giant fireball stretching the length of the tank lines, jerking unnaturally back and forth in convoluted patterns – bizarre – in the rampageous events unfolding, he heard nothing but the sound of his own heartbeat pounding inside his brain.

As he lay twisted on the ground, he raised his head and through half-shut eyes saw Uwe's blackened torso, his detached legs lying a metre away from where he lay.

"Aww, Jesus Christ … no ... no," Wilmot groaned. *Had he lost his legs as well?* He tried to look down the length of his body, but he could only rise enough to see that his shirt had been ripped open and his bloodied chest was exposed. He lay back, dazed and exhausted. His legs were still there, as were his arms. It wasn't a total surprise, for he couldn't imagine them flying off his body without him noticing.

The ground shook again, and a massive volcanic eruption of dirt and stones flew into the air and battered Wilmot's head and body. *It was raining fucking rocks!* He felt like a man from ancient times being stoned to death. Around him, men were being punished by a hail of bullets from an angry sky crowded with Allied PS 40 Warhawks and Spitfire fighter planes. The bastards were showing no mercy.

When a stone as sharp as a knife slashed his cheek, Wilmot's head whipped to the side. He felt nothing; no pain, no sound, no fear. *This is it,* he thought. *This is the end, and it's not as bad as I imagined it would be.*

# *Chapter Seventeen*

"Lie still, Obergefreiter, or I'll knock you out myself."

Wilmot squeezed his eyes shut, trying to be brave as a needle and thread went in and out of the tender, damaged skin on his face. He had tried to see what was going on more than once, but both times his eyes were hit by a brilliant white light that made his sore head thump even harder. He was alive. He knew that because no dead man would feel the agony he was experiencing. His backside was bouncing and banging off a hard surface while someone was pawing at his face – *the only one he had.* Panicking, he lifted his better arm and swatted the air with it. "Stop it," he croaked.

"Give him more morphine," the Oberarzt told his *Sanitätssoldat.*

The doctor waited until his medical assistant had injected the morphine then said, "We're going to have to keep him under while I stitch up the face wound. Tell the driver if he's not more careful, I'll end up suturing this man's nostrils closed – better still, ask him to pull over…"

Late in the afternoon, Wilmot's eyes flickered and eventually opened to a dimly lit space in the back of a canvas-covered truck. A few minutes earlier, he had come out of a dreamless sleep, and since then, his delicate eardrums had been battered with the sound of enemy aircraft buzzing overhead and ubiquitous vehicles and tanks punishing their engines on the hard, stony ground.

He covered his ears with his hands and groaned with pain as another explosion rocked the truck.

A man shouted, "Where am I? Aww, for fuck's sake, someone tell me where I am! Take me home … I want to go home!"

Wilmot finally managed to rise to a sitting position and wriggle his painful backside to the canvas wall of the vehicle, where he rested his back. He looked down. Thank God someone had dressed him in a pair of shorts. He didn't want to be known as the man who was caught with his pants down.

"Where am I?" the man was still shouting.

*He's in a bad state,* Wilmot thought. The poor sod's eyes were covered with bandages, as were his head, arms, and hands. He looked desperate, clawing at the air as if searching for something … comforting hands, probably.

"You're in the back of a truck," Wilmot shouted to the man above the exterior noises. "We're on the move."

Wilmot pressed the back of his head against the truck's soft covering, flapping in the wind. Exhausted by the effort it had taken to sit up, he wondered just how seriously injured he was. Someone had removed his shirt while they replaced his shorts. Blood was sticking to the thick black hairs on his chest and staining his skin, but when he touched the area, he felt no pain or bumps or cuts. His forearm, however, was bandaged.

His hand tentatively brushed the part of his face that was stinging and hot. It was covered with a linen strip and taped at the edges near his nose on one side and hairline on the other. Even through the morphine, he felt his pulse pounding through the wound. He knew it was a deep gash; he would have an ugly scar for the rest of his life. He remembered being battered by stones that had flown like bullets. He'd passed out, and his next memory was of being in agony while his face was being stitched up. That was when he knew he'd not been

captured by the enemy; he had vaguely heard someone
swearing and giving orders in German and had glimpsed the
Wehrmacht doctor's epaulettes.

Three people were in the truck with him: the noisy one
who looked like an Egyptian mummy, an unconscious man
with a face the colour of a Scotsman's arse and smelling like
the devil's breath, and a Sanitätssoldat, wearing the medical
corps' red cross armband on his shirt sleeve. He sat on the
floor with his bloodied head resting on his chest and his legs
at contorted angles. No one would feel comfortable sleeping
like that. He was dead.

The truck swerved as an almighty explosion struck
somewhere close by. The canvas cover ripped and kept tearing
into strips until it looked like a display of ribbons fluttering in
the wind. Wilmot coughed as the familiar war-stench of
petrol, cordite, and gunpowder filled his nostrils and mouth.
Burning vehicles that had been further up the column were
littering the road ahead, blocking the truck's path and that of
the long line of vehicles behind them. Twice, he clung on
when the ground vibrated, and he thought they were going to
lurch onto their side.

The unconscious man on the floor rolled about and bashed
his head against the bottom of the bench seats. Wilmot, in
terrible pain, got on the floor and pinned the man down while
the mummified man screamed with impotence, as he too fell
off the narrow ledge onto Wilmot's sore backside.

Pain engulfed every part of Wilmot's body. It felt to him
as though a steel scrubbing brush was shredding the skin on
his face and a crate of potatoes was resting on his arse, but he
couldn't lift the man's dead weight off him or take *his* weight
off the man below him. He squeezed his tear-filled eyes shut

as another explosion rocked the ground near the truck and lifted it into the air…

"Hello … hello, can you hear me?"

Wilmot opened his eyes to the blinding glare of late afternoon sun until the person speaking to him blocked it with his body.

"I'm alive?"

"You are."

"Did the other men with me survive?"

"The driver and one wounded man. The others are dead."

Wilmot was tearful as he was lifted and put onto a stretcher, then carried into another vehicle. Its thick canvas roof and sides were comforting. The brightness had gone, although it was stiflingly hot. Beside him, other injured men were groaning, and Wilmot's sweaty, blood-soaked body added to the already rancid stench captured by the truck's covering.

A medical assistant knelt over Wilmot, replacing the bandage on the latter's cheek. A drying cut above the medic's eye caught Wilmot's attention, but the man was ignoring it or didn't know it was there.

"Are they still bombing us? Am I badly wounded? When I was hit on the ridge, I saw my men getting strafed by enemy aircraft. I'm Obergefreiter Vogel from the 90th Light Infantry Division … did my men make it out?" Wilmot's barrage of questions poured out of his mouth, stopping abruptly when he realised … he had no memory of what had happened between falling unconscious on the ridge and waking up on the first truck. *Had hours passed or days?*

The medic tied off the new bandage and went into his pocket, bringing out a packet of cigarettes. He tapped the pack, lit the cigarette that popped up, and offered it to Wilmot.

"Thanks ... I needed this," Wilmot said.

Without answering any of Wilmot's questions, the medic left him to begin checking the other five injured men.

Wilmot watched the man at his work and was suddenly hit by a surge of emotion. Before he could stop it, a throaty sob left his mouth. Paul shot into his mind, then Max, Hannah, and even Frank Middleton. He loved them all so damn much. He'd do anything to see them again, to be a family. He sniffed and gulped painfully as the age-old question came to him: *Did any one of them think about him at all?*

The medic came back to Wilmot's side, rested his back against the truck's soft wall, and exhaled a long breath. He was about the same age as Wilmot. His sun-kissed golden-coloured hair was matted with blood, his face was white with sand, and his half-closed, haunted eyes fought to stay open.

"You're lucky. The others are either dead, or they won't make it," the man sighed.

"I'm sorry."

"We've lost a lot of men. Two ... three thousand, maybe. The enemy planes stopped coming after us half an hour ago, and their tanks are no longer firing. We're in the clear; for a while, at least."

He paused to stare at Wilmot's face. "It's not pretty, Obergefreiter Vogel. The skin on your cheek must have been hanging off you like a flap, but at least an Oberarzt had time to suture it before your medical truck was hit. You've got some shrapnel in your arm, and your lower back is black and blue."

*The man remembered my name,* Wilmot thought. "Will I be going home to Berlin?"

The man laughed. "I doubt it. You're not wounded badly enough for that."

"Shame."

\*\*\*\*\*\*

Ten days later, in a hole under a netted roof in another part of the bleached wilderness, Wilmot enjoyed a can of peaches, courtesy of the New Zealanders they had captured near the ridge that now was so far away. He sat beside Günter, the annoying soldier who had been digging the gun hole days earlier; he was one of the few men who had made it off that hill alive. For once, Wilmot was glad of the annoying Schütze's company. The man made it his mission in life to know what was going on. He was always lurking about and eavesdropping on conversations between officers. *He'd make a great spy,* Wilmot thought.

"Ten days, Obegefreiter, ten days it's taken for us to be able to eat and shit in peace. I dread to think where we'd be now had the Allies succeeded in cutting off our retreat. That damn word sticks in my gullet – *retreat* – running away, more like. I imagined us marching into Alexandria by now. Did you think we were going to make it there?"

"We don't get paid to think, Günter. We get paid to fight until we die or win."

Wilmot shielded his eyes with his hand and looked over to where the prisoners were sitting under the baking sun. "How many Allied soldiers did we capture?" he asked.

"I don't know, but the quartermaster reckons there's over two hundred of them. He wasn't happy being told he'd have to feed them. Did you know we got their commanding general as well?"

"No." Wilmot was more concerned about the loss of two Afrika Korps commanders. General Walther Nehring had been badly wounded in an air raid, and General Georg von Bismarck, commander of the 21st Panzer Division, had been killed by a mine explosion. The men were always jittery when high-ranking commanders got hit.

"Ach, it's all pointless when you think about it," Günter complained. "We didn't take a kilometre of ground on that El Alamein Line, and we lost nearly three thousand men and twenty-two tanks. If you ask me, we should call it quits here and get ourselves to Russia to finish off the Russkies."

*What the hell do you know about Russia and the Russians?* Wilmot threw the man a filthy look and said, "Go make yourself useful, Schütze. Your break is over."

Günter picked up his rifle, muttered something to himself, and left, leaving Wilmot to contemplate the last terrifying ten days.

*I'm a lucky bastard,* Wilmot thought as he stretched out his legs. Again, he'd made it out alive when many of his comrades hadn't. He recalled the man he'd been talking to on the El Alamein Line just before their world had exploded. He'd died, yet he'd been running only a few paces behind Wilmot. How was it possible that Uwe … yes, that was his name … lost both legs, but he, Wilmot Vogel, the man who always managed to survive when everyone around him kicked the proverbial bucket, got away with a cut to his cheek and a few bits of shrapnel in his arm? The men on the truck with him had died when the vehicle was struck from the air, yet here he was, sitting on his backside eating peaches. *I've got a guardian angel on my shoulder, or something magical is watching over me ... something keeping me on this earth. I'd like to say thank you, whatever ... whoever you are. And whatever you're doing, keep doing it.*

He got up to search for more food before the greedy pigs among them got all the good stuff. The landscape was littered with vehicles: tanks and armoured cars, trucks, tankers, half-tracks, and Volkswagen Kübelwagens. Most would need fixing before they moved on. Allied Spitfires had consistently flown overhead for days, but all had been quiet for the last two days, and German reconnaissance pilots had reported that the Allied column had halted ten kilometres to their rear.

Wilmot was glad of the break, as were the men snoring under their netting or eating captured food supplies, as he had been doing. He'd seen severely wounded men being evacuated, and a glimmer of hope had shone for a few hours as he had waited to be medically assessed. He was disappointed when a doctor removed some of his sutures and then told him, 'You're fit for duty. Try not to get sand in your wounds. Come back in two days to have the remaining sutures out and the wound cleaned and reassessed. That will be all.'

*Was the man off his head?* Wilmot had wondered, when he'd been ordered to take out his platoon to lay mines in a sandstorm five minutes after leaving the medical corps station.

He stopped walking to observe the prisoners who were corralled on a piece of ground encircled by guards, vehicles, and barbed wire. The poor buggers were sitting under the midday sun looking broken and miserable. A shiver went up Wilmot's spine. Reminded of his own time as a prisoner of war, he couldn't help but pity the men. He'd like to think they'd be dealt with better than he'd been treated in Russia, but he'd seen his fellow Germans involved in too many gratuitous executions in the Russian campaign to be confident of civility in the desert. Maybe it would be different here without the SS death squads around. Maybe the prisoners would go to a German POW Stalag instead of a concentration camp. Perhaps they'd be sent to Italy. *Ach, they aren't my problem.*

"Kick me again, and I'll rip your foot off your bloody leg!"

Wilmot turned to his right, catching the English voice with the funny accent. A German Schütze from the 90th was hitting the man in the face with his rifle butt. The victim, however, was not taking the beating lying down and retaliated by wrapping his arms around the German's legs trying to unbalance him.

The German and Italian guards didn't move to join or stop the assault. Incensed, Wilmot began to weave in and out of the prisoners' lines towards the man being battered by the rifle.

"Schütze, stop that, now!"

Ignoring Wilmot's command, the German turned his rifle on the prisoner and fired.

Wilmot stomped to the Schütze and ripped the rifle from his hand. Visions of Russian guards shooting German prisoners infuriated him further, and without thinking where he was and in front of whom, he smashed the weapon's butt against the soldier's forehead.

The Schütze looked up at Wilmot from the ground, shaking his head to clear it.

"Stand over there by that truck, and don't move from it until I come to you. Get up – move," Wilmot grunted.

The Schütze's victim lay on the ground, moaning. He was fortunate; the German had fired his weapon in anger without aiming, and his bullet had grazed the prisoner's shoulder.

Wilmot helped the wounded man to his feet, then looked closer at the injury. "I'll get a medic to sort that for you," he said in English. "Where are you from, soldier?"

"Auckland, New Zealand." The prisoner supported his injured shoulder by clutching his arm with his free hand, and then he gave Wilmot a bold stare. "Your English is perfect. Have you ever lived in England?"

Wilmot felt hundreds of eyes on him. The German and Italian guards, including an officer, were also observing the scene. "Right, you," he changed his tone. "Don't get into any more trouble … whatever it was you did. And tell the rest of your people to do as they're told."

"Where are you taking us?" the man dared to ask.

"Don't ask questions, either. We don't need to tell you anything."

"Obergefreiter, *kommen Sie!*"

Wilmot turned to see his Leutnant waving him over. He approached with a reticent step whilst searching for an appropriate answer to the reprimand he was going to get. This wasn't the first time he'd had a conversation in English with a prisoner. He'd given two of them cigarettes two days earlier, and his Leutnant had seen him on that day, too. *Was the telling-off going to be for hitting one of his own men or for being kind to the enemy?*

# *Chapter Eighteen*

"Heil Hitler!" Wilmot said, saluting his Leutnant.

"Yes, heil Hitler. Do you speak English, Vogel? I mean, do you speak it well enough to understand everything a man might say in that language?"

Surprised by the question, Wilmot said, "I'm fluent, sir. I understand it and speak it as well as I do German. You've heard me speak it more than once. Why do you ask?"

"Do you write English well?"

"I do ... as well as the next English person, I suppose."

Before speaking further to Wilmot, the Leutnant called over the soldier who had shot the prisoner. The offending Schütze, with a cut to his forehead thanks to Wilmot, stood to attention before the officer while giving Wilmot a defiant glare.

"Gather around me, all of you!" the Leutnant shouted to a group of German soldiers who were close enough to hear what was being said. "In years to come, history will talk about our behaviour today, and I refuse to let it dictate that we were cruel and disrespectful to enemy combatants."

*Apparently, he hasn't seen what the SS get up to in other countries,* Wilmot thought.

"While under my command, you will follow the rules and regulations of the Geneva Convention, and you will not ignore them because of anger or bitterness," the Leutnant ordered. "You will not shoot prisoners. You will not steal their food. You will not strike them or insult their flags. If I catch any of you mistreating the men in our custody, the whole platoon will be punished. We leave unwarranted violence to the SS in other battlefields far from here. Understand?"

The officer paused to stare contemptuously at the Schütze. "You think you're the bigger person, shooting an unarmed man?"

"I was…"

"Shut up. I saw the whole thing, and there's nothing you can say to justify what you did. Report to me in an hour. You're on extra duties until I decide whether to report your behaviour to a staff officer. If it were up to me, I'd have you court marshalled today."

"Yes, sir – and what of Obergefreiter Vogel hitting me?"

"You leave him to me. Hopefully, the gash on your head will remind you of your duty."

The Leutnant then addressed Wilmot, "Do you have anything to add, Obergefreiter Vogel?"

Wilmot's throat closed. He'd like to tell his men what it was like to be a prisoner under the whip of harsh captors, but he was still unable to talk about Russia without getting worked up. "Thank you, sir." He turned to the men. "If you lot ever get captured by the enemy, pray you don't get beaten up, starved to death, or shot. I've seen that up close. I know what it is to be those men sitting over there, looking scared witless. They are not animals … they are soldiers, fighting for their country. Show some damn respect for their ranks."

His speech didn't go down well. Cynicism sat in the eyes of the men staring back at him, but he didn't care what they thought. He had rank and the support of his Leutnant.

"Dismissed," the Leutnant told the men. "You, Vogel, come with me."

After a long walk, the two men approached rolls of barbed wire, and behind them, the command tents. The Afrika Korps normally slept outside: on the sand, in the backs of trucks or under vehicles. Wilmot had never been this close to the luxurious-looking command posts.

The Leutnant gripped Wilmot's bare forearm, halting the latter in mid-step. "If you ever strike a fellow German in front of prisoners again, I'll have you in front of our commander on an even greater charge than the one that upstart Schütze back there will face. Understand, Vogel?"

Wilmot drew himself to attention. *If that's the total sum of my reprimand, I'll take it.* "Yes, sir … sorry, sir, it won't happen again."

"Stay here until I call for you," the Leutnant ordered Wilmot before disappearing into a tent.

Minutes later, the officer returned and ushered Wilmot inside without an explanation.

Three men were standing around a table. Maps and other large sheets of paper with drawings on them were spread out and held in place by stones at the corners. Just before one of the men began rolling up the map, Wilmot caught a glimpse of it; riddled with pencil lines and circles and parts highlighted in red pen, it looked like they were holding an autopsy for the defeat they'd just suffered.

The men, two of whom were dressed in civilian clothes, had the typical intense gazes of the intelligence branch – maybe Abwehr, Army Intelligence. *Why do they always have to wear suspicious glowers on their pug-like faces, as if every person they met is guilty of treachery or deliberately letting down the Fatherland?* The other man, a Hauptmann, appeared more curious than suspicious.

Wilmot's resolve caved under their intense scrutiny, so he gave his best salute by clicking his heels together, stretching out a poker straight arm and snapping the words, "Heil Hitler," precisely as he'd been taught to do at SS basic training camp.

"Obergefreiter Vogel. Your Leutnant has been telling us about your language skills," one of the civilian-clothed men said.

"I am not a linguist, sir," Wilmot replied truthfully. "I speak German and English, that's it."

The man who had spoken wore khaki shorts and a shirt that was not military issue. His sunglasses sat on his wiry white hair like a decorative band, and a black chain that one would normally see around a person's neck was attached to their silver arms curled around the back of his ears. He was a strange-looking fellow, with a full beard and skin on his cheeks and forehead as tough as an old boot.

Wilmot's face reddened. No one spoke. The three men were content to stare at him and his lovely scar, blackened by the sun. *Should I ask why I'm here, or keep my mouth shut until someone asks me another question?*

"Come, sit, Obergefreiter. You're not in any trouble," the same man said, breaking the silence.

"Thank you, sir." Wilmot sat on a stool that sank into the sandy floor with his weight. He shuffled his still painful backside – contusions, apparently – then rested his hands on his thighs.

"Your Leutnant is impressed with your English proficiency."

Wilmot looked up at the civilian. "My mother was from London ... Kent, to be precise. We – my brothers and sister and I – spent our summers in England, so yes, I am comfortable speaking English. I also have an ear for its many accents, including the ones being spoken by the New Zealanders and South Africans we captured."

"*Sehr gut – das ist gut.* We lost two translators three days ago. They were killed when their truck was struck by allied air fire. We are assigning you to our intelligence unit. You will assist us during our prisoner interrogations, among other duties."

"I don't know how to question…"

The man laughed at the suggestion, and Wilmot's face reddened further.

"You will not be questioning anyone, Corporal. You'll transcribe what the prisoner tells us in English and then translate it into German, word for word. You will also search prisoners' belongings for intelligence materials and translate all written documents you find." The man picked up a piece of paper with typed words on it. "Read this. Tell us if it is good English, or if it can be improved."

Wilmot read through the three paragraphs, then said, "The level of English is intelligible, but it contains numerous inaccuracies that make it confusing. It's not of a high standard, sir. It wouldn't be clear to the person translating it to German, even if he were the one who'd written it in English to begin with. In paragraph two, for instance, he has written, *I saw eighty-nine troops and vehicles.* That doesn't make sense to me. He hasn't distinguished if it is eighty-nine troops *or* eighty-nine vehicles or, if both, how they are split."

Wilmot looked from one man to the other. German intelligence used prisoners to go after information about Allied troop numbers, plans, supply depots, locations of forces or aircraft, and anything else they could think of to give them the edge over the enemy. He had seen beaten prisoners nursing injuries sustained from interrogations. He couldn't think of a worse job for himself, but it was evident they had already decided to give him the post by the open way they were now nodding with satisfaction.

"We think you're the right man, Obergefreiter. What do you say?" the same man who had last spoken asked.

Wilmot still hesitated – *no, I don't want this.*

"Vogel? Answer the man," the Hauptmann snapped.

Wilmot flinched and replied, "Thank you, sirs. It would be my honour."

"Very well, collect your gear," the Hauptmann said to signal that the interview was over. "You'll be bunking in the command post area, and from this moment forward, you will not discuss your duties or share any information you might hear the prisoners give us, not even to the Leutnant who brought you here. I am now your commanding officer, and you'll receive your orders directly from me. Go to the quartermaster for *Feldwebel Wachtmeister* epaulettes. You are now my staff sergeant, to replace the one I lost in the attack."

Wilmot was stunned and, unable to find an appropriate response, nodded like a clown and stood to attention.

"Congratulations, Feldwebel Wachtmeister Vogel. That is all. Report to us at 1600 this afternoon," one of the civilian-clad men said.

Wilmot clicked his heels and left the tent. *Well, isn't life one big surprise?* he thought, walking back to his unit. He'd gone in there as a lance corporal and had come out as a staff sergeant with special privileges. He really was one lucky bastard.

# Chapter Nineteen

## Paul Vogel

*Łódź, Poland*
*4 September 1942*

In the Wehrmacht Command Headquarters, Paul spoke on the telephone to his superior officer, Oberstabsarzt Günter Mayer, who was currently on a visit to Warsaw.

The lengthy conversation was not going well. Paul's new posting to Auschwitz, to take effect the following week, had been a terrible blow, and as an added torture, he was being ordered to visit the Chelmno extermination camp today. As his temper flared, he tried to curb his anger. To hell with his superior officer's love of the word *insubordination* and to hell with Chelmno. He wasn't going.

"… I'll have no more of this defiance from you. Do you understand, Vogel?" Mayer said, after complaining about the problems confronting him in Warsaw.

"*Sir,* all I'm saying is that I'm in the middle of trying to organise the new mobile medical treatment centre in the ghetto. I have lost good people this past week, and the few remaining staff I have are trying to cope with the beginnings of a dysentery outbreak. Does it have to be today, sir? Do I really have to see what I've already witnessed at Brandenburg?"

"I don't care how many times you've seen it, Vogel. You *will* go. This order didn't originate from my office. Herr Bothmann, the Commandant of Chelmno, has personally asked to meet you. I've also had Kriminalinspektor Krüger on the telephone about it. He wants you to travel to Chelmno with him. He'll be waiting for you at Radegast train station at 1500, and you had better not be late for him."

Silence, then Oberstabsarzt Mayer continued, "Paul, I understand your reluctance. I agree with you. You should remain in the ghetto to deal with all the changes, but this is out of my hands…"

"Why does this Commandant –?"

"Don't ask me why Bothmann and Krüger are determined to get you there, just obey your orders. Krüger can be a vindictive bastard when he wants to be. Paul – Paul, don't make waves, you hear me? You know how much I rely on you, especially this week when I'm not in Łódź to run things."

"I hear you, Herr Oberstabsarzt. Thank you, sir."

Paul looked up at the wall clock – 1345 – he had little over an hour to get to the train station. He slumped in the desk chair, glad of a few minutes more to himself before having to give back the office to the Oberleutnant who'd let him use it. "Damn you, Krüger, what are you up to now?" he muttered.

Paul approached Fire Brigade Square where well over a thousand people were gathered. The *Sperrle* deportations were underway. The Gestapo and police had already removed over one thousand patients from the hospitals in the ghetto, including four hundred children from the paediatric centre. And during the next few days, Paul knew that the police and SS would systematically shut the schools and the rabbinate, as well as the other cultural institutions. The ghetto was preparing to become a massive labour camp, and anyone who couldn't pull their weight was to be murdered.

The *Jüdischer Ordnungsdiens,* the Jewish ghetto police, and the Sonderkommando, the ghetto political police, had sealed off the streets. After the hospitals had been evacuated, Paul had received news from a pale-faced Gert that the Reich had ordered the deportation of an additional twenty thousand Jews, including all children under the age of ten and all ghetto inhabitants over the age of sixty-five.

Paul foresaw the operation taking at least ten days to complete. Krüger had imposed a curfew, and he'd informed all remaining medical staff that they were not to treat patients during the deportation period. Doctors would get in the way, he had explained.

Paul lingered to observe the growing crowd of residents. They weren't there out of curiosity, for nothing would tear them away from the long, shady line at the potato store or clothes distribution depots. No, he surmised they were there because they'd been herded like cattle.

The sun's rays scorched the ghetto streets, biting through Paul's uniform and making his brass buttons burn. It was exceptionally hot for September. He scowled as Chaim Rumkowski appeared on a podium behind a lectern. Unable to control his tears, weeping like a child, and opening and closing his mouth as if catching flies, the elderly man was, at first, incapable of speaking.

Paul had come to know the leader of the Judenrat as an aggressive, domineering man, thirsty for power, impatient, loud and vulgar, and intolerant of any dissension. His tone this morning, however, was soft and sorrowful, as he asked his fellow Jews to hand over their children.

"A grievous blow has struck the ghetto. They are asking us to give up the best we possess – the children and the elderly."

The gasps from the crowd continued, as did Rumkowski, who became ever more fervent as his speech went on…

"… I never imagined I would be forced to deliver this sacrifice to the altar with my own hands. In my old age, I must stretch them out and beg … brothers and sisters, hand them over to me! Fathers and mothers … give me your children!"

The sun was stabbing Paul's wet, prickly eyes. The words and the pitiful, terrifying wailing among the assembled shocked faces blasted his ears. He put his sunglasses on and strode away; desperate to put distance between himself and the horrible scene he'd just witnessed.

*How must they feel? The same way I would if I had to hand over my Erika to be gassed.* During the last deportations, he'd been naïve and arrogant to think that he would kill to save his child. He had scorned the Jews giving their children up to the trucks, but today, he finally understood the meaning of pointless disobedience. Already, he was hearing rifle fire behind him. People were probably running back to their homes in the desperate hope of hiding their children before the Gestapo and SS invaded the tenements.

When Paul left the hospital earlier, he'd shadowed police officers in their search for that day's absentees. They had gone through the tenement blocks with magnifying glasses after the Jews had assembled for roll call and people were reported missing. During their hunt, they'd found babies and children in countless hiding places; some inventive, while others so obvious they might as well have had a sign above their heads saying, *I'm here.*

Three babies had been found in laundry baskets in the buildings' basements, crying loudly and alerting the Orpo long before they descended the stairs. Children had been crouched inside cupboards, in the shoddily made sewage system, under their own beds, and behind curtains – desperate, useless hiding places that earnt them on-the-spot death sentences, regardless of age or vulnerabilities.

To compound the terrible situation, the Łódź Jews now grasped the true fate of the evacuees. Already, baggage, clothing, and identification papers of their fellow inmates had been returned to the SS offices for *processing*. The death camp was no longer an inconceivable rumour in the minds of the ghetto's Jewish, Sinti, and Gypsy residents. It was a real extermination site a mere train ride away.

Outside Radegast station, Paul came face to face with Krüger. "Inspector, are we ready to leave?" Paul asked in a terse voice.

Krüger cracked his lips open. "Hmm, yes. My business is done here. We'll leave the trains to the Jews and the guards."

Paul sat in the front passenger seat of Krüger's Kübelwagen next to the Gestapo driver while Krüger sat in the back with his assistant, Graf, the man who'd taken Paul's fist on the nose in Alexanderhoffstraffe during the previous deportations. Paul kept his eyes forward, as the vehicle cleared the road exiting the station. It was going to be a long journey, and he wasn't in the mood for conversation with his two Gestapo companions.

When the Kübelwagen cleared the suburbs, Paul lifted his face to meet the warm wind hitting him face on. *I can no longer claim distance between myself and the Chelmno extermination camp,* he thought. For a long time, the place

had signified death … murder … wretchedness, but he had not
been personally connected to it; at least, that was what he had
told himself. Now, however, the murders perpetrated in the
name of the Third Reich would be his crimes, as they were for
those SS soldiers who had and were still to pull the gas levers.
He had reached a new low and was falling into the pit of evil
he had tried so desperately to avoid with his empty, pathetic
mantras…

"… wake up. We're almost there, Oberarzt." Graf poked
his index finger in Paul's back. "The Kriminalinspektor wants
to speak to you."

Paul twisted his sore neck from side to side to relieve his
muscle pain. His head had sat on his chest almost the whole
way. He'd been overcome by tiredness and had slept, despite
the rattling exhaust pipe on the military truck that had
followed them from the city. A few times, he'd woken, his
backside leaving the hard seat when the Kübelwagen went
over rocks or dipped into potholes in the road, but thankfully,
he'd dropped off again and hadn't had to endure Krüger's
droning, patronising lectures.

"Pull over to the side, driver." Manfred Krüger's
authoritative voice followed Graf's annoying pokes.

After being ordered to change places with the assistant,
Paul reluctantly got in the back. As always, the smile on
Krüger's face trembled, as though his lips were rebelling.

"Drive on," the Kriminalinspektor instructed the driver
before saying to Paul, "You slept most of the way. That's a
sign of having a peaceful conscience. Did you know that,
Paul?"

"I've not thought about it before," Paul answered, gearing
up for the tedious exchange that was coming.

"Well, it is." Krüger stared long and hard at Paul, holding the latter's eyes as he continued, "I hope your conscience is still peaceful after your visit to the camp. Certain aspects of the operation can be disturbing. Between you and me, I've often wondered if there might not be a more humane way to exterminate the Jews. After all, we are not barbarians, and what we do, we do for the Fatherland and for the Führer."

"And what in your opinion, would be more humane? The SS in the East have tried mass killing by gun, and that proved too traumatic for our soldiers. Perhaps they could try bludgeoning the Jews to death with clubs or simply halting all food deliveries to the ghettos and camps, in which case all would die, eventually." Paul's innocent eyes stared down Krüger, as he asked, "Is that sympathy for the Jews I hear in your voice, Inspektor?"

Krüger turned away to focus on the road ahead. "If such a thing as sympathy existed in war, no one would die, and soldiers would shake hands with the enemy and march homewards without a drop of blood being spilt. Empathy, thoughtfulness, even conscience, are luxuries we can ill afford. There is only duty – that is everything."

Paul's heart was thumping so hard he could feel it vibrating in his throat. His hatred for Krüger scared him, as did his own unrehearsed responses to the man's often ludicrous statements. "I agree, Inspector, duty is everything. This is all for the Fatherland and the Führer ... ah, and let's not forget his most ardent supporters in the SS who came up with the solution to the Jewish problem."

Now Krüger looked stumped for an appropriate response. "Yes ... of course. The SS High Command has played a major role in the Jewish Solution," he eventually stumbled. "No doubt about it, the gassing model is the quickest and least painful method ever to be tested. Herr Himmler and Reinhard Heydrich have developed a sterling plan. Do you agree, Paul?"

Graf, in the front seat, twisted his neck to hear Paul's answer.

"Yes. It was a *sterling* plan, indeed." Paul forced a smile.

Krüger continued, as though he were verbalising his thoughts and not caring if Paul were listening or not, "Not many people know this, but the SS cannot take the credit for being the first to gas prisoners. Gas vans were being used by the Soviet Secret Police ten years ago. In fact, it's a bit of a strange story … the vans were supervised by a man called Isay Berg. He was the head of the administrative and economic department of the NKVD of Moscow *Oblast* until he was arrested and convicted by the NKVD in '37 – he was probably gassed by his own men. Gassed by the men *he* trained!" He finally looked at Paul. "Ironic, eh?"

"It is," Paul replied drolly.

"How long to go, driver?" Krüger asked.

"Ten minutes if the road remains clear, Herr Inspektor."

"Before we arrive, there are a few things you should know about the camp," Krüger told Paul in a more formal tone. "Chełmno was set up by SS-Sturmbannführer Herbert Lange. He did a marvellous job getting things started, but he's recently been replaced."

"I see," Paul responded dutifully.

"Hmm, I thought you would have known the name, Lange. He worked at T4 on the euthanasia programme, as you did. You never met him in Brandenburg?"

Paul shook his head. He had no intention of getting into a conversation with Krüger about that first rotten period in his medical career or any period since.

"Lange toured this area with your father-in-law. Kriminaldirektor Biermann has a good eye and excellent judgement when it comes to site logistics. He recommended Chelmno – you see over there – just to the left of the trees?"

A large, brick two-storey country house stood in front of a treeline. "Yes," Paul answered.

"It's not visible from here, but the Ner River is beyond those trees. The camp is in a large forest clearing about four kilometres northwest of Chelmno. It's off the road to Koło where the prisoners must change trains. We use the manor house for admissions. Its rooms have already been adapted to use as the reception offices, including space for the Jews to undress and to give up their valuables. You'll shadow the Commandant's assistant today. Where he goes, you go."

"Do you know why the camp's Commandant requested me?" Paul dared to ask.

"No, you'll have to ask him."

Paul fought the urge to retort, *I already know. It's because my father-in-law is directing my future from Berlin and making it as ugly as possible for me.* He could think of no other reason. Instead, he kept his mouth shut and eyed the camp coming into view in a clearing to his left.

A high wooden fence surrounded the grand manor house and grounds. Another clearing further on, in what looked like a forest camp, was also fenced off. "What's in that clearing?" he asked Krüger.

"The Jews' final destination."

After manoeuvring the tricky country lane leading to the estate, the Kübelwagen pulled up outside the brown brick house. Krüger got out and threw over his shoulder, "Assistant Graf and I won't be staying long. We're going back to the ghetto as soon as I conclude my meetings. You'll have to make your own way back to Łódź. I suggest you find out the train times."

# *Chapter Twenty*

*Chelmno extermination camp, Poland*

A Gestapo Kriminalassistent by the name of Richter met Paul in the manor house's reception hall. "Heil Hitler. Good morning, Herr Oberarzt. I'll be showing you around the *palace* today," the friendly youth said, as though he were hosting a museum tour.

"Thank you, Kriminalassistent Richter," Paul responded, then followed the man in silence straight to the basement.

A thick wooden door stood at the end of a long passageway. Outside, three vans were parked side by side, each with a ramp leading to their back, double doors.

"Well, here they are," Richter said, his face as animated as a brick.

Paul studied them. They looked like any other military vehicles except they were clad in steel. The doors to one of the vans were open. He looked inside. A Jewish inmate was cleaning the floor. Paul covered his nose with his handkerchief and recoiled as the stench of excrement and vomit hit him.

"SS-Sonderkommando Lange was initially supplied with two vans. The men call them *Kaiser's Kaffe Fahrzeuge* – Kaiser's coffee vans. Each one carries about fifty Jews who are gassed here before the vans leave for the forest," Richter began, apparently smelling nothing out of the ordinary. "Another van arrived recently to deal with the larger numbers of Jews we're receiving, and, thank God, it has speeded up the procedure."

"I see," Paul said, still eyeing the killing machines. "How do they work?"

"Come with me. I'll show you."

Richter opened the back doors of another van and pointed to the floor inside. "The vehicles have been converted to mobile gas-chambers. The sealed compartments installed on the chassis have floor openings – about sixty millimetres in diameter – with metal pipes welded below, into which the engine exhaust is directed."

Paul's mouth became dry, and his throat constricted as he imagined how the victims spent their last moments.

"Innovative, is it not, Herr Oberarzt?" an *SS-Rottenführer* called out to Paul.

"Yes, Squad-leader... imaginative," Paul threw back to the man.

Richter continued, "I'm not an expert, of course, but I do know the system works every time ... the Sonderkommando have never pulled out a live Jew, which would be awkward, because they'd have to shoot him or her, and that would upset those prisoners still waiting to go into the vans. The exhaust contains large amounts of carbon monoxide. When a van is full, the doors are shut, and the engine is started. The victims are deprived internally of oxygen causing death by asphyxiation within minutes – and that's that."

*And that's that?* "This is not the first time I have been to a gas chamber. I know how the gas works," Paul grunted, "although it's a first to see them housed in the back of a van. I wonder who came up with that gem of an idea."

Richter swallowed hard, his Adam's apple shooting upwards in his throat then bouncing downwards into place. He frowned as he looked shiftily behind himself before stepping closer to Paul. "I'll be honest, sir, we didn't always get it right. At first, the vans left full of live prisoners who were gassed on the way to the graves at the forest camp. But one gas van broke down on the highway while the victims were still alive. Passers-by heard their screams, and there was a bit of explaining to do in the town afterwards. Soon after that, a van exploded while the driver was revving its engine at the loading ramp. The explosion blew off the locked back door and badly burned the living Jews in the gassing compartment. I suppose the commandant thought if there were to be disasters, they should happen inside the compound."

The young man's voice then lowered to a whisper, as more SS soldiers appeared. "The task of unloading the vans after each use is time-consuming and, as you experienced, quite unpleasant. Dying can take a while, and some of the Jews can't control their bladders or bowels. Commandant Bothmann made changes for the better when he took over from Herr Lange. Herr Bothmann modified the extermination methods by adding poison to the gas. Soon after his arrival, red powder and some sort of fluid were delivered by freight from Germany. The Commandant told me it was to be used to kill the Jews more quickly. I think this is a good thing for them, don't you?"

*Not killing them would be a good thing,* Paul thought, but was reticent to voice his opinion.

"It can be disturbing the first time you see it, Herr Oberarzt," Richter continued. "I've seen some victims take more than twenty minutes to die … and they're not quiet. The drivers … they hear the screams in the back. They get distracted when they're driving to the forest. Some are badly affected, and a few are transferred out, suffering from some sort of psychological breakdown. It's hard. We must put up a good front, but to be honest, sir, some days, I can't bear to be here."

*A Gestapo Kriminalassistent with a conscience? There's a novelty,* Paul thought. *How many other men working here were as disgusted as the young man standing next to him?*

Richter pulled himself up and looked sheepishly around himself again, as though he were afraid someone might have heard him airing his humanity.

Paul's tour was cut short when a group of men appeared.

"Who are you?" one of the men dressed in civilian clothes asked Paul.

Paul stood to attention, clicked his heels, and responded with an outstretched arm, "Heil Hitler. Oberarzt Paul Vogel. I've come from the Łódź ghetto."

"Ach, of course. It's nice to meet you, Oberarzt. I've heard a lot about you."

Paul, still thinking about the Jews' suffering in the gas vans, retorted, "And who are you?"

The man chuckled. "Forthright – I like that. I'm SS-Hauptsturmführer Hans Bothmann, the camp Commandant." Bothmann paused to address Richter, "You may go back to the office, Richter. I will attend to the Oberarzt."

"*Jawohl, mein Hauptsturmführer* – yes, sir," Richter said before leaving.

Looking again at Paul, Bothmann said, "Let's walk."

As they ambled together in the sunshine with Bothmann's entourage following meekly behind, Paul tried to reconcile the beauty of the countryside with the sinister camp that had been built in the middle of the forest. At Brandenburg, he had witnessed fifty Jewish children being gassed; here, that number would be tenfold, perhaps in one day.

"… and we have a rather mixed bunch here, made up of Gestapo, Criminal Police, and Order Police personnel," Bothmann broke into Paul's thoughts. "As your tour continues, you'll see them in action. We're going to have a very busy time of it this week, what with the Łódź deportations going on. After that, I'm not sure how long we'll stay open for business. I imagine we will continue to be busy until we run out of Jews and other undesirables." He grinned.

Bothmann led Paul to his office and invited him to sit in one of the plush armchairs. He ordered Richter, who'd arrived before them, to bring coffee before sitting in the chair opposite Paul.

"I knew your father, Paul. I met him on numerous occasions through Kriminaldirektor Biermann. I was sorry to hear of his death."

*Don't you know that Biermann thinks my father is alive?*
"Thank you. I miss him," Paul answered.

"Freddie Biermann has been a good friend to me over the years. He was my mentor when I attained the rank of *Kriminalkommissar* in 1937 and worked in the Gestapo office *Stapoleitstelle* in Berlin. I learnt a great deal from Freddie. He was a patient teacher, always willing to help and advise me, no matter the time of day or night. I was shocked to hear about his heart attack, but he assures me he feels well. He still goes to the Reich Security Office every day, so that's a good sign."

"It is, and may his health continue to improve." Paul forced out the words.

Bothmann grew quiet when Richter reappeared with a trolley carrying a coffee pot, two cups and saucers, milk, sugar, and a plate of biscuits. *There don't appear to be food shortages in this camp,* Paul thought, watching the man pour the welcome coffee into the cups.

"I had dinner with the Biermanns' on the evening before my departure," Bothmann continued when Richter had left.

Paul's eyes lit. "Did you meet my daughter?"

"Yes … Erika?"

"Yes."

"She's a pretty little thing. Your wife told me you haven't met the baby yet. It must be hard for you. Parenthood is the most marvellous thing a man could hope for."

"It is. I was hoping for leave, but I found out this morning that I'm being transferred to the Auschwitz-Birkenau camp next week." Paul took a sip of coffee then bit into the biscuit that tasted nothing like as good as it looked. "Is my wife well…?"

When Bothmann's answer was interrupted by a telephone call, Paul stared sightlessly through the open window. He was envious of the man. He'd seen Erika; had maybe held her in his arms. He'd spoken to Valentina; something *he* hadn't been able to do since before their child was born.

Paul received mail from Valentina on a bi-weekly basis, and the letters always enclosed up-to-date pictures of the baby. He loved getting the photographs, but his wife's writings didn't convey sentiment or affection. If truth be told, Valentina's penmanship was aloof and hurried, as if she'd been reluctant to write at all.

She spoke lovingly about the baby, her days in Berlin, the few-and-far-between air raids they were getting, which, she'd quickly pointed out, had no great effect on the city, and her desire for the war to be over. But she said nothing about her love for him or how much she missed him. Not once had she asked him if he had upcoming leave, or if they could go off together when such leave did come. And she never referred to anything he had told her in his letters.

He didn't know his wife, not the real Valentina, he'd concluded not long after she'd left Poland. In her letters, she prayed for a more peaceful future for the baby and herself but never mentioned him being with them. These ambiguities left him confused about how to reply. He was uncomfortable using terms of endearment when he no longer knew if his feelings were reciprocated. What had happened to their passion for each other? It had been intense, but apparently, short-lived from her end…

"Sorry about the interruption," Bothmann said, replacing the telephone in its cradle.

Paul, becoming angry as always when he thought about Biermann's influence over Valentina, lost his poise and grumbled, "Did my father-in-law ask you to send for me?"

Bothmann's eyes narrowed. "Yes, Oberarzt. He thought it would be a good experience for you. Now that the hospitals in the ghetto have been closed and your new posting has come through, he presumed you'd benefit from this visit – was he wrong?"

"No … excuse me, sir."

Bothmann lit a cigarette and studied Paul through a plume of smoke. "I get the feeling you don't approve of what we do here. Freddie – Kriminaldirektor Biermann – did mention your habit of questioning our policies. You do understand why we conduct these operations, don't you?"

That popular question again: *you do understand why we do it, don't you?* when it came to committing atrocities against the Jews. "Yes, of course, Commandant," Paul said. "We want to get rid of Jews in Europe and cleanse the Fatherland of their stench."

Bothmann's previously suspicious eyes widened with satisfaction. "That's a good answer, Paul. Exactly what I expect to hear from a loyal soldier of the Reich."

Paul smiled, concealing his sarcasm.

"Ach, I suppose we have it easy here." Bothmann relaxed in his chair. "The Jews come and go in the space of a day. You'll find that Auschwitz is a much more complex setup. Some Jews are disposed of upon arrival, mostly the children and elderly who are useless to our war effort; others live and work there, but they will all die in the end."

Paul, keeping his expression neutral, was aware that for the second time that day, he was being tested. After he eventually left Chelmno, he was certain Bothmann would report to Biermann in Berlin with his impressions of this meeting. For the life of him, Paul couldn't grasp why his father-in-law was still making it his mission in life to torment him. It wouldn't bring him any closer to finding the paintings or punishing Dieter Vogel.

"Do you need me to sign death certificates for the Jews arriving today? I'd like to make myself useful while I'm here," Paul said.

Bothmann raised a puzzled eyebrow. "Whatever gave you that idea? I have four doctors on my staff, all perfectly capable of dealing with the new arrivals. You won't have to get involved with the Jews at all. You will observe, and when our work is done, you can return to Łódź. I'll arrange for a vehicle

to take you to Kolo. From there, you can get the last train –
don't look so worried, Oberarzt, I will telephone your father-
in-law to tell him what a charming, helpful young man you
are."

Paul's chest was tight from holding in a bagful of
emotions he couldn't begin to go through. "When will the
prisoners arrive?"

"In an hour or two. They'll come into Koło railway station
first. It's about ten kilometres northwest of here. Our police
and SS will supervise the transfer of prisoners from the freight
train to smaller-sized cargo trains that run on the narrow-
gauge tracks to Powiercie station just outside Chełmno. Why
don't you put your feet up in the officers' mess? I'll send my
man to you when the prisoners get here."

"Thank you, sir." Paul saluted and went to the door.

"Paul … one more thing before you go. There's no need
for you to tell anyone about what you might see here today."

Paul nodded. "Of course not, Herr Commandant."

****** 

A Leutnant, who had been wearing his Waffen SS uniform
five minutes earlier, met the new arrivals at the double doors
to the manor house. Dressed now as a local squire and
sporting a Tyrolean hat, he announced to the Jews that some
of them would remain at the estate to work.

The Jews were processed as soon as they entered the
manor house. The German, still playing the friendly host,
gathered the arrivals around him in the reception hall.

"Good afternoon. Before you settle in, you must all take a
bath. Won't that be nice?" he asked the expectant faces.

Paul stared at the strategically placed plaque on the wall, saying, *Bathhouse,* with an arrow beneath pointing the way; a thoughtful piece of deceit.

"You must hand in your valuables to be registered," the *squire* continued. "These include wedding rings and eyeglasses. All hidden banknotes will be destroyed during steaming, so you must take them out and hand them over for safekeeping. Your clothes will be disinfected, but women may keep their slips on. Come with me – this way."

Paul trailed behind the group of one hundred fifty Jews whilst picturing what was to come. They were now going to remove their shoes and clothes and hand over precious rings and watches, eyeglasses and money that they had guarded on their persons for years, and they would do it with an air of optimism. Some of them were to work on the estate, they'd been told, and in their minds, they'd believe that the friendly-looking squire had no reason to lie to them. They were safe; the rumours of this being a death camp were unfounded.

Kriminalassistent Busch, Paul's new guide, led the first group of prisoners away for *bathing,* but Paul lagged at the back of the line to listen to the people in front of him whisper questions to others who shot back hopeful, albeit naïve answers: "I hope we get more food here. They'll need us to be strong if we're to work," an elderly woman wearing her fur coat in September said.

"Everything is going to be better from now on," the old man next to her responded, holding her hand.

"I agree. We're important to the Germans. They must have chosen us because we look useful," another elderly man decreed.

"If I'm any judge of character, that nice squire won't let the children starve," a woman threw over her shoulder to the first person who'd spoken.

"If we've been chosen to work, why did the children come?" another man asked, cutting the conversation dead in its tracks.

After stripping off in a large, bare room, the Jews were taken to the cellar and marched along the passageway. Paul, still following behind the group, saw a small detachment of Jews sorting and packing personal belongings at a line of tables in a room to his left. These men and women looked as miserable as he felt.

At the end of the corridor, the door opened onto the ramp that Paul had seen earlier. The first group of Jews crossed it, then disappeared into the back of a van, whose doors were immediately closed.

When he got outside by another exit, Paul observed a group of SS guards picking out Jewish men from another batch of prisoners. They were not being selected randomly, he noted; the chosen looked stronger and younger than the most elderly in the group. He began to shiver, even as the hot sun hit him. His whole body trembled, and his breath came in quick, shallow pants as it tried to seep past the lump of shame at the back of his throat.

"Come with me, sir," Busch said.

Paul's highly charged emotions were evident as he stared at Busch. "Come where?"

"The Commandant wants you to see the final part of the operation. It's a short drive in the Kübelwagen."

Paul jumped as the engine revved with the first fully loaded truck. The driver in the cab, wearing the SS death head pin, was about forty years old. He stared straight ahead, ignoring his surroundings and the guards standing at the side of the vehicle talking above the noise.

"Don't worry, we've got plenty of time to see the end results in the forest. It'll take about twenty minutes to finish that lot off," Busch nudged Paul.

In the clearing about four kilometres from the house, large open-air grids were already in the ground. Young Jewish men wearing striped suits and shackled with chains on their ankles were trying to run and jump around the perimeter of the grids under the watchful eyes of about fifty of the camp's Sonderkommando.

"What on earth are they doing?" Paul asked Busch.

"The SS hold jumping contests and races among the Jewish camp workers to deem who's fit to continue working. The losers are shot and replaced with new blood from the recent arrivals – it's a battle of the fittest here." The assistant's smug tone matched his apparent enthusiasm for the sport he was watching.

Paul was ushered to the first van when it arrived at the site twenty-five minutes later. Busch handed him a flashlight. "Take a look in the back of the van."

Paul turned on the torch and got behind the steering wheel, playing a role for the SS and Gestapo who were watching him. Between the driver's cab and the rear part were two peepholes. He flashed the light through them into the gas compartment and choked back a sob. The pile of mangled dead bodies, their loose, wrinkled skin with hardly any flesh underneath, looked almost cherry red in the strange light. Caved in stomachs with protruding ribs was a common sight to him these days, but these naked bodies were contorted, lying across, below, and above each other, displaying genitalia, saggy breasts, bony arms and legs with joints bulging like tennis balls. The gut-wrenching, unworldly corpses combined with the slack mouths on the open-eyed, terror-stricken faces, were enough to turn the strongest man's stomach to mush, and for the second time in his career, Paul vomited.

When his stomach had settled, he switched off the torch and jumped down to the ground, his face now a mask of indifference. He wouldn't apologise for the vomit running down the outside of the driver's door and staining his jacket, nor give an opinion of what he'd just seen; not to the dispassionate men ogling him.

"I've seen all I need to see, Kriminalassistent. Please take me to the train station," he uttered to Busch.

"I cannot. We haven't finished, Herr Oberarzt. I've been told you must go through the whole procedure," Busch retorted, without a hint of respect for Paul's officer rank.

"I don't give a damn what you were ordered to do! I must return to Łódź. I've wasted enough of my day and have more pressing matters to attend to." Paul gestured to the van. "These Jews have no need of a doctor's services."

Paul turned sharply at a loud creaking noise and watched as the van's door was opened and the dead bodies tumbled out of it and straight onto one of the grids.

"At first, we removed the corpses from the gas-vans and placed them in mass graves," Busch explained. "We filled the long trenches within weeks, but the smell of decomposing bodies began to permeate the surrounding countryside, including nearby villages. A few months ago, the SS came up with the idea of burning the bodies in the forest, hence these grids. Follow me. I need to take you closer."

Paul, conceding defeat regarding his demand to leave, crossed the few metres of burnt grass to the crematorium site. Standing closer to the corpses, he breathed in the sweaty stench of pre-death fear rising from the shallow pit. He recognised a naked child near the top of the pile. The little soul had fought for his last breath; his mouth was still gaping, his terrified … or were they puzzled and confused eyes … were open, and his bony arms lay across his caved-in tummy. He'd seen the little boy often playing with other children outside Kurt's tenement block. Once, Paul had given him and his friends a bar of chocolate to share between them. The lad's excitement had been precious. He swallowed the bile of disgust in his mouth and put on his dark glasses.

"The grids are constructed of concrete slabs and rail tracks," Busch was now saying. "We use pipes for air ducts and put in long ash pans below the grid. Because of the stench, the Jewish Sonderkommando had to exhume the mass graves and burn the previously interred bodies. Those men are also responsible for cleaning the excrement and blood from the vans."

Paul had seen and heard enough. "We're leaving now. I'll be late for the train, and I don't want to spend the night here. No argument, Kriminalassistent Busch," he said, already heading towards the Kübelwagen.

"I was told to take you back to the palace. You must be needing a coffee after your tour, but not a Kaiser's Kaffe … ja?"

# *Chapter Twenty-One*

*Łódź, Poland*
*10 September 1942*

The letter fell from Paul's hand and floated downwards in a
zig-zag pattern until it eventually settled on the floor to lie
face up. He looked at it; the words written in ink in his father-
in-law's flawless, elegant style. His flamboyant, oversized
signature; the seal of his own inflated ego, the brief, sharp and
to-the-point sentences without a hint of sympathy or respect
for the reader's feelings; all were quintessentially Fredrich
Biermann.

*Berlin*
*August 1942*

*Oberarzt Vogel*

*I'm writing this letter to inform you that your brother,
Schütze Wilmot Vogel, has recently been in Berlin. I spoke to
him whilst he was here, entertained him in my home, and
helped him secure a posting in North Africa. The fighting has
been heavy in that region – I hope my next letter to you will
not be informing you that poor Wilmot has been killed – it's
dreadful to hear of so many young men in Rommel's army
falling like flies in the desert.*
*Should he be unlucky, I shall, of course, tell you that
Wilmot died as a hero for the Führer,* Volk und Vaterland –

*for the Führer, for the people, and for the Fatherland – and that his sacrifice will not be forgotten. Unfortunate, is it not, Paul, that such grand applause is not something I could ever convey to anyone about you or your dear papa?*

*I informed Wilmot of Kurt Sommer's treason and subsequent death at the fumbling hands of your Jewish doctors. As you can imagine, he was upset and angry at Sommer's betrayal.*

*My daughter and granddaughter are both well in my care, and you no longer need to feel responsible for either of them. Valentina's feelings for you have changed, and she will be speaking to a lawyer about ending her marriage. Her eyes have been opened, Paul. Since her return to Berlin, she has discovered a new independence and what her true principles are. She is working with a women's society which devote their time to raising funds for soldiers on the front lines, and she also has a job at the Reich Main Security Office. Her disappointment in you shocked me, truly. 'Paul cares too much about the Jews. He embarrasses me and dishonours real Germans who are suffering terribly.' Her words, not mine, you understand.*

*I feel it would be better if you refrain from writing to my Valentina ... that is my wish. Her wish is that you sign the divorce papers and send them back to her as soon as possible so that she may look forward to a new and better life.*

*Kriminaldirektor of the Gestapo (retired)*
*Fredrich Biermann.*

Unlike the letter Paul had received from Biermann to inform him of his father's death, this one lacked warmth and instead displayed the Kriminaldirektor's contempt and intention to hurt Paul in every line, comma, and period. He was furious, yet unsurprised by his father-in-law's latest sick stunt.

Although devastated about Biermann's news of an impending divorce from Valentina, Paul claimed a modicum of personal satisfaction; he was not heartbroken, as a rejected husband should be, neither was he shocked or angry. How strange, that his love for his wife had died – where or at what moment, he didn't know – and that it had taken this callously given information to make him realise he no longer cared about her feelings, what she thought of him and his so-called love for the Jews, or what she was doing in her own life in Berlin. Biermann had prised his daughter and son-in-law apart like a wishbone, as though it were part of his game, and Valentina had allowed it to happen. He had no gaping hole in his heart, no desire to persuade her to stay. He was, instead, shattered about a future without his baby daughter in it. That pain was so immense, he could hardly breathe.

He sat on the edge of his bed, glaring at the letter, still enraged even though he'd read it four times in the last week. Biermann was now retired; forced probably, a sick old man who wanted to spend his remaining time on earth making the Vogels suffer for his failures.

He pitied his father-in-law, as he had when the man was in hospital, but he also hated him. He likewise despised the insipid Olga who could see no wrong in her sadistic husband … hated everything that damn family stood for.

Paul could see the future unfolding with startling clarity, and it was ugly and bitter. Now, he understood Valentina's coldness in her writings. She didn't love him either. He wondered, *had she ever?*

He picked up the letter, folded it neatly, put it into his rucksack, and then fished out an envelope containing another three-page letter from his bedside drawer. It had arrived six days earlier while he'd been at Chelmno, yet it had been written at the end of July. It was an infinitely more satisfying and truthful letter; so honest, in fact, he wondered why most of the lines had not been redacted.

Up until now, Paul presumed that many personal truths that were intended to pass between soldier and family were thoroughly scrutinised. In reality, a statistically insignificant number of letters had been controlled by censors since millions were being sent from the Western and Eastern Fronts. Officers he lived with had been speaking about the subject recently. They'd heard that it would take about one hundred fifty thousand censors to read all the mail going through the Wehrmacht Post Service, and as that was a statistical impossibility, they thought, writings with negative content about the Reich would be left largely unnoticed. Paul surmised that the policy was going to change soon. A new directive had been issued, according to Gert, who'd stated that the Army was now going to read all letters sent by soldiers to their families and friends. Gert had been unimpressed. "Good luck with that," he'd sniggered.

A warm smile replaced Paul's scowling face as he began to read Wilmot's letter:

*Berlin*
*July 1942*

*My dearest Paul*

*I may be shot at dawn for airing my thoughts, but I know many soldiers who throw caution to the wind to bare their souls to their loved ones. We must – we must share.*

*Well, big brother, you have probably been wondering what has become of me – where I am, where I have been, what I'm doing, and what has passed. Let me say first; my war has been full of surprises. In the beginning, it excited me, but then cynical perceptions of German righteousness crept in. Where is the honour in this carnage? That is the question I kept asking myself whilst in the East. Which military manual states that it is fair to shoot and kill an unarmed civilian when there is no imminent danger to oneself? Why must the gun be turned on children not yet able to walk or talk or comprehend conflict?*

*War is more terrifying than I could ever possibly have imagined, Paul, and not only because of the violence evoked, but also for the ubiquitous disregard for life. Our rifles have no boundaries. They find the smallest child, the crippled, the elderly, and all those marked with a yellow star and they kill with impunity – our bullets never miss those defenceless, unmoving targets, screaming for mercy when they have committed no crime other than offending the Third Reich with their existence.*

*Another revelation: I have discovered that this conflict has little to do with betterment for our people. I now see it as a grand display of abject cruelty of man against man, at times for a single frozen river or metre of icy tundra, or for nothing at all but our leaders' gratification.*

215

*Paul, I am no longer the man looking for glory that you waved off to Poland, for there is none to be found anywhere. The uncompromising, naïve soldier with dreams of invasion and armed with a God-given mission to rid Europe of those nasty creatures, the Jews, has died. Little by little, on a hundred battlefields, he was buried under a mountain of shame, and nothing but a confused and disillusioned shadow of himself remains.*

*I have witnessed the worst of mankind. I have been the worst man I could be; one our mother would scorn and spit upon. Our war in the East is not confined to military matters in which we are preoccupied with fighting the enemy and attempting to survive – instead, I, and others like me, have been forced to accept our leaders' perception of this conflict as also being an ideological struggle where we are duty-bound to destroy the enemies of humanity: Bolshevism, Asiatic barbarism, and the Jews, to name but a few of the offenders."*

*Contemptible as it is, many of my comrades found the special duties performed by the SS and defended by the Wehrmacht not to be abhorrent acts of mass murder, but rather a service to the German cause. But unlike those who agree with our high command, I find the killing of Jews and Bolshevik civilians to be both disturbing and beyond my comprehension of war. Indeed, I don't think I will ever solve the conundrum between duty and conscience. The line of human decency is thin and often blurred, but it never fades completely, does it? It always has and always will be that right is right, and wrong is wrong, no matter how we might want to distort their lesser merits. Or am I wrong in that assumption?*

*Despite my misgivings about the unwarranted slaughters going on, I am Germany; I am the Führer, still loyal to him. Perhaps Herr Hitler doesn't know all the facts? It is possible that rogue elements in our military have taken it upon themselves to carry out the slaughters I have witnessed? And even if he does know, now, more than ever, we must stand together, help each other, obey every order given, and believe in victory.*

*I shall not return to the East. I visited your father-in-law, Kriminaldirektor Biermann, here in Berlin and I asked him to secure me a posting that was not in the Soviet Union. I am certain he tried to help, but a strange thing happened ... the next day, the remainder of my leave got cancelled, and I was sent to North Africa. I won't say any more about where I am; suffice to say, I may not be able to write to you again for a while.*

*Paul, I kick myself when I think of the inflated pride and childish passion that divided us in our last short days together. Our rash debates seem inconsequential and petty now. We viewed the world through different lenses; each seeing a different political landscape, yet there was only one. We both heard on the radio and read in the newspapers the same words from the mouths of our government, but we had completely different views. We fought without knowing what was to come, what we would witness, what we were about to do, what the world would look like. For what it is worth, I am sorry for my part in our stupid spats.*

*I find it hard to believe that it's been over two years since we last saw each other on the threshold of war – you, a fledgling doctor, and me, an ambitious SS Stormtrooper – unwavering in our opinions and willing to disavow each other for the sake of contrary ideologies. I wonder if we are more aligned now that we have tasted war.*

*I am a senior lance-corporal, Paul, an Obergefreiter, a leader of men. I am also the recipient of the Iron Cross – yes, I can sense your disbelief, even from here. I'm a hero in the eyes of our Führer and to the men who follow me. I hope, one day, you and Max will also believe in the person I am striving to become – no saint, never that, but rather, a more considerate human being. How I wish I could adequately describe the moment the medal was pinned onto my jacket, and who pinned it on me, but as in the throes of battle, unless one is present, one can't possibly imagine the event.*

*Now, I must ask about you. For weeks … months, perhaps, I have toyed with the idea of writing to you. Where is Paul? I kept asking myself. Why has he not written a single letter to me, knowing that we are connected to the same military post service? Did he receive the notification from Kriminaldirektor Biermann of my capture and subsequent time as a prisoner of war in Russia? Did he know about the months I was missing, presumed dead? Did he hear about my reappearance after battling to get back to our lines, or that I now only have eight toes? Or did he not think to investigate my whereabouts and silence. All those questions have run through my mind, but I will never know the answers unless you decide to reply to this letter.*

*It is strange, is it not, that you and I no longer have a family to go home to. I was devastated to hear of our father's death, as I'm sure you were. I imagine our mother now, lost and broken. It breaks my heart to think of her grief and our inability to comfort her. It kills me every time there is mail-call and I receive nothing; as though my family has*

*disappeared from the face of the earth or I have ceased to
exist in their hearts.*

*I have shocking news now. When I returned to Berlin, the
house was in a mess. Someone had gone in there to
deliberately break Mama's cherished possessions. Nothing of
great value was lost, apart from the sentimental objects –
some of the ornaments and dishes will be irreplaceable to her.
Hasn't she been through enough? Who had a spare key, Paul?
The doors and windows were not broken. Who would have
done such a rotten thing to us? Kriminaldirektor Biermann is
looking into it. He was most helpful.*

*I want to talk about Kurt, but I cannot. I am disgusted with
him and glad he's dead. Sorry, but that is how I feel about the
traitor.*

*I am adrift, Paul. Please, write to me.*


*Wilmot hasn't received any mail from Łódź? That's
strange; the military post service is usually reliable,* Paul
thought, folding the letter with great care. Officers received
mail every day, and most were in reply to letters they had sent
to family; yet his letters, two to Wilmot and too many to count
to Valentina, were apparently not reaching their destinations.
Was that bad luck or something more sinister?

He put Wilmot's letter into his rucksack and felt his pulse
quickening. His eyes filled up, and he swiped roughly at them
with the back of his hand. It was too late to worry about the
Wehrmacht Post Service. It was too late for him to write and
receive letters, too late to turn back from his new path, even if
he wanted to.

Every nerve ending in Paul's body tingled with fear. The
previous night, he had received orders to report at 1200 to

Kriminalinspektor Krüger at Gestapo headquarters. The reason for the formal invitation, he believed, was his arrest and execution for the crime of aiding and abetting Jews to escape the hospital on 1 September.

Gert had informed Paul the previous day that they had captured an escapee hospital orderly. During the man's subsequent torture at the hands of the Gestapo, the Jew had apparently admitted that the German doctor had let him out of the hospital via the mortuary. According to Gert, Manfred Krüger's gleeful response had not been lost on those present. He had revelled in his plan to take Paul by surprise on the day after the deportations ended.

"Krüger wants to make a spectacle of the arrest, but he can't do it while the German police and SS are conducting searches for missing deportees and supervising the Jews getting on the trains," Gert had scoffed. "He wants the full attention of every soldier, policeman, and Jew in the ghetto when he drags you to the prison wall to be shot. You must get out now, Paul."

\*\*\*\*\*\*

It was 0700, five hours before his fateful meeting with Krüger. In the ghetto, he went straight to the new mobile medical centre where he found two orderlies and three nurses; all of whom had been spared the deportations. Amelia Bartek, the wife of the man Paul had smothered with the pillow, rushed to him as he entered the shell of an old clothing store in the street running parallel to Alexanderhoffstrasse.

Late at night, on the day of the hospital closure, he had returned to the abandoned building to collect Amelia from her hiding place in the pharmacy. The medical centre was in complete darkness, and the entrance doors were chained and padlocked in a purely symbolic statement, for most of the ground-floor windows were devoid of glass, and no one had bothered to board them up or clean the pavements that looked frosted over, as the broken glass sparkled under dimly lit lampposts. The door to the mortuary hadn't been secured, and most surprisingly of all, the area around the hospital had been deserted.

That day had been horrifying, with events that would, along with the Brandenburg gassings and Chelmno death camp, remain forever locked in his mind. But a glimmer of light had touched his soul when he'd found Amelia hiding in the exact spot where he'd left her many hours earlier. Since that day, they had worked tirelessly together to maintain some semblance of healthcare in the ghetto, and he had become fond of her.

He looked at a tearful Amelia now. Dawn was breaking; not quite day but with enough light streaming through the windows to see her pale complexion and wide, red-rimmed eyes.

"Herr Doctor, something terrible has happened," she told him.

The two orderlies, who were folding well-used material strips used as bandages, stopped working to join Paul and Amelia, their worried frowns mirroring her own.

Jakub, one of the men, shook his head and placed his hands on his hips. "I think we have a bigger problem than dysentery, Doctor. Cases of typhus are being reported in the city's east and west districts. The Generalgouvernement are not allowing supplies to come into the ghetto from outside.

People are saying we are spreading the disease to the Christians in Łódź, but it's just another excuse to starve us to death … that's their plan, you know."

"It's true," Kacper, the other orderly agreed. "I heard it from a man who heard it from a man who knows someone who works in the food sorting depot. I asked him … how can we spread typhus when there's a three-metre wall keeping us in here and away from the world outside? You see, Doctor? You see … again, we are being blamed for everything."

Paul raised his hand to silence the men. "Listen, all of you. I've heard nothing about this, and I would know long before you ever did if it were true. I'm ordering you not to spread rumours. Gossiping about such things could get you into trouble with the authorities. Not everyone wants to hear speculation like this, and eventually, someone will report you to your council leaders. You've been warned; not another word about it. You hear me?"

"Yes, Herr Doctor," the five people present answered in unison.

"Now, get back to work and think about how you're going to help the people *inside* these walls."

Paul was used to listening to the Jews gossiping about this and that. One of the most crucial aspects of their isolation in the ghetto was the curtailment of contact and relationships with the rest of society. The Jews had almost no access to outside information, including the progress of the war – something that would have a tremendous impact on their collective fate across Europe. The Germans had deliberately cut Jews and Poles off from such information by making it a crime to own a radio. All newspapers were banned unless they were German, and the publishing industry was strictly supervised and censored.

Three basic fountains of information were available in the ghetto: official information brought by the Germans who controlled dissemination through posters with propaganda, German movie chronicles screened in cinemas, news broadcast through *szczekaczki* – the annoying megaphones, or by the Jewish Council, who took their orders from the Gestapo.

The use of radio was illegal, but people on both sides of the ghetto wall took the risk to know what was happening in the wider world. Amelia had conveyed to him that many Jews thought the opportunity to hear a different narrative was worth dying for. She'd told Paul earlier that week that groups of people in the tenements got together in a basement after dark to listen to communiques broadcast from various countries. The radio was still active, even after numerous searches of the buildings – she wouldn't say which building had the radio, and he had not pressed her on the subject. The broadcasts spread hope, she'd insisted, and they counterbalanced the news spread by German propaganda.

Paul felt a rush of adrenalin course through him as he watched his staff keeping busy with their tasks. He went to the window, looked left, then right, and then turned back to the room. "Nurse Bartek, come with me. I have another job for you today."

Amelia took off her apron and donned her cardigan.

"The rest of you go home," Paul said. "There's no work for us today, by order of the Gestapo."

# Chapter Twenty-Two

Paul headed to the ghetto's gates with Amelia following meekly behind him. He said nothing as they walked in the soft-red glow of dawn, and she asked no questions. He didn't have to tell her anything. Jews didn't demand to know why they were following this or that order, nor did they ask why they were going here or there. They did as they were told, as quickly and efficiently as possible, and usually in silence.

"Good morning, Herr Doctor. Where are you going this early?" the policeman at the gate asked whilst ogling Amelia. "What's the Jew doing here? She can't go out."

Paul eyeballed the man and stuck his chest out in indignation. "I need a driver and car. There are reports of typhus cases in the city, and as senior medical officer while Herr Oberstabsarzt Mayer is in Warsaw, I am responsible for all emergencies that arise. If there is an outbreak, I must report it to the Generalgouvernement immediately. This nurse is my assistant. I need her to take notes – don't worry, she will not examine Christian patients, I know the rules." He paused to glare at the young man. "Well, where is my car?"

The youth went to the telephone in the guard box. "I need to clear this with Kriminalinspektor Krüger, Herr Oberarzt. The ghetto is under curfew while the deportations are going on."

"I know that. I helped arrange the curfew."

"Even so…"

"Even so, nothing. My orders come directly from the Wehrmacht High Command, and you will answer to them if

I'm delayed, not the Gestapo." Paul checked his watch for effect. "Every minute you keep me here, the threat of an outbreak grows. Do you know how quickly typhus can spread, hmm? Do you want this entire ghetto to be quarantined, with you locked inside it and under curfew with the Jews who are probably carrying the damned disease? My car. Now, before a full-blown pandemic hits this city and everyone in it, including you."

The young Orpo lifted the telephone and eventually asked the operator on the other end to send a car and driver from the carpool. Both arrived less than five minutes later.

Paul ushered Amelia to the vehicle's back door but was stopped in his tracks when the guard blocked it.

"With respect, Herr Oberarzt … of course, you … you can go, sir, but you cannot take this Jew with you. What if she tries to run away?"

"Don't be ridiculous. She'll be in my custody." Paul glared at the puce-faced lad whilst fishing out a notebook and pen from his jacket pocket.

The nervous-looking novice stared at it, then stepped aside as though the paper were a deadly weapon trained on him.

Paul unscrewed the top off the pen. "Give me your name. I'll be reporting you when I get back." His eyes blazed with anger, but privately, he felt sorry for the youngster who was probably experiencing his first days of his first posting in the German police force.

"Forgive me, Herr Oberarzt … my mistake."

Paul shoved Amelia into the vehicle's back seat with his notepad and pen still in his hand. He closed the door, then made a point of looking at the young man as he put his pad away. "Never question me again, understand?" he demanded, poking the guard's jacket with the pen.

The boy raised himself, clicked his heels, and said in a loud squeaky voice, "*Jawohl!* Heil Hitler, Herr Oberarzt!"

Two Jewish ghetto policemen opened the gates. Paul, still glaring at the German, knew he was disobeying one of the ghetto's standing orders; Jews were not permitted to leave without a letter stating extenuating circumstances signed personally by Krüger. He was also aware of the time. Soon, Orpo officers on day watch would arrive, and they would be infinitely more proficient than the raw recruit, who was now shivering like a shitting dog.

As the car revved its engine, the German guard gave way, then as if once weren't enough for him, he gave Paul another stiff-armed salute.

"Drive to the Feilenstrasse district. I don't know how far it is … its four stops on the tram. It used to be called Popiela," Paul instructed the driver.

"Yes, sir. I know it," the Schütze said.

Twenty-five minutes later, Paul gave the driver an order to pull off the main road and head down a narrow country lane. They were reaching the suburbs where there were green, open spaces, recently ploughed potato fields, and thickets of trees, parts of which had been gutted by the Germans for wood. "I'll tell you when to stop," Paul said when the car entered unfamiliar territory.

The driver hesitated halfway along the lane, which was more suitable for bicycles or cows. With his foot hard on the brake, he brought the vehicle to a complete stop and said, "I don't think we will be able to continue. The road is too narrow for this car. I should turn around, Herr Oberarzt."

"Very well. I must have made a mistake at the junction."

"I might be able to turn here, but I'm very close to the edge and … yes, there's a ditch and grass slope too…" the driver mused more to himself than Paul.

As the man popped his head out of the driver's window to get a better look, Paul removed the glass syringe from the metal box in his pocket. In it was a large, 2 grains dose of morphine from one of the two vials he'd uncovered in the pharmacy on that last day. Unwilling to use them and scared to be without them should a terrible emergency arise, he'd carried them in their container on his person, like ancient artefacts more precious than any amount of money. He hated having to use the medicine for this malign reason.

The driver turned off the engine, stuck his head out the window again to check how much room he had to manoeuvre on his side before going down a shallow, grassy embankment then sat back in his seat.

Paul pounced. Like a madman spurred on by a rush of adrenalin, he stabbed the needle deep into the side of the driver's neck, praying he had hit the jugular instead of the carotid, and emptied the syringe's contents with one quick depression of his thumb.

The driver began to thrash his arms about. The back of his hand inadvertently walloped Paul's cheek, but then he sighed with a resigned groan as the morphine began to work and his body grew limp. Out for the count, the man's eyes closed, and his head fell forward to thump against the steering wheel.

Paul panted, "Christ, Paul … get it in." His fingers were trembling, and he was having a hell of a job trying to get the syringe back into the tight-fitting metal case – he wasn't made for this sort of carry-on; he wasn't Max.

In the back seat, Amelia's eyes were wide with confusion, but she looked more composed than Paul, who had finally managed to replace the syringe container in his pocket.

He twisted his body to look at the woman he'd just brought to hell with him, and he was reminded of Judith Weber. Poor Judith; she was probably dead by now. He'd be more careful with Amelia. He would guard her with his life.

"You're a strong, level-headed woman, Amelia, and I want to explain what happens now. Whether you want to come with me is up to you."

"Why didn't you kill him?" she demanded, glaring at the back of the driver's head.

Again, Judith came to Paul's mind. Both women had hated the Nazi regime and had stood up to its authority in one way or another. "I'm not a murderer. When he eventually wakes up or is discovered asleep on the ground, he will tell the authorities I did this to him."

"Are you sure we shouldn't kill him? We could hide his body in the woods."

"No. I'm not going to conceal this crime. They already know I left the ghetto in this car with this driver," Paul explained. "Anyway, I'm not clever enough to come up with eloquent machinations. My brother ... well, he would have figured something out."

Paul got out of the car. He was beginning to feel vulnerable on this stretch of road and wanted to get away before being discovered. He opened the back door and took Amelia's hand. "They'll hunt me down as a deserter and you as a runaway, but by painting a guilty sticker on myself, the Gestapo and SS will leave the people of Łódź alone ... at least, that's my hope. We can't go back. We can never go back. We are fugitives now."

She nodded. Acceptance crossed her eyes as though she now understood Paul's madness and was glad of it. "Thank you, Doctor, for giving me this chance to live."

Paul struggled to pull the driver out of the car and laid him on the ground. "Help me strip him."

Amelia unclipped the driver's braces and trouser buttons, but then she stopped what she was doing to ask, "Why have you brought me with you? Why are you running away?"

"I brought you because I didn't want you to die." Paul was breathless with fear as he undid the man's shirt buttons, but he continued to explain his actions. "I found out through a friend that the Gestapo and SS suspect me of helping the Jewish staff escape the hospital. My friend managed to get my letter to another mutual friend. In it, I asked for his help in getting you and me to the Polish Underground Network – you know Doctor Anatol Nowak, don't you? He used to work at Hospital Number 4."

"We're going to Doctor Nowak's house?" she snapped, anger sparking in her eyes. "He was never nice to the Jewish hospital staff. Once, he shouted at me for dropping a tray – he told me to go back to the stinking ghetto where I belonged. He might report us. He looks like the type who collaborates with the Germans; I can spot them a hundred metres off. We had a few of them in our apartment block in the city..."

"Wait … stop. Anatol and his wife, Vanda, are good people," Paul interrupted her. "He's nothing like the man you thought you knew. Trust me, he won't throw us out. He knows we're coming, and he will help us."

"How do you know he'll help us?"

Paul looked down the road. "No more questions for now. Hurry, before someone passes by here."

Paul bit his lip as they worked on. He had answered Amelia truthfully, but he'd omitted the most important details, such as the many times Anatol had rescued Jews.

After the driver was stripped to his vest and underpants, Paul and Amelia dragged him down the grassy embankment and into the recently ploughed field. He laid the man in the hollow between two lines of furrowed ridges, careful to position him on his side with his top leg drawn up to prevent him from choking should he vomit before regaining consciousness.

"Let's go. He'll sleep for hours, but people will be waking up and travelling through here soon," he said, holding the man's uniform in his arms.

At the car, Paul instructed Amelia to get into the boot. "It's not far. Please, don't worry. It will be all right. I promise you."

"I know. It already is," she replied, with a certainty he found humbling.

# Chapter Twenty-Three

Paul was shivering as he drove in the direction of Anatol's house. His foot was jittering under the steering wheel, unnecessarily jumping from brake to accelerator and back again, as every nerve in his body fired up. He was feeling it now; the guilt, shame, and gravity of his situation.

To calm down, he pictured his twin's attitude after killing August Leitner; that event had happened a lifetime ago, yet he thought about it often. Max had not flinched or debated the rights and wrongs of his actions. He'd been unruffled and without a tinge of remorse – more – he'd had satisfaction written in his sparkling eyes and smirking mouth.

Paul recalled the advice Max had given him at that inn in Brandenburg. He'd overstated it, and it had stuck. 'To play a good game of subterfuge, a man must be paranoid every second of every day. He must see the very worst in people, focus on their most base characteristics before considering any positive qualities they might have. He must have an overactive imagination in which danger lurks on every corner and in every expression on every face in the street. No one is reliable until they have earnt your trust, tenfold.' Max had then chuckled, 'Calm down, Paul. What I'm saying is, it's always better to be safe than sorry.'

Paul, taking Max's advice to heart, looked in the rear-view mirror every few metres. As he turned into Anatol's long street bordered by woods, he was reminded of the forest in Dieppe where he'd been trying to get back to the Germans and away from the French. Now, he was running away from his own army towards the Polish Resistance.

Anatol's gates were ajar. Paul put the handbrake on when he got out of the car. His heart jumped erratically, and his face was creased with new worries as he opened the gates fully. Gert had confirmed that Anatol received the letter, but the former hadn't brought Paul an answer. *Had Anatol managed to make the arrangements? More importantly, had the Polish Free Army approved the request to take Amelia and himself in?* These questions would be answered within minutes, Paul knew, and when they were, he'd either be optimistic about his new future with the Resistance or looking at a short life alone and on the run.

He drove inside, got out and closed the solid gates behind him, then he steered the car to the back of the house where he parked on the grass lawn.

As soon as he'd opened the boot to help Amelia out, Paul caught the sound of footsteps behind him. He spun around and saw Anatol.

"We had no problems. I dealt with the driver, and I made sure I wasn't followed," he said while trying to read the stern-looking Pole.

Anatol gave a curt nod to Amelia, then gestured to the kitchen door. "Go in the house, both of you."

In the kitchen, Vanda stared at Amelia's ashen face. "You must be the woman Paul spoke of?" she asked, in a friendlier tone than the one her husband had used outside.

"Yes … I'm Amelia Bartek."

"I'm Vanda. Sit, Amelia. I've made herbal tea. It's a bit weak but it's hot."

"Thank you." Amelia removed her headscarf, which had a red cross sewn into the fabric. Her hair was dishevelled, and her shoes were dirty with baked soil that stuck to the leather. She looked confused and frightened as she took a seat at the table.

"Paul, a private word, please," Anatol said, already heading to the kitchen door that led to the hallway.

Paul smiled at Amelia before following Anatol. "I won't be long."

In the living room, Anatol said, "I've done as you asked, but with a couple of changes."

"Will they have me?" Paul asked, desperate to know.

"I don't know," Anatol said, closing the living room door. "The section of the Polish Free Army I spoke to scoffed at the idea. Their leader's exact words to me were, 'Are you off your fucking head?' Then I told him about your English connections, and he was intrigued. They will listen to what you have to say, but don't get your hopes up or think they'll trust those honest blue eyes of yours. You could as easily get shot."

Paul sighed with relief and then his legs buckled, forcing him to sit in an armchair. "Thank you, Anatol, that's all I needed to hear. To be honest, I didn't know what to expect when I got here. I imagined having to go on the run alone. Within hours, Krüger will have men hunting me. This has got to work ... I'll make it work."

Paul undid his jacket's buttons and expelled a long breath. He had no idea how Anatol had contacted the Resistance or where the group was based, but they were within his grasp, and he was hopeful, despite Anatol's bleak picture of him possibly getting shot by the people he was running to. "I won't hide like a rat down a drain until this war ends," Paul said, finding his voice. "If the Poles shoot me, so be it. I will *not* be a German who looks back and says I was following orders and had no choice but to comply. This war has wrung my soul like a wet towel. I won't take it anymore."

Anatol sat on the couch and said, "I understand why you're doing it. I just hope you know what's ahead of you. You can't go back to your wife or child, or to the German army with an apology for making a rash decision. You're out. You're now a wanted man with a price on your head, and the Gestapo will tear this city apart looking for you. Tell me, why did you bring Nurse Bartek?"

"I saw an opportunity to get her out of the ghetto, and I took it." Paul bit his tongue. This wasn't the time to talk about how fond of Amelia he'd become, or how much he wanted to keep her by his side. He was also disinclined to talk about the end of his marriage. "I went to Chelmno, Anatol, and the rumours are true … it's an extermination camp, using mobile gas chambers. The Jews are killed within an hour of arriving there. I watched the whole process from start to finish."

Anatol's face drained of colour. "All those people who were deported … all of them are dead?"

"Yes, and I now have first-hand knowledge of every moment the prisoners spent there before their executions. I took notes of the train stations that service the camp, what's inside the manor house, an approximate number of SS and policemen who work there, the methods they use to kill, the location of the crematorium grids … and names, too, as many names and their ranks as I could remember..." Paul tapped the side of his head. "It's all in here, Anatol, and I will pass every bit of information I have to people who can do something about it…"

"Do what?"

"I don't know … blow the damn place up! And maybe, maybe one day hold these people accountable."

Anatol leant forward in his chair. His stoic mask dropped, and in its place was the face of a broken man. "Vanda and I are also leaving the city this morning, and we're not coming back."

"Why in God's name would you do that?" Paul asked, aghast at the news.

"We don't feel safe anymore. The Gestapo detained my neighbours yesterday. They started at the corner of the street and took away the families from the first three houses. No one has come back home since. We're afraid they'll come for us too. As soon as Hubert arrives, we'll take his horse and cart and make our own way to the Home Army in Warsaw. It will take us at least four days to reach a safe house, but we can't risk travelling by car when the Germans are confiscating all vehicles registered to Poles."

Paul was upset for his friend. Poor Anatol and Vanda. They were losing everything. *Were they being overly cautious?* No. Paul knew exactly what the Germans were planning for the Polish people, and it would devastate them. He was struck by a more selfish thought, though; he'd been counting on Anatol to wear the Wehrmacht driver's uniform and drive the car: "What about the plan?"

"Don't worry, I've compensated for not being able to take you. You will be all right."

"No, I wasn't thinking … sod it, yes, I was. I'm sorry. I'm a selfish bastard, worrying about myself when you've got bigger problems to face." Paul's face reddened with guilt. He'd hoped to avoid this subject, at least today. Anatol was a proud man, and the Generalgouvernement's new *cleansing* policies and mass deportation of Poles were meant to strip the Polish people of their dignity and self-worth. He was ashamed to even talk about what he now knew to be true, but he'd be even more regretful if he didn't mention it.

"Anatol, I was going to speak to you about this on the journey, but I can see your problem is more urgent than I first thought," Paul said.

"What have you heard?"

"When I was at Chelmno, the camp's Commandant told me that the Generalgouvernement's new scheme is to deport twenty million Poles to Western Siberia."

"Ah. That I didn't know," Anatol said in a shaky voice.

"Bothmann, the Commandant, was blasé about it. He said the policy was for *much further down the road,* but I think it might have started."

Anatol's fidgety fingers ran through his hair and down the back of his neck. "Siberia, eh?" he muttered, looking shocked to his core.

"They're also planning the Germanisation of four to five million selected Polish people if they're deemed racially worthy." Paul then added, "The Commandant specifically spoke of an unspecified number of young Poles endowed with what the Germans call *desirable Aryan qualities* being taken to Germany to be raised by good stock. His words, not mine. If all this is true, Anatol, no one is safe; not the rich, the poor, the young, or the elderly … not even Christians."

While Anatol was trying to absorb the information, Paul measured his next words with great care. He intended to share

every piece of information he'd managed to wring out of
Bothmann on his visit to Chelmno. By doing that, he hoped to
buy his way into the Polish Home Army or one of the
affiliates Anatol had told him about some weeks earlier. He
now realised, however, how much easier it was to gain
unsavoury information than to impart it to those he cared for.
He was about to inform Anatol about something that was
going to crush him.

"I can see you know more..." Anatol said, almost in a
whisper.

"I do. Trust me, I'm going to tell you and your Polish
friends about every rumour, piece of mess-hall gossip, and
written order I've heard about or seen with my own eyes. I'll
blow the lid off Chelmno and what I know about the
Auschwitz-Birkenau camp and the others being built, but now
... right now, I'm finding it hard to give you news that makes
me ... I'm ashamed of being German."

"Say it, Paul. How much worse can things get?"

"Much worse. I think the Poles being selected for
deportation will be killed ... not all, but many of them.
Bothmann was quite open about Hitler's vision for your
country. He sees Poland as a laboratory for his racial theories.
He told me that the cost of reallocating Poles would be too
high and that *undesirables* would never reach their new
homes. Apparently, Hitler would rather spend money on new
infrastructure than feed Polish people forced to leave behind
everything they owned. Kraków and Lublin districts are to be
repopulated by German colonists once the Poles have been
removed..."

"Colonists? Is that what they're calling them?"

"Before I left Chelmno, he asked me to keep that information under my hat until it became an open official policy. I'm sorry, Anatol, had I known they'd already started this, I would have warned you sooner … somehow."

Anatol staggered to his feet, flinching as if he'd been physically struck. He stood behind the couch, gripping its fabric with tight fists and repeating over and over, "*Niech cię* – damn them to hell! Fuck the Germans! If they try to cleanse my country by choosing whom they see as the best specimens and by killing the rest as undesirables, we will piss on them. We will gather an army and destroy everything they try to build in this country. It's outrageous, even for Hitler – even for him."

Paul got to his feet, crossed the room to Anatol's side, and tried to calm his friend. "You know as well as I that Hitler is capable of this *and* more. He's already deported Communists and Catholic priests to the death camps – Christ, I can't believe I'm saying those two words together. You must have thought this was a possibility?" He felt a twinge of discomfort, realising how eerily his words echoed those Gert had spoken to him recently.

"Polish leaders, maybe, and Jews, of course, but not our children and the ordinary man and woman in the street. It makes no sense!"

"Anatol, let me finish. Please, you should know all of it."

Anatol wasn't listening. His face was ghostly-white, his eyes huge, and he was panting with rage, "How can I tell Vanda this? I am an only child, but she has four brothers and sisters, a huge family in Warsaw … Paul, how can I tell her?"

With no comforting response to give, Paul waited out the pause in conversation until Anatol could compose himself.

"I'm wasting time. Tell me the rest of it before Hubert arrives," Anatol finally said, sitting on a hard chair next to the sideboard.

Paul stood where he was and looked down at his friend. "According to Bothmann, the German policymakers foresee reducing lower-class Poles to the status of serfs, while deporting or otherwise eliminating the middle and upper classes and eventually replacing them with pure-blooded Germans. Hitler and his sidekick, Hans Frank in Kraków, want the Generalgouvernement to be their workforce reservoir for low-grade labour, like those in brick plants and road building. In other words, they're planning a great Polish labour camp."

Anatol scrubbed his face with his hands, as though he were cleansing filth off himself or trying to wake up. "Ach, I don't believe it. People like Hubert and I are valuable. We're doctors, for Christ's sake –"

"The Third Reich don't *want* Polish people with brains or wealth or holding any position of importance, and that includes scientists and doctors," Paul interrupted Anatol. "They want servants and slave labour with little or no education or culture – keep them ignorant – keep them submissive."

Anatol groaned as he rose. "And now they will kill whomever they perceive as the current Polish masters, as they did to our intelligentsia when they invaded. I will not forget any part of this conversation, Paul, but we'll talk more about this another time. Now we must go over your plan."

"Are you sure?"

"Yes, damn it. We must move forward, even in the face of defeat." Anatol cleared his throat and straightened his stooped shoulders. "We have considered a driver for the car and the uniform you brought. You will be surprised, I think. Wait here. I will fetch the man."

Paul was curious. He looked expectantly at the doorway and froze as Kurt Sommer's familiar face stared back at him. Already dressed in the unconscious driver's ill-fitting uniform, he looked broader and fitter; as though someone had plastered meat and new skin on his bones, then resurrected him to health. He wasn't the Kurt of old; his eyes wore haunting battle scars of the past, and he was thinner and much older looking than he'd been before the war. He had also grown a beard that almost covered his top lip and everything else beneath his nose to his chin. It was strange to see the grey bush on a man who was but thirty-five-years-old. No, he wasn't the Kurt of old, but he was a better Kurt than the half-starved man who'd been at death's door months earlier.

Paul began to chuckle, then the gurgling sound in the back of his throat flooded into full-blown laughter. He crossed the room in three long strides, pulled Kurt to him, then thumped him hard on the back with his palms and the laughter transformed to sobs.

"You're well, Kurt. You look good," Paul sniffed as he pulled away. "You've been here all this time? All this time, and I didn't know. Damn Anatol for not telling me. Ach, I don't care. Here you are, my friend, here you are! You beat Biermann, Kurt – you beat the bastard!

Kurt wiped his wet eyes and swallowed a lump of emotion. "*We* beat him, Paul … all of us." Then he cleared his throat again and gripped Paul by his shoulders. "I never thought I'd live to see this. I don't know what made you finally turn, but I know you well enough to assume it was a hard decision for you. I'm proud of you, Paul. Had your father lived, he would have been proud of you too."

"The decision was not as hard as you might think, Kurt…"

The creaking noise of the living room door opening broke Paul's moment of pure happiness.

Hubert, looking tense, looked from Paul to Kurt and back to Paul. "Sorry to interrupt this happy reunion but we need to get ready to leave now."

Paul crossed to Hubert and shook his hand. "It's good to see you. Are you coming, too?"

"No. I'm too old to leave all that's familiar to me. Besides, I have two cats and a wife who's not well. Come, you two, we must discuss your route."

As the men walked to the door, Paul held Kurt back. "No, no. This won't do at all. You cannot be a Wehrmacht driver with that beard on you. Come on, off with it." he cocked his head to one side. "Shame though, it looks good on you."

"Exactly what I said minutes ago," Hubert agreed, staring at Kurt. "As soon as we've finished talking, you can start shaving. I have the soap and razor ready, so no arguments."

Paul chuckled at the sight of Kurt, almost two metres tall and built like a Spanish bull, being told off by a short, old man.

# Chapter Twenty-Four

One of the four German soldiers leaning against an *Ursus A* lorry that was blocking the road ahead put on his helmet and raised his hand as Paul's car approached.

Paul swallowed the cotton-wool lump of fear at the back of his throat and kept his eyes on the back of Kurt's head as he gave instructions, "Kurt, let me talk to them, and for God's sake, don't get out of that seat. One look at those trousers of yours and the game is up. Amelia, focus on the seat in front of you. Do not look at the soldiers, and do not answer them even if they ask you a direct question. You're afraid, but we need you to look terrified. I am your enemy. I'm taking you from your home. Do you understand what I'm saying?"

"Yes, Doctor," she whispered.

Paul steadied himself for the interrogation to come. He'd put his plan together over a period of five days, and it was solid. Initially, he'd asked Anatol, through Gert, to prepare false medical orders that would allow Amelia to go with him. He'd then adopted the idea of stealing the car and driver's uniform in the hope that Anatol would drive them to the rendezvous site, where they'd meet with the Polish Home Army or their affiliates. It was, however, after he'd got confirmation that Anatol had delivered his message that he'd made his move, with only hours to spare.

Keeping his mind busy as the roadblock drew nearer, Paul imagined being a fly on the wall when Krüger discovered his prey had fled. *He will get straight on the telephone to Biermann in Berlin, furious that the arrest hasn't gone through. With a bit of luck, Biermann might have another heart attack,* Paul thought, as a second soldier up ahead raised his hand. He was going to get out of this alive and laugh at the Gestapo's defeat from a place far from Łódź. *Fuck their need for victory ... revenge ... hatred or whatever is in their sick, twisted minds! They aren't having me.*

Paul slipped his hand into his pocket and fished out the falsified orders he'd been carrying on his person for two days. "Now, Kurt."

Kurt stopped the stolen Wehrmacht staff car bearing German registration plates, beginning with WH for Wehrmacht Army and followed by five numbers. He had encountered two other military vehicles thus far on their journey to Warsaw. On both occasions, he flashed his lights and waved to the other drivers, receiving waves of greeting in return as the cars passed him.

"This is it," Paul muttered as two soldiers approached the car. His main concern was not the paperwork, but Kurt being ordered out of the vehicle by one of the four soldiers. He looked the part of a Schütze driver from the waist up, but he was comically lacking in his bottom half where his legs were too long for the uniform trousers, and his feet were in civilian boots.

Paul wound his window down as two soldiers came around to the rear passenger side of the car. The other two men leant nonchalantly against the lorry's bumper, smoking cigarettes and looking bored.

"Morning, Schütze," Paul said.

"Good morning, Herr Oberarzt. Heil Hitler," one of the soldiers replied with a brisk salute.

Paul gave the man the *lazy salute;* raising his forearm from the elbow until his palm was level with his ear. "Heil Hitler," he said then handed over his identity papers and the orders.

Amelia's genuine fear was apparent under the other Schütze's malign stare, yet when the soldier leant in through the open window, his breath smelling like a dirty ashtray, she managed to keep her eyes on the back of the seat in front, as instructed.

"Her identity papers?" the man asked Paul.

"She's a Jew. She has no papers. You'll read all you need to know about her in my orders," Paul retorted.

The soldier moved on to Kurt, holding Paul's paperwork in his hand without looking at what was written.

Kurt carried the identity documents of Paul's original driver. Looking nothing like the man, he had peeled off the photograph that had been glued to the first page of the *Wehrpass* book. He was prepared to answer questions, if necessary, having studied the man's biography. The Wehrpass included personal data of soldiers, extensive details of their careers, such as units served with, battles, awards, injuries, illnesses, promotions, and miscellaneous notes.

"I've just arrived in Poland," Kurt said as the soldier's eyebrows drew together. "I was in France, and I haven't had the time to get my picture renewed. You know how it is."

"My driver is an idiot," Paul grunted tersely. "He's got straw under that helmet of his, but if you want to blame someone, blame the clerk. He shouldn't have issued the identity documents until they were in order. I'll be reporting him when I get back to Łódź. Can we hurry this up?"

Undaunted by Paul's harsh tone, the soldier finally read the orders. "You're taking her to Warsaw?"

"Yes. I'm escorting her to a holding facility where she'll receive a rigorous medical evaluation. She's been nursing typhus patients for months but has never contracted the disease herself. Doctor Mengele, based at the Auschwitz-Birkenau camp, wants to run some tests on her to find out if she carries the illness, and why she's not become sick…"

The other soldier also popped his head through the open window to get a closer look at Amelia, studying her as if she'd just grown two heads in a laboratory jar.

"I wouldn't do that if I were you, Corporal. Doctor Mengele's tests will also confirm or rule out if she's contagious."

Paul stared down the soldier whose face was a picture of indecision. He'd taken a step back from the car but was apparently unconvinced of the story's validity.

"One moment, Oberarzt."

"No, I will not wait one moment, Schütze. Either check the legitimacy of my orders or get out of our way and let me get on. The less time I spend with this stinking Jew, the better."

The two soldiers went to the back of the car and opened the trunk. When they finished rifling through it, they returned to their vehicle where they huddled with their Gefreiter who was still leaning against the bumper of their truck. He looked at the documents while appearing to have one ear open to the Schütze who'd spoken to Paul.

"This is taking too long, Kurt," Paul whispered. "What are they talking about?"

"Stay calm, Paul," Kurt mumbled.

Paul, buckling under the agonizing wait, opened his door and got out of the car. "What's the problem here? You're wasting my time!" he shouted as he began to walk towards the four men.

The Gefreiter, deliberately smacking the documents against his outer thigh, strode towards Paul with his free hand on his sidearm and yelled, "Get back!"

Paul choked on adrenalin as the first salvo of bullets missed his right ear by centimetres. He fell to the ground like a dropped stag and lay on his stomach next to the corporal who was now also face down, but with two exit wounds in his back.

Mesmerised, Paul glanced up to see Kurt stomping past him while continuing to fire his Mauser C96 Semi-Automatic Pistol at the other soldiers, who were still scrambling to reach their weapons.

Paul heard Kurt's roar above the noise of bullets firing continuously from what seemed like a never-ending magazine. With primeval fear, he covered his head with his hands and squeezed his eyes shut while the persistent gunfire battered his ears. *Any second now, I'll be hit ... any second.*

The firing halted, the sudden silence a shocking contrast to the mayhem of seconds earlier. Paul took his hands away from his ringing ears but couldn't force himself to open his eyes. *A soldier will be standing above me with his rifle centimetres from my face. Kurt is dead; he must be with those odds against him. The crazy, hard-headed, stupid man...*

"Stay down, Paul!"

Paul's eyes shot open. *Kurt's voice?*

The dead corporal, lying half a metre from Paul, gazed unseeingly at the sky with one arm thrown wide and the other resting on top of the pistol he had managed to unholster before succumbing to Kurt's hail of bullets.

In a daze, Paul disobeyed Kurt and sat up to watch, like an impassive bystander out of harm's way. Kurt, looming large with his semi-automatic pistol gripped in his hand, checked the soldiers lying in front of the lorry. The soldier who had questioned Paul was wounded but grasping for the butt of his rifle, which had become entangled in its shoulder strap. He groaned with the supreme effort of reaching for it, alerting Kurt, who turned sharply and shot him not once, but three times to finish him off. Paul's mind had screamed, *look out, Kurt!* but like a damn mute, he'd been unable to verbalise his warning.

The sangfroid German Jew stood over the remaining two unchecked soldiers. They were dead, riddled with bullets, but grim satisfaction shone in Kurt's eyes as he fired his last rounds into them for the hell of it.

Paul lurched to his feet on legs that barely held him. He staggered towards the car to check that Amelia was all right, but before reaching it, he vomited as aftershocks surged up his throat. *I must stop this throwing up business,* he thought, with an almost-hysterical chuckle.

"It's over, Paul," Kurt's tinny voice sounded far away.

Paul wiped his mouth with the back of his hand and then straightened.

"Come on. We need to go – now, Paul!" Kurt's grating voice came at him again.

Paul, still not fully *compos mentis* and with his ears echoing the pinging of the bullets, straightened to see Amelia stepping out of the car. "My God, Kurt, what have you done? You nearly killed me!" he screamed as his fear morphed into anger. "If I hadn't hit the ground when I did ... what the hell were you thinking?"

"They didn't believe us," Kurt answered with a tone that broached no argument. "I saw the Gefreiter going for his gun, and in my book, that says he was going to make an arrest..."

"You couldn't have known that," Paul snapped. "I would have talked my way out of it."

"Paul ... look at the state of you. You would have stuttered your way to a bullet in your head."

Paul ran his fingers through his hair. He was still suffering a full-body tremble, as though a bloody earthquake were going off inside him, but he was also conscious of his impotence in the face of danger ... and in full view of Amelia. Embarrassed, he shifted his eyes to her. "Are you all right, Amelia?" he asked, busying his shaking hands by brushing the dirt off himself with his palms.

"Yes. You have blood on your face and jacket," she croaked, clinging to the car door for support.

Paul, unaware of how much of the dead corporal's blood had splattered him, brushed off her remark to salvage his pride with Kurt. "Where did the gun come from?"

"Under the front passenger seat. I put it there before we left the house." Kurt was checking the corporal's identity papers. "You should be more worried about where these soldiers came from," he suggested, holding up the dead man's Wehrpass book. "He was based in the Łódź Barracks."

"They're a long way from Łódź."

Kurt pulled down the lorry's back flap, jumped into the back of the vehicle and whooped with delight. "Yes! There's a nice cache of rifles and ammunition here. And what's this?" he then said, lifting a bottle of beer. "They've got a crate of alcohol as well. *Mein Gott,* Paul – whisky – help me take some of this stuff to the car."

"What about the bodies?" Amelia asked, as she and Paul hurried towards the lorry.

Paul shrugged. He was out of his league in this situation and would leave the decision to Kurt. He was the only one amongst them who knew what he was doing.

"We don't have time to move bodies. They can stay where they are." Kurt groaned as he handed four rifles down to Paul, who staggered at the unexpected weight, adjusted the load in his arms, and hurried them to the staff car.

"The Germans have half-cleared a forest about ten kilometres from here. Once we get in there, we'll hide the car and walk the rest of the way on foot. The patrol that comes across this will be stumped." Kurt grunted again as he bent over the side to hand more weapons to Paul who, this time, was better prepared. "There are three different country roads coming up at the next junction. They all lead to Warsaw, eventually, but we're not taking any of them."

"We're not?" Paul asked upon his return.

"No."

Kurt handed down more weapons, then he jumped off the back of the lorry. The case of beer and spirits waited just at the edge of the truck's bed. He lifted it, grimaced, and was forced to set it down again.

Paul returned and spotted the blood on Kurt's jacket. "Kurt, are you hurt?"

"It's just a graze," Kurt answered.

"Let me look…"

"I'm all right. We need to go."

"Look, I might not be the warrior and saviour you are, but you're no doctor. Let me look."

Kurt opened his jacket, gasping as his hand brushed the wound.

Paul studied it. A bullet had chipped the side of Kurt's torso just under his ribs, like a stone making an indent on the corner of a wall. It needed a couple of sutures but was not life-threatening. He pulled a handkerchief from his pocket and pressed it against Kurt's tender flesh. "Press that hard. I have a bandage in my rucksack…"

"Thank you, but there's no time, Paul. We'll do it when we get to our destination," Kurt answered with a terse shake of his head.

Paul ignored him, going to the back seat, digging into his bag, and returning to Kurt with the cotton bandaging. "Lift your shirt. You'll lose too much blood if it's a long walk."

Kurt glared but did as he was told, biting his lip as the bandage was pulled tight around him.

"I'll need to put a couple of stitches in there, but that will have to do for now."

Amelia let out a ragged sob several minutes after Kurt pulled the car around the lorry and drove through the adjacent grassy field. In a surprising move, she rested her head on Paul's shoulder and squeezed her eyes shut. "Thank God. I couldn't bear the thought of you being hurt."

Paul couldn't settle his uneven breathing, even though they'd now put kilometres between themselves and the German roadblock. He kept his eyes peeled on the road, but he couldn't stop thinking about the way Kurt had *enjoyed* killing the four men and how well he'd reacted under fire. The persecution of Jews, war, the ghetto, Biermann … these things combined had changed his friend's character. Kurt, the self-controlled and mild-mannered driver, had become a crazed killer revelling in his victory. Even now, he was unwilling to engage in conversation and focused instead on the difficult narrow lanes that sometimes ended at the edge of roadless grasslands.

*How many shots had the Germans managed to get off before being mown down by Kurt's bullets?* His proficiency with the lethal weapon and his cold-as-steel-nerves had been shocking. He and his gun had looked to be the best of friends, as if they'd worked many times together. *Maybe Biermann isn't a pathological liar after all?* Kurt had behaved like a seasoned killer; like Max, August Leitner, and other shady creatures in the Abwehr and British Intelligence Services. His eyes narrowed with anger as conversations with Biermann came flooding back, and despite the dangers posed by their current situation, he leant into the back of Kurt's neck.

"Were you a British spy, Kurt? Tell me the truth ... was Biermann right about you and my father being partners?" Paul demanded.

Kurt stared at Paul through his rear-view mirror. Amelia's body stiffened in the back seat, and she moved away from Paul's growing rage.

"Answer me, damn you!" Paul demanded, forgetting about the woman he'd sworn to protect.

Kurt took a sharp turn in the road and then drove towards a wooded area, thick with a mix of ancient and young leafy Caucasian oak trees. Just past the treeline, he manoeuvred the vehicle between two oak trees which looked like a giant arch conjoined at the top.

The car's left front tyre bumped over the roots of a tree and then kept bumping into loose branches and thick bushes until he was forced to stop and turn off the engine.

"We'll camouflage the vehicle, then walk the rest of the way. It's not far," Kurt said, struggling to get out of the car because of the branches.

Outside the car, Paul raised his eyes skywards. It was as if they had gone from day to dusk within minutes. The ceiling of oak leaves gave way to those of silver birch and aspen, shimmering translucently as a slanting beam of sunlight broke on their highest branches. He looked back the way they'd come and wondered how Kurt had managed to find his way in here until it dawned on him. "You haven't been at Anatol's house all these months, have you?"

"No. I've been with the Polish Underground Network for the last six weeks," Kurt answered truthfully.

"Well, at least something makes sense." Paul began to help Kurt cover the car with branches and leaves. For hours, Kurt had followed his map, and not once had he deviated from the narrow country roads winding through the rural landscapes or been fazed when he'd found himself in unknown territory. To Paul, it had been like travelling through a labyrinth of never-ending dirt tracks, all looking the same and bordered by identical landscapes, but it was now evident that Kurt knew the route well by the way he'd deftly taken every junction and turn with confidence. *Perhaps, then, Kurt was less of a crazed killer and more a ... trained one?*

Paul threw Kurt a look of disgust. Whether trained or crazed, the man he had respected was now a liar in his eyes. "I'm not going anywhere with you until you answer my questions." Paul's voice was calmer but still cold as he laid another branch on the car's roof. "Is my father alive?"

Kurt stopped what he was doing. His clammy skin shone as tiny shafts of light above broke on his face. "I give you my word, Paul, I will tell you everything you need to know after I get you to my people."

"You will tell me *now,*" Paul insisted. He had considered his father-in-law incapable of telling the truth. On the other hand, he had trusted Kurt's word with every cell in his body. "Kurt! I will not move."

"Yes, your father is alive." Kurt sighed with defeat. "He's in England with your mother."

Paul's rage reignited like a blazing flashover, and he pulled his arm back and swung a punch at Kurt's face. Lost to the unnecessary grief he had suffered since learning his father was dead and still not satisfied that he'd punished Kurt enough, he swung another right hook that hit Kurt squarely on the nose.

Kurt, who had not retaliated, moaned as he pinched his nostrils. Then he lowered his head and blew the blood out of them one by one.

Paul, still furious, went for Kurt again, but this time he was met by the latter's forearm smashing into his throat, just below his Adam's apple. Paul's legs collapsed beneath him. Breathless, he lay on his back, gasping for air and seeing thousands of sparks lighting the sky above him.

"I gave you the two, but that's all you get, Paul. Thank God, you're not Max. You hit like a girl," Kurt finally mumbled, as he pulled Paul to his feet.

Paul leant against the side of the car, panting with an almost hysterical hangover. Appalled that he had come to blows, he croaked, "I would have kept the secret…"

"I couldn't take the risk," Kurt cut Paul off. "You were too close to Biermann, and he would have wormed it out of you. I was following *your father's* orders, Paul, and I won't apologise."

"No!" Paul blazed, regaining his normal voice. "I cannot believe my father ordered you to keep Wilmot and me in the dark, knowing that we'd be grieving for him. Wilmot was in Russia. He must have been devastated."

"Your father kept your mother in the dark until she was safely out of Germany. You know Biermann. He would have stopped at nothing to get your papa back…"

"He knew! He told me my father was alive and I called him a liar. I trusted *your* word against his."

Kurt, ignoring his injured nose, pressed his hand on his recently bandaged wound. He looked genuinely regretful despite being the victim of Paul's fist. "I'm sorry for the pain I caused you, but I was right not to tell you, and I won't apologise for that. When we get to our camp, I'll take you through the whole story from start to finish, but first, we need to move."

Paul hesitated. "You had plenty of time of talk to me about it on the journey. At the very least, you should have warned me you already knew the people we're going to meet. I wouldn't have worried as much."

Kurt's stance stiffened, and his stony face was unreadable. "You should be worried. You should be very worried. It wasn't easy for me to gain the Poles' trust. They interrogated me and kept me under guard for days. It was after they'd verified my past association with London that they gave me any kind of chance to prove myself."

He pushed his bloodied fingers through his hair, then grunted, "You're a spoilt brat at times … know that? Anatol and Hubert risked their lives to get you this far. I vouched for you, but this meeting is still going to be hard, Paul. I'm surprised as hell they even agreed to it. You're not a German Jew; you're an enemy officer, and that means you will have to earn the Resistance leader's respect and trust on a minute-by-minute basis until he and his people no longer follow you every time you go behind a tree to shit. This is fucking serious, so can we forget your father for now and concentrate on us getting to where we need to be?"

"All right. I'm ready." Paul slung his rucksack over his shoulder. Kurt's remarks had stung; he had taken his driver and friend at face value, never realising how much attention Kurt had paid to a younger Paul. There had been times in Paul's past when he *had* behaved badly ... but it had never occurred to him that Kurt might have taken notice of the childish tantrums, rare though they had been.

Beside him, Amelia looked just as frightened as she had at the roadblock. She probably hadn't understood much of the angry exchange conducted in rapid German, but she'd have fathomed the physical violence.

Kurt led the way, Amelia followed, and Paul brought up the rear. He stared at her hair, breaking loose from its pins and lying in tangled waves down her back. *What must she think about my aggression?* He felt vulnerable, bared to his bones with the woman. They were not friends; at least, not yet. She'd always seen him as a German first, doctor second, person third, but in the space of a day, she was learning about his rare temper, possibly that he had a father in England, and that he'd lain on the ground squealing like a girl while Kurt was saving them. *What is she going to witness when we meet the Poles?* Being a Jew, they'd take her in with open arms, but if Kurt were correct, his introduction was going to be a much less friendly experience altogether.

# *Chapter Twenty-Five*

The six men appeared from behind the trees as though their bodies had been fused with the trunks. Armed with Mauser rifles, they surrounded Paul, Kurt, and Amelia, but their eyes and weapons were trained solely on Paul.

"Raise your hands above your head," Kurt instructed Paul, keeping his own by his side.

One of the men approached, a blink of recognition in his eyes. For a full thirty seconds, he studied Paul, his expressions changing as if he were an actor on stage using his entire repertoire: shifting his feet, cocking his head to one side, narrowing his eyes in anger, and then widening them in surprise. Eventually, he scowled then grunted a slew of Polish so quickly that Paul couldn't understand.

Paul panicked. The Pole was familiar. He'd seen him somewhere before. He couldn't recall where, but recognition had also flashed in the man's eyes when they'd stared each other down...

"He wants to search you, Paul," Kurt said, looking tense.

After the man patted Paul down for concealed weapons, he spoke to Kurt in Polish. The Pole showed concern over Kurt's wound, and when they finished talking, he gave Kurt a *well done* pat on the back. The two men were evidently friends.

"What happened?" the Pole then asked Kurt.

"A roadblock, about ten kilometres back. I don't think it was a checkpoint; not that far from residential areas and with the lorry they drove. They were thieving ... deserting ... who knows? They probably stopped to have a breather, and we happened upon them."

"And they shot you?"

"They didn't believe our story. I could see it was about to get ugly, so I fired on them before they shot the three of us in the car." Kurt grinned. "On the upside, I took a dozen rifles and alcohol off them."

"Hmm, bad news and good news, then. Tell them where the car is, Kurt," the Pole said, gesturing to three of his men. "They'll bring the contraband. You take the woman with you and settle her in at the camp. And get your wound seen to."

The man looked closely at Amelia for the first time. "You're the nurse?" he asked, as if he already knew the answer.

"Yes sir. I was a nurse in the Łódź ghetto hospital."

He looked at her cardigan with the yellow star sewn onto it, then talked to her in rapid Polish. "Kurt will take you to the camp. One of the women there will give you clothes. I don't ever want to see that star on you again or hear you say 'yes, sir, no sir' to any man. You hear me? You're free, and an equal to everyone else you meet until the day the war ends, or the Germans kill you. Go … and be welcome."

Then he turned his attention back to Paul and shocked everyone when he spoke in English. "You will come with me."

Paul whipped his head around to Kurt.

"Go. I'll look after Amelia," said Kurt, a flash of guilt on his face and just as quickly gone.

The two Poles pushed Paul about a hundred metres farther into the forest. He wasn't getting out of this alive. His chances had been ruined the moment he'd seen the man who'd done all the talking. The young Pole's voice had been familiar, as was his densely freckled face and lanky frame, and he now recalled where they'd met. An image of the man dashing towards the aircraft at the airstrip in Dieppe hit him as soon as he'd started walking. There was no mistaking it. It was Max's friend. Paul stumbled over a loose branch. He didn't stand a chance. The Resistance wouldn't trust a man who'd betrayed his own brother.

When they stopped walking, they found two armed men standing in front of a half-finished bunker. Three concrete pillars at the front, and concrete side walls held up a wooden slatted roof, four feet off the ground and partially concealed by unruly foliage resting on it. In front, steps led down to a narrow trench that stretched the length of the building's entrance.

"Get down the stairs," the English-speaking Pole snapped.

At the bottom, Paul was pushed inside the bunker. He straightened and began walking along a five-metre long passageway, lit by the Pole's battery torch. At the steel door at the end, the Pole pushed Paul aside, saying, "Wait here." Then he opened the door and closed it behind himself.

******

"It's true. He is Major Vogel's brother," said Darek Lukaszewicz, leaning across the table to the man sitting there. Behind the table, two narrow bunks were barracked military style, with blankets neatly folded at the foot of the beds and a pillow lying on top of them. A wooden crate with a storm lamp and book on it sat next to one of the beds, and above, more hurricane lanterns hung from thin wire that stretched at intervals for almost the length of the room.

"At first, I thought I was looking at Max dressed as a German, but then I noticed how scared he was," Darek continued. "I think he recognised me from France … not that it matters."

Darek sat, leaning in further towards the man he was talking to. "It's not too late to say no. We can kill him and be done with the problem. What do you want to do?"

Ever since Kurt and Anatol had informed him about the German doctor who was helping Jews in the Łódź ghetto, Romek Gabula had been anxious to meet him. He'd already learnt about Paul's existence through Darek, who months earlier, had told him the story of Max's brother escaping his custody at the airfield in Dieppe. By all accounts, this brother, every bit the Wehrmacht officer on the surface, was privately conflicted. His clash of conscience, according to Anatol, who'd approached him three days earlier, had turned to hatred for Hitler and his regime. He wanted out. He wanted to fight back.

Romek tapped his fingers on the desk. "I know you're against the idea, Darek, but Vogel's been passing on information and medicine to Anatol and Hubert for months. That, and his association with Kurt and Max is the reason I agreed to give him a chance. I won't go back on my word to Hubert and Anatol. I'm going to listen to what this Vogel has to say."

"You're the boss, but I won't trust a man who betrays his own twin brother," Darek retorted. "Romek, the minute you let him into our camp, he becomes a liability. Are you willing to risk the lives of our people because he's the brother of a man you were once fond of? I think you're making a mistake."

Romek's eyes blazed at Darek. "Were he any other German, I wouldn't even consider it, but it's Max's brother. It's not your job to question me, Darek. I am the one who will have to convince the other unit leaders to accept him, and, if I believe him, I will."

"I disagree. We do not fight with Germans and Jews. Let him and Kurt go to the units that deal with refugees."

Romek folded his arms and stared at the door. "We do not want Germans occupying our country, but they do. We do not want them using our land to build death camps where they gas and burn our people, but they do. We do not want to see our artists and poets and community leaders being executed, or our youngest and brightest being fostered by German people, but the Germans continue to do all these things. If we do not open our doors to Jews and Germans, refugees and dissidents, and anyone else who has a different religion and a different creed from ours, we are no better than the monsters we are fighting. If I am not satisfied with the man's answers, I will let you put a bullet in him before he leaves this bunker, and to hell with Max. Agreed?"

"Agreed," Darek grumbled, as he opened the door to Paul. "Get in here," he said, pulling Paul by the arm.

Romek was fascinated as he stared, blinked, then stared again at Max's double. Yes, they were identical, but Paul, who was standing to attention before him, looked like a man about to shit his underpants. This twin – Paul Vogel – also had a different *look* about him; a more innocent, less worldly gaze than Max's hardened, self-assured eyes that never flickered under harsh scrutiny.

"My God, it's incredible," he finally uttered in English, as if he'd just been inspecting a fine piece of art.

"I told you it was impossible to tell the difference," Darek replied, also in English.

Romek chuckled, "I can't decide who's the ugliest ... him or Max."

Paul's eyes widened. "You know my brother?"

"Yes. I know him well. We were close, once upon a time," Romek said.

Paul shifted his eyes to Darek and spoke in a high, accelerated voice as if this were his only chance to get it right. "I knew you'd recognised me from France, but I'm not the same man I was in Dieppe. I've chosen my side. I want to help you get the Germans out of Poland, to try and shorten this war, and save lives."

Darek clapped his hands slowly. "Bravo ... bravo! How long did it take you to rehearse that little speech?"

Romek, also amused by Paul's earnestness, said, "Sit, Paul – yes, I also know your name and where you met Anatol and Hubert. I've known about you for months."

"Then you know I'm sincere."

"Not yet."

Paul's eyes swept the room, as he took a seat.

"I see you're impressed by my home from home," Romek said, following Paul's eyes. "The Germans used this place for a brief time when they ravaged the forest for wood, but they didn't have the courtesy to finish the bunker's canals ... we did that. We also know they have much more complex bunkers in other parts of Poland, predominately in the Mazury region, north-east of Warsaw. The Germans have always excelled in reconstructing their home comforts. Tell me, Paul, have you ever been on a battlefield?"

Paul looked surprised by the question. "No. I've worked in hospitals and the ghetto," Paul answered, and then he asked Romek, "Aren't you afraid the Germans will come back here?"

"Yes ... and no. They think they've won this area. They've taken the wood they wanted, killed or transported the Jews who lived within a ten-kilometre radius of this forest, and they have moved on. If we're lucky, we'll have this place to ourselves –"

"We don't take anything for granted," Darek interrupted Romek. "We're well-armed and have the woods surrounded by men who'll give us fair warning of any German intrusion. People who come in here with bad intentions don't get out alive."

Romek was still trying to wrap his head around Max's brother being here. The subject of Max's family had never been raised in all the time they'd known each other. It was a no-go area as far as Max was concerned, and Romek had understood his friend's need for secrecy in his dirty world of espionage. He wasn't sure what stung the most; that Paul Vogel was German, making Max a German too, or that this Vogel was indirectly responsible for Klara's death.

"To be honest, I half-expected Max to turn up here at some point. He might yet show his face," Romek mused aloud. "But this ... this is priceless. Anatol and Hubert have sung your praises, as has Kurt, but despite your apparent, saintly attributes, you're still a German in Hitler's army, and I'm still deciding whether to take you in or kill you. Well, Max's brother, why should I trust you?"

"As of this morning, I'm in no one's army," Paul said calmly. "And I'm no saint. I suppose you shouldn't trust me; at least, not yet. I wouldn't, if I were sitting where you are right now."

Darek piped up again, "If we find out you're lying to us, we *will* kill you. We don't want prisoners here. They're more bother than they're worth."

Romek leant in, knowing he shouldn't be going down this rabbit hole when he had more pressing questions to ask, but he was desperate to know what had happened to his Klara in France. Heller had informed him that she was dead, but he hadn't said how it happened. He was covering up the truth. She had died in France in an *incident* that remained classified, Heller had insisted.

Darek, who had informed Romek that Klara had been in Scotland shortly before his time there, had been more enlightening than anyone at SOE or MI6. No instructor would talk to him about her, but he'd learnt from a loose-tongued trainee who'd met Klara, that she was desperate to return to France to finish what she'd started.

After a long silence, during which Romek tapped his fingers continuously on the table, he asked Paul, "Where did you meet the woman who abducted you in France?"

Paul visibly tensed. "Her? She was taking photographs at a party. She thought I was Max … an easy mistake to make … one people keep making."

"That I understand," Romek agreed.

"I've thought about that night a lot," Paul continued, "and I always come back to the same conclusion … if she had asked me my name before knocking me out, I would have told her who I was, and that might have been the end of it. I never saw her again after that first night."

Paul glanced at Darek then back to Romek. "Your friend here knows what happened in Dieppe. He saw me run away from Max after he'd rescued me from the Communists at the farm. I regret not getting on that plane with my brother. I don't expect you to understand, but I stayed behind because I believed it was my duty to help the ordinary German man and woman who lived in fear of the Nazi Party. I wanted to help the German army win the war as quickly as possible, to end the bloodshed." Paul scoffed at his own naiveté and hardened his tone, "This is not a war. It is the Fuhrer's attempt to annihilate the religious and social ideology of those he detests. Why, I can't say, but Hitler's magnetism still holds decent Germans in some pervasive, hypnotic state, which means that the bloodshed and gassings and executions of political and religious figures will not end with a German victory. My country, though it pains me to say it, won't stop its madness with victory; it must be defeated for the greater good, Hitler and his Party must be destroyed at its core, and every policy that lunatic ever came up with must be erased and never repeated."

Being allowed to talk uninterrupted spurred Paul on. "You may think I am perverse for wanting to see my country defeated, but I have hated myself since the day I arrived in Poland. I keep thinking ... if I had gone to England, I wouldn't have seen the atrocities that knot my stomach every morning when I wake up and every night when I try to sleep, but..."

"But you didn't go with him, and since then you've taken part in the slaughters you find so distasteful."

"Not taken part, no. Witnessed and not objected … yes, of those I'm guilty."

Romek's stomach was churning with anger and regret. Vogel was being candid, contrite, and owning up to atrocities he'd not yet been asked about. At this point, it was hard not to like him. "That woman who abducted you was my wife. She's dead because of you."

Paul's face reddened, and the fear that had begun to subside flashed again in his eyes and drained his visage of colour. "I didn't harm her, I swear it."

"I don't have proof, but I think she was killed because she took you to Duguay," Romek hissed.

"I'm sorry – very sorry your wife was killed, but like I said, I never saw her again after she left the basement."

"You didn't have anything to do with her after that night?" demanded Romek.

"I heard them arguing … her and the Frenchman. I couldn't tell you what they were saying, but I think she was trying to help me."

"Did you know about the people who were executed as a result of your abduction?"

"Yes. I take full responsibility for their deaths."

At least the man was honest, Romek thought again. Even Darek looked impressed by Vogel's frank admission of guilt.

"I was boxed in with the Gestapo. At one point, I think they thought I'd made the whole thing up. I never told them where Duguay's farm was or who'd taken me to Dieppe," Paul said, becoming agitated. "I spun them lies to protect my brother and the people who'd abducted me, including your wife … including your friend, here. I couldn't have their deaths on my conscience, but I had to give them something, so

I lied. The people of Dieppe … I didn't … if I could go back, I would change that part of my testimony."

Paul frowned as he undid his jacket's top button. "Being Max's twin has not been easy for either of us. God knows, I've thought that enough times in the last couple of years. It's like a damned cosmic joke … me bumping into his acquaintances when there's no reason on earth why I should ever have had contact with any of them – it's as if this war isn't big enough for both of us – like we've never been apart. I am him and he is me…"

Darek opened his mouth to interrupt, but Romek raised his hand. *Let the German talk,* he warned Darek with a look.

"Max is English through and through," Paul carried on with a voice that broke with emotion. "And he's a cold-blooded killer. I've seen him murder a man with his bare hands and look as though he had a great time doing it. He killed an Abwehr agent for me, and I'm glad he did it, but I'm not Max. I'm not a soldier. I don't have information on battle plans or troop numbers. I wasn't privy to military intelligence. I don't know how to fire an automatic rifle or kill a man in hand-to-hand combat, and I have never used explosives or heavy weaponry on a battlefield … I don't know..."

"Did it occur to you that you might not be of use to us?" Romek asked when Paul's voice broke.

"Yes, but then I thought about the ways I could be valuable. I know what's going on in the minds of the Occupying Army. I'm a doctor, and a damned good one."

Paul shifted in his chair, then clasped his hands together on the table. He looked determined to put his case forward, whether in a positive or negative light. "I have been involved in despicable crimes perpetrated by the Third Reich, and I will not give you tawdry excuses. Suffice to say I didn't want to follow my orders, but I did anyway. I watched naked men, women, and children being gassed to death and could see no way to stop it. I saw children being deliberately starved and left to die in freezing conditions because the Germans didn't want to give their parents wood to make a fire. I'm already cast to the wind as far as God's concerned, but in my defence, I did my best to protect as many Jews as I could, even when I knew I was being stalked by the Gestapo and facing possible arrest for treason…"

"And now you think that by helping us, your sins will be washed away?" Romek challenged.

"No, I don't think that at all. I'm here because it is the right thing to do," Paul retorted. *And because I don't want to die at the hands of the Gestapo.*

"I see. Tell me, why did you want to join us? You could have tried to get yourself to England. Or you could have hidden somewhere in Poland until the war ended," Romek said.

"I won't hide. I want to fight back. If you accept me, I'll pass on every sordid detail about Germany's policies concerning not only the Jews but the wider population of this country. But if you decide to kill me, do it after I give up what I know. You *must* tell the Allies what's going on in Poland."

Romek was impressed again by Paul's candour, but it was evident that Darek wasn't yet convinced of the man's motives, so he decided to push a bit more.

"Desertion … treason … those are monumental crimes. You must know that in any army, leaving your post endangers the lives of fellow soldiers. You will never be absolved. Even after this war ends, you will be viewed as scum by your military colleagues, and your neighbours … family … friends."

Paul nodded. "I've thought about the implications, yet here I am begging you to take me in. The way I see it, if more soldiers abandoned Hitler's regime, thousands of lives would be saved in concentration camps and ghettos. If camp guards refused to pull the gas levers and see to the trains being loaded, the system would fall apart."

"A rather simplistic view, don't you think?" Romek suggested.

"Maybe, but one simple soldier cannot change events. I'm a man of no consequence. I can't up-sticks, go to Berlin to plant a bomb under Hitler's feet and blow him to smithereens, but I can draw back from an unjust war of aggression … call it a tepid form of resistance from someone who will not watch another van full of people being gassed, burnt, or starved to death." Paul went deeper. "I believe the Reich is underestimating their records of absentee soldiers. Every day, I see the disgust for murder on the faces of some SS and Schupo policemen. I know for a fact that they, and perhaps others, would gladly stop what they were doing were they not afraid for their families' safety in Germany."

Romek was intrigued. "You've heard this being said?"

"No … at least, not openly. But I've seen the look of revulsion on soldiers' faces, and I've seen the officers ignore it. Take the Kriminalinspektor in Łódź. He's a swine. No one would say it, but more than a few of the men I shared a mess hall with would have no objection to him being assassinated – fuck it, I'd be willing to go back there to help you kill the bastard."

"Go on," Romek said.

"His name is Manfred Krüger. He's the present head of the Gestapo and responsible for making the Jews' lives miserable before they're sent to their deaths in the extermination camps. He's just rounded up over fifteen thousand people in the last twelve days, including five thousand children. They've all been murdered at Chelmno, and he enjoyed every minute of the deportation process."

"Jesus Christ…" Romek's voice petered off. His hands gripped the corners of the table, and his breath was laboured. "F-fifteen thousand?" Every cell in his body demanded that he take revenge on *all* Germans, starting with Paul Vogel, yet the man's honesty was compelling, as was his apparent desire to atone for his sins and switch sides.

Romek rose on shaky legs. He had lost his appetite for this interrogation. The news that Vogel had just given him was shocking, and he needed to process it alone. He looked at Darek whose face was set to burst with rage, while his hand was itching to unclip his sidearm's safety clasp. He knew Darek's temper. Any minute now, he was going to put a bullet in their guest's head.

"Darek, meet me outside," Romek snapped, trying to pull Darek from his murderous thoughts.

Darek got up, hatred spitting from his eyes as he pushed his chair back. When he left, he slammed the door behind him, making Paul flinch.

"There will be a guard outside," Romek said, going to the door. He curled his fingers around the doorknob and turned back to Paul. He felt sick to his stomach. If he didn't leave, he would be the one shooting Paul, not Darek. It might just take killing a German to calm him down.

"You've given me a lot to think about, Paul Vogel."

"Is Max doing well?" Paul shouted behind Romek before he left the room.

Romek turned again and glared at Paul's concerned face. "He was the last time I saw him. I'll send one of my men with a plate of food for you. Get comfortable. You will be here for a while."

# Part Two

*"I cannot see an end to this conflict, but I do see a flickering light, like a candle flame struggling to ignite in a gloomy basement. Every day I see it grow stronger, as we begin to fight back with hope and the will to do battle with giants."*

Paul Vogel
1943

# Chapter Twenty-Six

## The Vogels

*London*
*16th March 1943*

Max arrived in London on a rainy spring morning. At Oxford
Circus, he got out of the car that had picked him up from the
aerodrome, telling the driver he'd walk the rest of the way. He
needed a cup of English tea in his favourite café before his
meeting with Jonathan Heller, and he wanted to pound the
streets of his beloved capital.

London had been hit from the air numerous times since
he'd left for Cairo months earlier. Rubble from buildings
destroyed in the Blitz had been contained for safety and
cleared away from roads and pavements, but signs of
destruction met him on every corner of every street. The
bombings had not been as intense as they were in 1940, the
driver informed Max, but every day and night, Londoners
carried their gas masks over their shoulder and headed to the
shelters and tube stations whenever the sirens went off.

As always, MI6 headquarters was a flurry of activity.
Instead of stopping to chat with those he knew, Max headed
straight to Jonathan Heller's office and found a familiar face
welcoming him home.

"You're looking well-tanned … been anywhere nice,
Major?" Marjory, Heller's secretary, smiled mischievously

from behind the desk with her trademark plastic rose sitting in a tubular vase.

She was always well-turned-out, Max noted, smiling affectionately. War or no war, she sported a nicely styled hairdo and a face smothered in face powder and lipstick that was never smudged. But even she looked exhausted beneath the cosmetics, like most Londoners he'd seen on his walk. "You're looking as lovely as ever, Marjory," he said with a mock bow. "Is he here?"

"He's waiting for you, Major. Go right in."

Heller rose and walked around the front of the desk to greet Max, a nod of satisfaction infringing upon his staid, professional face. "You made it, then. Those supply planes are not the most comfortable, are they?" Heller commented, shaking Max's hand.

"No, they are not. I was lucky. They let me squeeze on at the last minute."

Heller went to the door and opened it halfway. "Bring the usual for the major and myself, Marjory," he instructed.

When he returned to his desk, Heller said, "You look none the worse for wear."

"And you look knackered, Jonathan. Everyone I saw on my walk here seems to be exhausted and depressed. I'm feeling guilty, to be honest. Life in Cairo is slow and easy, and downright jovial compared to London's misery."

"We're all feeling a bit down in the dumps, I suppose. We've got used to air raids, and we're even getting numb at seeing dead bodies in the rubble afterwards. We had a terrible accident in the East End at the beginning of the month, though. A bloody awful thing."

"What happened?" Max asked, taking a seat.

"The air raid sirens went off in the evening. A crowd started rushing down the stairs to the Bethnal Green tube station shelter, and someone tripped on the wet concrete. The people behind the man went tumbling down like bloody skittles, making a mountain of bodies at the bottom. Most of them died from crush injuries and asphyxia. It's estimated that over a hundred men, women, and children fell within the first fifteen seconds. A survivor reported that, unaware of what was happening in front of them, people kept surging forward into the supposed safety of the shelter. Christ, I can still see it … over one hundred and seventy people dead within minutes."

Heller, looking deeply affected, gritted his teeth. "The public story is a German bomb scored a direct hit ... damn irony of it all was that no bomb struck and not a single casualty was the direct result of military aggression. The real reason for the deaths is classified, Max, so mum's the word in public. Londoners have gone through hell. We don't want them to be afraid of using the tube station shelters."

Stunned, Max could only utter, "Good God."

Heller let out a tired sigh. "I don't know. I sometimes wish I could get out in the field with you and away from this place." He smiled, trying to shrug off the terrible disaster and his bout of dejection. "Still, a nice run out to Bletchley today will do me a world of good. I've informed your parents and Judith that you'll be with me. Your mother squealed down the phone and promised to bake something."

Marjory brought the tea for the men, and when she left Heller did his *nervous dance* in his chair followed by two coughs to clear his throat. "Before we get down to our business, you should know that Romek is in London."

Max, who had been pouring the tea into the cups, paused with the utility-issue white teapot in the air. "I thought he was in Poland?"

"He is; he's based in the Warsaw area, but SOE brought him back to report to the Polish, British, and American governments on the situation over there. He's done the rounds. In two days, he met with Polish politicians in exile, including the Polish prime minister, members of the Socialist Party, National Party, Labour Party, People's Party, Jewish Bund, and Po'alei Zion. He even managed to get a meeting with Anthony Eden, which I also attended."

Max could imagine Romek blasting his way through those meetings with the most important Poles in Britain and demanding that something be done about this and that. "What sort of help was he asking for – I presume he wanted something?"

"He wants better resources and money, of course, but he's more concerned about the conditions in the Warsaw, Bełżec, and Łódź Ghettos. He had microfilm with him, with information from the underground movement on the extermination of European Jews and murder of Ethnic Poles and other minority groups. He has detailed testimony from someone who witnessed the execution process at Chelmno death camp. The killings come under the auspices of the *Sonderbehandlung* – Special Handling Unit. We also have detailed reports on them."

Heller picked up his teacup, grimaced because it was already lukewarm, and then banged it down on the saucer. "Damn it, Max, I wish we had nipped the Jewish problem in the bud in 1940 when you came back with the intelligence on Brandenburg."

*No shit. You should have at least tried to do something; you had enough evidence back then.* After a quick assessment of Heller's mood, Max held that opinion and gave another instead. "We suspected it would get a lot worse, yet we will probably continue to sit here fuming about it until the war is over. Then, we will make up a plausible excuse for not stopping it in its day. I wonder what history will say about us knowing of this brutality but ignoring it."

Heller snipped the end of his customary daily cigar with his silver clipper while expelling an irate sigh. "Unfortunately, you might be right. I can picture us in twenty years saying it was easy for Hitler's Germany to kill Jews because they did it. The Allies will say it was impossible and too costly to rescue the Jews because they didn't do it. Like you, I can see the Jews being abandoned by all governments, religious and church hierarchies, and societies, but I also see thousands of Jews surviving because of the underground networks Romek spoke about. The Poles are doing a bloody good job, Max. Maybe his defecting to the exiled government wasn't such a bad idea after all."

"Maybe," Max mused. "How was he with you? Displaying his usual self-aggrandising nature, no doubt."

"Pleasant enough. He asked for you. Do you want to see him? He's in London for another three days."

Max toyed with the idea as he lit a cigarette. It might be good to clear the air, close that book properly with a goodbye instead of with the note and trickery at that bed and breakfast in Camden. But did he want to see the Pole's, sullen, resentful scowl demanding to know why he, Max, had not said anything about Klara's death? *No, bloody right I don't.* He had three days or so in the country before returning to North Africa. He'd rather have a harmonious time.

"No. I'll pass," Max eventually said.

"Probably for the best." Heller's eyes narrowed as he expelled a thick plume of smoke. "Although, he did want to talk to you about a mutual acquaintance…"

"Oh?" Max's first thought was of Florent Duguay.

Heller's lips spread with satisfaction. "Yes. Oh."

"What's that cheesy grin for? What aren't you telling me?"

"The mutual acquaintance between you and Romek is your brother Paul."

Max laughed. "Impossible. It can't be?" Max felt his stomach fall then rise again like an ocean swell. "Did Romek say he knew Paul?"

Heller smiled again. "Oh, yes."

"How – where – for God's sake man, tell me?"

"Paul deserted the Wehrmacht six months ago. He's with Romek's Polish Free Army unit. He –"

"What –?"

Heller raised his hand to silence Max, who was rising from his chair. "Wait … sit down, Max. I don't know anything else. I didn't get the chance to ask Romek about the circumstances of how they'd met, only that they are together."

"My God. Does my family know?"

"Your parents and Hannah have known for a while. The news was sent to London through an encrypted transmission last year with the request that I be informed." Heller went into his drawer, picked up an envelope and handed it to Max. "Romek gave me this letter from Paul. It's addressed to your parents."

Max was crying; not blubbering like a baby, but quietly shedding tears. "This is … my God, it's bloody marvellous! I'm shocked, but I shouldn't be … or maybe I should be. Paul must have gone through hell to take such a massive risk."

Max's words trailed off as he stared at the envelope in Paul's handwriting. "I've changed my mind; I *will* see Romek. Can we arrange a meeting before I go back?"

"I already have."

For the next hour, Max and Heller talked about Operation Lanner Falcon, although it was not a detailed discussion since they were both going to Bletchley Park to meet with the people involved in the mission. Max was surprised to hear that his father, Theo Kelsey, and Judith were the operators who had been collecting his information from Cairo. To him, the Bletchley circle who did the actual talking to the Abwehr had been nameless, faceless agents he'd relied upon to translate his intelligence into cohesive and believable facts that they then twisted to mislead the Germans. Judith, especially, came to mind. He wondered now if he would have altered the way he'd given his information, specifically when some of it had come from suspected female German sympathisers from Cairo's nightclubs.

"There was some concern about you killing the Muslim Brotherhood man, Sarraf. I'd like the full story. Obelisk was furious … said you went in gung-ho and put the operation at risk before he'd even left Egypt."

"Rubbish. I killed the man because he should never have been involved in the first place. Don't look at me like that, Jonathan. Had you been there, you wouldn't have hesitated. He murdered John Bryant, and there was no way in hell I was going to trust him with my life the way Obelisk did – you should be thanking me. I saved the section money by getting rid of the Arab."

Heller didn't deny it, nor utter a word, instead, he stared Max down.

Undaunted, Max continued, "After we got rid of the body, I went back to my apartment, feeling much better that the weasel was out of the picture. I heard the next day that the military police had found his body, and after that, nothing … *nada*."

Heller still didn't look convinced. Max stubbed out his cigarette, and unwilling to back down, said. "When we meet with Obelisk this afternoon, you must make it clear to him he's not to get anyone else involved in the Lanner Falcon operation. German sympathisers in Egypt are seeing Rommel conceding ground in Libya, and they're getting desperate. Some of them are making mistakes and coming out in the open to look for support. Obelisk did a brilliant job, but he's far too extroverted for my liking."

When Heller took a telephone call, Max tried to settle the growing excitement in his stomach. He was both jubilant and worried about Paul's desertion to the Allies and was finding it hard to concentrate on the Egyptian operation. He hoped to calm down before they got to Bletchley, but he probably wouldn't. The minute he saw his father, he'd be begging him to rip open the envelope and read Paul's letter and to hell with other matters.

Max's heart was pounding. It was not yet time to ask *the* question; not until the business part of their meeting was over. He felt like a bucking racehorse waiting to come out of the starting stall, wondering if Heller had managed to do the colossal favour asked of him the week before. Putting protocol aside, Max had made a personal request directly to Heller in a radio transmission.

*Sod it,* he'd thought when he found out he was returning to London. The war interrupted lives, took blossoming love affairs from the young, separated children from their parents, and often stole a soldier's chance to say goodbye to elderly relatives. He'd jumped in with both feet and capitalised on the only opportunity he might have for a bit of happiness for the foreseeable future; Cairo and the Western Desert's front lines were beckoning, and he wouldn't come home for a long time.

Heller hung up, looked at his wristwatch and said, "I think we'll call it quits here. Fancy a spot of breakfast before getting the train?"

"That sounds good, but before we go anywhere, will you tell me?"

Heller cocked his head to the side, looking confused. "Tell you…?

"Damn it, Jonathan, am I getting married or not?"

Heller dropped his façade and had a good chuckle. "Ah, Max. See, this is an example of why you're a top-notch agent. You've probably been sitting there biting your lip since the minute you walked in here. Go on, admit it."

Max laughed, "Of course, I bloody have."

"You hid it well."

"Jonathan?" Max demanded but with humorous eyes. "Remember, I am an expert in interrogation techniques. *Well?*"

"Hmm … are you getting married? This is the question." Heller shuffled through the mountain of papers in the filing tray, then lifted a large manila envelope. He was still tittering to himself, which in turn, let Max know it was mission accomplished.

"It wasn't easy getting this," Heller said, handing Max the envelope. "I managed to get the Town Hall Registrar in Charing Cross to issue me the special licence, but only after I told her it was an emergency for an officer who was leaving the country and hadn't the time to post or read the banns over the three weeks normally required." Heller laughed again. "You should have seen her face. She told me she heard those words every day from young, lovesick couples, and I should stop wasting her time. She wouldn't even consider it until I showed her your deployment orders for this Thursday..."

"Thanks, Jonathan. I owe you." Max pulled out the document. *Marriage solemnised in the parish of...*sat at the top, awaiting the Vicar of St Mary's Parish Church, Bletchley, to complete the details on the licence, then pronounce them husband and wife.

"I'm getting married," he said aloud. "Me ... I'm getting married."

# Chapter Twenty-Seven

*Bletchley Park, MI6 Section*

Max and Heller entered Hut 6 at Bletchley Park for their meeting with the team who were involved in Obelisk's Operation Lanner Falcon. Jonathan joined the group of people already there and took his seat at the top end of the conference table. Max, however, stood just inside the door, his eyes focused on the woman he loved. Overjoyed at seeing Judith, he ignored the others, including his father, Theo Kelsey, a much fitter-looking Obelisk, and three men he didn't know at all.

Judith, beautiful as always, was also glowing with happiness; something that had been missing when he'd first met her. Her eyes were bright, her cheeks flushed with joy, and her soft, plump lips trembled with emotion. "Max…"

He hurried to her, whispering her name as he crushed her to him. "Ah, Judith, my darling … my darling." He breathed in her perfumed skin and the smell of her newly washed hair. Then he kissed her, on and on, knowing it was wrong and not giving a damn…

Dieter coughed and uttered good-humouredly, "Hello, Son. It's good to see you, too. While this is touching, perhaps you two lovebirds could leave your … erm … greeting until after the meeting?"

Elated, Max forgave his father's interruption and pushed Judith gently away. "Later, darling," he said, lifting her hand and kissing it.

When he'd pulled Judith's chair out for her, he went to Dieter and finally greeted him with a brisk handshake and a back-slapping hug.

"You look well, Father. Not sure about the beard, though. You look like Santa Claus," Max said.

"Mr Heller thinks so too, but I'll tell you the same as I told him – your mother likes it. She thinks I look rather dignified and mysterious." Dieter grinned warmly at Max as he sat again. "It's good to have you home. How are you, Son?"

"I'm well, Father."

Max smiled sheepishly at Theo Kelsey who was sitting next to Dieter. He stretched out his arm to shake Theo's hand. "Theo – have you forgiven me yet?"

"Yes, that goes without saying, Major. Good to see you back in one piece, sir."

Max finally gave his attention to Obelisk. "You're looking better. When I saw you last, I didn't think you'd survive the flight home. Well done."

"I'm a new man, Major, and looking forward to going back to Cairo. I'm not happy in your English climate," he said in his lilting Italian accent.

After shaking hands and being introduced to the three other men at the table, Max sat next to Heller at the top end, four chairs away from Judith. He wanted to leave with her right now. He wanted the wedding over so he could spend the whole night with her…

"What do you think of our Judith being involved in the operation?" Dieter asked, interrupting Max's pleasant thoughts. "A nice surprise, eh, Son? I brought her in so she could keep an eye on you."

"Oh, Papa, that's not true. You said you thought I'd be an asset. Don't listen to him, Max," Judith giggled.

Max melted at the sound of her voice. *She was calling his father* Papa. *A nice touch from his parents!*

Any further conversation was cut short when Heller, looking official as he perched his glasses on the tip of his nose, said, "Right, let's get to it, shall we? We can celebrate Max's return after we've seen to business."

Max nodded and grew serious as he began to report on the latest political and military happenings in Egypt. "You'll find Cairo quite a different place this time around," he told Obelisk. "The Egyptians have finally written off the Axis forces. There's not one person in Egypt who thinks Rommel can break out again."

"I presume Egyptian shopkeepers have removed their German and Italian welcome signs?" Obelisk queried.

"Yes. They know we're not going anywhere. In a show of good faith, British authorities lifted the embargo on our soldiers using the Egyptian entertainment establishments that had put up the German signs. On the surface of things, all is forgiven, and we're in favour again."

Heller said, "I believe we might be looking at the beginning of the end of Operation Lanner Falcon in Egypt."

"I'd say we were closer to the end of the end," Dieter disagreed. "Last October, when Rommel retreated against our superior numbers, he didn't halt westwards of El Alamein to regroup, he withdrew all the way to Tunisia. His questions to Max ever since then have been more about whether the British 8th Army were pursuing him than what British battle plans were. He knows he's not going to make another breakout. He's finished."

"Rommel is never finished. He's a Houdini," Obelisk said. "He always manages to turn a retreat into a new offensive."

Heller nodded. "True, but on this occasion, I have to agree with Dieter that he will not breakout again."

"He did rebuff the American 1st Army at the Kasserine Pass," Theo joined the conversation.

Heller picked up a file. "Yes. We've received these casualty numbers and reports for the damage he inflicted on one of the American armoured divisions, and they're more severe than we first thought."

"Precisely my point. Rommel does the unexpected," Obelisk insisted.

Heller nodded his agreement. "We must come up with a decent intelligence strategy that will hinder any plans he *might* have for another push forward. This is a priority."

Max, thinking about the presence of American top brass in Cairo the previous week, said, "As always, the Yanks came in gung-ho, thinking they had all the answers against the Desert Fox, who's been there for years and knows the terrain. They weren't as cocksure of themselves when their top brass returned to Cairo red in the face."

Heller paused to address Obelisk and Max. "Max is right. The 1st Army were as raw as hell. They couldn't handle the landscape and the damage it did to their tanks and vehicles. Had it not been for the experienced British troops who counterattacked, Rommel might have exploited his earlier gains. Max, what do you hear over there? What's the mood of the Egyptian government?"

For an hour, Max informed the others about the current situation in Egypt: the latest chatter regarding King Farouk and his government, information on the Muslim

Brotherhood's activities, obtained via Gaidar, and the recent discovery and subsequent arrest of two women caught spying for the Germans.

For the first time since the meeting began, Max felt uneasy talking about his job in Egypt in front of Judith. It was one thing for him to cavort with people for information but quite another to court attractive young women to learn their darkest secrets.

"The women are Italian sisters who once worked for the Italian Legation. I met them at the Nightingale Club and got close to them ... in the platonic sense, of course."

Dieter's somewhat rare sense of humour displayed itself. "Judith trusts you, Max. Don't you, dear?"

"Carry on," Heller said, not the least bit impressed with Max's personal relationship interrupting the meeting.

Obelisk asked, "Are you talking about the Bianchi sisters? Good lookers?"

"Yes. That's them," Max answered, throwing Obelisk a filthy look. "After meeting with them a few times they became rather talkative. They swooned over my German accent, hated the British, lamented the internment of Egypt's Italian male population, and tried to find out from me if I knew of any Italians still at liberty in Alexandria or Cairo."

Heller raised his hand to silence Max, then he spoke directly to Obelisk. "I already know about this case. One of my officers arrested the women. According to Max, Cairo's British socialites are still gossiping about the affair. I want you to find out through your many friends over there if the Italians were working with anyone else. My interrogators have hit a brick wall with the women ... they've stopped chattering." Heller nodded to Max to continue.

"Armed with my suspicions, Gaidar Shalhoub conducted a dawn raid on the women's house and came face to face with an old woman lying in bed in the first room he came to. She screamed, then had a convulsive fit. Gaidar doused the old woman with a bucket of cold water to bring her around, then the two sisters rushed into the bedroom and went for Gaidar and the two military policemen with him. They were screaming their heads off, apparently, and accusing Gaidar of killing their mother. Poor Gaidar had two nasty fingernail scratches on his face the last time I saw him."

Dieter and Kelsey chuckled. Even Heller found the imagery amusing, allowing himself a rare smile.

During the pause, Max smiled at Judith, who beamed at him in return.

"Anyway, the old mother didn't die, but Gaidar's search of the property did find some interesting information. There were two lists of names … one with Italians in Egypt loyal to the Axis countries and another with those who opposed Mussolini and Hitler. He also found a code book, but no radio transmitter. My concern is that Axis supporters still at large are beginning to panic and will try any way they can to get information to Rommel. If that happens, it could put Obelisk's operation on the ropes."

Heller added, "We know from our conversations with the Germans that Obelisk is still the German spymaster in Egypt. The Abwehr have no idea he has been out of action all this time, thanks to our team here, but if they begin to receive contradictory intelligence from loyal agents placed in the region or fanatical supporters clinging to hope, our misinformation programme could crash. It is imperative we don't let this happen."

Judith finally spoke, "Excuse me, Mr Heller. If there are *women* in Cairo trying to communicate with Rommel, albeit they failed on this occasion, where does Obelisk even start to uncover more German or Italian spies?"

"Good question, and one I can't answer, Judith."

"I can. Ask Max. He managed to get into bed with them … not physically speaking, of course," Obelisk said, and received another filthy look from Max.

"There is no easy way to uncover a spy," Heller continued, his eyes warning Obelisk to shut up. The Italian's cheap shots had not gone unnoticed, and he made certain Obelisk knew that. "I asked Max to highlight that one incident – that minor success with the two Italian sisters – because it demonstrates the gravity of the situation over there. We have cemented Obelisk's credibility in German eyes, but we can't assume they'll continue to believe him when there are more desperate attempts to save Rommel's desert campaign by people who know we're winning the North Africa war."

Dieter carried on, "No side is infallible when it comes to the intelligence war, but I think it's fair to say that we have the upper hand. We have better cryptographers, and we use the information gained from Enigma selectively so we can benefit from the source without giving away that we have it. I feel that instead of worrying about what German spies will do, we make damn sure we do our jobs to the best of our abilities."

"History is on our side," Heller mused. "When Rommel went on the offensive last summer, he put out false radio signals and deceived us about the location of a convoy of tanks. That trickery allowed him to gain the element of surprise, and the tactic hurt our troops, struggling to hold their ground. I hope, and I believe we have learnt a lesson from that subterfuge. The Abwehr, on the other hand, still believe in Obelisk and his lies, so I agree with Dieter; we must continue to capitalise on his good name until the end."

# *Chapter Twenty-Eight*

After a private meeting with Obelisk, who was returning to Cairo that night, Max joined Dieter and Judith for lunch at the local pub.

Laura was waiting in the ladies' domain, the pub's snug, and ran into Max's arms in a flood of tears. "Oh, my darling boy, you're home safe and sound. I feel as though you've been gone for years."

"Most soldiers are, Laura," Dieter reminded her.

"Oh, hush, Dieter." She kissed Max again. "I have my boy back. Look at him, tanned and … yes, I think you've filled out, Son."

Embarrassed, Max pushed his mother gently away and flicked his eyes to Frank and Hannah, who were standing behind his mother, both wearing broad smiles. He kissed Hannah, then hugged Frank, the last person he'd thought he would see today.

"Well, this is a surprise. When did you get back, Frank?"

"A week ago."

"We're going back to Scotland. Isn't that marvellous, Max?" Hannah said, clinging to Frank.

"That's good news, you two," Max said, trying to curb his envy. *If only he and Judith could go to some remote place for a while.*

"I know you can't say what you've been doing or where you've been, but I've got so much to tell you, starting with Paul's situation," Laura said.

"I know about Paul, Mother," Max said in a much softer voice.

Laura continued to blether as she shimmied her way along the window banquette behind Judith and Hannah. "I wish we could get word from Wilmot. Wouldn't that be wonderful? Oh, I do wish someone in Germany could send us news of him. Dieter, do you think the Red Cross has delivered the gift parcels we sent him?"

Dieter, with a rare look of disapproval at his wife, sat opposite her and hissed, "Don't mention Germany, Laura. I've warned you about that before."

Laura gestured with her head to an old couple sitting at a table by the window. "Oh, stop it. There's no one here but Mr and Mrs Barclay from the paper shop, and they can't hear us from way over there. Honestly, can't we have one conversation where we're not minding our volume and p's and q's?"

Max reached over the table and squeezed Judith's hand. He was desperate to go for a walk with her alone, kiss her in their derelict barn, and hold her in his arms in a way he couldn't do in public. But he was also excited to see Frank home. It would be the perfect family reunion were Paul and Wilmot here. His eyes widened with a thought. "Where's Jack?" he asked Hannah.

"Mrs Allerton next door is babysitting."

"He's no longer a baby. He's a little boy now and becoming quite the handful. Strong as an ox, Max," Frank said with a proud voice.

"Hannah was shocked to see Frank turn up last week," Laura said, "but I wasn't. I told her a fortnight ago that he'd be coming home. We've almost won the Middle East, I said, and the army will have no need to keep him out there. And here he is, our Frank."

Laura then gripped Max's hand. "Oh, Max, you've no idea how happy I am to see you. Judith didn't sleep a wink last night. Isn't that right, Judith? Tell me, Son, what did you think when you heard the news about Paul...?"

"Let's order our food before we overload Max with information and questions, shall we, dear?" Dieter suggested to a weepy Laura when the waitress appeared.

"We've got minced meat pies and mash, or cheese sandwiches with pickled onions. I'm afraid that's all we've got until we get our next order of ration coupons," the young woman said.

"We should all have the minced meat pies. Then tonight we can have a light supper," Laura advised the family.

"I'm sorry. We've only got three minced meat pies left," the girl muttered.

"Could you not have said that right at the beginning?" Laura snapped.

Dieter patted Laura's hand. "Darling, you must calm down. It's not the young lady's fault."

"I'm sorry, dear," Laura apologised to the waitress. "Please bring the minced meat pies for the men. Us women will have the cheese platters."

Hannah ordered a cup of tea. The three men ordered pints of beer. Judith, who was not going back to work that day, asked for a small glass of sherry, and Laura, after raising a disapproving eyebrow, followed Judith's lead.

When the waitress left and his mother was quiet, Max found his opportunity to ask the question he'd dreamt about asking for months. "I have a question for Judith, and I'd like you all to hear it," he said, stopping any new conversation short.

Dieter raised his eyebrows. "A question? Hmm, interesting."

Max opened his leather briefcase, pulled out the manila envelope and then infused the moment with drama. "Do you know what this is, Judith?"

Judith giggled. "No, but you're going to tell me, aren't you?"

"Jonathan arranged a special licence for us. We can get married tomorrow at Bletchley Park. That's … if you still want to be my wife?" Max grinned as her eyes grew teary. "Is that a yes?"

Judith, Laura, and Hannah squealed in unison; drawing more stares from the Barclays at the window table as well from as the men in the main bar who were no more than translucent silhouettes on the other side of the snug's glass partition.

"We're getting married tomorrow?" Judith asked, her voice breathless with excitement. "Oh, my goodness, will Papa and I get time off work for the wedding? Mama, what shall I wear? Where are we getting married, Max?"

"We'll find something lovely for you to wear, dear," Laura jumped in before Max had a chance to answer any of Judith's questions. "I have my sewing machine at hand, and a few nice dresses we can tinker with. You'll look beautiful, whatever you put on." Then her mood darkened. "Max, you should have given us more time to prepare. Wait until I see that Jonathan Heller! He should have told us. Judith *is* the bride, after all. And what are we supposed to give people to eat and drink?"

"Mother, one step at a time," Max said as patiently as he could. *Maybe I should have asked Judith after lunch when we were alone?* "Don't blame Jonathan. I specifically asked him not to say anything in case I didn't get home in time. Besides, I wanted this to be a surprise."

"Max is right, dear, you mustn't say anything to Mr Heller," Dieter also warned Laura. "He had a hellish job getting the date to coincide with Max's leave…"

"You knew about this?" Laura snapped at her husband.

Max jumped in. "I don't have leave, as such. I'm returning to London day after tomorrow."

"No! So soon?" Judith cried.

Max cursed himself for letting the happy moment slip away. Again, he should have told Judith this rotten news without an overactive audience. "I'm sorry. I've been posted again…"

"What sort of job is this, Max? Two days? That's all they give you after you've been away for months?" Laura was furious.

"Laura, Max is fortunate to be home at all," Frank said.

"We can't take anything for granted, darling," Dieter said, his tone warning her to calm down.

Max squeezed Judith's hand while giving her an apologetic smile. "You understand, don't you, dearest?"

"I do … of course, I understand. I'm just … well, I can't say I'm happy about it. On the other hand, I'm going to become your wife tomorrow! I couldn't wish for anything more than that."

Judith whispered to Laura in German, "I think Mr Heller did marvellously, considering I don't even have a birth certificate."

Max, not hearing what she said, told the family, "The army chaplain at Bletchley Park has agreed to conduct the ceremony."

Still not happy, Laura asked, "And what time will that be?"

"We're slotted in for eleven o'clock tomorrow morning. I thought we could come back here to the pub for a few drinks and cake … sandwiches maybe," Max suggested, as Laura's frown deepened. "You mustn't go overboard, mother, so don't go inviting everyone in the street. When Paul and Wilmot come home, and we're all back together as a family, we can have a proper wedding reception."

"Oh, this is impossible. How am I supposed to alter a dress for Judith this afternoon?" Laura grumbled.

"Stop it, please. It's perfect," Judith said, looking irritated. "I don't care what I wear. I'll stick a flower in my hair, and if I may, I will wear one of your nice coats, Hannah?"

"Of course," Hannah said, throwing her mother a look that said, *Be quiet.* "In fact, you can have my wedding dress if you don't mind wearing it second-hand." Hannah's eyes brightened with tears as she looked at Frank. "When we got married, I wished the family could be there to see me in my outfit. Now they will see it, and I couldn't be happier. You wouldn't mind that would you, darling?"

"Not at all," Frank said, lifting Hannah's hand and kissing it.

"I will be honoured, Hannah. Thank you," Judith said, giving Hannah a peck on the cheek. She looked at Laura and gave her a radiant smile. "It doesn't matter what we eat or drink, or don't have, for that matter. I'm happy Max thought of all these arrangements when he must have had a million other things to worry about. I'm going to be his wife tomorrow, and that's the most important thing," She then whispered across the table to Max, "*Ich liebe dich* – I love you, Max."

Max felt sorry for Laura, who still looked peeved at not being allowed to make all the arrangements. "I wish Paul could be with us tomorrow, but in a strange way, he will be. I have another surprise for you, Mother," he said, retrieving an envelope from his pocket. He was taking a risk, springing an unopened letter on his parents when he had no idea what his brother had written. He imagined his father would find it distressing since Paul thought him dead. And he had no idea what his mother would do if it contained bad news.

Max laid the envelope on the table whilst looking behind himself. The Barclays, who had been sitting at the window table had left, and there was hardly any noise coming from the bar area behind the partition. Still, Paul's letter was private; certainly not for public consumption. "This letter is from Paul," Max told his father as he pushed the letter along the table. "Don't read it aloud. I don't know what's in there."

Laura tore it from Dieter's hand. "Bring your chair closer to me. We'll read it together."

Max, desperate to get the letter himself, stared at his mother and willed her to hurry up and start reading.

Laura squealed again as she pulled out an envelope from inside the larger one; this one also bearing Paul's writing but saying: *From Wilmot.* Tears rolled down her cheeks as she handed it to Max. "This is better than all the Christmases and birthdays I've ever had, put together. At last. My boys … my two boys! Read it, Max."

"For God's sake, Laura, will you just read? I've got to the bottom of the first page, waiting for you," Dieter said, his irritation growing again.

Max skimmed the pages, drinking in Wilmot's bold writing, but feeling disappointed that many lines and words had been redacted, leaving what seemed like an anonymous person talking about personal feelings. Even so, the words he *could* read were more than enough to raise goosebumps on his arms.

He imagined Wilmot writing it, where he'd been, how he'd looked and felt at the time. His young, wild, mischievous brother was not known for displays of affection, but in this letter, he'd clearly wanted to convey his love for his family.

When he'd finished, Max looked up, wiped his wet eyes and then exchanged letters with his mother and father who were also crying. "There's not much in it, but it's enough to know he's well," he told Hannah, whose hungry eyes were staring at it.

Judith looked on, appearing reluctant to interrupt, and when the waitress returned with the food, she quietly organised the plates herself.

Max began to read Paul's handwriting, which was almost identical to his own penmanship.

*My dearest family*

*This letter is coming to you thanks to my friend and comrade, R, who took me in ... a long story, and now is not the time to tell it.*

*I am now doing what I trained to do. My talents are being put to much better use than they were in my previous employment – I can imagine the shock on your faces when you learn where I am and what I am doing. If I were with you in person, I would, of course, tell you why I decided to change the course of my life, but I am not and will say only that it was the right choice; the only choice.*

*My dear family, I see all the ugliness of the world unfold before my eyes, but I am also witnessing truly heroic acts by men and women who seem to have no fear against Germany's mighty army. Please forgive me for not being more specific with names and places. I am presuming this letter will get to you safely without being intercepted by the enemy, but if, God forbid, it is, it will leave no trace of my identity or those of my friends.*

*I have a daughter. I never got the chance to meet her, but I have seen her angelic face in photographs. Will I ever hold my child in my arms? I don't know. My marriage is over, and though there are many reasons why it failed, B was the biggest factor. He is an odious man; a greedy, deceitful tyrant, and a liar. He made my life hell, but he is also guilty of atrocities against the people who were in his care. I no longer love my wife, for I see B in her eyes and words and political beliefs. I wonder if she is already teaching our baby the racist hatred she espoused.*

*I ask you this, even assuming I will not get an answer ... is my father alive as B claims or was this revelation another of his lies? I am praying that the answer to that question will find its way to me.*

*Finally, as I can say no more, I want to tell you, my dearest ones, that I have heard from another family member. I enclose his letter, redacted as you can see, but with his love for us all clearly visible.*

*I love you. I miss you all terribly. I cannot see an end to this conflict, but I do see a flickering light, like a candle flame struggling to ignite in a gloomy basement. Every day, I see it grow stronger as we begin to fight back with hope and the will to do battle with giants.*

*I am forever your loving son and brother. May God allow us to reunite one day; safe and well!*

Dieter and Laura were silently waiting for Max to finish Paul's letter. When Max lifted his head, Dieter looked furious.

"I knew it. I damn well knew it … Biermann is still investigating me." He gripped Laura's hand. "Now you know why I couldn't tell you the truth about my disappearance. He's still on to me. I swear to God, if he harms a hair on Paul's head, I'll kill him."

"Father, maybe we should talk about this when we get home. It's a lot for you to take in, and this is not the place," Max said, still digesting Paul's news.

"Ach, no one is listening to us. It's almost 2pm, closing time and we're the only people in here, and I know that's old Mr Robbins in the bar through there. He's as deaf as an ornament on a mantlepiece."

"You've changed your tune," said Laura wiping her eyes with her handkerchief. "Dieter, please forget about Freddie Biermann. Let's just be happy our boys are alive – oh, I wish I knew what our Wilmot was saying. Who would have scribbled all over his letter like that?"

Max could think of two people: Paul or Romek. "Paul probably redacted most of it because he wanted to keep Wilmot's identity safe should the Germans in Poland, or the

British authorities here, confiscate the letter from the courier who brought it. One can never be too careful, Mother."

"Max is right, dear," Dieter said. "The most important thing is that we know our boys are okay. This calls for a celebration."

Although Dieter was being valiantly cheerful for Laura's sake, his face couldn't hide his anger or concerns. Max, who had learnt about Kriminaldirektor Fredrich Biermann's relationship with his father, also worried about the consequences should Biermann report his suspicions about Dieter to the SS or Gestapo, or God help them, Himmler himself. Paul was now a deserter, according to Romek via Heller, and that made him safe from his father-in-law's ire unless the entire Resistance network and Polish Free Army fell with Paul in it. Wilmot, on the other hand…?

Laura, gripping Wilmot's letter in her hand, described her youngest son as a child to Judith. "He was a little saint, my Wilmot, always wanting to help me in the kitchen and with my grocery shopping. And he was strong. He could carry two bags that were almost as big as himself. He was a pensive little boy … liked to read a lot, and always played soldiers. I'm surprised he didn't come out of me wearing a uniform."

Max chuckled. Wilmot had been anything but saint-like. His mother had missed out on his younger brother's epic temper tantrums and his time in Dachau prison camp. She must be talking about another little boy.

Max took another look at Wilmot's letter. The black ink covering the words underneath was indelible, as it should be, and no amount of chemical help would make it fade. Disappointed, he replaced it in its envelope and handed it to Hannah.

As he finished eating, Max let his mother, Hannah, and Judith discuss the wedding. His father looked on but was still frowning, and Frank, who had to wait until after lunch to read the letters, was still going through them.

"Don't let this Kriminaldirektor Biermann get to you, Father," Max whispered, surmising that was who Dieter was thinking about.

"I want to kill the man," Dieter blazed through gritted teeth. "Yes, I might do that someday."

His parents would never know who *R* was in Paul's letter, Max thought, as the women continued to discuss flowers and dresses. They knew nothing of Klara, who had died serving Britain. His mother would continue to live in blissful ignorance while he and others like him delved into the deep, murky waters of espionage and war. He was excited about marrying Judith, and of having her to himself for an hour after lunch, but now he was also eager to see Romek and learn how he and Paul had come to meet…

"… Max … Max, do you agree?"

"Sorry, Father, I was in a world of my own. What were you saying?"

Dieter flicked his eyes to the glass partition behind him, then spoke softly in Max's ear, "I was saying Paul must continue to think I'm dead…"

"Who's dead?" Laura demanded to know.

"No one, dear," said Dieter, giving Laura a pat on the hand.

Laura asked, "Can I write to Paul?"

Dieter shifted his eyes to Max. "Can she?"

"Yes. I'll get a letter to the courier before I leave London."

"I presume it's that *R* man he mentioned," Laura said, with an exaggerated look behind herself.

Judith's eyes widened. "May I write something to Paul, Max?"

Max, reminded now that Paul had no idea Judith was in England, said, "That's a marvellous idea. I wish I could be there to see the look on his face when he reads that you've become his sister-in-law."

Laura expelled a contented sigh. "This is the best day I've had in years."

# *Chapter Twenty-Nine*

*London, England*

The warm, sunny part of the day was minutes old; fifteen, to be exact. Earlier, the rain had pelted down, soaking Max as he'd hurried towards Baker Street. Spring in England was a delight, for it often brought surprising weather changes that confounded meteorologists and those fond of predicting nature's plans. One never knew what to wear, or if they should bring their cumbersome umbrellas.

Max stood opposite the pub. He was anxious and dreading the forthcoming meeting with Romek. He gazed at his gold wedding band and conjured up the previous day's events to give himself courage. Judith had looked radiant in the small army chapel at Bletchley Park. Their marriage ceremony had been short but poignant, the party afterwards, attended by close friends, had been a joyful occasion.

Heller had paid for the bottles of champagne he had acquired from God knows where, and he had also arranged for the honeymoon night in a room above the pub. It had been glorious, Max thought. He and Judith had made love, talked, made love again, caressed each other's bodies, and neither had slept for more than an hour.

He stepped into the road and began to cross. He would hold these memories fast in his heart, summon them often, use them as a shield against the turbulent war he was yet to fight in North Africa. *Not even Romek can take away the love and joy I feel,* he determined as he entered the pub.

The pub, situated in a narrow street behind Baker Street, was packed with men in uniform, and every chair and table in the place was occupied. Max spotted Romek sitting at a round table no bigger than a serving tray. He waved and was rewarded with one of Romek's icy scowls.

Disappointed, Max made his way to the window. He had hoped his old friend might stand, shake his hand, smile, or give him a nod of recognition, but no, if anything, Romek looked angrier than the day he found out about Klara's affair.

Max sat on a stumpy-legged stool, brushing knees with Romek because of the lack of space around them. "Romek, you look well," he said, wishing he'd stayed with Judith in Northamptonshire for another hour, and to hell with the Pole. "I heard you wanted to see me."

"I see you're still the officious Englishman with a rod up your arse. Or should I say, German? You kept that gem to yourself, didn't you?" Romek responded with a clipped tone. "*Hideout?* It's a bit of a stupid name for a pub. Looks like half the British army is in here. Maybe they should try fighting instead of drinking?"

Max looked around, deliberately ignoring Romek's slur against British soldiers. The place was noisy, pint glasses were chinking as men knocked them together in numerous toasts to something or other, and voices were raised to combat the pub's terrible acoustics. "I've seen worse names … *The Dog and Bull, The Hedgehog and Goat, The Double Tree.* Who knows why they come up with these names?"

Max had no drink, but men were queuing at the bar two deep, and he didn't feel like standing up there for half an hour for a pint of beer. "Has your trip to England been successful?" he asked to breach Romek's wall of silence.

"Probably not. I was promised resources, but I didn't get what I came here for. They're disgusted by the information I gave them on the situation in Poland, but they won't do anything about it. I even managed to get a meeting with Anthony Eden, your British Foreign Secretary, but he spent most of the time shaking his head and saying, 'Hmm, dreadful.' The murder of hundreds of thousands of Poles, whether Jewish or otherwise, is a problem the Allies don't know how to handle, and by the time they get their collective arses together on this, millions of men, women, and children will have been killed."

Romek surprised Max by going into his briefcase and taking out the two-page letter, held together by a clip. "Here, read it, everyone else has."

*"For nearly a year now, in addition to the tragedy of the Polish people, who are being slaughtered by the enemy, our country has been the scene of a terrible, planned massacre of the Jews. This mass murder has no parallel in the annals of mankind; compared to it, the most infamous atrocities known to history pale into insignificance. Unable to act against this situation, we, in the name of the entire Polish people, protest the crime being perpetrated against the Jews. Let it be known that all political and public organizations join in this protest.*

"I hit the same brick wall when I returned from a mission in '40. I told them the Jewish situation was going to get worse," said Max handing the letter back.

Romek returned the letter to his briefcase, saying, "I'm not the first Pole to bring this information to our governments. Witold Pilecki, a Polish Underground intelligence agent in the

*Armia Krajowa,* the Polish Home Army, volunteered last year to be imprisoned in Auschwitz. He sent numerous reports about the camp and genocide going on to Polish resistance headquarters in Warsaw through the resistance network he'd organised in Auschwitz. As far back as March '41, Pilecki's intelligence was being forwarded via the Polish resistance to the British government in London, but the British authorities refused the *AK* reports on atrocities as being gross exaggerations and propaganda of the Polish government."

Max was stunned. "Bloody hell. I didn't know, Romek."

Romek shrugged, "What could you have done? I've managed to secure a meeting with President Roosevelt. I'm hoping the Americans will have bigger balls than their European counterparts."

For a while, the conversation centred on this topic, but, worried about time and how long it would take him to get back to MI6 headquarters, Max eventually changed the subject to a more personal one. "Romek, I want to thank you for delivering my brother's letter. My family were very happy to hear from him. No, that's not true … they were overjoyed. We're all grateful to you."

"I brought the letter because I promised your brother, I would deliver it by hand. I didn't want to see you, Max."

Max, who'd expected this response, said, "That's fair enough."

Romek twirled in a semi-circle on his stool to confront Max face on. His expression softened, and for a moment, Max saw his old friend from Poland as he clasped his hands, placed them between his open legs, and leant in until they were within hugging distance.

"I'm here for two reasons," Romek said, his cold voice belying his facial expression. "The first is to demand information from you, and the second is to fulfil my promise to Paul. The deal is, you tell me what I want to know, and afterwards I pass on your brother's messages."

"As long as I don't cross any secrecy laws, I agree," Max responded with an equally frosty voice, already suspecting the conversation would turn to Klara's death. Heller had ordered that Romek be kept in the dark about how she had died, but Max had always thought it an unreasonable request. Romek deserved to know what had happened to his wife. "What do you want to ask me?"

"Tell me where Klara was when she died, and how she died. The truth, Max. I don't want to hear any more bullshit from your lot."

"I don't blame you," Max answered, noting Romek's blink of surprise. "I believe she was at Duguay's farm. The truth is, I've wanted to talk to you about this since last year, and if you hadn't left me looking like a fool at that Camden Town bed and breakfast, I would have given you the full story, despite Heller's orders not to tell you. And before you ask, he didn't want you to know because he thought you might do something that would damage our French operations."

Romek surprised Max by passing his half-full pint of beer across the table. In the spirit of their past friendship, Max accepted, raising the glass in a silent toast before taking a couple of swigs.

*Romek has every right to know the truth and make of it what he will,* Max thought again. "Klara parachuted into France for SOE. She was to supervise Florent Duguay and his partisans and the British radio operators who were due to arrive two days after she did. I can't tell you what happened after she got there, but when the agents arrived at the farm, Duguay told them Klara was dead. According to him, she suffered a broken neck while parachuting in. He even showed the agents her grave."

Romek looked furious but said nothing.

Max continued, "The agents reported in to SOE headquarters with the news about her death, but a few days later they sent another transmission claiming they'd overheard a conversation between three of Duguay's men. In it, the Frenchmen spoke about Duguay's direct involvement in Klara's death; more, they called it 'Duguay's execution.' One of our agents went as far as to say the Frenchmen were worried for their own necks should they prove inadequate in Duguay's eyes."

"Duguay … the bastard…" Romek muttered.

"There's more," said Max. "Sometime during that night, the two agents dug up Klara's grave and found a bullet hole in her skull. They concluded that Duguay murdered Klara, but Duguay has never admitted his part in her death."

Waiting for Romek to explode, Max added, "I've told you everything I know."

Romek's jaw muscles danced under his skin, but he seemed incapable of speech.

"I'm sorry, Romek," Max said.

"Did the agents confront Duguay?" Romek asked, his expression murderous.

"No. He doesn't know they exhumed Klara's body."

"You're telling me he has not been dealt with – no one has even questioned him?"

"I don't know. That's the truth."

Romek finally leant back on his stool, giving Max room to breathe. "I'm going to kill the communist pig."

"We need Duguay's partisans," Max reminded Romek. "When the conflict in France is over, Duguay will be brought to justice..."

"No. He won't be put on trial or questioned by your British authorities. When this is over, I will kill Duguay myself, and I'll have no interference from you or anyone else." Romek's eyes blazed again. "I'm warning you, Max, say and do nothing. She was mine ... my wife ... my Klara. I will be the one to see to this; only me."

"You have the right," Max agreed. "All I ask is that you are patient."

Romek stared at his glass with unblinking eyes.

"Romek, give me your word. Romek! I'm disobeying orders by telling you this..."

"Yes. Yes, fine. I will wait and plan and dream, and when the time comes, I will savour the moment. But God help any man who takes that moment from me, and that includes you."

Romek finished his beer in four large gulps, then he banged the glass on the table. "I want to be sure you understand this, Max. You go near Duguay, and I'll kill you."

Redness spread from Max's neck onto his face as guilt dissolved any retort he might have. "I hear you."

Romek took a deep breath, then shifted uncomfortably on the hard, wooden stool. "Now, I will give you what you want ... Paul asked me to relay two messages. He wants you to know that he redacted your brother Wilmot's letter because of the sensitive material in it involving enemy combatants. Your younger brother went to Berlin and then to the Afrika Korps in North Africa in August last year, but he has not written since then. Oh, and someone broke into your house in Berlin – destroyed everything in it."

Max digested the news that had come from Romek in a detached tone. It was worrying that Willie was in the Western Desert where the Germans were desperately clinging to hope and fighting like cornered rats against combined Allied forces. *And who the hell would break into my parents' house?* Thinking aloud he said, "I thought Wilmot was in the East … Russia, Poland, maybe. The Afrika Korps are taking a beating…"

"Good."

"Yes, good."

"Do you want the second message?"

"Yes, please."

"Paul wants you to get to know his daughter. Should anything happen to him, he asks that the family makes sure they have access to her after the war."

Max's eyes filled. "Damn it, I hate what this war has done to us. The way we casually talk about our mortality." Then his teary eyes pleaded with Romek. "I hate not knowing what Paul's got himself into. Can you tell me anything?"

"He's saving Polish lives. He's well, as much as any of us can be when we're sleeping rough most of the time. He is a good doctor, well-liked, and a better man than you or I will ever be. That is all you need to know."

"Are you treating him well?"

Romek's eyes narrowed in anger, and Max was instantly sorry for asking the question. "I didn't mean *you,* per se, I meant … it must be hard on him to be the only German fighting with Poles against his own countrymen … that's what I wanted to ask."

"I told you he's well-liked, but he's not the only German. We also have Kurt. You know him."

Max stuttered, "Kurt ... Kurt Sommer ... our family driver?"

"Yes. Kurt is also in my unit."

Romek then told a stunned Max the story of how Paul and his colleagues had smuggled Kurt out of the ghetto. Kurt had been in hiding for three months after being systematically tortured by the Gestapo, and when he was well enough, he volunteered to serve in the Armia Krajowa.

"Kurt is also popular with the Poles. He has proven his loyalty to us tenfold. In fact, he's in charge of a *special* unit," Romek said, adding the slight emphasis.

"Doing what?"

"*What* doesn't matter."

Max nodded. "I'm trying to take this in. Sorry, I shouldn't have asked. Thank you, Romek. Kurt is the most reliable man I know."

Although shocked to learn Kurt was a Jew, Max was even more surprised to hear that he'd spent time as a ghetto inmate being tortured every day by the Gestapo. *What had happened to make all that come about, and who sent him to Poland?*

Max's brow wrinkled with unwelcome thoughts; if Paul was with Kurt, wouldn't he already know that their father was alive? If that were so, he'd also know that the family was lying to him when he received the letters Max had in his pocket. "My family has been worried sick about Paul and about Kurt. We were talking about him yesterday, wondering what had become of him. Again, thank you for taking him and Paul in, Romek. You have my eternal gratitude."

Romek sniggered. Animosity flooded his face as he wagged his index finger in Max's direction. "I didn't do any of this for you. Believe me, Paul and Kurt's relationship to you didn't do them any favours. If anything, you made it harder for them to win my trust. In fact, had I not seen straight away that Paul's character was entirely different than yours, I would have killed him."

"For God's sake! I'm sick of the jibes and the knives you're sticking in me every five minutes," Max finally snapped. "I know how you feel about me. You don't stop reminding me what a disappointment I am to you, but Christ … I wish I hadn't left my family to meet with you today."

Max got up to leave, despite being desperate to hear more about what had precipitated Paul's desertion from the German Army. He had had enough. He wouldn't beg the petty-minded Pole or kiss his damn feet for information or spend any more of his precious time in his company. "I know you hate me, and you'll never forgive me for being a deceitful swine, a rotten bastard, a backstabber … but you need to get over it. For Christ's sake, let it go."

After he'd unburdened himself, Max cursed his own stupidity. Whilst rebuking Romek, he'd forgotten about the letters he was carrying for Paul. He went into his coat pocket and brought out one envelope containing notes from his family, including one of his own.

"This mail is for Paul. If not for me, will you give it to him on my mother's behalf?"

"After all you've done and said, you want *me* to do you a favour?" But then Romek gestured to the envelope. "Give it to me."

"Thank you," Max mumbled, as Romek slipped the envelope into his briefcase.

Romek stared up at Max, a flash of regret crossing his soulful eyes. "This meeting was a mistake. This isn't the first time I've come back to London, and it won't be the last, God willing, but we won't meet again. I don't forgive you. I never will, and I will *not* let it go, not today, not ever." He gestured to the door. "Go ... and take you tender conscience with you."

Max swallowed painfully. "I understand. Goodbye, Romek, and good luck."

After Max left Romek with the same coldness that was in their icy hello, he took a brisk walk across Regent's Park to settle his nerves. Then he returned to MI6 headquarters for his final briefing with Heller and the other relevant intelligence sections that dealt with North Africa.

His final orders received and with only twenty minutes until he had to leave for the designated RAF aerodrome, Max sat in the staffroom and quickly scribbled a letter to his parents with news of Wilmot, Paul, and Kurt's situations. He handed it to one of the secretaries to put in with the next Bletchley mail drop. Before leaving the offices, he placed a telephone call to Judith to tell her that he loved her and to further commit her sweet voice to his memory.

On the ride to the Royal Airforce aerodrome, he went through his meeting with Romek. He looked at his wedding band, which Romek had either not noticed or had not wanted to comment on. The Pole would find out eventually, for Paul would read about the marriage in the letters he and Judith had sent him and would tell Kurt and Romek the good news. Romek's resentment would grow, no doubt, when he learnt that the man who had stolen his wife had married a new lover. *To hell with Romek,* Max thought. He was done feeling guilty.

"We're here, sir," the driver said, pulling up at the gates to the base.

Max got out of the car to a gust of wind that almost blew his cap off. He signed in at the guard house then walked to the Aerodrome's main building. He was nervous. No Cairo awaited him this time – fiery sand and desert battles lay ahead.

# *Chapter Thirty*

## Max Vogel

*Tunisia, North Africa*
*25 March 1943*

Max arrived at the front immediately after the Allies' failed assault on the German defensive lines at Mareth. The British Eighth Army had managed to establish a bridgehead west of Zarat, near Tebaga Gap in eastern Tunisia. It was close to a low mountain pass located in rocky, broken terrain that led to the northern and eastern coastal plains, much of which were uninhabited. It was not where they had expected to halt, however, and the mood was grim.

Since his return to North Africa, Max quickly learnt the differences between operations in the field and raw combat. The intelligence services were involved in a more subtle and cohesive conflict where one sought to outdo an enemy on a mental rather than physical level and defeat foes by using information as its primary weapon. The chaos and violence of open warfare had taken him to a place he had only experienced briefly once before; the long twenty-four hours he'd spent in Poland on the day the Germans invaded that country. Here in Tunisia, there were no made-up names or nationalities to hide behind, no hotel rooms in which to sleep peacefully, no games or trickery, and no retreat. This was not

323

the civilised, although at times dangerous, war he was used to, and his fear was palpable in his dry, scratchy throat.

On his second day there, Max was summoned to Command Headquarters, which was located inside a subterranean cavern dug into the side of a rocky hill. He had seen many such dwellings in this area, for west of the Matmata Hills, harsh temperature changes and lack of moisture forced the indigenous people to live in rock-cut or quarry caves, as they had for thousands of years. Now, these former Tunisian homes were being sequestered for the Allies' needs. Staff officers slept in them, men from the army signal and administration branches worked in them, and some were being used as temporary field hospitals until the army's next major advance.

Max squeezed his eyes shut and then slowly opened them to adjust to the dimness inside the cavern. The air was fresh with a strange light breeze that entered from some unseen orifice in the rock and circulated sufficiently to dry his sweaty face. He removed his hard helmet, tilted his head back to the aerated spot above him, breathed deeply, and enjoyed the heaven-sent respite. He had not been given a temperate cavern to work from; instead, the intelligence branch had tents that were unbearably hot during the day and freezing cold at night. On missions, he was usually the senior officer, but here, with every man and his dog present, he was a small toad in a large pond.

In the first cavern, a soldier sat on a stool banging furiously on the keys of a typewriter that sat on a rickety wooden table. Another British private leant against a granite wall watching the man work. His helmet, tucked under his arm, was white with stone and sand dust, and he held his rifle loosely in his hand, letting its strap trail on the ground. He raised his stooping figure to full height when Max appeared and said, "Major."

"Where is the briefing being held?" Max asked.

The corporal at the typewriter started to rise.

"No, Corporal, carry on with what you're doing," Max said, thinking how bizarre it was to see a clerk inside a cave.

"The general's 'ere, Major, sir," the private said with a cockney accent. "Briefing's in a cave right down there, right at the end. Yer can't miss it."

Max nodded and made his way along the passage that had been pointed out to him. It was lit by paraffin Tilley lamps supplemented with additional candles in wall brackets.

General Montgomery and his staff officers were talking about the map that was pinned to a wooden easel. It was a small room, forcing the men to bunch together from the front to the exit. Max had arrived late for the briefing, having just been informed about it, but Montgomery, standing on a crate so he could see everyone in the room, spotted him and called him out for his tardiness.

"And who are you?" Montgomery's booming voice asked.

Max cleared his sand-filled throat. "Major Vogel, General. I apologise, sir. I got the message –"

"Ah yes, Major Vogel. Colonel Jenkins has something for you. He'll get to you when we've finished here. In the meantime, listen in to what the colonel has to say."

Max had never spoken to or seen General Montgomery before today. He'd also never heard the men say a bad word about him. *Monty,* as he was affectionately known by his troops, was a living legend in their eyes. He was admired for his brilliance but also for his somewhat unorthodox and eccentric habits, such as the way he dressed; he looked as though he were on his way to play a spot of golf, with his short-sleeved khaki shirt and a green silk scarf hugging his neck, tucked in cravat-style above the top button.

Not involved in the following day's attack, Max's mind wandered to a conversation he'd had on his way to the Allied Front with a couple of Eighth Army drivers. Here in the desert, General Montgomery was surrounded by doting devotees.

'E don't get on that well at times wif' 'em other bigwigs. I ain't never spoken to 'im, but 'e ain't done no wrong by us. We'd follow 'im anywhere. Ain't that right, Alfie?' one of the men asked his colleague.

'That's right, Jim.'

Then Alfie told Max, 'Monty don't like them Yanks that much eiver, but who the 'ell does?'

Alfie then gave an even stronger opinion, probably because Max had no rank insignia on his combat uniform and had not told the men who he was. 'Some of them British officers are right pansies compared to Monty. I ain't talking 'bout them wot gets their 'ands dirty, but most don't know their arses from their elbows 'alf the time. We 'ave faith in the general. 'E's a real man's man wif' us lot.' Max didn't volunteer that officials in London, including Heller, were often frustrated by Monty's arrogance and disdain for military procedures.

Max, nudged accidentally by the lieutenant standing next to him, pushed his thoughts of Montgomery aside and gave the briefing his full attention.

"…tomorrow, the New Zealand Corps will start their assault into the Tebaga Gap on a two-brigade front; however,

Operation Supercharge II will begin tonight with RAF heavy bombers attacking German transport and communications hubs. These attacks will be followed by fighter-bombers who will begin relays of low-altitude pattern bombing to disorganise the Axis forces and take out their airfields. And these will continue as we move forward." Then he addressed General Montgomery. "Sir?"

Montgomery stood again on the crate, puffed out his chest, and began with a rebuke. "Although it was not a fiasco, I don't want a repeat of last week's failure to break out. Penetrating the German lines and establishing a bridgehead west of Zarat was all well and good, gentlemen, but it was not good enough. We must be able to take ground and keep it. We cannot allow another German counterattack by the 15th Panzer Division to destroy our pocket."

Montgomery's small round eyes swept the room and the men in it. He had a compelling gaze. "If we are going to take the German defences at the Mareth Line, we need to get across the Wadi Zigzaou with a strong enough force to remain on the other side of it. We will not retreat to this side again like a flock of damn ducks going forwards and backwards from shore to shore." He walloped his fist into his open palm. "The Mareth Line is the Desert Fox's last stand. It will be his final battle – it will be our final major battle in North Africa – we know it, and *he* knows it. We are going to chase him all the way to the Mediterranean Sea…"

Max knew Montgomery was talking about Field Marshal Rommel, often known as the Desert Fox. It was rumoured in Westminster that the general refused to say Rommel's name and had ordered his men not to speak it in front of him.

Monty, it appeared, was jealous of Rommel's godlike reputation.

"…we know the bulk of the Axis forces are holed up in reinforced French fortifications that are protected by the two steep-sided ravines, the Wadi Zeuss and the Wadi Zigzaou which we *failed* to take and hold last week," Montgomery, again emphasising the word *failure,* stared accusingly at his officers. "We also know that the gap between the two Wadis is filled with minefields and that the Axis main defences are on the north side of the Wadi Zigzaou, which means we have to go through highly explosive ground – yet we will not stumble, gentlemen … not this time …no, I will not allow it. We will break out of here and take this line, or by God, we may live to rue the day we let Rommel slip through our fingers."

Colonel Jenkins, who had done most of the talking, remained behind after Montgomery left, followed by a flurry of nervous aides-de-camp and other officers. Max, waiting for Jenkins to call him over, was disappointed he hadn't got the chance to speak to the general after all and wondered what his orders were.

The colonel lit a cigarette, plopped into a wooden chair, and then finally called Max over. "Major Vogel, what I'm going to ask is not in your job description, but we are in full battle preparations, and we need every man in the Eighth to be ready to move with their units." The colonel drew on his cigarette and then dropped his superior rank façade. "I'll be honest, Major … we don't have the right men to pull off this job. Don't get me wrong, we do have soldiers who might qualify, but they don't have enough experience. You, on the other hand, are *old hat* at this, *and* you've recently arrived … you're fresh, yes?"

Max nodded, wishing the man would get to the point.

"Of course, your intelligence subordinates are available, but the general believes this is too damn important to send in an untested man. You understand, don't you, Major? I mean, you'd think we'd find German speakers who could handle this, but bottom line, when the general and I spoke yesterday, you came to mind … well, you are German by birth, after all … you'll fit right in. I was saying last week…"

"What is the job, Colonel?" Max interrupted before the rambling fool digressed to a conversation that had nothing to do with whatever his bloody orders were.

"You're going out tonight," Jenkins said, as if the outing were to the nearest pub for a pint.

"Yes, sir," Max responded, going straight into his pocket for his cigarette packet.

"The general needs … *I* need you to get across the Wadi Zigzaou and into the Mareth Line dressed as a German officer."

Max inadvertently gulped. "I see."

"You must collect as much information as you can on Axis troop numbers, how many panzers they have within range, and what air strength they have available to them."

Max was genuinely confused and struggling with the questions on the tip of his tongue for fear of sounding impertinent or cowardly. By his speech and haughty bearing, Colonel Jenkins had evidently been an old school, plum-in-the-mouth, Army Officer Cadet who probably still had his valet with him and thought he was a member of the aristocracy. He'd most likely never been behind enemy lines.

He was the sort of condescending prig whose power far exceeded his brains and experience.

"I've only now arrived, but I assume you've had reconnaissance patrols out, and Axis prisoners to question?" Max questioned his superior. "Tell me, Colonel, will anything I bring back be so vitally important to you that you have to mount such an operation hours before a major battle?"

When Jenkins glared with narrowed eyes, Max followed his questions with a veiled rebuke of his own. "With respect, Colonel, but shouldn't you already have the intelligence you need?"

"Yes, yes, of course we have intelligence," Jenkins snapped, looking annoyed, "but General Montgomery insists on knowing if Field Marshal Rommel is at the Mareth Line, as we suspect, and if he is, how many staff officers are with him. You see, it is the size of the officer contingent that matters, Major. If most of Rommel's staff officers are with him, it means they have nothing much of anything left in their secondary lines. You do understand that tomorrow's ground attack could herald the last major battle of the North Africa campaign?"

Max's brain started screaming, *Suicide mission. This is a bad joke!* before Jenkins had finished speaking. But the colonel wasn't laughing.

Max, rebelling against the ridiculous order, shot back, "You do know I am representing the Foreign Office in Westminster? I am not under Eighth Army command..."

"I know who you are," Jenkins spat, taking the gloves off, "and you can wipe that smugness off your face. You are wearing a military uniform, are you not?"

"Yes, but..."

"And you are in North Africa, not London, am I right?"

"Yes, sir..."

"Then whilst you are here you will follow orders, whether you find them distasteful or not. Am I correct, or am I missing something?"

"Yes, sir, you are correct. But it's my duty to inform you that if I am captured wearing a German uniform, I will be interrogated or shot or both. And if I am questioned, I will be carrying a considerable array of classified MI6 material in my head. Am I really the man you want for this job...?"

Max turned sharply as the noise of heavy boots thumping the ground grew louder.

Six men approached. They halted together and saluted first Colonel Jenkins then Max, who wore a murderous scowl.

The captain of the squad ordered his men to stand at ease. "Reporting for duty, sir," he said, also standing easy.

"Captain Scott. Good, just in time," Jenkins said. "This is Major Vogel, British Intelligence. He's your mission tonight."

"Sir?" Captain Scott queried, looking almost as confused as Max had been earlier. "Begging your pardon, sir? You're sending an officer ... a major behind the lines dressed as a German Leutnant?"

"Yes. Why do you chaps not understand what I am saying? Major Vogel has spent almost the entire war, thus far, behind enemy lines. I'm sure a few more hours won't do him any harm – am I right, Major?"

"Yes, sir. I don't see any problem at all," Max answered, tongue-in-cheek.

Missing the sarcasm, Jenkins continued, leaving Max's protests behind him. "Captain Scott is one of the unit leaders of the Long-Range Desert Group. They come under the direct command of GHQ Middle East now, but General Montgomery wants this done, and what he wants, he gets. The LRDG's will be guiding you into position. And Major? You'd better make it back on time because these chaps are out again tomorrow with the 2nd New Zealand Division, who are spearheading our offensive."

Max knew all about the LRDG. They were hardened men – mostly British, Indian, or New Zealanders – who had volunteered for the unit that had been formed specifically to carry out deep penetration, covert reconnaissance patrols and intelligence missions behind Axis lines, predominately Italian. Experts in desert navigation, they often guided other units, such as the Special Air Service, and secret agents such as himself across treacherous desert terrain.

"Captain, why don't you brief the major. I'd better get off," the colonel said, and he left without another word, as if he'd completely lost interest in the whole thing.

Scott unrolled his map and placed it on top of the one that was already pinned to the easel. His six men stood in a relaxed position as they eyed up Max, who had so many questions it felt as if fireworks were going off in his brain.

"Major, we'll be using two of our own vehicles. We'll halt one kilometre from our target area, then lead you on foot to within four hundred metres of the German perimeter. From there, you'll go in on your own." Scott pointed to the map. "These are the main German fortifications on the Mareth Line. We expect you'll find Axis Command Headquarters in one of these bunkers here."

Max nodded. "Carry on, Captain."

"To the rear of the bunkers are numerous machine-gun posts, but the two on the eastern and western edges of the hill behind the main fortification line don't have direct line of sight to the ravine because of jutting rocks. If you can take out one of those two-man dugouts, you should be able to slip behind the Axis lines."

Max stared hard at the map. It was not enough for him to hear that two machine-gun posts didn't have a direct line of sight because of jutting rocks. He needed more to go on. A mapmaker used collected data and attempted to represent it visually on paper. He used encoding, applied generalisation, symbols, and standardised production methods that would, hopefully, lead to a depiction that could be interpreted by the map user in the way the mapmaker intended.

"Sir?" Scott prompted after a long pause.

"One minute," Max mumbled, refusing to be hurried. If he got this wrong, he could walk headlong into a machine-gun post staring him in the face or be sprayed with bullets by one before he got within fifty yards of it.

For a full five minutes, Max searched and decoded the symbols, patterns, gradient percentages, distances, and rock formations and eventually came to his own conclusion. "Take me to the flat ground on the most eastern part of the hill. That'll be my way in, and I won't have to kill a German to do it."

Scott gestured to one of his men to mark the map and route they'd now take whilst he continued to brief Max.

"We'll have six hours in total, sir, to get in and out and add on travel time. We haven't managed to get as close to the Axis fortifications as you will tonight, but we've seen enough to know they're short on heavy weaponry..."

"You've been close enough to see that?" Max asked.

"Yes, sir. We've been under their noses in this desert for more than two years."

One of the other men butted in, "I don't think anyone is underestimating the fight we're going into tomorrow, least of all General Montgomery. The Mareth Line is a natural defensive position, and its fortifications are as strong as hell."

Scott asked Max, "Were you involved in the assault last week, sir?"

"No. I arrived at the front a couple of days ago," Max answered.

"Ah, fresh meat … begging your pardon, sir," the other man apologised after Scott threw him a filthy look.

"General Montgomery wasn't happy about that failure to take the line," Scott began again. "He tried a flanking attack to the south, around the German right flank, but he underestimated the danger the two Wadis posed, and his 30th Corps, New Zealand, and Free French troops were pushed back. Don't get me wrong, he did manage to make this bridgehead, but he hates to lose a fight with Rommel." Scott, a man in his early thirties, had a mop of blond hair, similar in colour to Max's. He also sported an unruly, thick beard, which the officer enforcing the book on uniform standards had apparently overlooked.

Max scratched his own sand-coloured hair and stared again at the map. *If they already know that information, why the hell am I going in there?* All eyes were on him, and he forced a tight smile. If, in his old age, he remembered any rule from his time in the army, it would be that he mustn't look scared or hesitant in front of lower ranks. "What firepower are you bringing, in case we're detected en route?"

Before Scott could answer, a man wearing a well-worn German Afrika Korps uniform, displaying the rank of *Gefreiter* – corporal – joined the group. He saluted Max with an outstretched arm and a "Heil Hitler." Then he introduced himself in perfect German with a Bavarian accent. "Gefreiter Hans Winkler. I'll be going in with you, sir."

Max gave the short, stalky man with greying hair and a sun-beaten face an easy smile and asked a question of his own, "Do I take it you are fluent in German, Sergeant?"

"Yes, sir. My grandfather is from Munich. He's been speaking German to me all my life. I lived with him in Munich for six years after my parents died, but I haven't heard from him since '39. I worry about my old *Großvater,* sir – he's a Jew. What are your orders, Herr Major?"

"I don't have any orders yet, Sergeant Winkler. Get yourself something to eat. I'll meet you in an hour."

*Poor sod. His German grandfather didn't stand a chance.*

*Jana Petken*

# *Chapter Thirty-One*

Max was dressed in what he presumed was a dead Leutnant's Afrika Korps uniform and helmet. He also carried a rucksack full of German-issue military accoutrements, Mauser rifle, and goggles, and he had the German's *Wehrpass* identity book in his pocket, minus the photograph. He surmised the Germans would be far too busy trying to stay alive to demand his identity papers.

As he made his way to the transport, he vowed to report Colonel Jenkins to Heller. He wouldn't do it because Jenkins was a plonker but for the sake of other men who might be put in the same position; one where Jenkins' incompetent orders might be an irrefutable abuse of power. His job, Heller had told him before leaving London, was to gather intelligence from captured German and Italian prisoners and to draw updated, detailed maps of Tunisia to give to the cartography unit. Five cartographers had been killed recently whilst on missions, and Max had expected to go behind enemy lines to compile maps of enemy positions and any plausible routes they might take because that meant looking outwards from their locations. Not this, though; this was a job for an NCO, not a bloody Major!

While waiting for the last of the seven-man LRDG team to arrive, Max looked over the two vehicles they were using to get to the Mareth Line. The *Willys* MB Jeeps were unlike any others in service in that they had been stripped of all non-essentials, including doors, windscreens, and roofs. They'd also been fitted with bigger radiators, condenser systems, built up leaf springs for the harsh terrain, wide, low-pressure desert tyres, sand mats, and channels. Each vehicle also had map containers and a sun compass. Max, although familiar with the all-purpose Willys, had never inspected one. They'd been designed for the American Army to provide a convertible small car body so arranged that a single vehicle could be interchangeably used as a cargo truck, personnel carrier, emergency ambulance, field beds, radio car, trench mortar unit, and mobile anti-aircraft machine gun unit. They were the *stars* of the show, as the Americans liked to boast.

"We're ready," Captain Scott announced as he appeared, "and I've got bad news. Your extraction time has been brought forward to avoid the main part of our air attack. You and Sergeant Winkler will have no more than two hours to get in, collect the intelligence, and then get out. Sorry, sir. Orders from Colonel Jenkins."

Max shrugged as he got into the back of the second Jeep. He wasn't surprised, truth be told. "The less time we spend there, the better, Captain."

Scott gestured to his men to get into the first Jeep where Sergeant Winkler was already seated, then he got in beside Max.

Max's backside thumped against the hard seat as they began the short but treacherous drive to the German Lines. Scott had predicted it would take no more than half an hour. In preparation for the following day's attack, he and his men had conducted a trial run of the route they were going to take and had also investigated a second course in case the first one was blocked.

Allied soldiers were nervous but also expectant, Max had noted as soon as he'd arrived at the Eighth Army's lines. For the first time, an RAF air attack would be carried out in tandem with ground troops and forward air controllers advancing with the lead forces. The army's orders were to smash their way through the Axis lines and within two days reach El Hamma, to the north-east of the Tebaga Gap, where they'd continue to push the Axis forces northwards and towards the sea. Tomorrow would be a pivotal day in the war, and it would also be bloody...

"You know the reason Monty's sending you in there is to find out if Rommel's around," Scott remarked, jerking Max from his thoughts. "I swear he's obsessed with the Desert Fox. He probably has wet dreams every night about the day he captures the man."

"If that's true, he should go in there himself tonight," Max grunted.

"I agree, sir. This is bad form."

With his eyes shut, Max visualised the operation in his head. In his mind's eye, he saw Winkler and himself already integrating with German and Italian soldiers and masking their subtle questions about troop numbers, weaponry, plans, and where their highest-ranking officers were located.

As they neared the drop-off point, Scott ran through the weapons they were carrying, should they get caught in a firefight during extraction. The LRDG men were using their standard Short Magazine Lee–Enfield No.1 Mk III, and .38 Enfield, Webley & Scott, and .45 Colts. Each Jeep was also equipped with a Thompson sub-machine gun and several types of hand grenades, some extremely powerful. Max and Winks were going in with Mauser rifles, Luger P08 pistols, and knives.

Whatever happened behind the line, Max had made it clear to Scott he was not to wait past the designated pick-up time. If worst came to worst, he and Winks would make their own way back to the Allied positions, some of which would be moving forward within hours. It had sounded like a straightforward order when Max said it, but as the vehicle got closer to the rendezvous point, he regretted opening himself up to the possibility of being stranded.

After marking the spot and leaving the rest of the team, Max and Winkler set off on the last sprint to their target location. The sky was clear and quiet, and being one day short of a full moon, bright enough for the men to see a good few metres in front of them.

When the two men were three hundred fifty metres in and on high ground, Max looked through his binoculars and spotted the Axis' outer defence perimeter. Hundreds … thousands of men were positioned on the plain bordered at the far end by a low ridge. Max looked at his map. According to it, twenty metres on the other side of the incline were the main fortifications and command bunkers with trenches leading from one to the other.

He looked through his binoculars again, focusing this time on the ridge itself. It too was packed with soldiers along the scrubland line. Then he drew his finger across the map following the route he'd marked earlier. "We'll cross further east and skirt the Axis flank all the way to the ridge if we have to, but we'll probably find an opening before that," he whispered to Winkler.

Max and Winkler used rock formations and scrub for cover as they moved across the rocky terrain in a north-easterly direction. When they were as close to the Axis perimeter as they were willing to go, they crouched behind a waist-high rock.

Max peered up at the sky. It was happening already – early – far too early. The sound of approaching Allied heavy bombers and Spitfires was growing louder and louder until the rumbling noise of the engines was deafening. He nudged Winkler, who was still sweeping his binoculars across the black sky. "Any minute now, hell is going to descend on this line."

"Bloody marvellous. For once, they're early," Winkler muttered.

Max calculated that the RAF and Northwest African Tactical Air Force would hit the Axis Airfields first, not the line itself. Max had learnt at General Montgomery's briefing that RAF forward observation officers had prepared pilots by nominating landmarks, and they would already be marking targets with red and blue smoke. Once the main ground attack began, friendly troops were to use orange smoke, and the artillery would fire smoke shells to signal to the aircrews; however, none of that helped Max now. He, Winkler, and the men waiting with the two LRDG vehicles were in as much danger of being blown up as the Axis troops were. *Damn Jenkins.* He'd either miscalculated the start time of this mission, or he didn't give a damn.

"On the upside ... at least we won't need to take out any machine-gun dugouts. As soon as the first bomb hits, this lot will run for cover, and that will let us in as though we were invisible," said Max, focused on the mission now.

"Well, that's something I suppose. Who was the clown that thought this gem of an op up?" Winkler asked.

Max shrugged, unwilling to admit it might have been the mighty Montgomery. "We'll head straight for the bunkers on the other side of that ridge," he said instead. "We're not going to hang around. We've got approximately forty-five minutes to get what we need but if you think you've got enough in the first five, get out. Understood?"

"Understood," Winks mouthed, putting his binoculars away.

The ferociousness of the first bomb blast took Max by surprise, but it also surprised the Axis troops on the ground who were fifty metres from Max and Winkler's position. Max took in a long deep breath, exhaled, and then breathed in again. "See you at the extraction location."

A second, deafening Allied bomb hit far too close to the men for comfort, then another blast vibrated the ground beneath them as they lurched to their feet and ran into the chaos.

Axis soldiers were running in numerous directions, making it easy for the two men to blend in. Some were scrambling over the ridge to get to the bunkers on the other side, others were running away from the hundreds of parked vehicles, while those frozen with fear were trying to take cover beneath them.

It took twenty long strides to run up the gentle rise. Max looked down on the bunkers on the other side, some twenty metres from where he was, but then he craned his neck to look up at the sky as the shrieking whistle of a bomb descending from an unseen bomber behind the clouds of smoke grew louder and louder.

*Move? Stay?* his mind screamed. He made for the lip of the ridge with the throng of men looking for cover and was about to go over the edge when an earth-shattering explosion impacted with the lower ground behind him and took his legs from under him. Max fell with the blast wave and rolled down the hill like an Easter egg.

At the bottom, he was kicked in the face by a man's boot, then two other soldiers landed on top of him, crushing the air from his lungs and provoking a sharp pain in his side.

Conscious but dazed, the men eventually got off Max. All around him, men were bloodied from numerous gashes and cuts. An outstretched hand grabbed Max's arm and pulled him to his feet.

"Herr Leutnant, what do we do?" the young Schütze yelled.

Max gazed through blurred eyes at the boy's red face. The whole world appeared to be lit up in an orange glow reflected off burning vehicles. Blood was still running into the Schütze's left eye from a gash showing his eyebrow bone, but he was oblivious to it. "Get to your bunker, Schütze. Find your squad and get your eye seen to," Max said.

The boy started to move off but then fell unconscious at Max's feet. Overhead, Spitfires were diving towards Max, appearing as though they were personally targeting him. He bent down, gripped the boy under the arms, and then flung him over his shoulder in a fireman's lift.

The low-flying Spitfire was spraying bullets in a straight line about twenty-five metres to Max's right-hand side. Men, being picked off and falling as they ran towards a bunker further along the line, didn't stand a chance of evading the flying monster coming in low enough to show the teeth painted on its nose. And above, the sky was no longer black but red, and covered with a blanket of grey smoke clouds enshrouding the moon and stars that had been so bright an hour earlier.

Max, with nowhere to hide except for the closest bunker situated ahead and to his left, stumbled on with the Schütze slung over his shoulder and himself groaning in agony with every step he took. *I've broken a rib,* he thought, as he staggered like a drunken man. *At least one.*

At last, Max and the unconscious soldier reached the trench leading to the bunker whose roof was about three feet above ground. At the bottom of the crowded narrow channel by the entrance, Max heard a man say, "I'll take him, Herr Leutnant." Max couldn't see the person who'd spoken through the smoke that cloaked the area, and he staggered in a circle as the voice repeated, "I've got him, sir."

"Good. Look after him," Max said, dropping his burden as gently as he could.

Max, still in pain, but now relieved of the painful weight, pushed his way inside. As he'd suspected by the number of men wearing red crosses on their sleeves, this bunker was a makeshift hospital. He turned and made his way outside again to a world on fire.

Outside, much of the noise had abated, and men were scrambling to organise defensive positions again. The bombs and bullets had stopped falling, but the RAF were probably getting ready for their second pass; the next of many more air attacks to come throughout the night. Max's body shuddered with relief, and in the respite, he headed to the next bunker along.

The massive underground keep was full of men, weapons, supplies, and crates of ammunition. Soldiers seeking shelter against the back wall ignored him and carried on readying their rifles and machine guns by going through boxes of bullets and filling machine-gun belts. *They look as terrified as any sane man would,* Max thought, including himself in that analogy.

"Herr Leutnant – Herr Leutnant, are we moving out?" a man with a bandage on his head asked Max, who was looking for their operations centre.

"Wait for your orders, Gefreiter," Max answered tersely and walked outside.

Max struck gold in the next bunker. It stood to reason as soon as the bombs started falling, the German Command would hold some sort of top-brass briefing, despite the confusion outside. Soldiers were being strafed by aircraft machine gunners and blown up by bombers, their transport and communication lines were probably down already, and staff officers commanding tens of thousands of men would want orders from the top of the chain.

With an officious stride, Max entered a room chock-full with officers and NCOs. He remained unobtrusively behind the pack and near the bunker's entrance where a wall of sand dust obscured the fires outside. A heated debate, as fiery as the air raid itself, was taking place. At first, the men spoke in raised voices, but then they began shouting at one another as a new wave of bomb attacks shook the walls and ceiling and filled the place with even more clouds of dust, smoke, and falling debris.

A fierce argument broke out between three officers, including the one who seemed to be heading the briefing. Max recognised the commander from MI6 photographs. He was Colonel General von Arnim. *If he is here at Mareth, is it probable that Rommel is not?*

The debate centred around whether the 1ˢᵗ Army should withdraw immediately to Wadi Akarit or try to hold on for the 15ᵗʰ Panzer Group's counter-attack, which would give them cover to slip away later. The general was opting for the first option, but the other officers were trying to overrule him.

Max, listening intently under the noise of the new air attack, learnt that a radio communication had gone out to their reserve divisions before the lines had been cut. He also found out where the 15ᵗʰ Panzer Group were positioned, that the 1ˢᵗ Army had little air support left, and that their heavy weapons, along with the bulk of their transport vehicles, had been destroyed. Then, the jewel in Montgomery's crown came during a yelling match; the crux of the matter was that Field Marshal Erwin Rommel was no longer in North Africa and had returned to Germany.

Max checked his wristwatch and exited the bunker. Time was up, and as he'd predicted, he'd learnt nothing he deemed *new*, apart from the information that Rommel was not in Tunisia. Satisfied that would appease Colonel Jenkins, who would scurry like a rat to Montgomery with the exciting news, Max decided to get the hell out of there.

Chaos, destruction, and pain met Max when he returned to the plain behind the ridge. With careful steps, he made his way through the encampment that had housed thousands of men before the first air attack began. It now looked like a massive vehicle graveyard on fire. Soldiers were valiantly trying to douse the flames with buckets of sand and collecting ammunition crates that hadn't been blown up. Smoke, looking like giant grey shadows rising from the earth, filled the sky to the north, east, and west of the Mareth Line where the bombers were now targeting. Piles of rocks that had spewed from the ground like geysers littered the area pitted with craters and dead bodies still burning.

Half-blinded by dirty smog that stung his eyes and fighting against excruciating, breath-stealing pain in his chest and side, Max hobbled on in a south-westerly direction towards the rendezvous point. As he zigzagged in and out of the lines of destroyed vehicles and injured men, he was struck by a horrible thought: *I hope my Wilmot isn't here. I feel sorry for the poor bastards.*

Max reached the rendezvous location with ten minutes to spare. His crown was bleeding, his jacket sleeve torn and bloodied, and the pain in his side left him gasping for air. At a row of rocks surrounded by ugly shrubs and a couple of sad-looking, stunted trees with barely a leaf between them, he got on one knee, flashed his torch three times, and received two flashes in return. He groaned as he rose to his feet again but found he couldn't straighten because of the pain in his ribs. Nonetheless, he advanced, stooped over, to the two well-camouflaged vehicles and the LRDG men manning their sub-machine guns.

Scott came forward and helped Max to one of the Jeeps. "How bad are you, Major?" he asked, frowning with concern.

"It's my ribs … has Sergeant Winkler returned?" Max panted.

"Yes, and he brought a gift for you."

Max went to the second Jeep. Winkler was standing in front of it, rinsing his blackened face with a handful of water from his canteen. A thick line of drying blood stained his left arm, and he had two cuts on his face; one above the eye and the other on his hairline.

"I think I came out of that better than you did," he said, taking in Max's pitiful, bent over appearance.

One of Scott's men was guarding a terrified-looking German Hauptmann with a deep gash on his left shoulder.

Winkler grinned at Max, then he gestured to the prisoner. "I met this Kraut here on my way out. He was running away so bleedin' fast, the silly sod nearly overtook me. Are you interested?"

Max regarded the German captain in his early twenties and said, "This is your lucky night, Hauptmann. You're coming with us."

# Chapter Thirty-Two

## Wilmot Vogel

*The Mareth Line, Tunisia*
*25 March 1943*

For days, Wilmot and the 90th Light Division had been running for their lives under cover of 15th Panzer group fire. The tanks had successfully counterattacked the Allied bridgehead west of Zarat, allowing the remnants of the infantry divisions to reach the Mareth Line, a complex of interconnecting defensive fortifications, but there was nowhere left to go from there.

Wilmot lay on his stomach inside one of the Mareth Line bunkers as the enemy's fifteen-minute-long air attack continued. His rifle peeked out of a hole in the wall, big enough for his head to get through, but too small to be called a window. In front of him lay a landscape of rocky terrain, and to his west, the Matmata Hills, currently being overrun by the Allied forces. He was half-blinded by white flashes and becoming deafened from the ferocity of the attack. The Royal Air Force's merciless bombing of the German positions was causing rock formations to explode into the air like massive eruptions of yellow-ochre dust. Tracer fire shot down from the heavens like falling stars, and quick flickering lights in the black sky looked like children's sparklers. Flash after flash afflicted Willie's dirt-filled, stinging eyes, and booms, detonations, and the piercing, whistling sound of bombs dropping were making his ears bleed.

He and everyone else in his unit had been hopeful at the beginning of March. After months of retreating, it appeared that Field Marshal Rommel was going to attack. Three German armoured divisions, two light divisions, and nine Italian divisions launched Operation Capri, attacking southward in the direction of Medenine, the northernmost British strong point. The attack was repulsed, however, with massed artillery fire that knocked out fifty-five Axis tanks. And with that defeat, all hope was lost, or so he believed.

Wilmot's belly rumbled. It was either craving food or swirling with the bitter bile of fear. In the last two days, frequent bouts of nausea had made it impossible for him to eat without throwing up. It had been two days since he'd held solids down; four hours since he'd had his last drink of water.

The soldier behind him sat with his back against the wall, battery torch in one hand, a folded map in the other. He was talking to himself, as he did quite often when he was scared. The short stocky man, as bald as a baby's bottom, was twenty-two years old, but he held the record in the platoon for not one but three bullet wounds from earlier battles. None had been life-threatening, the medics had declared, but Wilmot had fought for him to be sent home. He was suffering from shell shock and a brain injury that doctors had not diagnosed. At times, he rambled like an idiot. He froze when confronted by danger, which was most of the time, and he asked the most stupid of questions; one being: 'Are we winning, Willie?'

Wilmot blinked as bursts of white hit his retinas again. Earlier, he'd observed his infantrymen lifting, carrying, and passing around boxes of ammunition to the other shelters, but now, apart from men in gun holes surrounding the bunkers, no one was venturing outside; instead, hundreds were pouring in. He retracted his weapon and stood it against the wall. Bloody stupid idea pointing his rifle at … what? If an enemy soldier came within range, it'd be all over before he got his first shot off.

He slipped his hand into his pocket, then hesitated as Egon, the soldier reading the map, looked up expectantly at him.

"We're not going to be here much longer, Egon," Wilmot said taking out a pack of cigarettes. *Should I give Egon one or not?* He had two left with no expectation of getting any more.

"I know, Willie. Are we winning?"

Wilmot, a staff sergeant, had told his men to address him by his Christian name when they were out of earshot of the officers. It didn't matter to him what he was called nowadays. All he and his unit had done in the past four months was flee westwards, through Libya and into Tunisia like a gang of bungling fugitives being chased by the British and Americans and the rest of the bloody world combined. The men respected him; that was what mattered the most.

"Schütze Gier!" Wilmot shouted to one of his men. "Tell our men to move back from the outer wall. No one goes outside, understood?"

"*Ja, Feldwebel,*" Gier shouted back.

"Come with me to the back," Wilmot then told Egon.

When the men huddled near the back of the bunker, Wilmot took out his flask and finally took a sip of water to ease his burning throat. He looked at his men and all the other soldiers he didn't know and saw his fear reflected in their eyes. Apart from random periods during their chaotic retreats,

351

discipline was still important to the men of Army Group
Africa, as it was now called. It had changed names many
times since Wilmot had joined the desert war – back in
February, it had been re-designated as the Italian 1$^{st}$ Army and
put under the command of Italian General Giovanni Messe.
Rommel had then been placed in command of a new Army
Group Africa, created to control both the Italian 1st Army and
the 5th Panzer Army. It was at that time that the remnants of
the Afrika Korps and surviving units of the 1st Italian Army
retreated into Tunisia.

The rank and file didn't care what grand new titles the
higher ranks came up with for their army; they still called it
the Afrika Korps. They were hardened veterans and wouldn't
allow themselves to fall into permanent disarray. He laughed
to himself. His term, *hardened veterans,* wasn't strictly true,
for raw recruits, young and old, including some Poles and
Czechs, had been arriving even as the army was on the run in
what must be the longest retreat in history. Some of them
hadn't even fired their weapons in combat. Shooting a rifle
with one's back to the enemy was a waste of bullets and not
easy to do.

The noise of the British bombs and bullets continued to
deafen the men, and it was compounded by Allied ground
aircraft flying almost at head height and screaming in every
fifteen minutes or so to pick off anything that moved with
their machine guns. Wilmot put his helmet on. The Mareth
Line was untenable, and any minute now, he'd be called to a
briefing where he'd receive orders to withdraw immediately
from this position.

Wilmot pushed the horrible thought of retreat to the back
of his mind, and instead looked again at the packet of

cigarettes clutched in his hand. Nazi Party members were a load of hypocrites. The Reich was anti-tobacco. They condemned its consumption and had limited the cigarette rations issued to troops. They'd banned smoking for the common man on buses, trains and trams while they, the upper echelons of the ruling party, enjoyed smoking big fat cigars and turning the air blue with cigarette smoke in their private clubs and restaurants. Who cared whether tobacco was good or bad for people? It was the only luxury he had, and he was more likely to get blown up than develop an illness because of smoking.

"Will you stop staring at me?" Wilmot finally snapped at Egon. "I'll give you my last cigarette, all right?"

*Egon might be daft in the head, but he's good at looting and might get hold of some more later,* Wilmot thought, lighting Egon's cigarette for him. He liked to pick the pockets of fallen comrades, claiming that his dead German friends wouldn't mind sharing what they'd left behind. It was an unsavoury practice, but none of the men thought taking from the dead was a sin, and he, as their staff sergeant, didn't either. *Why should we leave stuff behind for the enemy?*

Egon gave Wilmot a virtually toothless grin. He'd lost four of his front teeth a month earlier when he had fallen and hit his mouth against a rock. "You know I'll share whatever I pick up in the future, Willie. It won't be long until we get to Tunis. Do you think they'll let us sleep in real beds?"

As the withering fire of the British army wore them down, the two men enjoyed their final cigarettes in a moment of relative peace. Both heard the blasts, felt the vibrating bangs that hurt their heads, suffered the dust and bits of debris falling from the ceiling and gushing in through the holes in the bunker's outer walls, but every now and again they got a jolt of optimism, as German anti-aircraft guns fired into the black sky. The men were calm as they puffed away, as though they were watching a movie unfold outside.

"Have you ever read a book called *The Alamo?*" Wilmot asked Egon.

"No, what's that?"

"Not what, where. It was an American fort in Texas. The story goes that a handful of men tried for days to hold out against a massive Mexican army."

"How did that go for them?"

"They all died, but it was the way they fought to the last bullet that got me. The story reminds of me of what we're going to finish up like … fighting over the last bullet. It's a good book. You should read it one day."

"Hmm, *ja,* I'll do that, Willie."

Wilmot had lost his belief in the Afrika Korps' infallibility, and his prior faith in victory was now vacuous. The way he saw it, they were no longer seeking victory but forestalling defeat. Not something he would say to anyone else, but they all thought it. He was getting to the stage where he wanted it to end, regardless of the humiliation at the beating they'd taken.

"What are you looking at on the map?" Wilmot asked Egon.

"Where we are."

"You know where we are. This is the Mareth Line."

"I know that, Willie. I was seeing how far Tunis is from here. A man can get confused by geography when he's been chased across a desert for months on end, looking at the same landscape. Look here…" Egon highlighted the map with his torch and drew his finger to the edge of it. "We're going to end up swimming to Sicily if we're not careful..."

"*Feldwebel Wachtmeister* Vogel!"

The soldier, his face black with gunpowder, crouched down as he hurried to Wilmot's side.

Wilmot looked at his half-finished cigarette and sighed. *Typical.* "Do they want me, Schütze?"

The man panted, "*Ja,* Feldwebel Wachtmeister … I think we're moving out."

"Of course, we are," said Wilmot, rolling his eyes sarcastically.

In the adjoining bunker, Wilmot joined a packed room of officers and staff sergeants. The commanders and staff officers were huddled around a map while the rest of the men couldn't see a thing. On his way there, Wilmot passed lines of injured soldiers being treated by members of the medical corps, which included one Oberarzt. *Poor devils,* he'd thought, seeing the medics trying to stem the blood flow from a screaming man's gut. They weren't going to get out of this alive. Only the fit and strong would be able to run through this terrain to relative safety. A German graveyard of vehicles and tanks, along with dead soldiers of all ranks, stretched all the way back to Libya, and from what he was seeing, the Allies were blowing up damaged Panzer tanks and transport trucks. Transport was going to be a problem for the wounded.

The men at the table were strangers to Wilmot, apart from his Leutnant, an aristocratic sort of fellow who claimed his family had blood ties to the old Kaiser. He was, for all his pompous speeches, a hard bastard in terms of discipline and a damn good leader.

Wilmot listened to the brash discussion going on. The rumours that Field Marshal Rommel had left the desert and was in Germany because of illness had been circulating for days. 'That's all they are – rumours,' Wilmot had told his men. They'd find out for themselves soon enough if they were accurate. Wilmot, knowing that Rommel *had* left and that his successor was General von Arnim, kept the information to himself. Thinking that Rommel was still with them gave the soldiers hope, and that was all they had left. He wouldn't take it from them.

An explosion hit near the bunker's roof, and the items on the table rattled. Dust and bricks fell from the ceiling, narrowly missing the division's senior staff officer, and large cracks in the roof ripped across the thin layer of plaster.

"... our position is strengthened by these hills and rock formations, but even with these well-constructed defences, we can't hold them back. They're throwing everything they have at us and smashing their way through solid stone," a major was saying. "We received orders from Berlin to fight on until the last drop of Afrika Korps' blood is spilt, but Field Marshal Rommel left instructions that we were to retreat to save lives if we think we cannot hold. That time has come. I will not watch the men die for the Reich's convoluted pride."

*Thank God for Rommel,* Wilmot thought.

"With respect, Herr Major, I disagree. We should fight on. If we can hold them back now, the Italians will eventually reinforce us," a Hauptmann with one bandaged eye said.

Another shell hit, forcing the major to shout, "No, Hauptmann, we will not *carry on!* Maybe you haven't noticed, but we're pinned down! That means no supplies or men can get through to us. *Generalleutnant* Gause suggests we withdraw immediately to our secondary defensive positions. He's out there and knows more than we do in here. Our anti-tank guns will try to check the Allied advance to give us time to get away."

General von Arnim removed his cap and scratched his sand-coated hair as he looked at the men. "We're outnumbered two to one. We've lost thousands of men and our support and mobility from the air." He threw his hands up. "They've liquidated our aircraft and have practically wiped out our tanks. You tell me, Hauptmann, how are we to face over a thousand Allied tanks, not to mention the hundreds of Allied guns pouring in on this sector? I'm stating a fact … if we don't go now, we won't get out at all!"

"We have the 15th Panzer Group on our secondary defensive line. We have not lost yet, Herr General," the Hauptmann insisted.

Wilmot jumped as the ostentatious major slammed his fist onto the steel table. "Those tanks went up against the lead units of the American forces and ran into a minefield. The American artillery and anti-tank units opened fire, and our 10th Panzer Division lost thirty tanks within an hour. The tank commanders who survived have limped back to Gabès. We should withdraw!"

Emotions were running high. Wilmot, sharing the universal agony of imminent defeat, remained silent as the officers continued to spar with each other. He glanced at the other staff sergeants present and guessed they were praying for the retreat to go ahead. One was staring at the floor, shifting his feet in some strange, mournful dance, another was staring up at the dust-filled air, gritting his teeth, and an officer was leaving … *my God, the man is a carbon-copy of*

*Max and Paul.* A lump sat at the back of Wilmot's throat, and for a second, he thought about following his brothers' double, so he could look at the man's face again. *My brothers – Christ, how I miss them.*

Wilmot focused again. The sooner they reached the sea and got themselves to Sicily to regroup, the better, he had concluded hours earlier. The North Africa campaign was over; at least, for the moment. That had been evident when the intelligence services he was working with dismissed him.

In retrospect, that job had lasted about five minutes; he had never translated a single interrogation. The Abwehr, not prone to admitting defeat, had abandoned their operations when it became evident that they had no means of collecting enemy prisoners while on constant retreat. They'd tried a couple of times to send men behind enemy lines in darkness to capture live prisoners, but most of the soldiers they sent died on the missions, and the survivors didn't bring back a single Allied soldier. Even the Abwehr had lost all hope for a comeback. They'd burnt their intelligence tents with everything in them. Luckily, though, he was able to keep his promotion in rank.

"… *nein … nein,* Herr Major, I must object. If Field Marshal Rommel were here, he would order us to hold…" another officer had now butted in.

"You know that's not true, Josef," Wilmot's Leutnant interrupted the man.

"It is true! The Americans have been unable to exploit our failure in the minefield, and our 10th and 21st Panzer Divisions are still counterattacking up the road from the salt marshes at Gabès at the coast. And the coordination between the Allied air and ground forces remain disjointed. It is our right … our duty to the Fatherland to keep our guns firing…"

"Enough!" the general shouted as part of the brick wall in the next bunker blew inward.

The table vibrated again, the room filling with dust particles and smoke. Men were on the ground, and some were heading to the exit. The general, screaming now above the blasts, issued his final orders. "We are moving out, now. The injured that can walk, will walk, those who cannot will be put on what transport we have left."

"And if we don't have enough room to take all of them?" the sparring major shouted back.

"Their wounds will be treated by the enemy when they are taken prisoner." As he rushed towards the exit, von Arnim threw over his shoulder, "Heil Hitler!"

"Heil Hitler," came the muted responses.

Wilmot ran back to his bunker, past fires and dead men and through what looked like an impenetrable cloud of smoke.

Egon and the other surviving members of Wilmot's unit were outside their section of the bunker with their rifles and rucksacks already on their backs. The front wall and trench had blown in.

Wilmot looked at the partly destroyed building and felt sick. "How many men were in the collapsed area?" he asked.

"About twenty. They're probably all dead, *Feldwebel Wachtmeister*."

Wilmot had missed the beginning of the briefing, but he'd heard enough to believe that the North Africa campaign *was* over. One of two things could happen now: he and his men would be captured by the enemy, or they would be killed.

Egon giggled as the first of many Africa Korps' platoons began to slip away from the Mareth Line to the noise of Panzer cover fire. "Ach, it's ironic."

"What is?" another man asked.

"Us, being in this place. Apparently, the French built the Mareth line in the 1930s to stop Italian fascists from occupying French Tunisia, and here we were with the Italian First Army, trying to defend the place against the rest of the world – hilarious."

*Egon isn't stupid after all,* Wilmot thought as he prepared to lead his men out of yet another hell hole.

# Chapter Thirty-Three

*In the hills south of Tunis*
*Tunisia, May 1943*

After a hard struggle, the remnants of Wilmot's 90th Division and Italian 1st Army eventually crossed the central plains of Tunisia to the comparative safety of the hills west of Tunis and Bizerte. The men were exhausted, hungry, and short of ammunition, but despite the pressure and hopelessness of their situation, they had, for weeks, bitterly contested the Allies' mountain redoubts south of the Tunisian capital.

Above them, allied air forces bombed, blasted, and strafed the Germans and Italians with impunity until the thin Axis crust of a line began to decay, and gaps appeared or were pushed aside. Men were dying by the hundreds, and the wounded were receiving little more than battlefield first aid. The British and Americans had everything in the air that could fly and everything on the ground that could shoot, and they were bringing their concentrated fury to bear on the outfought, outgunned Afrika Korps.

Wilmot was sick. He thought he might be dying. His legs wobbled when he walked, his ribcage protruded like the Atlas Hills under his skin, and he was sweating by the bucket load. From behind a rock, he prayed an Allied soldier would appear and order him to surrender. He begged God, if such a thing existed, to shroud him in the luck that had kept him alive until now. He wanted to live, not end up like his mates lying around this hill … like garbage.

One by one, the German defences were being taken out. Dead Germans lay unburied, and their flesh was being devoured by vultures and carrion-eating kites, feral dogs, and flies. One after the other, their redoubts were being smashed, supplies were obliterated, and the surviving infantrymen were running out of bullets.

Wilmot had no idea how many men in the 90th were still fighting on this hill, but he believed the number was now down in the low hundreds. He also had no way to verify the orders being chaotically handed out, for it had been two days since he'd seen an officer of worth. His Leutnant had been killed a month earlier, and the Hauptmann he'd spoken to last had instructed the men to carry on fighting until their last drop of blood. 'Stand and fight. Transport planes full of reinforcements are flying in to help us,' the officer had said, looking and sounding like the bloody liar he was. *Where is the bastard now? Is he dead, or did he surrender as so many others have, on some other godforsaken hill?*

When the redoubt to his left was hit, Wilmot ordered his remaining men to abandon their posts. Fuck the officers, and fuck Adolf Hitler. His men lacked ammunition, and no more was coming. No magic carpet carrying crates of rocket launchers or fresh-faced men from Berlin was coming, either, and he and his men weren't going to die on an officer's say-so.

On shaky legs, Wilmot stumbled through a world of black smoke, tripping over dead comrades, some with uniforms still smoking with gunpowder. From one destroyed redoubt to the next, he shouted the same words, "Move back … move back … move to surrender!"

Egon, who'd been injured yet again, limped behind
Wilmot as he manoeuvred through the labyrinth of crushed
rocks and corpses. Men followed without question,
abandoning their holes in the ground and tiny caves carved in
the rock faces until a rifle shot behind them stopped them in
their tracks.

"Get back here! You will fight! *Bewege euch Schneller –
sich zu ergeben ist Verrat und wird von einem
Erschießungskommando bestraft* – man your posts, now – to
surrender is betrayal and is punishable by firing squad!"

The Oberleutnant, screaming at the men to return to their
posts, had appeared from nowhere.

Wilmot charged back through the group of soldiers,
seething with rage. The coward had probably been inside one
of the hill caves, too scared to come out until the weapons had
stopped firing. Of course, he didn't want the men to abandon
the position and leave him on his own; he wanted them to
cover his arse and take the flak!

"With respect, Herr Oberleutnant, I will not order my men
to die –" Another explosion hit, covering the men with debris.
"Get down!" Wilmot shouted to his men, as he and the
Oberleutnant also dropped to the ground. "Take cover!"

In the distance, Wilmot saw enemy troops, for the first
time looking like men instead of marching ants on the plain
below. "I respectfully advise a full withdrawal from this hill.
It is lost, sir," Wilmot tried again, getting to his knees and
hunkering on the ground.

"*Nein!* Get your men back into their positions, or I'll have
you shot! We will not surrender – no surrender, men!"

Wilmot glimpsed two of his men falling to enemy bullets –
allied rifles were now in range, and within the hour, British or

American soldiers would be overrunning this location. Still hunkering, he shouted to his men, "Abandon your positions. Follow me. We *will* surrender!"

The Oberleutnant had scrambled to his feet, waving his Walther P38 pistol in the direction of Wilmot's men. "I will shoot! Get back here! I will..." he screamed.

Wilmot, still on his knees, raised his rifle, and fired three shots into the officer while he was still barking orders.

"It's over!" Wilmot yelled at the soldiers.

The officer dropped to his knees, stared at Wilmot in disbelief, then fell forwards until his face smashed into the ground.

Wilmot bellied towards his men like a lizard; afraid to rise, afraid to move too slowly. Against the cacophony of weapons fire that was hammering their eardrums, he screeched, "If any of you have objections to me killing our officer, it is so noted. Do you want to live?"

"*Ja! Ja,* Feldwebel!" the men shouted back.

"Then follow me. We're going to surrender to the enemy."

Wilmot's heart thumped in tandem with the shell blasts that were obliterating their defensive positions, now behind them. He quickened his step, screaming, "Come on!" as he staggered downwards on uneven paths towards the plain.

Almost at the bottom, he threw his rifle on the ground. Its magazine was half full, but he'd use it no more. "Death or capture!" Wilmot now shouted.

The men behind Wilmot also threw their rifles away and then without being instructed, raised their arms high in the air with their face and neck scarves waving in their hands. They weren't white flags, but near as damn it.

Finally, with no more deaths, the group reached the open plain at the bottom of the path. Wilmot panted, made a fist with his raised hand and halted his men. "We surrender!" he shouted in English when his platoon confronted American soldiers.

******

A few hours after their capture, the German and Italian prisoners rested on a wide, open plain packed with tanks and trucks, half-tracks, and bulldozers, a sea of defeated Axis troops, and the American army in all its glory.

Wilmot and the remnants of his platoon had not been the first group of Axis forces to be captured, for when they'd arrived at this place, which was as crowded as Berlin's train station on a national holiday, he saw thousands of Afrika Korps men, standing, sitting, and lying down under American guard. From what he'd gathered from other prisoners, men had been capitulating since midday the previous day.

He was now trembling like a man doused in icy water; he realised how fortunate he and his men had been to abandon their position when they did. Weapons fire was still echoing down from the hills, swarming now with Allied soldiers who'd climbed rock faces using grappling hooks and ropes. The Germans and Italians who had decided to remain would not be as lucky as those who had volunteered to lay down their arms. They were idiots, but more honourable than he'd been when he'd shot his superior officer, he supposed.

Allied soldiers, mostly Americans, looked as exhausted as Wilmot felt, as they stood in groups surrounding the tens of thousands of Afrika Korps prisoners. *Tens of thousands?* Over one hundred thousand, easily, and they were the ones Wilmot could physically see. Axis troops were still coming in on foot in tens, twenties, hundreds at a time, and being escorted by more Americans with their distinct helmets and American flags waving off their vehicles in the blistering hot breeze.

Wilmot sat on the ground beside Egon, who'd taken off his cap and boots and was moaning with satisfaction as he wriggled his toes. His bald head was pitted with tiny cuts and stained bright red, and his cap was ripped and full of holes; he probably didn't even know it.

"Put your cap back on, Egon," Wilmot ordered. "You'll burn your head."

"All right, Willie. You won't leave me, will you?" Egon asked, as he put on his cap and pulled it down his forehead.

Although he acknowledged his fear, Wilmot also admitted that he was not as afraid now as he'd been on the hill when trying to defend their indefensible position. And he was certainly more optimistic than he had ever been as a prisoner of the Russians. Americans were more civilised than the Russkies who'd meted death sentences to their prisoners on a whim. These people here wouldn't do that. They would follow the Geneva Convention, as Field Marshal Rommel had. He wasn't going home, but he might survive this catastrophe.

When he and his men had come upon the Americans, he'd half expected to be mown down by semi-automatic rifles. Only later did he deduce that the Americans must have spotted his platoon-sized group waving scarves in their raised hands from a distance. The enemy soldiers hadn't panicked or looked surprised. They'd been prepared to receive prisoners, as though waiting for them to turn the corner.

As the buzz of voices around him grew, Wilmot reached more conclusions. The Americans' calm acceptance of seeing Axis forces surrender could only mean that the Afrika Korps was giving up everywhere. When he'd arrived at this huge rallying point, he'd estimated that about half the one hundred thousand Axis troops already there were German. Field Marshal Rommel's successor, Generalleutnant von Arnim, had been positioned further south. He must have witnessed his artillery and panzers being wiped out; the landscape was ablaze with burning trucks and tanks. The hills to the south of Wilmot's position had also been pounded for weeks, and he believed that von Arnim and the Axis forces on them were either dead or captured.

For the first time, a mixture of excitement and disbelief rushed through Wilmot, as the unthinkable became a possible reality. He lurched to his feet and approached an American soldier with his helmet sitting cockily on the back of his head and his jaw jumping up and down as he chewed gum.

"Excuse me. Can I ask a question?" Wilmot asked in perfect English, tinged with a German accent.

"No." The soldier's eyes went to the Iron Cross pinned to Wilmot's collar, then they shifted to Wilmot's face and the unkempt beard, red-rimmed eyes, and ugly black scar running along his cheek. "You speak English? Where are you from?"

"Berlin. My mother is English ... from Kent." Wilmot's mouth was dry. He swallowed painfully and asked his question despite the initial *no.* "Have we all surrendered? *All* of us? Is it over?"

"Yep. You're beat ... done. Go on now ... back to your friends."

Wilmot began to walk away, sad yet elated at the same time. *Christ, I don't know I feel.*

"Hey, you, Jerry!" the American behind him called.

Turning around, Wilmot walked back to the man he'd been speaking to. "Yes?"

"Your guys put up one hell of a fight. Ain't no shame in being beat when you've given it your all," the gum-chewing American said.

"I know," Wilmot answered and surprised himself when his lips spread into a broad smile. "We did fight well, didn't we? Tell me something … had you heard of the Afrika Korps before you came to the desert?"

"Sure, ain't no man here who ain't heard of Rommel and his Afrika Korps."

"Is that right?" Wilmot nodded with satisfaction.

"What's your name?" the American asked.

"Wilmot. Staff Sergeant Wilmot Vogel," Wilmot answered, a touch of pride lacing his voice.

"Call me Victor."

Wilmot went back to his men. He sat down and scratched his head. *Was that a smart-arse connotation for the American victory or the man's real name?* Wilmot shrugged and mumbled, "Ach, who cares?"

Well into the night, the dusty plain continued to fill up with surrendering Germans and Italians. Wilmot had not moved from his original spot since being dismissed by the American earlier that day. He was desperate for a drink of water and a secluded place to do his business. His eyes swept the area. *A private place?* Stupid git, he couldn't even see a spare centimetre or two to squat, let alone a tree or bush to go behind.

His head jerked upwards as the atmosphere changed. Men were cheering and whooping. Vehicle horns were blowing from British trucks, LRDG vehicles, and British Jeeps, along with the Afrika Korps' nemesis, the Eighth Army.

"Shit. Talk about adding insult to injury. Now the British have shown up to stick their snotty noses in the air," one of Wilmot's men complained.

Egon, who'd been dozing, woke up with the noise. He sat up, groggy-looking, and asked, "Willie, where will they take us? Or do you think they'll let us go? Or maybe leave us here?"

Egon was rambling again with that far-away look in his eyes. To imagine the enemy setting free hundreds of thousands of Axis soldiers, only to confront them again another day was a ridiculous notion, but young Egon didn't see it that way.

"I don't know where they'll take us, but it will be under lock and key, Egon," Wilmot told the disappointed man. True, he didn't know where they'd end up. *Britain? A prison camp in the desert, then somewhere else later?*

Humiliation set in as Wilmot observed the Allied troops' celebrations. They even had cinematography cameras filming the Axis prisoners. As it panned around to Wilmot, he smiled for the camera, then in defiance, gave it his middle finger.

Later that night, Wilmot curled up in a ball, closed his eyes, and wondered if history would judge the Afrika Korps as cowards who had given up. The Axis army wasn't riddled with disease, shrunken with hunger, barehanded, or naked under the sun. They had deliberately laid down their weapons after reaching the conclusion that their aircraft had flown until they'd been wiped out, guns had fired until there was no more ammunition, their tanks had carried on firing even after their petrol was depleted, and soldiers had carried empty rifles even after there was no more ammunition. In the end, they'd recognised a superior power in the long and bitterly fought battles throughout North Africa ending in Tunisia. They'd been clever enough to know when to call it quits. That wasn't cowardice; it was smart.

# Chapter Thirty-Four

## Paul Vogel and Romek Gabula

*Bielański Forest, near Warsaw, Poland*
*July 1943*

Bielański Forest was situated eight kilometres north of Warsaw and was, perhaps, too close to the city for comfort. It was made up of Mazowiecka Primeval Forest and was also connected to Kampinoski Forest by a narrow strip of woods, making it a warren stretching for over three kilometres from one end to the other. The Germans, who probably found it too inaccessible for their transport and too large to control on foot, had not ventured close to the hidden Polish campsite for over a year. The men in Romek's unit were reasonably confident of their concealment; however, Romek insisted that the perimeters be constantly watched, and men patrolled those areas on a rotational basis.

At sunrise, Paul left his well-camouflaged shelter to see to the overnight fire used for cooking. The men or women on night watch always made sure there was a boiling pot of water ready when the sun rose, for just before dawn, all campfires were doused so no tell-tale smoke would advertise their presence to the enemy.

Afterwards, he returned to the shelter and the blanket on the groundsheet inside that hid Amelia's half-naked body.

"Wakey, wakey," he said in English while pulling the blanket down to her waist. "Wake up, darling. I'm making coffee," he repeated in his best Polish.

Amelia pulled Paul to her, parted her lips and purred, "Not before you kiss me good morning."

Paul gripped a handful of her hair and gently tilted her head back before his lips met hers in an ardent kiss. After a while, he felt his passion grow and pulled away. *Shame,* he thought, gazing at her sleepy face. As much as he'd like to make love to her again, he had work to do. "Satisfied?" he asked.

"Yes … for now."

Paul stroked her cheek, then drew his finger down her hairline and across to her lips. "Darling Amelia, if it weren't for the dangerous world beyond the forest treeline, I could imagine you and I being content here, despite the nits, creepy-crawlies and discomforts."

"Me, too," she said softly. "I can see our children climbing trees or fishing with you and learning to hunt for their dinner, and having dirty faces and long, wild hair. The thought of a life here doesn't scare me at all."

He kissed her again. "You, my love, have a vivid imagination; but you're right, it's not such a hardship, is it? Living rough, eating sporadically … improving my Polish to more than courteous phrases and medical instructions?"

"You're being hard on yourself, Paul. You understand most of what's being said now, and the men appreciate your determination to learn. I've heard them speaking about you. They trust and respect you."

"Finally," Paul sighed with contentment. "After three years in the country, and ten months living with Poles, I'm enjoying being able to converse and understand what's being said around me. I *almost* feel accepted – you know Darek hasn't called me *German swine meat* for at least two months."

He laughed. "Ach, Amelia, if it weren't for the horrors of war that fill our world, I would say I've never been happier than I am now."

Outside, Paul smiled to himself as he spooned ersatz coffee grains made from roasted acorn and chicory root straight into the boiling pot of water before it went cold. He loved this time of the day. The forest, home to rich fauna and flora, had everything a small army needed to survive. There was an abundance of clear water streams and rivers deep enough to bathe in and cook with and with which to fill copious buckets to quench one's thirst on these hot summer days. There were roots, leaves, and seeds that could be foraged and eaten, and edible berries and fungi ripe to eat by autumn. Game was also on hand, although hunting posed its own dangers. Whilst chasing down a rabbit, one of the men had been set upon by two local policemen who were known to collaborate with the Germans. They, too, had been looking for food. The surprise meeting had turned into a brief firefight, with Romek's man winning but sustaining a leg wound in the process.

Danger was ever-present. The men had to eat, therefore fires had to be lit despite the threat of being spotted by the enemy. They had to stray outside their encampment to find protein sources, such as wild boar, deer, fox, rabbit, martens, squirrels, and the many different bird species that supplied fresh eggs during springtime. Every day posed new threats, yet the Resistance had found some semblance of normality deep in this woodland sanctuary.

Paul, now a fully-fledged member of Romek's unit, felt quite at home when he and Amelia stayed in their makeshift semi-sunken branch shack in the forest, sometimes for two or three nights in a row. He was taking this new period of his life in his stride and was fully committed to Romek, who had probably saved his life by taking him in…

"Paul, did you make some for me?"

Startled, Paul looked up, beamed at Kurt, and then stood to hug him. "Kurt, you're back. I was beginning to worry about you. It's been weeks … almost two months since I've seen you."

Kurt sat on another log next to the smouldering embers. His face was drawn, and his eyes were dull with grief. "I shouldn't have been able to take you by surprise like that. I thought Darek was training you?"

Paul chuckled. "I have been training. Since I last saw you, I've learnt the art of shooting a pistol and rifle, how to correctly throw a grenade, best an opponent fighting hand-to-hand using knives and fists, and conceal myself from German patrols using what's available in the forest. If you had told me you were coming, I would have wrapped myself in leaves."

Paul stirred the pot, trying to dissolve the granules that were like hard stones. "Darek gave me my own rifle, so that's a good sign?" he muttered, more of a question than a statement. "I'm not a bad shot, as it happens."

After Romek had convinced his superiors and other unit heads to accept Paul, he gave the latter an ultimatum. On paper, the choice had been a simple one: regardless of his position as doctor, more adept at saving lives than taking them, Paul was to either vow to kill Poland's enemies, should that need arise, or forget about fighting with the Poles and take the deadly consequences of being captured by them.

'You're either all in, or you're not in at all. I have vouched for both you and Kurt, and if you let me down, I will pay a

374

heavy price for my failure,' Romek had stated after subjecting Paul to weeks of interrogations and virtual captivity.

'I'm all in, but I'm a doctor, not a fighter. I hope you will use my skills wisely,' Paul had responded, feeling both relieved and anxious.

Paul poured coffee into two rough-hewn wooden cups and handed one to Kurt. He'd let Amelia lie abed a while longer. They had walked and foraged for hours the previous day, and she was tired.

Kurt, his head down, his hooded eyes staring at the dying embers of the fire, exhaled a painful sigh.

"What is it?" Paul asked.

"I saw Anatol and Vanda on my travels. They send you their love."

"Are they all right?"

Kurt looked up. Tears slipped from his eyes, and he let them fall.

Paul's stomach lurched with grief as he imagined the worst. "Oh God, what's happened?"

"The SS arrested Hubert and his wife. Anatol got word from Gert in Łódź that they were both executed." Kurt cleared his throat as anger replaced his sorrow. "Sixteen people were put against the wall of a building in Łódź and gunned down by an SS firing squad. The Germans called them 'hostages.' They wanted the people involved in the raid on the weapons supply depot in return for the lives of Hubert and the others. Five German soldiers were killed in the attack, and four of ours didn't make it out. Gert deserted. He's gone to the east of the country to join a Polish Home Army unit – good for him."

Paul kicked the hot remains of the fire, thinking back to his early days in Poland when he had discovered Hubert and

Anatol's human smuggling activities. Hubert had been one of the bravest and most loyal men he'd ever met. Not once had he refused to help a Jew escape or to treat one when injured or sick. "Damn it. We should have tried harder to convince Hubert to come with us. No house is worth dying for, no matter how long his family has lived there."

"Paul, some people don't want to run away in fear. They want to cling to what's theirs ... to what brings them comfort. It's not about a house's bricks and mortar, it's what's inside it ... familiar objects, photographs of family, an old armchair that's been comforting for years, a knitted bedspread, a china cup. Hubert told me the last time I saw him that he wouldn't let the Germans chase him out of the house he, his mother, and his grandfather were born in. His wife was ill, and the Jews..."

"What about Jews?"

Kurt finally lifted his eyes to Paul. "... Hubert was sheltering Jews in his attic. He had five of them up there."

"Ach, Hubert," was all Paul could manage.

"Damn it, Paul, I can't wrap my head around what our countrymen are doing here." Kurt also kicked the hot ashes, spreading them more evenly. "I was in a town called Słonim last week. There's hardly anyone left alive. Almost twenty thousand Jews have been murdered. A few weeks ago, a Ukrainian SS squad executed over one hundred Poles, along with the town's priest, for sheltering Jews in their church. I'm ashamed of where I come from. I'm so damn angry, I want to kill every Wehrmacht, Gestapo, SS ... whatever their nationality ... fucking policeman in Poland!"

Paul killed the last of the fire with a handful of soil, deeply saddened by Kurt's news. "Hubert and his wife were heroes,

Kurt. That's how I'll always remember them. And yes, good for Gert."

Kurt cleared his throat, his face full of pain as he snapped a twig and threw it on the ground. "Romek is here as well. He wants both of us to attend his meeting."

Paul stood. Romek, whom he hadn't seen in almost a month, was back, which meant changes were coming. "Now?"

"No, in about fifteen minutes. Sit. Time enough to finish drinking your shit excuse for coffee."

Paul glanced surreptitiously at his tent, and Kurt laughed. "And how is the lovely Amelia?"

"Fine. She's asleep," Paul said with a red face. After a rocky start together, during which Paul had slated Kurt for lying about Dieter, the two men had finally agreed to be honest with each other about everything. Everyone in the unit knew about Paul's affair with Amelia, and no one cared or gave it a moment's thought, apart from Paul, who felt the guilt of a married man going behind a wife's back. *Stupid,* he admitted. His signature was probably on divorce documents by now, forged by Biermann himself. For all he knew, Valentina might have remarried a staunch supporter of Adolf Hitler; a high-ranking officer, perhaps. *So what?* It was his angst over never having met his one-year-old daughter that gave him sleepless nights, not heartache for the child's mother. He often wondered what he'd ever seen in the woman … or had *he* become unrecognisable of late?

Kurt, studying Paul's pensive gaze, said, "Enjoy what you have with Amelia. Don't ever feel sorry for finding love. God knows, I wish I could." Then he gave Paul a playful push. "Ach, come on, boy, it's your duty to have a good time for all those people we've seen die. If we can't have fun, what's the point of it all?"

"I know that, Kurt. How are things with you? Are you still doing what you do?"

"Yes. Why do you find it so hard to say the word?"

"You mean *assassinate?*"

Kurt chuckled, "Ach, Paul, if only it were that simple."

"Will you tell me about it?"

"Do you really want to know?"

"I do." Paul sipped the coffee, not quite boiling hot anymore, but warm enough. "How do you find your victims?"

"First thing you should know is that they are not victims. Every one of them deserves what they get from us."

"Is it wide-scale … the collaborations?"

"No, not wide-scale … in fact, it's marginal. The tragedy is that it takes only one collaborator to get dozens of good Poles killed. Most of the German collaborators are those in possession of Volksdeutsche ID cards and come from the German minority enclaves. We have men who track down the people who are actively reporting on their neighbours to the Generalgouvernement. They're put on a list, which is then handed over to the Underground Court. You think I spend my days shooting people?" Kurt chuckled at Paul's sombre expression. "Not true. We kill very few Poles. They're sentenced and punished by the Home Army Court."

"I didn't know that."

"There's a lot you have to learn, Paul. For instance, the level of help the Germans are getting goes much deeper than that from ethnic Germans. It's sickening to the people here when they find out that an unsympathetic Polish neighbour has reported a family hiding a Jew in their street, or that the *szmalcownik* – blackmailers, are extorting money to keep their mouths shut about the whereabouts of Jews. We also have the ethnic Ukrainians to deal with. Many of them are pro-German, as are the Jewish collaborators from Żagiew and *Group 13*."

"Group who?" Paul asked.

"*Group 13*. There was talk of these people when I was in the Łódź ghetto. The *Trzynastka Yiddish* Network was a Jewish collaborationist organisation. The Underground knew about them, but they couldn't get to them because they were based inside the Warsaw ghetto. It was said they worked for the Germans to curtail the black market, but they were the biggest racketeers of them all. They used everything from blackmail to extortion and murder. They even ran their own prison."

"Good God. No, I've never heard of them."

"Probably because most of them were executed by the Germans last year in one of their cleansing operations. We're still after one of its leaders … a man called Abraham Gancwajch. He and a few surviving members of the group re-emerged posing as Jewish Underground fighters. We caught and interrogated some of them and found out they were still working for the Germans … still working for the people who wiped out most of the members of their group … unbelievably stupid people, clinging to the hope they'll be spared for being traitors to their own kind."

"Were they spying on the Underground?"

Kurt sipped his coffee and grimaced. "*Scheisse* – shit, Paul, this tastes worse than it smells." Then he continued, "Yes. They were spying and hunting down Poles hiding or supporting Jews. We believe Gancwajch is somewhere in Warsaw and receiving his orders directly from the Gestapo.

We have a kill on sight order for that *drecksack* – dirty bastard."

Kurt's foot shot out in anger again, this time disrupting the stones around the fire's ashes. "Fucking barbarian. I'll spit in his treacherous face when I find him – betraying his own kind…"

"Kurt, you're wanted. You too, *Lekarz*." Darek joined the men at the fireplace and gave Paul's foot a playful kick. "Come on, breakfast is over."

Kurt raised his eyebrow at Paul, and uttered, "*Lekarz?*"

"They've stopped calling me derogative German names. I'm just plain *doctor* now," Paul shrugged good-humouredly as he threw the remains of the coffee onto the last of the cooling ashes.

# Chapter Thirty-Five

Fifteen men, including Romek, were already assembled at their command centre a short distance from the main campsite. Romek, who was in deep conversation with one of the men about a recent mission, spotted Kurt and Paul arriving and called them over. "We'll finish this after the meeting, Jan," he told the Pole he'd been speaking to.

"Good morning, *Lekarz* – Kurt. Good to see you both," Romek said, shaking Paul's then Kurt's hand.

Darek said, "This must be important, Romek. We haven't had a meeting like this in a long time. How did you manage to get everyone in the same place?"

"With great difficulty, Darek – great difficulty."

Romek raised an eyebrow at Paul, then nodded with approval. The latter's rifle was slung over his shoulder. He wore a pair of cotton jean trousers and a threadbare blue shirt. His hair was longer, his stubble thicker, and he no longer looked like a German officer or a frightened rabbit, as he had the first time he'd been in the company of hardened Polish soldiers. "Paul, don't go far. I want a word with you in private when the meeting ends."

Paul nodded. "Yes, Romek."

Romek then turned his attention to the men who had travelled long distances over dangerous terrain controlled by the Germans. Every man present, apart from Kurt and Paul, had gone through some measure of SOE training at Audley End in England. Romek had recently spent a week at the training facility, completing an advanced explosives-handling course. It was run by the Polish section of the SOE, and they guarded their autonomy as they would gold bars. Unlike other national sections, the *Cichociemni* – created in Britain to become the elite, special-operations paratroopers of the Polish Army in exile, ceased to be SOE soldiers as soon as they touched down on Polish soil – instead, they came under Home Army command.

Romek looked at the men forming a semicircle around him. He was their equal, not their leader, but his job was markedly different than theirs. His superiors called him a liaison officer, but he saw himself as a glorified messenger going between the Polish leadership in Poland, the Government in Exile, and the Allies. He wondered, *how will these fighting men take the good and bad news today? How can I uplift them but also make them hate the Germans even more?* Both positive and negative emotions made for more determined soldiers.

"I know the risks you've taken to get here, but I have news that needs to come straight from my lips to your ears," Romek began the meeting. "I've come from the *Delegatura.* Our supreme political body is finally expanding its operations and financing more programmes. Since last year, it has granted over twenty-nine million zlotys to the *Żegota* Organisation, which assists Polish Jews, and it will continue to provide for them."

While the men murmured their approval, Romek sneered, "The British and their allies have their fingers up their arses and will do nothing to help the Jews or non-Jews in Poland; yet our countrymen, even under German occupation, have managed to find and deliver the money to assist thousands of extended Jewish families."

Romek had started the meeting with good news, but as he swept his eyes across the line of tired-looking men who battled the behemoth German occupiers daily, it was hard to imagine them being uplifted by anything else he might say. All Poles were shrouded in yet another layer of grief after the uprising by the Jews in the Warsaw Ghetto in April and May had ended in total defeat for the Jews and other minorities who lived there. Since then, the Germans had liquidated the ghetto and sent thousands to the death camps.

He cleared his throat and informed the men, "Szmul Zygielbojm, the Jewish member of the National Council of the Polish Government in Exile, committed suicide last month."

Some of the men gasped but made no verbal response.

Romek continued, his sorrow mirroring that of most of the men while he explained what had happened to those who didn't know who Zygielbojm was. "After years of protesting against the Allied governments' indifference toward the destruction of Poland's Jews and minorities, he found out that his wife and son had been killed during the Warsaw Ghetto uprising. Before Zygielbojm took his own life with an overdose of sodium amytal, he wrote a letter that condemned the Allies' blatant disregard for the genocide we are witnessing in our country."

Romek's anger and disgust grew every time he acknowledged his failure to stir the British into action over the horrific slaughter of Poland's Jews, as well as, now, the many Polish non-Jews. "I have also tried everything to wake up the British and Americans. I showed them pictures. I handed over microfilm and eye-witness testimonies that Kurt and our German doctor, Paul, wrote in detail. Nothing came of my efforts."

Romek's hands were shaking as he took out three folded pieces of paper from his trouser pocket. In them were lists and copies of official encoded communiques that he had already deciphered and would later re-read carefully, so as not to miss anything important. "We are not Polish Jews, but they are our brothers and sisters. They have no outside help, apart from that which comes from our Polish Government in Exile, but let no man here be in doubt that we *will* punish the German collaborators who report on Jews in hiding and the people who are helping them."

Romek waved the page in his hand. "Our government has reinforced our mandate with this decree." Then he began to read an excerpt:

*Any direct and indirect complicity in the German criminal actions is the most serious offence against Poland. Any Pole who collaborates in their acts of murder, whether by extortion, informing on Jews, or by exploiting their terrible plight or participating in acts of robbery, is committing a major crime against the laws of the Polish Republic...*

"...it is signed by General Władysław Sikorski, our Prime Minister and Commander-in-Chief of the Polish Armed Forces, and dated, May 1943." Romek held up the page again for effect. "This cannot bring back the men, women, and children who perished in the ghetto, nor can it bring back the uprising survivors who were taken to Auschwitz – God help them, they are probably dead by now – it cannot stop the SS from imprisoning Christian men and women who refuse to join the *baudiensts* when requested. We all know these forced labour battalions are nothing short of enslavement of the

Polish people. And this decree cannot stop the Third Reich's attacks on Catholic priests in the Wartheland where it is estimated that almost nine hundred Polish clergymen have either been shot or imprisoned in Germany's Dachau camp."

Romek, a Catholic who had always attended Mass on Sundays with Klara, had been dismayed to read the Home Army's latest statistics on lost clergy. His face reddened as his anger grew with every word he spoke. "I have the statistics right here. The Catholic Church is being decimated! The Germans have confiscated properties and funds, and lay organisations have been shut down. In almost every arrest of any clergy, monks, diocesan administrators or officials of the Church, a collaborator has testified against them or reported them to the Generalgouvernement for aiding and hiding Jews."

The men, silent and wholly focused on the information being given to them, were as enraged as Romek, which was precisely what he wanted to see.

"We are on the front line, and as such, we must act on behalf of our government and for all the *Szmul Zygielbojms* who no longer have voices. People acting against the Jews or their rescuers, whether blackmailers or others using extortion or other means, must be punished by death."

"Yes. Agreed – death!" some of the men echoed Romek.

Again, Romek paused to give the men time to take in this nasty piece of business. His eyes settled on Darek, who was whispering to Kurt and probably discussing more of what had been said. Both men were nodding, not only with apparent satisfaction but also with enthusiasm.

Romek now changed the subject. It was time to mix in some positive news. "Since our amalgamation with the

*Związek Odwetu* and *Wachlarz* groups at the end of January this year, our new *Kedyw* Unit has grown to over two hundred thousand men and women in arms. With this growth in our army, we can no longer base ourselves solely in towns but will now be forced to set up more forest camps like this one. We're also going to organise bigger and more central weapons and munitions factories, military schools, intelligence, counter-intelligence, field hospitals, and a communication network…"

"Will we still have time to kill Germans?" Darek chuckled.

"Yes. Our commander, Brigadier-General Fieldorf has decreed that *Operation Heads* will also be stepped up." Romek answered Darek. "But we can only be successful with the continuing cooperation of the *Związek Harcerstwa Polskiego* – the *Grey Ranks* in the Underground Paramilitary Scouting and Guiding Association. They are essential to our operations and plans for our eventual uprising in Warsaw and other major cities. Be heartened, all of you. We are now taking the fight to the Germans in a way they have not yet experienced. We're going to send them back to their Fatherland with their dicks up their arses!"

Again, the men nodded and murmured their desire for action.

"We can do this," Romek continued his upbeat message. "We have already proved to the Germans that we will not bend to their will. Who would have thought it possible that we could achieve what we did in March in Warsaw, eh?"

Romek paused again when he noted some puzzled faces. Some of the men had evidently not yet heard of that successful operation. "We sent in twenty-eight members of the Grey Ranks, along with SOE trained agents, and not only did they meet their objective, they surpassed it. Their mission was to free one of our troop leaders and his father from the hands of the Gestapo. When the Scouts attacked Pawiak Prison, Jan Bytnar and his father were in a prison van outside awaiting transport to Gestapo headquarters at Szucha Avenue. The assault took the Germans by surprise, and our people freed Bytnar and twenty-four other prisoners with him."

Romek observed the men. Used to hearing appalling news, they now looked like schoolboys celebrating a victorious football match. If they were not worried about making a racket, they'd yell a victory song right now, to add to their backslapping and handshakes, which were just as encouraging.

To keep the men's feet on the ground, Romek finished on a low note. "Bytnar died four days after the rescue due to injuries sustained at the hands of his interrogators ... but as a free man."

Darek piped up, "And not without being avenged. Last month, the Scouts assassinated both Gestapo officers involved in Bytnar's torture. Romek is right, we cannot only protect our Jews and fellow Poles by punishing collaborators; we can also beat the Germans." He looked apologetically at Romek. "Sorry for interrupting you, Romek."

*It is wonderful to see the men in such high spirits,* Romek thought. Even Paul, who seemed to understand most of what was being said, looked enthusiastic about killing Germans. "Darek is correct, we *will* be victorious, but we also have a long, dangerous road ahead of us. Selected *Kedyw patrole* – the scouting patrols, will now carry out missions across the country. You will continue to operate in small groups, and meetings like these will become rare. Most of our current operation objectives will remain the same but will be on a bigger scale. We will sabotage railroads, bridges, roads, and supply depots, primarily near transport hubs in Warsaw and Lublin. We will burn trains and fuel depots, destroy weapons factories working for the Wehrmacht, and liberate hundreds of prisoners and hostages, and we will do all those things under the Germans' noses *because we can.*"

Given that it could be one, two, or even three months before the unit leaders reunited again, Romek wanted them to have one more reason to hate the Third Reich. The information he was about to give them was not new, but the scale in which these German atrocities were growing had shocked even him.

"Comrades, it's no secret that the Germans are abusing and raping our women, but I think you will be as outraged as I am when you hear this…" Romek's throat was dry, and his voice was hoarse from continuous talking and with emotion. "Mass rapes are being committed against Polish women and girls before they are shot in punitive executions. Large numbers are being rounded up and forced to serve in German military brothels utilised by German soldiers and officers. I intend to free as many of our women as we can by carrying out raids on the brothels and by stopping the transports being used during the mass captures in our cities."

Romek appealed to his men's visible outrage. "I have not received orders to target these establishments, but our Government in Exile doesn't need to know every single operation we carry out. Think of your sisters, your daughters, your mothers losing a child as young as fourteen to a German pig who'll hump her until the day of her eventual execution. We will begin these missions in Łódź. Are you with me?"

There was a resounding *yes* from the men.

******

After the meeting, Romek spoke to the men individually. As officers, they would take their orders from central command back to their units. Romek passed on specific target lists for sabotage operations and attacks on depots and small supply convoys, and, in some cases, he gave coordinates and times for supply and weapons drops in their areas.

Finally, he got to Paul, Kurt, and Darek. "Operation Heads has a new target." Romek looked at Paul. "Captain Wójcik, who will run the operation, has already filed a report about Gestapo Kriminalinspektor Manfred Krüger to Commander Fieldorf, and the Special Court of our Underground State has sentenced the Kriminaldirektor to death."

Paul's eyes widened with surprise and pleasure, but then his conscience woke up. *It's good news, but am I a rotten doctor to feel happy about a plan to murder Krüger?* At times, it was hard to reconcile who he'd been with who he was now...

"Well, Paul. This is what you wanted, no?"

"Yes, it is. Glad to hear Krüger's promotion will be short-lived."

"Excellent news. When?" Darek asked.

"You'll leave for Łódź today, and you will be taking Paul with you."

"Are you out of your mind? Paul doesn't have the experience or the know-how!" Kurt looked horrified.

"But he does know the target. His insight into Krüger might be useful."

Darek, seemingly not bothered whether Paul was going or not, asked, "Who else is going on this one?"

"A platoon of one of the Scouting battalions will carry out the execution. You and Kurt will be giving cover fire, and Paul will deal with any wounded."

Paul, curious about the timing of this assassination, asked, "Is there a reason why you're targeting Krüger now?"

"Yes. Krüger is still policing the Łódź Ghetto and prison, but since his promotion, he's increased the number of public executions and civilian roundups outside the ghetto wall. His police force is sealing off whole streets and trapping anyone who's in them. Tram and trainloads of people, regardless of work documents, are being herded into trucks. We believe he's sending them to concentration camps, including Auschwitz. Every day, he's publishing lists of his hostages to be shot in reprisal for civil disobedience or attacks on German soldiers. We want rid of him."

"I'll be happy to kill that bastard," Darek spat.

Paul's smile was wide with satisfaction.

# Chapter Thirty-Six

Paul was both excited about and dreading his first combat mission. Accustomed to staying behind at the farmhouse or in the forest, he wondered how he'd handle the violence up close. He was glad he was going to witness the assassination first-hand, but he was also terrified of returning as a German traitor to the city he'd escaped nine months earlier.

He wanted Manfred Krüger dead, not out of sick revenge or even personal hatred, but for the people of Łódź who might stand a chance of surviving the war should the Kriminaldirektor not exist. Perhaps he was naïve to think that the next Gestapo chief would not be as evil or find gratuitous killings as enjoyable as Biermann and Krüger had, but if he were going to kill a man in cold blood, he'd cling to that hope.

Paul found Romek sitting on the bank of the stream that ran past the camp. His eyes were closed, his feet bare and resting on the white pebbles on the stream's bed. The two men had not seen each other since April when Romek had finally returned from England with the letters Max had given him for Paul.

"How was your assignment? Did Darek give you a hard time?" Romek asked, wiggling his toes under the water.

"No. It's clear he's not keen on having me here. Don't get me wrong, he doesn't disrespect me or … ach, never mind. He's a good leader. We worked well together, and to be honest, I was too busy to take any notice of his personal feelings towards me." *That wasn't strictly true,* Paul thought.

Darek had made it apparent to the other men in his unit that he wasn't happy about having a German anywhere near him.

"Any trouble with Germans at the farm?"

Paul had been reasonably relaxed at the farmhouse. It was owned by Alojzy, a Resistance fighter who delivered milk and eggs to the German garrison two kilometres south of the farmhouse. German and Polish police collaborators had slaughtered the Jews in the nearby village, and without their presence, German soldiers no longer had any reason to go to the farm. It was an ideal hiding place – if there was such a thing as ideal. Polish combat units frequently congregated there before or after missions, especially if they had wounded fighters with them, and Paul had been comfortable on the nights he stayed there.

"No trouble as such," he finally said. "We had a couple of frights. The first occasion was when we spotted a German patrol heading across the field towards the house, and the second time, a lone German on a motorcycle came for food. Alojzy has a great pile of straw and manure in his courtyard. It sits on top of the trapdoor to a bunker in the ground. As soon as the lookout saw the Germans, I got down there with the wounded man I was treating."

Paul had been much busier than he'd ever imagined he would be before his first stint at the farm. It had been nothing like his time with Florent Duguay's Partisan group in France. Here, in Poland, he felt he was in a bona fide army. "I saw a lot of wounded men, Romek. What's going on?"

"It's as I said at the meeting. Our army is growing. We're going to surpass a quarter of a million men and women at arms soon, and with those numbers, we must expect greater casualties and wounded." Romek smiled. "Don't worry, we have plenty of Jewish doctors helping out."

Romek threw a stone into the water. "Amelia will start training today."

"For what?" Paul asked with a worried frown.

"She'll learn how to shoot a gun, same as everyone else. If we need her nursing skills, we'll use her, but she needs to be able to fight, too ... or she can leave. I can't have bystanders, and you can't have her around just to keep your bed warm at night."

Paul bit back his retort. Whatever he said, he'd be in the wrong. He wasn't happy about Amelia being given a weapon, but this had been inevitable, he supposed. "I understand. You won't have any trouble convincing her. She's been desperate to pick up a gun."

For a while, Romek spoke of his failure in England to get support for the Jews as well as the Poles now being persecuted in the Nazi cleansing programme, but after a while, he turned to a more personal subject.

"A British agent arrived in Warsaw last week." Romek went into his pocket and brought out an envelope. "He gave me this to give to you."

"Max?" Paul asked, his eyes shining with hope.

"No," Romek spat. "When you've finished here, you'll find me with Darek and Kurt. Don't be long."

As Romek began to walk away with his socks and boots in his hand, Paul wondered why he always appeared angry whenever Max's name was mentioned. He had not had the courage or opportunity to ask Romek, but now that they were alone, it was the right time if ever there was one.

"Before you go, can I ask you something?" Paul called out.

"What?" Romek turned around.

"You don't say much about him, but I get the impression you and Max are not friends. What went on between the two of you?"

Romek considered his words a moment, then said, "He was a friend, once upon a time … like a brother to me. I saved his life in the North Sea and sheltered him in Poland before this war even began. I shared my dinner table with him, and, apparently, my wife as well. Let's say, I think him a selfish bastard, no longer worthy of my trust." Romek turned to walk away again but threw over his shoulder, "However, if Max were in trouble, I'd save his life a second time, and I've no doubt he would save mine."

Paul, still not much the wiser about Romek and Max's past association, ripped open the envelope and gasped when he saw his father's handwriting. He squeezed his eyes shut, feeling both elated and bitter. His greatest joy in years had been receiving the letters from the family in April. He was an uncle to a boy called Jack. Judith Weber was not only alive, but she was now his sister-in-law; he'd look forward to hearing about that story when he was reunited with his brother. Frank Middleton was, at the time, well and somewhere in the Middle East. His mother was happily living with Hannah and her grandson, and everyone was healthy and united. But the truth about his father's situation had not come in those letters, and he'd felt betrayed by Max ever since.

Finally, swallowing his hurt pride, Paul began to read the letter from the father he'd thought dead.

*My dearest Son*

*I imagine you feel let down, angry, and betrayed by all of us. You must believe me when I say I hid my real situation from you to protect you and your mother, but mostly to protect myself. Now that you probably know the truth from Kurt, I beg of you, do not blame him or Max. They followed my instructions and are not at fault. Ask Kurt to tell you everything, from start to finish. I cannot say anything else, for if I tried to explain to you on paper, it would only be half the story. Just know that I love you. I am proud of you. We all yearn for the day we can be reunited with you and your younger brother.*

*Your loving father*

Paul turned the page over – blank.

*Was that it; a few lines? A short rationalisation to make up for the years of grief and lies?* He scrunched the paper in his fist, then ripped it up into tiny pieces. One day, he might forgive the subterfuge that had caused him such misery and had given Biermann his moments of gloating joy, but not now.

He got up, slung his rifle over his shoulder, and headed to the encampment. He was going to murder a man today – he, Doctor Paul Vogel was going off to kill with his gun. *Jesus, who the hell was he?*

Paul found Amelia and kissed her hard on her mouth. He breathed in the fresh scent of river water and soap on her hair, savoured the softness of her skin, the beauty within her and without. "You're going to start weapons training today. You have your wish, *kochanie* – darling. Promise me you won't volunteer for anything? We'll talk about this when I get back, all right?"

Tears ran down her cheeks. "I promise I won't. I … I'm sorry for being like this. If you were going anywhere else, I wouldn't be as upset, but Łódź … *Łódź,* Paul."

He kissed her again. "I'm going to get rid of the man responsible for the deaths of our friends." He was always reticent to mention her late husband, even though he'd told himself a hundred times his death had been a mercy killing. "I want to go, Amelia."

"I know, and I love you for it." She stared at him, as if looking deeper than his outward appearance. "Are you ready to fire your rifle, Paul? To kill fellow Germans if you have to?"

Paul held her hand, raised it to his mouth, and kissed it. "Yes, of course. How can you even ask me that?" He let her go. "I know what I'm doing. I knew this day would come. I love you, too, my sweet Amelia."

After his goodbye to Amelia, who was staying with Romek at the camp and then moving to an undisclosed location for training, Paul joined Romek, Kurt, and Darek. The latter held a glum and openly hostile expression, Paul noted. Apparently, Romek had briefed Kurt on *Operation Krüger* before Darek, and he had also named Kurt the team leader. Darek, who had never fully accepted having to fight alongside the taller, stronger Kurt, was taking what he saw as Romek's *betrayal* to heart, and that did not bode well for what was going to be a high-risk mission.

\*\*\*\*\*\*

At midnight on the third day of their journey from the forest near Warsaw, the men arrived at the rendezvous coordinates in the woods, three kilometres north of Łódź. There, they met up with the ten members of the Combat Sabotage Unit taking part in the plot to kill Manfred Krüger.

One of the men present; a seventeen-year-old called Bogdan, veteran of numerous firefights with German patrols, greeted Paul with a bear hug. "Lekarz Paul, I like ... I feel better now that I see you," the boy said in stuttering German.

Bogdan turned to the others standing behind him, saying in rapid Polish. "Doctor Paul may be a German pig, but he saved my man-parts for me." Then he undid his trouser buttons and pulled down his trousers and undershorts. "Look, my wound is all healed, and I'm in fine working order."

"You're still a virgin, Bogdan," one man stated, and the group laughed. As the men tittered with amusement, Bogdan turned back to Paul, spread his legs and pointed to the scar, a couple of centimetres from his manhood, and it was his proud manhood that now stared Paul in the face. "Good work, eh, Lekarz?"

Paul chuckled. "A decent job, even if I say so myself. Thanks for showing me, Bogdan."

Darek and the other Poles standing behind Bogdan laughed again, and Paul felt the day's tension leave his body.

"Bogdan, put your arse away. We have a lot to get through," the mission's overall leader, known as *Wójcik,* said,

Darek, Paul, and Kurt sat on the ground. The last fifteen kilometres of their journey had been on foot across country, and they were ready to drop.

"I will translate for you and Kurt, should you get lost in the discussion. It's important you know all the details. I don't want you two making a mess of things," Darek said.

Wójcik began, "Our spy in Łódź has been monitoring Kriminaldirektor Krüger's movements over the last two weeks. We know where he lives in the city, where he routinely goes, and how he gets there. But we have two problems with him. The first is that he never walks in the open, much less alone. Even if he's travelling a block or two from his house or office, he uses a driver and car, a black Opel Admiral limousine. The second is that he doesn't always leave his house, but instead has his Gestapo officers and other authorities going to him."

"Are you planning an attack on his car or on his house? If it's his car, we'll need some heavy firepower," Darek said.

"We have it, Darek. I've brought ten men and enough assault weapons to take out a street of Germans. The assault will be on the Kriminaldirektor's car, and this is how it will go. Our first executioner will be armed with an MP 40 sub-machine gun, by courtesy of some dead Germans, Vis pistol, and Filipinka hand grenade. Our second-in-command and security screen will carry grenades. The second executioner will use the Sten sub-machine gun and grenades. The third will drive an Adler Trumpf-Junior and will be armed with a Parabellum Luger P08 pistol and grenades. Our covers will have sub-machine guns, Parabellums, and grenades. Bruno, here, will drive an Opel Kapitän and will be armed with two Parabellums and grenades. We will also have another man driving a Mercedes 170 V and armed with two Parabellums and grenades. And we will have three men covering signals."

Wójcik paused for questions. When there were none, he continued, "Despite our falsified identity papers, we can't take the chance of driving cars in civilian clothes through numerous roadblocks in the city, so we will walk to the cars, which will be parked reasonably close to the hit zone. We expect this to turn into a street battle. Krüger always has an escort when he leaves his house, and there are at least three German checkpoints in the vicinity. Stay sharp and remember your training. Not all of us will get out of this in one piece."

Paul, who had observed each man nodding as Wójcik had gone through the roles they would have, wondered what parts Kurt, Darek, and he would play. He threw Darek a filthy look; for some inexplicable reason, the Pole had given him a rifle only to confiscate it later. 'You won't need that, Doctor,' he had stated.

Paul looked around at the other men who were going to carry a huge cache of guns and grenades on their persons and in duffel bags. He wasn't sure what he'd expected, but not this large gathering with men talking of expected firefights and street battles. He was terrified.

Darek, on the same train of thought as Paul, asked Wójcik, "Where do you want us three?"

"You and Kurt will give cover fire. The doctor will be travelling in the Mercedes with his medical supplies. Keep him safe. We will need him."

*Jana Petken*

# Chapter Thirty-Seven

At 0909 the next morning, Manfred Krüger left his home in the German named Kanalstrasse. Oblivious to the plot against him, he lit a cigarette, got into the back of his limousine, and opened his briefcase.

Members of Wójcik's combat unit were in place, with the first lookout standing near the entrance to a park opposite Krüger's house. As soon as he saw Krüger's car going through the open gates, he gave the signal to the next man further along the street.

As Krüger's vehicle approached the junction at the end of the street, the Adler Trumpf-Junior, carrying the driver and the two executioners, swerved in front to block its path. Immediately, the two fighters jumped out of the Trumpf, approached Krüger's car, and fired on it from close range, killing the driver and wounding Krüger.

The Mercedes had arrived on the scene seconds after the first gunfire popped in the morning air. Paul, sitting in the passenger seat, watched the bloodied Manfred Krüger fall out of his car and begin to crawl away from it. Holding his breath, Paul then saw the driver of the Trumpf jump out of the car and run towards Krüger.

Unthinking, Paul left the Mercedes and followed the driver to where Krüger now lay exhausted and dying from a wound to his neck. He raised his hand to the hole spurting arterial blood and tried to speak.

"You're dead. Go to hell," Paul heard himself say in a stone-cold voice.

Krüger stared up at Paul and his terrified eyes widened with confusion. "Y-you…" he gasped.

The driver aimed his pistol and finished off the injured Krüger with a gunshot to his head, then snapped, "Doctor, get back to your car."

On his way back to the vehicle, Paul observed one of the executioners searching Krüger's dead body for documents while the other man was taking the briefcase from the back of the car. Frozen, with only the thought of Krüger's death on his mind, Paul watched in awe as the other getaway vehicle moved into position, just as the German guards stationed nearby opened fire on the assassins.

Paul's driver opened the car's door to get out, shouting at Paul to take cover. Paul, still mesmerised by the intense firefight ensuing between the Germans and the covering team, now including Kurt and Darek, watched as three of the combat unit's men fell to German bullets, including the driver who had called to him.

Bullets sprayed Paul's car, but instead of running away from them, he jumped in and took cover in the narrow space between the front and back seats. All sensible thought deserted him, apart from his inner voice screaming that he didn't want to die. Seconds later, grenades went off, rocking the car as Paul struggled to get out of it again before it was blown up with him inside.

In the street, Paul's eyes stung with smoke and the stink of gunpowder and cordite rushing up his nostrils. "Withdraw!" Paul heard someone shout in Polish, but he was already on his way to Darek, who was lying wounded on the ground. Machine-gun fire was deafening, and the chaos was compounded by the fog the weapons produced. Bending down, he gripped Darek's shoulders and began to drag him along the ground toward the Mercedes behind him.

"Get in the car!" Kurt shouted as he yanked Paul's hand off Darek and pushed him roughly into the vehicle. Seconds later, Darek was being thrown in beside Paul, as though he weighed the same as a sack of bread.

Paul, panting for breath, lay across Darek's bloodied body as bullets continued to spray the air. He raised his head as Kurt got in, started the engine, and drove off, hitting a German soldier blocking their path. Then the car slowed, the front passenger door opened, and a Polish Scout jumped in, with Kurt driving off before the car door had closed.

Gunfire struck the back window, smashing its glass into various-sized shards that left small, stinging cuts on Paul's head.

"Stay down, Paul!" Kurt shouted, as the car swerved and screeched around a tight corner.

Minutes felt like hours to Paul in the back, unable to see or hear anything but the bright flashes and deafening noise of deadly weapons. With his face pressing against Darek's shoulder, he imagined a violent car chase and then being caught and executed on the spot. Out of the ten combat fighters, he'd seen three go down, but he had not seen any dead bodies apart from Krüger's and his driver's. He had no idea where they were or whether Darek's injuries were life-threatening. Petrified to move, unwilling to see the danger or to confront death in the face, he covered his head with his hands and prayed.

"See to Darek, Paul!" Kurt shouted.

At last, Paul came to his senses. He looked out of the window, saw no German soldiers running along the road after them or other cars chasing them, and he became the doctor Darek was counting on.

When he'd ripped open Darek's shirt, popping all its buttons, he gasped. "Kurt, we need more than the first aid I can give. We need a hospital surgeon or another doctor to transfuse and suture his wounds – now! If not, he won't make it!"

****** 

Kurt contacted doctors in the vicinity known to defy the Germans and assist the Polish Underground, but after five vain attempts to gain access to the physicians on his list, he and his passengers abandoned the city and headed to the prearranged rendezvous site in the woods where they'd slept the previous night.

Five others, including Wójcik, had also made it *home* using one car. In their frantic bid to escape, the men had been unable to get to two of their wounded comrades lying on the ground or to reach the third car. But Wójcik *had* managed to carry a third wounded man and put him in the car's trunk.

"Where is Szymon?" Kurt's Polish passenger asked Wójcik after the latter had explained what had happened.

"I managed to get a local doctor from my list to take him. He'd lost a lot of blood. I don't know if he'll survive."

"And the men we left behind?"

"Dead or captured," Wójcik spat. "If the Gestapo or SS have them, they'll die anyway…"

"But they might talk about us during torture," the man pointed out.

"What if they do talk? All Poles are wanted men whether we behave like angels or kill like demons. We'll have to change our identities and the location of our base again like we always do."

Paul, who'd been trying to deal with Darek's wound, lifted his head and shouted to the men, "I need light, your torches and your medical supplies. All of them."

The bullet had entered Darek's right upper quadrant, but there was no exit wound. Paul had stemmed the bleeding as best he could in the car, but he was more worried about what was going on inside the chest. "Hurry up!" he shouted again.

"Lekarz ... Paul, don't let me die. I like you ... better than ... your brother," Darek panted.

"I'll do my best." Paul, who had been putting direct pressure on the wound using a ripped piece of Darek's shirt as a pad, now removed it from the injury site and looked properly under the light from a battery torch that young Bogdan held.

Darek lay on a tarp. He was suffering from shortness of breath, his lips were blue-tinged, and he was becoming drowsy, sweating heavily through shock and confused. The chest wound was bubbling blood with each inspiration and expiration.

"Will he live?" Wójcik asked.

"I don't know," Paul answered truthfully. "He's losing blood, and air is being sucked into the thoracic cavity through the chest wall instead of into the lungs through the airways, which will collapse the lung into a pneumothorax. In layman's terms, he won't be able to breathe. And he has a bullet in him."

Paul went into the medical case that Romek had given him. The standard tools doctors needed to, hopefully, save lives in the field of battle were in it. One of the other men also brought his medical rucksack from the other car, along with bottles of sterile water. He also had a small sack of coals; one of the few commodities in Poland that was easy to come by.

"This is a fight against time. I only have a chance of saving him if you two work quickly and obey my instructions," Paul told the two Scouts assisting him. "Light the fire, Bogdan, and keep it going as hot as you can … get that bicycle pump I saw in the boot of the car, pump air through that onto the fire like a bellows at the smithy." Then he spoke to Andrzej, the other lad. "You hand me my instruments as I command and keep this light steady on Darek's wound."

Paul spread the contents of both bags onto the clean ground sheeting that he'd laid out next to Darek. He sighed with relief when he saw the metal case with the nine-centimetre-long, large-bore needle he'd been looking for. He had never done this chest procedure himself but had observed Hubert do it once in Hospital number 4 on a man who'd also been shot by a German patrol and had survived. Although he had to work fast, he needed to take great care that the needle was not angled toward the mediastinum to avoid injuring any of the mediastinal structures like the heart, trachea or oesophagus with their major nerves and blood vessels.

"More light here," he demanded, as he began to insert the needle between the second and third intercostal space at the midclavicular line, just above the superior aspect of the third rib. He paused, and satisfied with the insertion, shouted, "Silence, everyone!" Then under torchlight and in the quiet, he heard the rush of air leaving the bullet hole and saw some bubbling blood seepage as the contents of the damaged thoracic cavity started to drain.

"We can't stay here," Kurt told Paul.

"Darek's survived this long, and while he's unconscious, let me try to get the bullet out of him before you write him off."

"Yes," Wójcik agreed. "You will have the time you need, Doctor. He's too valuable to us to leave in the back of a car to die. Do what you must to save his life."

At Paul's insistence, Wójcik, Kurt, and the three other men left Paul and his two assistants to deal with Darek.

Kurt drank greedily from a flask of water, then rinsed Darek's blood off his shaking hands. "How many Germans did we kill?" he asked the other men with him.

"We got our target, and that's what's important," Wójcik said.

"One less Gestapo chief to worry about. This is a great coup for us," Kurt agreed.

"We must have killed at least six soldiers and policemen, but we would have got even more had Bogdan not fumbled like an idiot with the case of grenades," a man with a cut on his arm said with an angry shake of his head.

The case carrying a dozen grenades had been sitting on the Triumph's bonnet. "Don't blame the lad, Albin. The lock on the case was defective." Wójcik grew serious. "They will hit us hard for this."

"We will take the pain," one of the other Poles said. "Killing the man known as *the sadist of Łódź* is a great victory for us. We are telling the Nazi scum that no German commander is safe on Polish soil. We will have their SS, military, and Gestapo leaders so afraid they will run back to Germany claiming their nerves are shattered."

Paul had organised Bogdan and Andrzej, the latter of whom couldn't stop shaking. Andrzej was passing Paul the medical instruments on command while Bogdan was heating the tip of a pair of Spencer Wells forceps in the fire. Paul was not optimistic. He'd given Darek a little morphine to ease the worst of the pain, but he couldn't afford to depress his respiratory system further as his breathing was already shallow and his pulse dangerously weak.

Paul used the sterile water to wash the wound site and saw two large blood vessels, which he clamped with two pairs of forceps. Then he cauterised the smallest seeping vessels.

Distracted by groaning, he looked up to see Andrzej swaying on his knees beside him, the torch waving like a flag in his hand. Any minute now, he was going to fall flat on his face in a faint. "See to the fire, keep it as hot as you can," he hissed at the grey-faced boy. "Bogdan, get over here."

After the first smaller blood vessels were cauterised and seemed to seal the bleeding, Paul then used the finest catgut available to sew the biggest bleeding vessels and tie them off. As he released the forceps, he saw the absence of blood. It was working. "Good ... good," he mumbled, but then he looked at Darek's face.

Bogdan tugged Paul's rolled up sleeve. "*Lekarz* – Doctor – I think he is dead."

Paul, so intent on doing things right, of making every step the correct one, of remembering everything from his training, had not thought to check Darek's breathing. He had died in his deep, painless, morphine-induced sleep. Seconds ... a moment

… five minutes earlier? Time had been blurred by Paul's frantic attempts to save him.

When a blood-soaked Paul joined the group, he was unable to look at the expectant faces, and instead, focused his eyes on the ground. "I'm sorry. I couldn't save him. I tied off the arteries, but the bullet was in too deep, and he'd already lost too much blood. I managed to cauterise the small vessels with…"

"Paul – Paul – we know you tried your best," Kurt interrupted him.

Wójcik displayed his anger by banging his fist on the car's roof. "Bastards … bastard cowards! I *planned* for medical evacuations. I bribed doctors in four different districts to treat our men in the event of injuries. I had a list of houses where Jewish doctors were hiding with false documents that *we* arranged for them, but our Polish practitioners are too cowardly to put their lives on the line for those of us who are trying to free them." Anger, hurt and tension were palpable as the men approached Darek's body.

"We will bury Darek here, and then we'll dump the cars and go our separate ways," Wójcik said, breaking the strained atmosphere.

Later, the men stood over Darek's crude grave where Paul reflected on his treatment regimen, step by step, second by second. *Maybe Darek had been a dead man the moment he was hit? Maybe Darek lasting several hours after being shot had been a miracle? Maybe no one could have saved him? Maybe* I'm *not a good enough doctor? What the hell did it matter?* Paul screamed the questions in his head.

After one of the men said a prayer in Polish, Paul kicked away his self-centred thoughts to make room for his anger.

"Had a hospital or doctor with a proper table and organised sterile instruments accepted Darek, he'd have had a better chance of coming out of surgery alive, instead of dying in a wood, under crude lighting, and inadequate medical instruments."

"We have already discussed that," Kurt said.

"Wójcik, can I have a word with you before you go?" Paul asked the leader as the men headed to their cars.

"Doctor?"

"You've seen what happened here. May I request that your men steal better medical equipment? If you are going to conduct operations like this using multiple men, you should have proper combat medicine in the field of battle – or at the least, a safe house in which to operate."

"Paul, we've already talked about that," Kurt repeated.

The men stared in silence at Paul as the depth of his rage surfaced. "I'd like to go on more of these missions with you. I want to be on hand with my medical kit *and* a gun. I might have shot the man before he shot Darek this morning. I can do much more than sitting in a farmhouse in the middle of nowhere or in a forest waiting to be called out."

"Paul? You're not a killer. When you take a man's life, you never get it back. It is gone … a part of you is gone, too. Don't do this to yourself," Kurt said, his low tone laced with regret.

"Do what? I *liked* seeing Manfred Krüger die in front of me, but I am fuming that we lost Darek, so don't tell me who or what I am, Kurt. I'm done being passive. I'm as committed to this unit as any other man here." Paul looked back at the grave. "Darek gave me a rifle, yet I wasn't allowed to carry it this morning. I want in on these operations, and I want my fucking gun back!"

Wójcik nodded. "We'll be glad to have you, Doctor. I will speak to Romek."

# *Chapter Thirty-Eight*

## Max Vogel

*Algiers, Algeria,*
*July 1943*

Max drew his already damp white handkerchief across his perspiring brow, wet hairline, and the back of his neck. The offices of the Allied Forces Headquarters in Algiers were hotter than one of those saunas he'd tried whilst on a mission to Finland before the war began, and it was only 0900 hours.

He looked out of the window at the clear blue Mediterranean Sea. The docks were busy; ships in harbour were loading American soldiers and Axis prisoners after unloading incoming supplies and reservists. The building Max watched from was situated high on the hill above the sparkling blue sweep of the Bay of Algiers with panoramic views over whitewashed colonial palaces and palm-treed gardens. It was beautiful from this vantage.

Below him were the not-so-picturesque streets where urchins and thieves resided. Arabs and Algerian French swarmed markets under the watchful eyes of the extremely tall and thin fez-wearing Senegalese troops equipped with huge hobnailed boots. They often kicked their fellow Muslims without provocation or grounds for punishment.

Since his arrival, Max had noted that the French were happy to – no – *wanted* to shake the hands of British and

American soldiers. The Berbers, on the other hand, were more interested in profiting from the Allies' presence. He thought it strange that the French called this city the jewel of the Mediterranean, for most of it reminded him of Cairo at its dirtiest and smelliest. He hated Algiers and Tunis, and he was tired of the constant need to take cold baths.

"Major Vogel, the colonel will see you now."

Max turned from the window, nodded to the white-faced corporal, and then followed him into the passageway leading to the hub of operations. One could always tell the difference between new recruits and veterans by the colour of their skin and whites of their eyes.

Office doors and windows were open all along the corridor, and ceiling fans swirling above the desks were silent in comparison to the noise of men and women in uniform typing furiously. The fighting was over in North Africa, but not the arduous task of keeping track of whether British soldiers who had fought the battles were dead or alive.

Colonel Harold Hepiner, known as *Harry* by his officer colleagues, greeted Max with a handwave to the visitors' chair in front of the desk. "Major Vogel … you still here? I thought you chaps would be gone by now."

"As long as there are German and Italian prisoners in North Africa, I'm stuck here, I'm afraid." He'd been in Tunisia and then Algeria for almost four months. After the guns had grown silent, he'd spent his days and nights interrogating high-ranking German officers, including German Afrika Korps commander, Generalleutnant von Arnim. Now, he was going to do something for himself, off the books, and without permission. Oh, he knew his chances of finding Wilmot alive and in Algiers were miniscule, but his parents would never forgive him if he didn't try every trick up his sleeve to get answers. He was not a man to disappoint his mother.

Harry lifted the lid off an Arabic copper box sitting on the desk and offered Max a cigarette. "Help yourself."

"Thank you, sir," Max said, taking one while observing the colonel searching his drawer for something or other. Harry, a younger man than Max, had shot up the ranks with two battlefield promotions. He had strong Mediterranean features and skin as dark as the natives. He was an extrovert who smiled often, drank a lot of whisky, sang well, and frequently escorted not one but two European ladies to functions at the St. George Hotel. Most of the British officers Harry socialised with thought he had a beguiling air of self-confidence, but Max saw a rather arrogant fellow who could be annoyingly vocal with his personal opinions. Even so, he had paid in blood for the privilege of being an arsehole at times, and for holding the rank of colonel. He'd lost a hand at El Alamein and had shrapnel embedded in his face, dangerously close to his right eye. It was an unsightly scar, but women found the man irresistible.

After striking a match against the Swan Vestas box, Harry proffered it toward Max to light his cigarette and grumbled, "Damn shame about this heat, what?"

Max inhaled, blew out the smoke and sat back in the hardback chair with ornately carved wooden arms. *Sitting right underneath the ceiling fan is a joy, and Harry has nothing to complain about,* he thought. "Colonel, I won't beat around the bush, I'm here to ask a personal favour."

"I see; and here's me thinking this was a social call. I do hope it won't take up much of my time, old chap. I'm swamped with one crisis or another. Those damn Yanks are making things bloody difficult around here, that's all I can say."

"Yes, well, when the Americans are in town, they tend to take over through sheer numbers and raucous voices. What are they up to now?" Max asked out of politeness.

"They're competing with us for Arab labourers on the docks. The blasted cheek! They're offering the locals double the British daily wage, and the greedy wogs are deserting us en masse. They have a lot to learn, the Yanks. Doubling the rate won't make the locals work harder, it'll mean they'll work one day and sleep in the sun the next. I'll be glad to see the back of the bloody clueless – babes in the wood, if you ask me – Americans."

Max, nodding and agreeing with the man because he wanted something from him, neglected to say that without the Americans, they might not be in a fancy office with a fan in Algiers but would probably still be fighting in the desert where Harry would find whisky and women in short supply.

"About the favour, sir?" Max tried again.

"Yes, of course, Max. What can I do for you?" Harry asked.

The colonel was the officer in charge of prisoner movements, and all prisoner records went through his office. He also liaised daily with his American counterpart, a Lieutenant Colonel Maddox, who had, thus far, refused Max access to his prisoners. Max had been astounded at the knock-back. American and British intelligence services usually worked well together, and Maddox, knowingly or unknowingly, had been unjustified in his decision to keep his prisoner records to himself.

"As you've probably guessed by my surname, I have a bit of German in me…" Max began.

"Really?"

"Yes. My father was a Berliner."

Harry laughed. "That's more than a bit, old chap. I'd say that was half. I take it your name is Maximilian?"

Max spread his lips to hide his irritation. Harry and other officers of all nationalities who'd socialised with him probably knew about his German heritage. He wasn't undercover or using a false name, and he was in uniform. It didn't matter one iota to anyone that he was part German, yet not one person had ever asked him to his face about where he came from in Germany or about the origins of his Vogel surname; they preferred to whisper about it behind his back.

"That's right. My name is Maximilian Dieter John Vogel … John being in honour of my British grandfather," Max said, quietly mocking Harry. "The thing is, Colonel, I have a brother, Wilmot. He got left behind in Germany when the war started, and like most men his age, was conscripted into the army. I found out a couple of months ago that he was serving in the Afrika Korps –"

"Good God, man, that must be a bit on the strange side for you, what with you interrogating the buggers," Harry interrupted with a gaping mouth.

"Yes. You'd be surprised by how many Germans with British citizenship left England to answer Hitler's call."

"No, I'm not surprised at all. Half the Afrika Korps officers speak the King's English better than the average Northerner." Harry puffed on his cigarette, looking intrigued by Max's admission. "Any other brothers serving in Germany's armed forces?"

"No, no more brothers." Max sat back again. He didn't have to mention Paul. Wilmot was all that mattered here.

"Fascinating. I'm dying to know more. This will make for good dinner conversation." Harry's eyes lit up, as though he'd had an astounding thought. "You must come to a party tomorrow night at the St. George's. It's being hosted by the new Governor General of Algeria – name of Georges Catroux – some sort of French liberation fighter, apparently."

"That sounds nice. I'll look forward to it. Now about my favour?"

Harry rolled his eyes and threw up his hands in an apology. "Yes, of course. I'm all ears."

*Thank God,* Max thought. "I've been trying to track down Wilmot. To be honest, I was hoping I'd find a record of his name on the prisoner lists I received while conducting my interrogations at the holding camps, but I've finished the job and come up empty."

"Hmm, I can't say I'm surprised. It must be like looking for a flea in a pepper pot. You do know we captured over a quarter million Axis soldiers in Tunisia alone?"

"Yes, sir, and about half that number are German –"

Again, the colonel interrupted, this time raising his hand to silence Max. "Old chap, this is a delicate subject … perhaps not one we should be having, but I must ask … do you have evidence your brother is alive? Like us, the Germans and Italians suffered massive casualties. Between the Americans and ourselves, there must be over a thousand Axis troops being treated at our field hospitals, and their dead are still lying in the Western Desert somewhere between Tunis and the railway hub at El Alemain."

Max let out a tired sigh. He'd exhausted himself with the question: *is Wilmot alive?* After going to every prisoner holding camp in the area, talking to Germans, either during interrogation or in a more casual way on his own time, he was at his wit's end. No one had heard of Lance Corporal Wilmot Vogel who might have served as a Panzer driver or even a cook in God knew what division, company, or platoon.

Dropping the *sir*, as he usually did with Harry when they socialised at the St George, Max finally answered, "Look, Harry, I know it's a long shot at best, but I promised my mother I would find my baby brother or learn what happened to him. You're right, I don't know if he's alive, but I do know I've exhausted every avenue on the British side. I don't think there's a German or Italian officer that my men and I have not questioned, and I ordered my men to ask about Wilmot. I must have spoken to thousands of German rank and file since the day the Axis troops surrendered. I've checked all the military hospitals and army medical posts, and I've watched hours of Pathe newsreels, shot from the end of May in Tunisia until today. My only option now is to leave this in the hands of my fellow British intelligence officers while I go to the Americans in an unofficial capacity. And I'm going to have to get a move on."

"Ah, Max, now there's your problem. The Yanks want to keep their administration of the American controlled prisoner camps separate from ours. They weren't happy that your chaps got to General von Arnim first, and they're not best pleased about having to accept tens of thousands of Germans on American soil. God knows what their civilians back home will make of having to receive sunburnt, battle-hardened veterans of Rommel's infamous Afrika Korps."

"They've already taken a hundred and fifty thousand off our hands," Max reminded the colonel. "Even before the North Africa invasion, Churchill convinced the U.S. Joint Chiefs of Staff to begin taking prisoners."

"I know the statistics, Max. I have them right here on my desk. The Americans understand we're unable to meet food and housing requirements set by the Geneva Convention for prisoners, and they, like us, don't want thousands of German POWs on Europe's soil. But it doesn't mean they're happy about the situation. They certainly won't want a British Intelligence Officer waltzing into their domain and asking to see the name of every prisoner they have. Hmm, yes, this is most unusual – I don't know what else to say to you."

In a coded transmission, Heller had informed Max of Churchill's recent trip to Washington. It was, in principle, to talk about the planned Italian Campaign, Heller said, but he'd added that the Prime Minister had shared the passenger ship, the *Queen Mary,* with several thousand Axis Prisoners of War. The United States was wholly unprepared to deal with enemy soldiers on this scale, and it was understandable. Their nation was gearing up its war industry and training troops, and officials had to figure out how to house, feed, and secure incoming POWs in a timely fashion.

Max now played his last few cards by pouring compliments on Harry. The man lived to be the centre of attention. "You've handled our prisoner situation admirably, Colonel. Your records are impeccable, and, I'm betting, much more comprehensive than those of the Americans who are handling the bulk of the Axis forces. There's not a more popular figure in Algiers than you, and I'm guessing you know everyone who's anyone on the American side. You could get me inside their camps. They respect you."

"Are you still living in the officer's mess on HMNB *HMS Hannibal?*" the colonel asked, looking quite proud of himself at the effusive acclamation.

"I am."

"All right. Let me make a couple of telephone calls. I'll contact you at the base if I have something. I can't promise anything, Max, but I'll do my best for you."

"Thank you, sir." Max stood, saluted, then left, praying that Harry wouldn't procrastinate on this. Prisoners were already being shipped to the Port of Oran, where they were to be housed in tents surrounded by barbed wire until the United States and Britain were ready to take them. The bulk of the Axis troops were to be shipped across the Atlantic on cargo ships that had brought troops and equipment from America for the eventual invasion of Europe. After unloading their cargoes in Britain, many of these ships, dubbed Liberty Ships, had been earmarked to either return empty to the United States or carry wounded American soldiers. He'd already had the heads up that the vessels were on their way to Oran. He was running out of time in his search for Wilmot.

# Chapter Thirty-Nine

## Max Vogel

*London, England*
*4 September 1943*

A heavy downpour accompanied by a strong wind met Max as soon as he'd climbed the last step leading from Piccadilly Circus Underground Station to the street. He ran to the nearest doorway; a closed fish and chip café, already sheltering an elderly man from the rain and wind that was turning umbrellas inside out.

The white-haired, balding man wore a raincoat two sizes too big for him, drowning his frame and giving him a frail, vulnerable appearance. Not so frail, however, when he poked Max in the back to get attention. "They should call this a *sidepour* instead of a downpour. Bleedin' wind and rain together set my headaches off every time," he complained.

After the oppressive heat of North Africa, Max was enjoying the crisp cold air, its sting on his desert-lashed face, the wet streets, and the sound of heavy rain. He turned his head and grinned at the man. "There's nothing like a good drop of rain on the face to freshen up a person."

"Where've you been, Son?"

"The desert," Max answered.

"Ah, I know all about that place," the man raised himself to his full height. "I was in the Boer War, end of '99. Bit more south than where you lot were fighting. Well done out there, boy … cheered me up no end when you got that nuisance Rommel out of Africa."

Max breathed deeply, and London's ubiquitous aromas crept up his nostrils: petrol fumes from the trams, buses and trolleybuses, manure and sodden grass from Regent's Park, wet animal smells from Regent's Park Zoo, and even the somewhat obnoxious odours coming from an overflowing bin at the edge of the pavement; all gave him a sense of being home, with all things familiar.

"That bloody stink of old fish and chip paper, still smelling of fat and vinegar, puts you off fish and chips for life, don't it, Son?" The elderly man pointed to the bin and shook his head in disapproval. "I came across the river from Battersea to treat meself 'ere today. This place used to 'ave the best 'addock and chips in all of London … s'ppose they've closed today 'cos they can't get the fish as regular nowadays … bloody war takes the fun out of living, don't it?"

"That's true," Max nodded, as he poked his head into the street and lifted his face. The rain was still heavy, and the sky was slate-grey with not a white or blue patch in it, but he'd be there all day if he didn't make a move. He looked at the old man's disappointed face, went into his pocket and brought out five shillings. "There's a nice restaurant around the next corner on the left. You have a good day. Mind how you go." He smiled as he gave the pensioner the money.

When he arrived at Piccadilly's Regent Palace Hotel, Max went straight to the restaurant where Jonathan Heller was already seated at a table. Upon his return from North Africa the previous night, Max had been surprised to find the note in his post box at MI6 Headquarters. *Meet me tomorrow at 1300 at Regent Palace Hotel for a spot of lunch. Take the morning off.* Jonathan was buying him lunch, and in one of London's finest restaurants where much of the food was by far *off ration* and exclusively available to the wealthy. Something was wrong.

The two men shook hands. Max sat, and within seconds a waiter was asking him what he wanted to drink. "Scotch, if you have it," Max answered the stooped man who looked to be a stone's throw from his eightieth birthday.

"I must say, this is nice, Jonathan. What have I done to deserve this, apart from getting home alive?"

Heller shrugged. "I thought for once in our lives, we could have an out-of-office meeting. You've just got back and have your reports and debriefing to get through this afternoon. I wanted to give you some time to settle in before going to headquarters." Heller sipped his whisky, then coughed twice as he set it down.

*Shit. Bad news is coming,* Max predicted. After all their years working together, Max knew Heller's *tell* as well as he knew his own face in a shaving mirror. "This is not a social outing, then. What's going on, Jonathan?" he asked outright.

"That depends on what you call social. I aim to enjoy my lunch…" Heller was saved by the waiter who brought Max's drink.

"Can I take your order now?" the man asked, peering over his rimless glasses perched on the tip of his nose.

"I'm having the *Chaufroid de Volaille Yorkaise* – chicken and potatoes to us mere mortals," Heller said.

"I'll have the same," Max told the waiter, without taking his eyes off Heller.

After the waiter left, Max persisted, "Tell me … why are we here?"

"You're leaving the country at midnight, for France … Paris."

Max downed his whisky in one, swallowing the burn of the bitter news he'd heard with the whisky. It would be his last alcoholic drink today. No going to Bletchley this evening to see Judith, to take her out for a drink at the local pub where he'd hoped to book a room for a romantic night with her. No talking to his parents about Wilmot, or seeing his sister and godson, Jack, or hearing about the latest news from Frank and his cousins in Kent. *No bloody time for anything!*

"Are you serious? I've spent nearly six months away." Wracked with disappointment, he added, "Whatever this is … why me?"

Heller, annoyed by Max's terse question, retorted, "The agent I was supposed to use was killed in Paris yesterday. It's Mike Preston, Max."

"Christ … I'm sorry to hear that," Max said, shame replacing his earlier petulance. He and Mike had come up the ranks together, but they hadn't crossed paths in over two years.

"Does Linda know?"

"Yes. I sent a man around to Mike's house early this morning." Heller gripped his empty tumbler, and like Max, looked as though he wanted another. "Losing men never gets any easier, does it?"

When the waiter returned with plates shaking in his weak, old hands, Max stood and took them before gravy splashed over him. "Thank you," he said with a respectful tone.

After setting Heller's dinner plate in front of him, Max looked at his. The mushy green hill with three small chicken fillets strategically clinging to it, surrounded by fried onions and boiled potatoes separated by green leaves looking like soggy weeds, turned his stomach. He was no longer in the mood to eat after hearing that Mike was dead and he was going to France. "I don't care how much poking around the chef did to enhance the appearance of this food, it still looks inedible. I should have had spam in one of its many forms," Max said, then he apologised. "Sorry, Jonathan. I'm being an ass. Call it travel fatigue, war fatigue, whatever. I'm being an obnoxious prick. I appreciate the gesture of lunch."

"And, so you should. I'm personally paying for this."

Max tried to slow down the angry pulse banging against the side of his neck by drinking the tumbler of water the waiter had brought to accompany the whisky. "What can you tell me about the mission, apart from it's in France?" he finally asked.

"Nothing, at least not here and not now." Heller swept his eyes around the room, then added quietly, "Anthony Eden and Stuart Menzies will be at your briefing later today."

Max's level of interest rose tenfold, even as the volume of his voice fell. "The Foreign Minister and Chief of MI6 in the same room? Must be big."

"It is, but for now, eat your lunch and tell me about Wilmot. Your mother was hounding me for months for news, and when she found out you'd seen him on an American film reel after the surrender, she sent me a cake. I'm surprised she didn't write to you a dozen times while you were in Algiers."

Max rolled his eyes. "Oh, she did, but as usual, I replied with a rundown of my daily diet, how hot the weather was, and my assurances that I was well and not in *too much danger*."

Max stabbed his chicken and grumbled, "Damn it, Jonathan, I was so close to seeing Willie in person before he was shipped out. I missed him by hours." Max had been in constant touch with Heller, keeping him abreast of the information he'd picked up from German and Italian Staff Officers. Anticipating victory in North Africa in March, MI6 had been keen to get their hands on the most up-to-date intelligence before the Americans. Max had honed in on Rommel's successor, Generalleutnant von Arnim, practically stealing him away from American intelligence before they could get their paws on him. Even as Allies, they were in constant competition with one another, as Harry in Algiers had pointed out.

"It's a damn shame, Max. When you told me you'd seen Wilmot on an American Pathe newsreel and that you were heading to Oran on the coast, I thought you might manage to track him down."

Max chuckled to himself, "I was crying and laughing at the same time when I saw him. The camera was inches from his face. He was smiling into the lens as if he were deliberately mocking the Yanks, and then he gave the camera the middle finger. I'm surprised they didn't edit him out altogether – ach, that's my brother for you – always has to get the last word." Max grew serious. "To be honest, I got a bit of a shock when I saw his face. He was gaunt, black rings under his eyes, hair sticking in every direction from his head, and an ugly black scar from his outer nostril to his hairline. God knows what sort of hell he's been through…"

"Same hell as all soldiers – Allied or Axis. Was he always a strong supporter of the Third Reich?"

Max, taken off guard by the question, especially coming from Heller who should know better, retorted, "He's no fanatic, if that's what you're implying. If he were, the SS wouldn't have thrown him in the Dachau prison camp." Max apologised again. "Sorry, Jonathan. I had enough of having to defend my brother in Algiers. I told the Americans, and I'll tell you. Wilmot is a man who is – was – proud to serve his country. That's all."

To get over the uncomfortable silence that followed, Max and Heller tucked into their dinners.

Max, having controlled his emotions, then continued, "After finally seeing a list with Willie's name on it – he's a Staff Sergeant, apparently, which is probably why I didn't get the response I was looking for from other German prisoners – I presumed he was still a corporal…"

"Or they didn't want to tell you they knew him," Heller suggested while chewing a piece of chicken.

"Yes, there is that."

"How was the treatment of prisoners out there?" Heller asked.

"Good. No nonsense, no war crimes to deal with, or gratuitous executions on either side. Field Marshal Rommel adhered to the Geneva Convention, unlike the SS and Gestapo butchers in Europe. I tracked down some British Eighth Army soldiers who'd been captured by the Afrika Korps. They were at an abandoned Wehrmacht medical post near Bizerte. The men's wounds had been treated, and a German doctor and three corpsmen had remained with them even after their unit had left to surrender."

Heller stretched out his hand and patted Max's arm. "I know you're disappointed, Max, but Wilmot is alive and will probably be treated lawfully in an American Prisoner of War Camp. If I were your parents, I'd be glad he's going across the Atlantic. At least he doesn't have to face the prospect of fighting in Europe. His war is over, Max."

# *Chapter Forty*

Anthony Eden, the Foreign Secretary, and Stuart Menzies, the head of MI6, walked into the conference room together. Both men were accompanied by their secretaries, who attended presumably to take notes of the meeting. Max was not surprised so few people were present. The mission was evidently a huge deal, but it was also designated *top secret*.

The discussion began not with the subject of Max's impending mission to France but with Hitler's disasters at Stalingrad and the Allies' Italian Campaign. The Foreign Secretary was animated with an indelible smile on his lips that held firm even as he spoke; a rare sight for a politician nowadays.

"… Hitler's withdrawal from Kursk in July has forced the Germans to go on the defensive in Russia. The Red Army has already begun the liberation of Western Russia while in Italy, General Alexander's Fifteenth Army Group, headed by General Clark's Fifth Army and Montgomery's Eighth Army, is doing better than expected. Gentlemen, Herr Hitler is now fighting the war on two fronts, and I believe he will not be able to maintain his occupations in Western and Eastern Europe for much longer." Eden nodded to Stuart Menzies to continue.

"Despite our recent strategic disagreement with the Americans over whether to invade France now or stick with our policy to centre our operations in the Mediterranean, we have, I believe, reached a mutually approved plan."

Menzies poured water from a jug into his glass, but continued to talk as he did so, "Great Britain and America have committed most of our combined forces to an invasion of France early next year, but we are also fully involved together this year to take Italy off the table."

"Out of the conflict altogether?" Heller asked Menzies.

"That's the plan, Jonathan. Popular support in Italy for the war has been declining since Mussolini's arrest and imprisonment, and we believe we are now in position to remove Italy from Germany's clutches."

Menzies then addressed Max directly, bringing him into the conversation for the first time. "Major Vogel, yesterday, at an Allied military camp at Cassibile, Sicily, Brigadier-General Castellano of Italy met with General Eisenhower's Chief of Staff, General Bedell Smith. In the meeting, both generals signed an agreement, which stated that the Kingdom of Italy was surrendering to the Allies. This event was, and still is, top secret, and it won't become public knowledge in Italy for another four days when Italy's new Prime Minister Badoglio will make an official announcement to the Italian people."

Max was pleased but not astounded by the news; he'd seen and spoken to hundreds of demoralised Italian prisoners in Algeria and Tunisia. They'd been short on weapons, aircraft and men, and after constantly withdrawing from their defensive positions, their officers were utterly fed up with the whole thing. To hear today that one of the Axis countries had officially capitulated lifted his spirits no end. Now, the Allied Generals would seriously eye the European Continent and make their plans to invade with one great, consolidated force.

Eden continued, "We are assuming the man you are going to meet with in Paris will not yet know about yesterday's armistice agreement in Sicily. It will be your job to not only repeat to him what we are telling you today, but also to leave no doubt in his mind that we are gaining the upper hand in this war, period. You, Major, will also falsely inform the gentleman that General Eisenhower himself was present at the surrender, and accompanied by as much pomp and ceremony as you want to invent. He must get our version of the event and not Herr Goebbels' embellished list of reasons as to why this is not a catastrophe for the German people."

"Yes, sir, of course." Max, intoxicated by Anthony Eden's enthusiastic response over Italy's momentous surrender to the Allies, felt his expensive dinner dancing in his digestive tract. This was a real breakthrough – a pivotal development that would change the dynamics of the war – a game-changer.

Although eager to know the name of the man he was to meet with in Paris, Max was savvy enough to bite his tongue. Heller had once told him, 'One must wait for announcements from a member of His Majesty's government. Mere mortals should not steal their leaders' thunder.' Max glanced at Heller for a clue, but in return got a glare, saying, *don't ask me.*

For another half an hour, the men continued to speak about Mussolini's demise and their ambitions for Italy's new role in the war, but then to Max's relief, they turned their thoughts to France.

"Max, before Mike Preston was killed, he and his team had prepped for this meeting tomorrow in Paris," Menzies said. "I'm sorry you're being thrown in at the deep end, but arrangements have been made and we cannot afford to miss an opportunity to speak to such a high-ranking German official."

*For God's sake, say the name,* Max thought, as he nodded dutifully.

"You were the obvious choice," Menzies added.

"I presume if I'm the obvious choice, I'll be dealing with a German-speaking man?" Max dared to say."

Anthony Eden smiled. "Correct. The German in question is Admiral Wilhelm Canaris."

Max looked at each man in turn, his mouth gaping open, his tongue suddenly covered in cotton, his brain frazzled. "Canaris … the head of the Abwehr?" he finally managed to stutter. "Sorry for my surprise, but I never imagined…"

"Good," Heller said, interrupting Max. "No one is supposed to imagine he could be playing both sides."

Max, stunned to hear that the man in question was Stuart Menzies' nemesis in Germany, stared at the file that Heller had pushed towards him. The photograph of the white-haired man in his fifties, wearing the uniform of the German *Kriegsmarine* with his rank of admiral clearly visible on his shoulder epaulettes, was one he had seen many times both before and during the war.

Even before Hitler's invasion of Poland, Canaris was known as an inveterate nationalist who had been quoted as saying numerous times; 'I feel that Adolf Hitler's party is much better than anything that has gone before.' As far back as the Brownshirts' demise and their leader's assassination in the *Röhm putsch,* Canaris had preached for wholehearted cooperation with the new regime.

As he scrolled down the page, Max came to a telling paragraph that had encompassed MI6's view of the Abwehr chief. In it, Canaris was again appealing to the German military to support Hitler. Max raised his head to his superiors, who had sat in silence as he'd read excerpts from the documents. "I've been studying Admiral Canaris for years.

He was quoted many times, appealing to the military to recognise the Führer. I'm hardly surprised by anything nowadays, but this is quite the revelation."

"Your shock is understandable, Major. It's hard to conceive that the man who first suggested the use of the Star of David to identify Jews is an anti-Nazi, British Intelligence asset, is it not?" Anthony Eden said with a victorious smirk.

"Not quite an asset, sir," Menzies contradicted Eden like a gentle schoolmistress. "Canaris turned from Hitler because he believed from the outset that Germany was going to lose another major conflict. We must remember that whatever he says or does, it is for Germany's benefit, not ours."

"Yes, quite … quite right," the Foreign Secretary graciously agreed.

"Whatever his game is, he wants the Führer gone," Menzies continued, "and that's good enough for Winston Churchill, who's taken a personal interest in these meetings with Canaris."

Now that Max knew who he was going to meet, he needed every bit of information on Canaris he could get his hands on. "Do we know when and what turned the admiral towards our side?" he asked Menzies.

"Mike Preston first met Canaris in Spain in '41. Apparently, the admiral became concerned about the direction Hitler was taking when he voiced his intention to absorb Czechoslovakia," Menzies answered.

Heller added, "It goes further back than that. In 1938, Admiral Canaris sent his emissary, Ewald von Kleist-Schmenzin, to London to secretly discuss the situation with MI6 and some of our politicians. I was present at the meeting where Kleist informed us that Canaris and other unnamed

German military and government officials were planning to capture and unseat Hitler and the entire Nazi Party before the invasion of Czechoslovakia began. And unsuccessful as those ambitions were, we suspect that Canaris is still as supportive of overthrowing Hitler today as he was five years ago."

Max, forgetting the esteemed men sitting at the table with him, mused, "Call me a sceptic, but I recall a certain mission to Holland to meet with German anti-Hitler generals, and instead of sharing a plot, we lost two of our best agents, who are to this day, as far as we know, still being held in a German prison camp."

"Jonathan, give the Major the *other* file on Canaris," Menzies said, then addressed Max. "In those pages, you will find our assessment of Canaris' integrity as a British collaborator and records of every meeting he had with Mike Preston. You'll find it interesting reading."

Max took the file and asked," Did the admiral ask for this meeting, or did we?"

"He did. Now, let's get down to the nitty-gritty, shall we?"

******

After Eden and Menzies left, Heller and Max discussed other matters. Marjory brought tea, but for the first time in over a year, she apologised for not having sugar. "I'd have thought one of you boys could pinch some sugar on your travels," she said, teasing Max.

"That will be all, Marjory," Heller said good-humouredly.

Heller, looking like a man who was bursting to share a secret, lit his one cigar for the day and relaxed into his chair.

"Well, now that we've got that over with, I can tell you what's to become of you when you get back."

"I'm coming straight back, then?" Relief washed away the strain on Max's face. He'd been worried sick that he'd be ordered to remain in France in Mike Preston's place.

"If all goes well, you should be back here within the week." Heller puffed on his cigar, the secretive smile still playing on his lips. "In preparation for the eventual Allied invasion of France, our Secret Intelligence Service is collaborating with American and Free French allies to create special teams of agents. The programme, codenamed, *Sussex,* will begin next week at an undisclosed location. You will be on the first course with two other officers. The second course will begin in September with a further ten officers."

Max was interested, for two reasons; firstly, Heller had mentioned an Allied invasion of France, which could mean a shortening of the war. Secondly, the course was being held in Britain, meaning he'd probably get some free time to spend with Judith.

"What's the idea behind *Sussex?*" Max asked, after lighting a cigarette.

"Agents, men, women, or mixed, working in pairs will be dropped behind enemy lines to provide front-line intelligence after our allied landings on the continent. I wouldn't look so damned happy about this, Max. This is Menzies' baby and he personally asked for you. Once you're out there, you won't get back."

Max gave Heller a careless shrug. "I'm glad we're thinking about taking this war to the next level. I sometimes think we're getting too bloody comfortable with the status quo in Europe. I'm for kicking the Germans all the way back to Berlin as soon as possible, aren't you?"

"Damn right, I am." Heller handed Max an envelope. "Your orders and your objectives. Make sure you destroy what's in there before you leave the building."

Heller rose and pushed his chair back. "I hope you understand now why I ordered you not to tell Judith or your family you were coming back yesterday?"

Max had been disappointed, but he agreed with Heller's thinking, "I do, sir, and given the secrecy surrounding this mission, I think it's best if I was never here. See you when I get back. I'll bring sugar for Marjory."

# Chapter Forty-One

RAF Tempsford in Bedfordshire had been designed to look like an ordinary working farm. Used by 161 Squadron, it was the main base of operations for SOE and agents from other intelligence sections conducting top secret missions on the continent.

Upon Max's arrival at the base, he reported to Tangmere Cottage, situated opposite the main entrance. After signing in, he was taken to a local hotel where he spent an hour and a half in a bedroom, lying on top of the bed and thinking about this and that, and going around in circles until his nerves were shattered.

For a while, he tried to anchor his thoughts with Judith, but instead, they returned to the mission. He'd been involved in a lot of dangerous and significant operations since 1938, but this one would probably define his war, his career. Wilhelm Canaris was not just another foreign agent, or a German officer claiming to be anti-Hitler and against the policies of the Third Reich; he was someone who had the power to end this war with a single blow against the Führer. Canaris' file was a comprehensive record of small but pivotal acts in favour of the Allies and against his own leader; however, it also contained contradictions, such as his discordant acts of killing civilians and executing Allied soldiers.

The admiral was not the first high-ranking German officer to make overtures to MI6, but in this case, the British Foreign Secretary and Stuart Menzies believed in Canaris' desire to oust the Führer and were willing to throw all their resources at the admiral in pursuit of their shared goal.

'The admiral wants to talk,' Stuart Menzies had said. That was all he could tell Max about the purpose of the meeting.

*Admiral Canaris wants to talk,* Max repeated to himself, and for the first time in memory, he questioned whether he was up to the job.

When the call came, Max was ferried to the *Gibraltar Farm,* the nickname for the cluster of farm buildings within the airfield's perimeter track. He and one other man, a French SOE agent who had been a pilot in the French Armée de l'Air, stood in the hangar going through the final briefing with the captain of the Westland Lysander Mk III aircraft. Max recognised the pilot. He was involved in the Carpetbagger project, which had been created to fly *special operations,* to deliver supplies to Resistance groups in enemy-occupied countries, to deliver personnel called *JOEs* to the field, including SOE and MI6 agents, and occasionally to extract personnel from the field.

He'd been the pilot of the plane that had carried Darek and Max back to England on the night Paul had run from the airfield near Dieppe, and by the look on the Scotsman's face, it was clear he also remembered that night.

"Oh aye, so it's you again? I hope you're in a better mood tonight than you were the last time I saw you. You had a few prime words to say that night, didn't you, sonny boy?" the pilot said, nodding in remembrance.

"I'm in a much better mood today, Captain," Max told the man. "I apologise for my bad language. It was a difficult mission."

"Aye, you lost a man if I remember correctly. Bet you got a bollocking for that when you got back home, eh? Och, it happens to the best of us. Right then – let's get started, shall we? We've got a nice night for it. Perfect skies, a full moon, and no strong headwinds to worry about."

After the pilot went through the flight plan with the SOE agent who had selected the French airfield, he said, "As usual, we'll face the risk of German night fighters on our flight path. If the sky's good for us, it'll be good for them too. Aye, you can guarantee they'll be out tonight. You will sit in the rear cockpit," he informed Max. And to the Frenchman, "You will be in a pannier underneath the storage area in the fuselage. What are we carrying?"

"Wireless equipment and four crates of weapons."

"Fine. When we land, I'll be picking up a downed airman, so get off this plane as fast as you can and stay out of my way." Then the pilot gave the men his obligatory warnings. "Remember, if we're met by Gestapo instead of the Resistance, keep the bastards busy while I get my Lizzy back in the air. This is an expensive piece of machinery, and my life is much more valuable than yours."

*He's probably right*, Max thought. Pilots, especially for missions like these, were in high demand. He liked the Scotsman. He was earthy, and his banter was evidently helping to keep the French SOE agent's nerves at bay. The young man had looked terrified when he'd walked into the briefing room. Max recalled his first time going into France and being dropped off, not knowing if friend or foe would be on the airstrip to greet him.

Once Max was issued with his firearm, a small Beretta 418 with a 25 ACP cartridge, he went through the contents of his rucksack. At MI6 Headquarters, he'd gone to the clothing department where he'd been issued a suit, two white shirts, two ties, and a fedora hat. He'd also been given a soft, brown leather briefcase in which were a selection of fake Swiss watches.

MI6 and SOE were inventive when it came to their outfits for male and female agents. They were aware of national and regional differences in fashion, and since 1940, they'd either sourced outfits, shoes, and suitcases from second-hand shops or bought them from refugees who'd fled Continental Europe for the British Isles.

Max recalled a fitting he'd had with a French seamstress. She'd told him, "We get our shirts from refugees, and we take them apart to check the shape of the collar and the stitching on the seams. You would be surprised to know, Major, that something as simple as the stitching on a seam will advertise to the keen eye whether a garment is British or French, Dutch or German."

Max's favourite seamstress, who'd outfitted him numerous times, had remarked a few months earlier that European stocks were depleted, and MI6 and SOE had been manufacturing their own *authentic* continental clothing and luggage to outfit their agents for over a year. She'd gone on to say they were using clothing companies owned by refugees, who were already well-versed in the sewing styles of their native lands. He hoped his suit and shirts wouldn't be too wrinkled by the time he reached Central Paris. Strange to be thinking about clothes at a time like this, but better that triviality than thinking about being shot out of the sky or shot on the ground by Germans.

As he boarded the waiting aircraft, Max's nerves stretched taut. An agent should be on the ground in France, waiting for the aircraft's arrival. He or she would guide the pilot in with either a bonfire or bicycle lights or storm lamps. The pilot had to spot the minimal ground signals, but he also needed to navigate by visible landmarks in the moonlight to correct dead reckoning. 'Any man who says he's not afraid on these flights is a liar,' Max had assured the Frenchman before they'd boarded.

After the aircraft landed on a narrow airstrip about fifteen kilometres from the Paris suburbs, Max was escorted in a farm truck by two members of the Paris French Resistance, who had worked in tandem with the dead Mike Preston. When they reached a more populated area, the men continued the journey on foot to the Port of Gennevilliers, which was situated about six kilometres from Paris. There, Max spent what remained of the night on a Resistance-owned river barge that was hauling building materials.

The following morning, Max dressed in his Rolf Fischer outfit and armed with a briefcase of watches and his Swiss identity papers made his way to the safe house in the centre of Paris, first by barge and then using the Paris Metro system.

Max's two-man team were already in the safe house, situated near Notre Dame in the *Place des Vosges.* Trained in Britain, the Frenchmen had been members of Mike Preston's team and were still shaken by his death.

"What happened to Major Preston?" Max asked in French before the men began to discuss the forthcoming operation.

"He got caught in crossfire near a checkpoint in the street behind the Cathedral. The SS were chasing Jews, and the major got hit. He was in the wrong place at the wrong time, nothing more. A freak accident – *ça schlingue!* It stinks, but that's what happened."

"And his body?"

"They threw it on the back of a truck along with three dead Jews. We don't know where they took him, or what identity papers he'd been carrying on his person."

With Mike's unfortunate death still on his mind, Max was taken through the plan for the impending meeting with the Abwehr chief. Mike had put it in place the day before he died, and the two agents were clear on their joint purpose and the identity of the man they were escorting to the prearranged meeting place.

"Admiral Canaris will be in a Wehrmacht-licenced staff car displaying the serial numbers of the Abwehr," one of the men informed Max. "Jacque, our British agent, will be driving him. He is a man Canaris has met before, and he will explain to the admiral that Mike is no longer in the picture. He will also vouch for you, Major, before Canaris thinks about calling off the meeting."

The other Frenchman took over and pointed to a map of Paris, laid out on the table. "Jacque will park the car in this narrow, one-way traffic street near the river. We will arrive before the admiral to check the area and make sure we are not being tailed."

"I will get in the back of the vehicle with Canaris. The vehicle should have darkened windows, so I will blindfold him," the first Frenchman to speak, said.

The other man continued, "And I will arrive at the meeting place first, to watch for suspicious activity in the area."

"Good, and where will I be?" Max asked, still studying the map.

"You, Major, will make your way to the Convent of the Nuns of the Passion of our Blessed Lord on Rue de la Santé and wait for us there. The Mother Superior is expecting Mike's successor, so please identify yourself by giving her this note."

Max unfolded the piece of paper and read the one line: 'In God we trust,' it said – short, simple, and probably a predetermined code that one of the men had given her. "She will recognise this?" Max wanted to confirm the note's validity.

"Yes. This and only this will get you inside."

"She has been working with us for over two years. She was fond of Major Preston," the first Frenchman added.

Max arrived at the convent without incident. It was a glorious day. French people were going about their business. German soldiers were, as usual, behaving like tourists; taking photographs with cameras attached to leather straps hanging around their necks whilst slouching on hard-backed café chairs with glasses of wine or beer in their hands. In a more sinister fashion, German SS squads were also driving and walking in the streets and going into shops and cafés, presumably to check identity papers. Since November 1942, the whole of France had come under direct German control, apart from a small sector occupied by Italy. Mass deportations of Jews had begun around the same time, but even now the Germans were hunting them down. Paris, as wonderfully picturesque as always, felt like a place untouched by war, apart from the insidious presence of the occupying army.

Whilst waiting, Max got comfortable in one of the two armchairs in front of the fireplace in the Mother Superior's private sitting room. He was going into this meeting blind, but he was experienced enough to know that patience would be critical.

He was also awed by the German who was, hopefully, going to arrive any minute. Despite Canaris being MI6's direct opponent, he was also someone whom many at headquarters respected. To admire one's enemy was not necessarily a conflict of interest, Max believed. Wilhelm Canaris had had a stunning military record that went back to 1905, long before many current SIS agents had even been born. Indeed, Canaris' heroic exploits in the Great War were obligatory reading for trainee officers at *spy school.*

At the age of seventeen, the admiral joined the Imperial Navy, and by the outbreak of the First World War in 1914 was serving as an intelligence officer on board the *SMS Dresden.* It was the only warship that had managed to evade the Royal Navy for a prolonged period during the Battle of the Falkland Islands in December 1914, and it was primarily due to Canaris' skilful evasion tactics…

Jerked from his thoughts when the door opened, Max leapt to his feet and stood to attention when one of the French agents ushered the blindfolded Wilhelm Canaris to the second armchair and seated him. Max, his pulse dancing in his neck, said, "Remove the blindfold." Then he sat opposite the admiral.

One of the French agents brought in fresh coffee in a green and white floral coffeepot with matching milk jug, full of milk, and two matching cups and saucers. He left immediately without saying a word or acknowledging the German, dressed in his civilian clothes.

Max remained silent whilst Canaris grew accustomed to the room's brightness. The other MI6 agent sat in a chair beside the door. He was not there to participate but to confirm Max's account of what was said during the meeting to MI6 in London.

Canaris' innocent round eyes settled on Max. Both men, looking like two fighting cocks weighing up their opponent before a battle to the death, remained reticent until Max broke the silence in German.

"Coffee, General?" Max offered.

"Thank you," Canaris said, without taking his eyes off Max's face.

After they both had their cups filled, Max offered Canaris a cigarette from his silver cigarette case. Canaris accepted but lit it with his own lighter.

*He looks much older than he does in MI6's most recent photograph of him*, Max thought. His hair was whiter, his pallid complexion more wrinkled, especially around the mouth where it turned down at the edges. "What message would you like me to convey to my government, Admiral?" Max asked.

"Straight to the point. I like that," Canaris answered as he lifted his china cup to his lips. "Tell me, what do you know about me?" he asked, after sipping his coffee and replacing the cup on its saucer.

"I know you are a respected admiral in the Kriegsmarine. You are also the head of the German Abwehr Secret Service. You are a man of deep principles, and you have a strong sense of duty. You are not an ardent follower of Adolf Hitler, yet you do his bidding both in Germany and in the occupied territories where you have killed hundreds … thousands of people."

Max, willing his hand not to shake, took a sip of coffee before continuing; his mouth was as dry as the desert sand he'd left. "Despite the deaths of civilians at your hands, Admiral, I also believe you are not an inherently bad man, but rather someone who must pose as a trusted friend to the Führer in order to survive whilst trying to bring down his regime."

"What else have you heard?" Canaris asked, looking impressed by Max's candid impressions.

"September 1942, you allowed a train with five transport wagons to make its way to Auschwitz with nine hundred Jews, most of whom were from Holland. At the same time, you paid for train tickets from Berlin to the Swiss border, for twelve Jewish men, women and children who were carrying falsified identity papers that you provided. Upon being questioned in Switzerland by MI6, the men and women stated unequivocally that they owed their lives to you, Admiral. I also know that you have given vulnerable people token training as Abwehr agents and then issued papers allowing them to leave Germany, which makes you, in my eyes, a paradox of good and evil."

Canaris' eyes widened in surprise at the mention of evil, but Max had decided before the meeting began to be honest. He was not there to smother the man in compliments but to have a deep, meaningful conversation. Why else would both men be taking such risks, if not to open a discussion seeking a way to end the war?

"I ask myself every day if I am a good man or an evil one without redemption," Canaris said after a long pause, during which both men had filled the silence with yet more coffee drinking. "I fear I will never know the answer to that question.

When the Führer wanted to invade Czechoslovakia, I went as far as to arm shock troops to be used to arrest him when the time came. That plan came to nought. Then your Neville Chamberlain came, and my close associates and I believed Germany would take the road to peace."

"As we all hoped," Max said.

"Yes, as we all hoped." Canaris sighed, as though with a distasteful memory, "I complained to my superior when the first synagogues fell in Berlin, and the future for the Jews looked bleak, but nothing came of my protests. I protested again in 1939 when I saw the sickening destruction of Warsaw and the mass graves being dug for *undesirables,* so you see the pattern? I was becoming an annoying fly in the Reich's ear, and to carry on ... to survive in a position from where I could do some good, I had to temper my ... disillusionment with the Nazi Party with an apparent willingness to carry out the Führer's policies. Exactly as you perceived."

Canaris leant in towards Max across the small glass table that separated them. "If my circle of friends and I could find a way to get rid of Adolf Hitler in a violent coup, what terms for peace would Germany receive in return? You must take this question to Winston Churchill on my behalf. It is my reason for being here."

Max held his lips in a tight line, but Canaris reiterated what he'd said.

"My similarly-minded colleagues and I believe this is the only way to end the war, but should we succeed in killing the Führer, we would want *good* terms for peace."

"Then, that is the message I will convey to my Prime Minister, Admiral," Max said, knowing damn well that

Winston Churchill's answer would be, *nothing but unconditional surrender.*

Max, mindful of the time and that he still had to get out of France the same way he'd got in, wondered what else Canaris wanted to say. What he had already said could have been sent to London in a coded transmission; *why had Canaris wanted to meet in person?*

Canaris twisted in his chair to look at the French agent. Then he turned back to Max. "I would like five minutes alone with you."

"You can speak freely in front of my colleague, Admiral," Max responded with a nod to the Frenchman.

Canaris shook his head, "Ah, but I don't think you would like that."

Max was intrigued. "Wait outside," he instructed the French agent.

When they were alone, Max asked, "What can I do for you, sir?"

"You can tell me … did your father kill my Abwehr agent, Captain August Leitner?" Canaris asked, then grew quiet, his eyes watchful.

Robbed of speech, Max stared like a torpid fool at Canaris' expectant face. Unable to come up with a single retort of denial or an honest answer that would not have dire consequences for his family in the future, he clawed his mind for a response. For the first time in his career, his ability to smooth talk and tell plausible lies had abandoned him.

"Come now, don't be shy – you are Major Max Vogel, are you not?" Canaris, clearly enjoying himself, asked.

*Honesty,* Max reminded himself. He couldn't lie his way out of this one; Canaris was too bloody important, and he already *knew* the truth. "Let's say I am Major Max Vogel, Admiral. Why would my father have anything to do with an Abwehr agent? If you knew him, you'd know that Dieter Vogel was a businessman who cared for money, not politics or military matters. You must also know he's dead?"

Canaris smiled, and undeterred, said, "Yes, but at the time, your father was alive and the last person to see August Leitner before his unfortunate accident." Canaris then shocked Max with a deep-throated chuckle. "I sent Captain Leitner on Operation Brandenburg. I have a thick file on every member of your family. I have looked at your photograph, and that of your brother Paul many times. And I have long suspected your father of murdering Leitner to protect your doctor brother who has recently deserted the army and his country."

"My brother – a deserter? No..."

"Major, we are both sitting here together and conspiring to kill Adolf Hitler. Perhaps you can appease my curiosity, hmm?" Canaris cocked his head to one side, observing Max's reddened face and eyes that couldn't quite hide their fear. "Had I wanted to, I would have arrested Dieter Vogel before he ... *died,*" Canaris finally said. "Tell me ... did your father kill Hauptmann Leitner?"

"No, he did not, sir," Max answered, and it was the truth.

After the two men had parted company, Max remained glued to the armchair. It was hard to take in, to believe that his cover and position had finally been burnt. *Mirror* was smashed to pieces, and Rolf Fischer was dead in the water.

He could imagine Heller's reaction, and it wasn't going to be pretty. *You cannot operate for MI6 if the head of the damned Abwehr knows who you are. Christ's sake, Max, you're finished here. I've lost you to that bloody SOE again!*

*Jana Petken*

# Chapter Forty-Two

## Freddie Biermann

*Berlin November 1943*

Freddie Biermann looked at his dinner plate and grimaced in disgust. The cooked rice mashed into patties and fried in mutton fat had been okay the first few times he'd eaten it, but the *ersatz meat,* as it was commonly called, was beginning to turn his delicate stomach. "This again, dear?" he asked Olga, who passed him a slice of her homemade bread, made with ground horse-chestnuts, pea meal, potato meal, and barley. He looked at it and shook his head. "Have we nothing else?"

"No, Freddie, we have nothing else, and neither does anyone else in our situation," Olga replied sharply.

Valentina, looking thin and pale, pushed her fork into the rice patty and moaned, "If only you could get your old job back, Papa. Frau Hoffmann, who works with me at the donations for Russia depot, says her husband gets extra meat rations because he's in the Gestapo."

"I won't have that man's name mentioned at my table, Valentina," Biermann frowned at her.

"Try not to be insensitive, darling. He stole your father's job, remember," Olga reminded her daughter.

With his wife and daughter watching him, Biermann dug his fork into the patty, lifted it to his mouth, and then shoved the rice in as if it were torture. He looked at Olga's expectant face and swallowed without a scowl. "Nice, darling," he repented to keep the peace.

With tears in her eyes, Valentina broke off a piece of crusty bread. *She looks sad all the time,* Biermann thought, giving her a tender smile. "Eat up, Valentina. You work too hard at the Reich Security Offices. You should stop volunteering at that donations place on your day off. Let the army look after its soldiers. That's what they get paid for."

"I don't mind. I'd rather help there than work in Prinz-Albrecht-Strasse."

"Someone has to bring a little extra money into this family," Olga rebuked her daughter again. "If it weren't for the little extra bits and pieces *you* get from Ernst Kaltenbrunner's offices, we'd be starving."

"We're not starving." Biermann chewed another mouthful of the disgusting food he was eating. No point arguing with his wife or Valentina about the rotten conditions in Berlin. 'Things are as they are,' he'd pointed out on many occasions. He'd allowed Valentina to go back to work not because she got extra scraps from the SS, but so she could find a good, loyal man who supported Nazism and the policies of the Third Reich; someone who would make her forget her disastrous marriage to that traitor, Vogel.

Sometimes he thought she still loved Paul Vogel. Since her divorce, which he had obtained for her using dubious but effective means with the help of a good lawyer and forged signatures, she'd rarely spoken about the deserter. But Biermann had caught her once or twice looking at a photograph of her wedding day. She kept it in her purse along with photos of Erika.

"It's about time you found yourself a nice officer – SS, perhaps. Herr Himmler looks after his men, especially those serving under him at the Reich offices," Biermann told Valentina.

Valentina frowned. "All the typists say it's not the same there since Reinhard Heydrich's assassination in Prague. Everyone is miserable."

"He was a good man," Olga said, although she'd never met Heydrich.

"Did you know he flew nearly one hundred combat missions for the Luftwaffe?" Biermann asked.

"Yes, Papa. Is it true he once had to make an emergency landing in Russia behind enemy lines when his aircraft was hit by Soviet anti-aircraft fire?"

"Yes, although he never admitted it happened. Ach, Ernst Kaltenbrunner will never fill Heydrich's shoes ... no one will."

Valentina set her knife and fork neatly together on her plate, then gave her father an inquisitive look. "Papa, did they ever find out who killed Manfred Krüger? I liked him. I could have seen myself with a man like that."

"Tragic ... despicable," Olga said shaking her head.

"They probably won't find the men who killed him," Biermann said. "Still, plenty of Poles will have paid with their lives for the murder. Manfred won't get justice, but at least his family will know we punished the people who supported their son's assassins."

"I don't understand those Poles, Freddie," Olga said. "Bad men kill and then they let their countrymen pay the price while they hide like rats. They're such cowards."

Biermann, still furious about Krüger's assassination in the streets of Łódź, made his feelings known. "It is inconceivable that a man surrounded by Gestapo officers and Orpos could have been gunned down in the open like that. It's the Kriminalassistents who were with him that should be shot. It wouldn't have happened to me. I'd have been much more careful."

"Oh, Freddie, please, don't talk like that. I can't bear to even think of you being shot by those criminals. Thank God, we left that place when we did," Olga said.

Valentina went to fetch Erika, who was crying in her cot in the next room. When she returned, she handed the seventeen-month-old to Olga. "I hate night shifts. I can't remember the last time I picked her up when she woke up in the morning."

"Look at her," Freddie mused with pride. "The perfect blonde, blue-eyed Aryan. At least, Vogel did that right."

Long after Olga had retired for the night with Erika and Valentina had left for work in the offices of the *SS-Obergruppenführer und General der Waffen-SS*, Biermann retrieved the envelope he had received earlier that day from the sideboard drawer. He hadn't shown it to Olga or his daughter. He saw no need for them to know that Wilmot Vogel was in America in a prisoner-of-war camp.

He pulled out the one-page letter from inside the outer envelope; another envelope, addressed to Oberarzt Paul Vogel, was also inside, still sealed. He read Wilmot's letter for the second time:

*Dear Kriminaldirektor Biermann,*

*I am in the United States of America as a prisoner of war. I was captured in North Africa and will now spend the remainder of the conflict in captivity, far from my family.*

*I have not sent a letter to my mother, as I don't know where she is. I have, however, enclosed one here for my brother Paul. You have been so very kind to me, but I wonder if you could do me yet another favour and pass on this letter to him in Poland.*

*I do hope your health continues to improve. Please give my love to your family and to my niece, Erika.*

*Yours faithfully,*

*Wilmot Vogel*

Biermann ripped open the other envelope that had already been censored by American and German officials and taped closed numerous times, by the looks of it. *What did it matter?* Paul Vogel, the traitor, would never see its contents anyway.

The long letter had been redacted in numerous places, but there was still plenty of reading left. Biermann looked at the slightly ajar living room door and got up, wheezing as he walked to it. After shutting it, he poured himself a small, illicit brandy, then sat in his armchair once again to read Wilmot's letter.

*My dearest brother,*

*Still nothing. No letters, no news, no hope left that you will write to me. Are you even still alive, Paul? Is Max, Mother, Hannah? If not, these words will go nowhere. They will have been written like the many thousands of other words penned to you, my family, but never sent. Maybe I just like writing – maybe I should keep a diary or journal in which I can air my love and thoughts for you all – perhaps I no longer fill your thoughts, Paul, and you are done with me?*

*My war is over. I survived Russia and then the bleached desert of North Africa. I fought a good fight in both those lands, Paul, but I am now beaten, finished, and will spend the remainder of this war in a far-off land across the Atlantic Ocean.*

*It's not so bad, you know. The Americans bear no resemblance to my sadistic Russian captors; they are firm but fair. They do not shoot us like dogs nor starve us until we are bones covered in skin pitted by the scars of war. I suppose I must say that I am one of the lucky people who ended his fighting days with both body and mind intact. Always the optimist, eh?*

*I was brought to America by ship. I was afraid, Paul, not for my life as a prisoner, but of being on a ship that could be sunk by our own U-Boats. It was a strange notion and one I shared with the other thousand or so POWs on that ship. I swear, I hardly slept during that two-week long voyage.*

*We arrived in New York on a Sunday evening, and I will never forget the moment when the American guards pulled the porthole shades up as the ship passed the Statue of Liberty. It was an unbelievable sight. The shore was full of people. They were almost dancing and looking bright and fresh, as though the war had not touched them at all.*

*Most of the prisoners on the ship were seriously wounded, and they received excellent medical treatment as far as I could tell. I was uninjured, but I've had my fair share of wounds. Maybe one day, I can show you my scars.*

*It took several days to get from New York to the town of ... I am sorry, I cannot tell you where I am, only that it rises high on the plains of the Midwest and has a spartan environment – large swathes of land, the likes of which I have never seen – fields that go on forever without a house in sight to blemish the tranquillity it brings to one's often chaotic thoughts and memories of burning buildings and cities wallowing in dust.*

*When we arrived at the town near to the camp, its inhabitants waved and cheered on the American guards marching us in file down their main street. It was an almost friendly atmosphere. Unlike the last time I was taken captive, I did not get pelted with projectiles, spat upon, nor insulted for being German. Despite all that had happened, I was proud to be a Feldwebel Wachtmeister – staff sergeant, in the Afrika Korps.*

*The food is good, Paul. The barracks are not too uncomfortable – fifty beds in a long hut of which there are three hundred in total. We have a canteen hall where we can even buy American beer at 15cents a bottle and other things like cigarettes, razors for shaving, soap, combs, and sometimes American candy, although chocolate is not on offer often. We get 80 cents a day and this covers our purchases in the canteen.*

*I work on a wheat and corn farm. It is over 200 acres in size. A man could get lost easily it is so big. The farmer has three daughters. I like the youngest one, Dorothy – she likes to be called Dottie – she is a nurse in the camp hospital. Of course, I like her only in my dreams, for I can never forget that I am a prisoner; the enemy of the American people.*

*I have much more to tell you, brother, but I fear it would be censored both here and in Germany, so those thoughts and observations will have to wait until we are reunited.*

*Herr Kriminaldirektor Biermann will, hopefully, pass this letter to you. I'm certain he is as kind to you as he has been to me.*

*Take care, Paul.*

*Your loving brother,*

*Wilmot*

Biermann ripped the three-page letter into tiny pieces, furious as he thought about Paul Vogel's betrayal and resenting Wilmot Vogel's apparent contentment, or as near as damn it. He laboured to his feet. His breathlessness always worsened when he was angry or upset – Christ, what life did he have when he couldn't even vent his emotions for fear of his heart stopping or exploding in his chest – *what sort of life was this for any man?*

He tossed the fragments of Wilmot's personal writings into the dying coal fire, watching the pieces fall like snowdrops onto the red embers. Mindful of Olga finding the brandy-smelling glass, he took it to the kitchen and rinsed it out before replacing it in the cabinet. He was too exhausted to go up the stairs to bed. He'd sleep on the couch wrapped in the blanket Olga had knitted for him. He slept there quite often these days.

Tucked in, he sighed with tiredness but also with anticipation. It was his birthday the following day; one he thought he'd never see. The ladies of the house had something nice up their sleeves for him. Valentina had the day and night off, and although they hadn't mentioned his big day, he knew his wife and daughter well; they were planning something.

*Jana Petken*

# Chapter Forty-Three

Biermann held onto the railing and had to stop every so often to catch his breath. It had been a while since he'd walked down these stairs to the newly named Victory Club, and he was determined to make a dignified entrance. People were going to see the old Freddie; the Kriminaldirektor, not the sick, elderly man he had become. He wasn't going to allow anyone to pity him or catch him labouring for breath, not whilst blood still flowed in his veins. His friends and ex-colleagues were on the other side of the double doors, and when they opened, he'd hear shouts of, "Surprise!" and he was going to stride in, head held high.

As the doors opened, a veritable sea of uniformed and civilian-clothed men and women clapped their hands. The drummer on the bandstand gave Biermann a dramatic drumroll as lights flicked on and off, heralding his arrival. He halted, genuinely surprised to see the number of people who'd made the effort to attend his fifty-fourth birthday party. He hadn't been forgotten after all; he was still a force to be reckoned with in Berlin – the indomitable Fredrich Biermann. His tight smile cracked, and people applauded more raucously as an embarrassed, authentically happy grin replaced it.

Tired after shaking hands with SS officers, Gestapo, and Orpo ex-colleagues, Biermann finally sat at a table for eight whilst other guests took their seats at adjoining tables. His eyes swept the room again, and this time he took more notice of who was there. He waved to his ex-subordinates from the Gestapo office, his secretary, who'd brought her husband along, his fellow officers from the SS floor and their wives; even Martin Bormann's two aides, his old drinking partners, had come despite their heavy workload. The womanising Major Hess, who had drafted Wilmot to North Africa, unsurprisingly, was nowhere in sight.

Two Gestapo officers from Department E – security and counterintelligence – shared the Biermanns' table. The men had brought their wives. They were acquainted with Valentina, for they worked with her on the charitable donations committee. Alfred Hoffmann, the Kriminaldirektor who'd stolen Biermann's job, as the latter viewed it, was in full uniform; *he's ramming his position down my throat,* Biermann thought as the man took his seat opposite. The pup had risen in the ranks quickly by succeeding others who'd been posted to occupied countries and concentration camps, *not* because he was good at his job. He was sloppy – everyone knew it – but no one cared about skill and ethics nowadays. It was all about quantity and speed, not quality.

Biermann threw his daughter a surreptitiously disapproving glare, which she failed to see. She should have asked him beforehand to choose his dining companions. The trouble with surprise parties was that people often got the most important details wrong through thoughtlessness.

"Papa, this is the Frau Hoffmann I've been telling you about. We work together at the donations depot."

"Nice to meet you, Frau Hoffmann. My daughter speaks highly of you," Biermann said, his *charming face* back on.

"And my wife speaks highly of your Valentina, Freddie. You don't mind if I call you Freddie?" Alfred Hoffmann butted in.

"No, I don't mind at all," Biermann lied.

Hoffmann gave Valentina a sickly-sweet smile and a compliment to boot. "It's kind of you to give what little spare time you have to the *Volunteers for Russia*. You're looking beautiful tonight, my dear." Then he asked Biermann, "And how are you enjoying your retirement, Freddie?"

Biermann, still inwardly fuming at his daughter's tactless choice of table companions, managed to maintain the smile on his face long enough to reply to his successor's question, "I don't like it at all. I had a few more good years left in me as far as I'm concerned. How are you enjoying my office?"

Hoffmann sat across from Biermann at the round table. He raised his full water glass and took a sip as if he wanted to ponder the question before giving his answer. "It has its ups and downs like all jobs, I suppose. To be honest, I'd rather be playing a more active role. My place is in the streets or keeping order in our prison camps. I've never been happy sitting behind a desk. They should have kept you on, Freddie. You were the master organiser."

Biermann chuckled at the praise, mollified more than he would ever admit. He warmed marginally towards Alfred Hoffmann. *Perhaps he wasn't such a bad fellow after all.* "I agree, but I was sacrificed for a younger, fitter man. Ach, I suppose I should be thankful for what I've got."

Waiters went to every table, setting bottles of champagne, wine, and jugs of beer and water on the crisp white tablecloths which would be stained with spilt drinks by the end of the night. Then the hostesses began collecting ration stamps from the diners. Biermann panicked. *How much was this going to cost him? Did he have enough stamps? Did anyone?*

He'd not set foot in the Einstein Club, as it had previously been called, since his return from Poland. 'Going to a nightclub will be too much for you, Freddie,' Olga had suggested. Yes, such an outing would tax his weak heart, leave his lungs gasping for breath when he exerted himself, and make his legs as fragile as a new-born foal's; yet, here he was, out and about, witnessing the humiliating war-wrought changes to his city, and what taxed him most was whether he had enough to pay for the three of them. It was ... unbearable.

On his way to the club, he'd been dismayed to see that living conditions for the ordinary Berliner had deteriorated. Display shelves in shop windows were mostly bare. There were fewer trams on the road, more underground shelters were being opened, and now this, having to hand over colour-coded stamps to get food and sundries in a restaurant that charged a fortune for menu items and boasted mediocre service to add insult to injury. Even the wealthy were suffering, he presumed, although he was confident the powerful and well-connected would continue to get whatever their hearts desired, one way or another.

He glanced around the room. His guests were looking happy enough, but he was a good Gestapo officer; one of the best – maybe *the* best Germany had ever had. Since walking into the club, he'd seen through the jolly, relaxed atmosphere to the tension beneath. The war was not panning out as the Reich had predicted, and every Hitler supporter in this room agreed with that assessment. *How do I know this?* Biermann mused. *Simple; everyone else is thinking the same treacherous thoughts as I am.*

German occupation across Europe was at its height, and apart from a few skirmishes in Poland against its criminal element, the Fatherland was succeeding in its plans to get rid of European Jews, some ethnic factions, and other indigenous peoples to make way for hard-working Germans. But they had lost North Africa and their Italian Allies, and behind Goebbels' optimistic tone was a whispering wave of uneasiness over the news from the Eastern Front and Stalingrad in particular. *We're not winning. We are holding on,* Biermann truly believed.

"Do we have enough ration stamps for all this?" Biermann quietly asked Valentina when an attractive young woman came to collect the stamps from his table.

"We've all had to get used to the hardships," Hoffmann said, apparently lip-reading Biermann's concerns from across the table, "but you mustn't worry about money or stamps tonight. We've banded together for your birthday..." He leant towards Biermann and whispered, "Ernst Kaltenbrunner himself contributed," before resuming his normal tone. "We all think very highly of you, Freddie. In fact, I wanted to talk to you about work. Maybe tomorrow..."

"Now ... now will be fine, Alfred," Biermann stuttered with excitement.

Hoffmann gave the girl his and his wife's stamps, then told Biermann, "I will have to get your security clearance back, but if I can, and I believe I can, I'd like you to handle some administration jobs for me from home. Every day, I'm losing personnel to the SS authority dealing with the growing number of concentration camps, and I don't have time to go through the paperwork that piles up on my desk. I don't want to give it to my grunts. They don't understand what it is to be meticulous, even when they're given a somewhat tedious job. You understand, don't you, Freddie? Have a think about it and let me know by the end of the evening."

Biermann's heart skipped a beat, but it was a pleasant murmur for a change. Hoffmann couldn't handle the job. *Ha, I knew it,* he thought. "I don't need to think about it, Alfred. If you can get me cleared, I'd be honoured to help you out, whatever the task at hand is."

Olga allowed Freddie a small glass of something that was far too sweet and dark to be called Champagne but pleasant enough, regardless of being a poor imitation. The band was now playing smooth background music that would ramp up later and get people on the dance floor, and Biermann was happier than he'd been in a long time. *Good things come to good people,* he decided, grinning at everyone who raised their glass to him. This was the best birthday present a man could hope for; his pride and dignity back after he had thought them lost.

Biermann began to relax after he'd eaten a decent meal starting with eggs with a creamy Mornay sauce and followed by chicken and potatoes. During the evening, toasts had been made, and kind things had been said about him and to him. The accolades reminded him of how much he missed his career and the social aspects that went with it. He was going to enjoy himself tonight, for Olga and Valentina's sake, and after tonight, he was going to turn the page and become the man he'd been before this sad, self-pitying shell of a person had taken over.

When the band played one of the most popular songs around, *Berlin bleibt doch Berlin – Berlin is still Berlin,* Valentina danced with a rather handsome SS Hauptmann. Biermann looked on with pride. His daughter was radiant. She was the most beautiful woman in the room, leaving even the attractive female singer in the shadows. He was indeed a proud father.

A hostess came to the table offering cigars. Biermann took one but held it between his fingers for only a few seconds before Olga snatched it from him.

"Now, Freddie, you know what the doctor said," she reminded him before giving it back to the woman.

To hide his embarrassment, Biermann chuckled to Hoffmann, "Wives. What would we do without them, eh?" Then he changed the subject, "Tell me, Alfred, why did they get rid of the Einstein name for the club?"

"Because of Einstein's Jewish connections. The owner was persuaded to replace *Einstein* with a more appropriate name," Hoffman answered, then tapped the side of his nose as if to say, *it was my doing.*

"Aren't the Einstein family non-observant Ashkenazi Jews?" Biermann asked, already knowing the answer.

"I don't think they're religious at all," Hoffmann replied.

"I know Albert attended a Catholic elementary school in Munich – I met him a couple of times."

"I don't know why the club was called *The Einstein* to begin with," Siegfried, the Gestapo Kriminalinspektor also at their table, joined the conversation, "Einstein renounced his German citizenship in 1896 and took Swiss citizenship in 1901. Why should we name things after him? He didn't want anything to do with us, did he?"

"Where is he now?" Olga asked.

Hoffmann replied, "Some say he's in America. After he left Berlin's Prussian Academy of Sciences in '33, he left the country and hasn't returned since. I should know, eh?"

"Of course, you should, dear. You *are* head of the Gestapo, after all," Hoffmann's pretty, petite wife joked.

At eleven o'clock, Valentina and Olga suggested they leave. They'd eaten the birthday cake, everyone had sung *happy birthday* to Biermann, and the neighbour looking after Erika would be wanting to go home.

"I've got work in the morning, Papa," Valentina said.

Biermann was peeved. He didn't want the evening to end. He was exhausted but not yet ready to leave the company of men with whom he could hold a real conversation about the war and Berlin's latest intrigues and gossip. He'd missed these discussions with his peers.

Hoffmann spoke to Greta, his wife, who suggested to Olga and Valentina that they should share Hoffmann's car and driver with her.

"An excellent idea, Hoffmann agreed. "Let us men stay a while longer?"

"I'm not sure…" Olga hesitated.

The other women were also getting ready to leave, as were Martin Bormann's aides. Biermann hadn't had the chance to speak to them all night apart from a few pleasantries when he'd arrived. He urged them to stay a while longer, and they agreed, then he told Olga, "I'll be fine, *mein Chatz*. Let me have this night to remember."

"I'll bring him home in one piece," Hoffmann reiterated to Olga and Valentina, who placed her arm into her mother's crooked elbow and pulled her along, teasing her about her overprotectiveness.

Sixteen men joined Biermann by adding their tables to his. The band started to kick up a storm, and as if by magic, dancing girls appeared on stage, dressed in not much more than underwear. The atmosphere turned boisterous minutes after the ladies left, and Biermann, euphoric after one brandy too many, asked the waiter for another. "Now we can enjoy ourselves, eh?" he said, full of bravado.

Fifteen minutes later, a massive explosion at street level shook the ceiling's crystal chandeliers. Glasses on the tables vibrated, some tipping over, paintings fell off the walls, and the lights went out. Air-raid sirens wailed above ground, but then that familiar sound was smothered by more explosions that made the band's drum skins vibrate by themselves.

Biermann and his companions finally reacted as dust particles and plaster from the ceiling rained down on them with another fierce blast that almost blew the entrance doors off their hinges.

Hoffmann went to the stage and shouted as men were dusting themselves down. "This is no ordinary air raid. It's a full-blown attack," he gasped as if the realisation were coming to him as he was speaking the words. "*Mein Herren,* we're in one of the safest places in Berlin. We should remain here until the attack is over."

Another blast forced Hoffmann to jump off the stage and crawl beneath the nearest table where he joined the other men. Biermann, gasping for breath and unable to get to his feet or onto his knees, remained in his chair and put his hands over his ears as they popped from the pressure waves. As he listened to the club's walls grumble and groan under the increasing proximity, frequency, and severity of the bombs, he imagined his Berlin engulfed in flames. This was it. The massive attack the Führer and his cabinet said would never come.

Biermann, the only man not taking cover, grunted his hatred of the Allies. Weeks earlier, Joseph Goebbels, the Reich's master of propaganda, had called for *total war* in the *Berliner Sportpalast* newspaper. Well, it appeared he was getting what he wanted: the destruction that war brought was now on their doorstep.

As another bomb dropped, Biermann finally got down onto his knees and covered his head with his hands again. He and a few other men came out of hiding, however, when the doors were thrown open, and two SS drivers followed by one Gestapo chauffeur ran in to take cover.

"What's happening up there? How bad is it?"

The SS Hauptmann, a man Biermann had been fond of when he'd worked in Prinz-Albrecht-Strasse, checked his driver's wound. All three drivers were bloodied, having been caught by the blown-in window glass from their vehicles.

"Herr Hauptmann, we've shut the doors up top. There are fires everywhere," the shaking driver said while pressing a napkin against a cut on his hairline. His voice was quivering, almost inaudible at times, despite there being a lull in the bombing. "I think the whole city is on fire, sir. We ran for it when bombs took out the streets parallel to the club. We can't get out of here until they douse the flames and clear the rubble. It's a mess, sir, and if the fires spread, the top floor of this building will burn."

"We can walk out of here," Hoffmann said, as another Royal Air Force attack on the German capital began and brought down part of the ceiling.

# Chapter Forty-Four

At dawn, an hour after the last bomb had struck Berlin, Biermann and the other four remaining partygoers left the Victory Club. Most of the men, including members of the staff and entertainment group, had left at 0300 during a pause in the air assault. They'd believed it was over, but it was not, and the bombs continued to fall for several more hours. As Alfred Hoffman had noted earlier on the stage, this was unlike anything Berlin had ever seen.

At street level, Biermann, Alfred, and one of Martin Bormann's aides looked to commandeer transport to take them home. All three men were desperately worried about their wives who had left the club some twenty minutes before the first strike. Biermann and Hoffmann, aware that their wives and Valentina had left in the same car, discussed possible routes the driver might have taken. *Did he go east and drop off Frau Hoffmann first, as Biermann had suggested, or did he take Olga and Valentina west to their house and then carry on to the Hoffmann's home?* Speculating over this and that was agony, for the telephone lines were down, and only when the men reached home would they know if the women were safe.

The area was a mess, the street-level shop above the Victory Club a burned-out shell. Fires were still blazing from all directions, and the streets were littered with cement, bricks and rubble, which were already being cleared away by soldiers.

Biermann sat on the window ledge of the damaged clothes store next to the club's entrance while Hoffmann went in search of a driver and vehicle. 'I am a Kriminaldirektor,' he had growled three times to Biermann, 'and if I want a driver and car, or whatever drives with wheels, I will damn well get one. And if the worst comes to the worst, I'll get a horse and cart!'

When he eventually returned to Biermann half an hour later, it was in a Wehrmacht car bearing the registration number of the engineers and demolition branch and carrying a *Hauptmann der Pioniere* – engineer captain – and his driver.

"I've given the driver your address. He'll try to get you home first, Freddie, if the road is clear enough, of course," Hoffmann said after Biermann got in the car.

"That's kind of you, Alfred … I hope our houses are still standing. Hauptmann … driver … I appreciate this, very much."

"I will try my best, Herr Kriminaldirektor," the driver called out.

"I can't believe what I saw when I left you," Hoffman said, getting into the back seat beside Biermann. Then he spoke to the Hauptmann sitting next to the driver, "Tell Herr Kriminaldirektor Biermann what you've seen since you left your barracks."

"There's almost total devastation in some areas. The Tiergarten and Charlottenburg, Schöneberg and Spandau were all hit," the Hauptmann said, twisting in his seat to look at Biermann. "Fires from the explosions are still burning, and several firestorms have ignited. The *KaDeWe* department store took several direct hits, and an allied bomber crashed through its roof. Its entire upper floor is engulfed in flames. I got reports that the Kaiser Wilhelm Memorial Church is badly damaged, as well as the residential areas to the west of Tiergarten and Charlottenburg. I'm afraid our journey of a few kilometres may take quite some time."

"Hauptmann, do we have any idea how many casualties there are so far?" Biermann asked, trying to settle his breathing and the nauseous gurgling in the pit of his stomach.

"It is too early to know, but we have to assume it will be in the thousands, with hundreds of thousands made homeless … but they're estimates going on what we've seen."

"*Mein Gott* – dear God, no," Biermann moaned. "This is inconceivable."

The journey had taken hours, but at 1000, the army engineers' vehicle arrived at the bottom of Biermann's tree-lined street. The trees were not on fire, the houses were still standing, but the church and a row of shops were burning at the street's entrance, and rubble blocked the vehicle's way, as it had many times on the journey that had been painstakingly slow. The driver cut the engine. "I'm sorry, I can't go any further," he said.

"I'll walk you to your door, Freddie," Hoffmann said.

"I can manage, thank…" Biermann began, but then he relented and allowed Hoffmann to help him into his house, through his front-door frame devoid of glass.

When they entered. Biermann shouted up the stairs. The place was freezing and as quiet as the despair he felt. Both men stared at each other, thinking the same thing but afraid to say the words: Olga and Valentina were not at home, and neither was Frau Mayer, the neighbour who was babysitting Erika.

"I'm betting your Olga and Valentina are at my house," Hoffmann finally broke the tension between them. "They probably dropped Greta off first and then decided to stay there when they heard the aircraft."

Biermann let his tears fall; the worry and fear leaving his body with loud, gut-wrenching, panicking sobs. "We've gone through this scenario several times, but now that I'm home and they are not … I feel … I don't know…" Biermann then pulled himself together and apologised, "Go on, get yourself home to Greta. I'll wait for my Olga and Valentina to come back. Promise me, Alfred, if you hear something … anything, send news?"

"Herr Biermann, Frau Biermann!" a woman's voice shouted through the broken door. "It's me, Frau Mayer!"

Biermann sat in his armchair, done in, unable to exert himself further.

Hoffman went to the open door and returned with Frau Mayer, who carried Erika in her arms. "You're not alone now, Freddie," he said, his relief palpable. He nodded to Frau Mayer, then made his exit.

Frau Mayer burst out, "Mein Gott, I was worried…"

"Have you seen them?" Biermann asked, even though he knew it was a stupid question.

Frau Mayer looked confused. "No. Erika was with me all night. We spent most of it in our garden bomb shelter – God bless my husband for insisting we get in it. I was terrified, but this little thing didn't cry much at all. She was as quiet as my eldest granddaughter, and she's just turned seven. Where are Olga and Valentina?"

Biermann was inconsolable. Hoffmann had left, and he had no idea how he was going to look after Erika on his own until Olga and Valentina came home.

Frau Mayer was making them a drink, crying as she did so. When she brought it to Biermann along with his long-overdue medication, he took them off her with shaking hands.

"Please, can you take Erika across the street with you again, Frau Mayer? It's a lot to ask, I know, especially after the night you and your family have had, but I really don't feel well. To be honest, I can't see me coping, not today ... not until I know my wife and daughter are safe. Please ... I'd be grateful?"

She didn't want to. He noted her tired face and disappointment.

"Please, Frau Mayer. I might be able to do something for you one day," he said, stooping to begging.

Before she left with the baby, saying she'd be back that afternoon, Frau Mayer helped Biermann to the couch, and when he lay down, she covered him with a blanket.

Biermann instantly fell into a procession of nightmares that woke him up every few minutes. He could neither stay awake nor gain proper rest. Olga ... her dear face kept swimming in and out of his mind. His heartbeat was dangerously fast, the beat pounding in his head, yet he was also drowsy and light-headed, feeling sick and more scared than he'd ever felt in his life. He was as weak as a mewling kitten and helpless to act; that was the worst of it. *They will come home soon,* he kept telling himself. And when they did, they'd tell him of their close call with death, for they would not be unscathed. Then after the shock had died down, all three of them would thank God they were alive and well. *That's what will happen.*

At 1400 hours, the front door opened. Biermann, who was still drowsing on and off, had failed to hear the knocking. He struggled to sit up. Two Gestapo officers in civilian clothes, their fedoras in their hands, walked into the living room.

Biermann recognised both men. "Müller … Schmidt?" he stuttered.

"Herr Kriminaldirektor," Müller said. "We are very sorry, sir. Your wife and daughter died in the air attack, as did Kriminaldirektor Hoffmann's wife. Please accept our heartfelt condolences."

Biermann lay under the blanket and remained there long after the two messengers had left. For hours, he mouthed, "My Olga – my love. My Valentina – my little girl…" then, occasionally, he'd remember that Frau Hoffmann had also been killed, and mouth, "So very sorry."

Frau Mayer came with Erika and left again with the baby as soon as she heard the news. Biermann hoped she'd never come back with his grandchild. What good was he to her? *His Olga – his Valentina, his little girl – they were gone.* He was broken, never to be whole again. He could not conceive of the tragedy at all, for it was unimaginable that his wife and child had been taken from him forever. He did not deserve this horror.

"Mein Gott, why?"

# Part Three

*We fight today so that tomorrow men can be free to love whomever they choose, worship whatever Godly presence sustains them through their darkest days, and walk untethered by religious labels, badges, or racial stigma.*
*We fight so we can wake one day to a brighter dawn.*

Kurt Sommer
Warsaw, August 1944

# Chapter Forty-Five

## Wilmot Vogel

*POW Camp Concordia,*
*Cloud County, Kansas,*
*United States of America*
*20 April 1944*

After finishing his first woodwork project, Wilmot tidied his workspace, said goodbye to the American guard called Bill, and then left the hut known as the *Hobby Hall*. Apart from the time he'd made rough, crude spears from branches in the Russian forests, he had never carved anything. He was proud of himself. His twenty-centimetre tall horse, with tail and mane being the hardest parts to create, was ready to be painted. It would be black; Dottie's father had a black horse, she'd told him. Ah, Dottie ... he couldn't stop thinking about her.

It was a dry spring evening with a strong wind that brought wheat seeds across the plains and into Camp Concordia. Kansas, a state located almost dead centre of America, was flat and so vast that the fields seemed to go on ad infinitum. The change of scenery and his day job at Mr Barrett's farm made Wilmot feel he was more than just a prisoner of war. A guard waited beside Mr Barrett's truck each morning and accompanied the eight German labourers to and from the massive farmlands, which were situated two miles from the camp, but their presence was not threatening. Unlike the Russians, they didn't train their rifles on the prisoners but were more subtle in their approach, as if they were convinced no German would want to escape even if he found the opportunity. They were probably correct in most cases. With no money or identity papers, where would they run to? There was a big wide ocean between Camp Concordia and Germany, and he, like many other fellow prisoners, was glad he was out of the conflict. He already had enough nightmares to last a lifetime.

Wilmot loved the outdoors; being in a field without Kübelwagens, motorbikes, tanks, and rocket launchers was significant. Having no soldiers, machine guns, or aircraft overhead buzzing and dropping bombs every five minutes was more peaceful still. Being a prisoner of war in the hands of the Americans was not what he'd hoped for, but, in retrospect, it was a damn sight better than what he'd left behind in the desert.

His easy stroll back to his barracks halted when he reached the camp's hospital. She might be there – Dottie, the trim brunette with coquettish dimples and open, expressive face that lit up when she spoke – she had recently graduated nursing school but was already a supervisor in the POW camp's surgery department.

He had gone through a medical examination upon his arrival at Camp Concordia from New York. When he saw her, he'd thought her pretty, but when she opened her plump ruby-red lips to speak to him, she disintegrated his gloomy cocoon of defeat. 'Good morning, Staff Sergeant. How are you doin' today?' she'd asked him.

He also recalled a particularly glorious day at the farm when Dottie had been home from work. It was lunchtime, and Mrs Barrett asked Dottie to fetch a bucket of water from the well. He'd volunteered to carry it for her, and on their way back to the house, she had asked him, "Have you ever been in love, Willie?"

He was honest with her in his reply, as he was whenever he spoke with her. "Love is a phenomenon I've never dealt with before, Dottie. I'm not charming like my twin brothers. I don't have my sister's knack for captivating an audience when I speak, or my father's power of persuasion. I'm more reserved ... like my mother."

"But, Willie, I think you have all the qualities you've just mentioned."

He blushed. "Ach, I suppose what I lack in social graces, I more than make up for in my enthusiasm. And I am very enthusiastic about you, Dottie. I can hardly sleep at night for thinking about you. I can't explain this nervous fluttering and dizzy pleasure that warms me every time I see you. I think I might be in love."

She had beamed at him, as though his declaration had pleased her...

"Where are you going, Willie?" Egon, appearing from nowhere, asked

Startled from his dreamlike state, Wilmot retorted, "Where did you come from this time, Egon? Jesus Christ, it's like you're deliberately lying in wait for me behind some bush or wall. Have you got nothing better to do than jump out at me every five minutes?"

Other prisoners relentlessly teased the lad. "Look, it's Willie Vogel's shadow," they'd call. The loquacious Schütze with the concentration of a gnat worked in the mail sorting office for an hour or two a day and spent the rest of his time writing in his journal or wandering aimlessly around camp waiting for Wilmot to return from the farm.

The men's catcalls were not malicious. Most of them were protective and patient with Egon's idiosyncrasies. It was well known that the twenty-four-year-old was slow in the head. He lost track of time; sometimes, he had no memory of what he had done ten minutes earlier, yet he recalled his war in North Africa with startling clarity and spoke about it often, even when the topic was not welcomed.

The rumours said that he bore more physical scars than any other prisoner in the camp, and Wilmot believed that could be true. He'd seen Egon wounded many times over, shrugging off less-serious injuries as though they were scratches on his fingers. The man was a hero, although now he clung to Wilmot like a barnacle, reacted physically to loud noises, and often peed himself when he was scared or alone for any length of time. He was brain damaged, and for this there was no cure.

"I know I'm forgetful, Willie, but I can't remember where I'm supposed to be going half the time," Egon often said after he woke up in the mornings.

"Have you been for a walk?" Wilmot asked Egon now.

"No. I went to look for you in the Hobby Hut. I think we have to go to our barracks now."

Wilmot looked longingly at the hospital hut. If Dottie was on duty, he wanted to tell her he had a present for her. He studied Egon. He never knew if the lad were giving him real messages, or if he were retelling a message from days earlier.

"Are you certain we have to report to barracks now?" Wilmot asked again.

"It's the Führer's birthday, Willie."

"Oh, is that right?"

With Egon trailing behind him, Wilmot headed towards their hut, passing some of the three hundred or so other huts that made up much of Camp Concordia's one hundred fifty-eight acres. He'd been in captivity for six months, and during that time he'd learnt not to disobey orders or be late for lectures or spur-of-the-moment meetings such as this one. *Bad things happen to rebellious prisoners,* he thought, waving to the American guard who usually accompanied the prisoner farm labourers to Mr Barrett's. *And the bad things are usually instigated by other Germans, not their jailors.*

"Hey, Willie. Nice evening, ain't it?" said John, one of the guards.

"It is, Corporal. You have a good night," Willie called back.

At 2000 hours, Wilmot and Egon entered Hut 67. Wilmot looked down the length of the long dormitory where fifty men lived and slept. The prisoners had reshaped the place by moving the beds around, and they now ran in a line parallel to the walls, which gave more floor space in the centre aisle. Wilmot was fed up with this nonsense; most of the men were already dressed in their uniforms and had also pinned their medals on. It had to be Jürgen's idea; some of the men secretly called him Staff Sergeant Himmler-Schatz, such was his admiration for the SS chief.

"Shit … don't tell me Jürgen's going to inspect the troops again," Wilmot whispered to Egon. "I don't think I could stand another of his lectures."

With Egon following him, Wilmot crossed the room to Günter, the Schütze who never stopped moaning about something or other. Wilmot often recalled that terrible day in North Africa in which Günter was digging a gun-hole whilst complaining about not having water. The horrific air attack the Allies had launched that morning still stuck in Wilmot's mind; not so much because of Günter, but for the dreadful sight of Uwe's legs being blown off and himself losing his trousers. After that day, Günter's glum disposition had worsened, but Wilmot had lost too many friends to count and now appreciated those he had. Despite the man being intolerable at times, Günter was one of Wilmot's closest companions and loyal to a fault.

"What's going on here, Günter?" Wilmot asked him.

"The officers have ordered us to celebrate the Führer's birthday. They pooled their daily beer coupons and have provided us with two crates of beer. Let's see how far they go, eh. I don't want to, Willie. I'm tired. It's all right for them … they don't need to get up at the crack of dawn and work in the fields all day. I managed to get a good book from the library, and I wanted to read it before lights out. I'm sick of this parade-ground rubbish. *Diese Fanatiker haben zu viel Macht* – these fanatics have too much power. I've been saying it for a while now."

Three or four other men with whom Wilmot had served were also complaining about the unwanted celebrations.

"We don't want any trouble. If the guards find out we're shouting our heads off for Adolf Hitler, we'll be punished," one of the men said.

"Have a word with Stabfeldwebel Weiner, will you, Willie?" another man begged.

Wilmot's fellow staff sergeant, Jürgen Weiner, sat on the edge of his bed, bending down to tie his boot laces. Wilmot had long since acknowledged that they would never be friends. Apart from making the hut and shower room's cleaning rota together once a week, Wilmot stayed as far away from Weiner as possible. He was an intense sort of fellow, always wound up like an alarm clock. He had an invidious character, as though he didn't feel comfortable in his own skin. He demanded discipline and loyalty to the Reich, and he hated Wilmot's relaxed relationship with the lower ranks.

It had become apparent in the first couple of weeks at the camp that radical and aggressive Hitler supporters stalked every hut. The pro-Nazis amongst the general population were loud, demanding, and found every opportunity to remind their fellow prisoners of their duty to the Fatherland and Führer. Weiner was one of those men.

"What's going on, Jürgen?" Wilmot asked pleasantly enough.

Jürgen looked up and folded his arms across his chest. "What do you mean, *what's going on,* Willie?"

"I *mean* why was I not informed about this? And why are you not giving the men the choice to attend or not?"

"Unlike you, I still follow orders," Jürgen retorted. "Look at you ... you've become soft-bellied like that fool, Egon, who follows you everywhere. Are you telling me you don't want to celebrate the Führer's birthday? Is that what you're saying?"

Wilmot measured his words carefully before saying something he would regret later. Jürgen was a rat who reported prisoners' indiscretions and disobediences directly to the officers who were known to live by the Third Reich's rulebook. Upon their arrival at Camp Concordia, the

American commander had separated enlisted men from officers to break the chains of command. Those deemed to be *hard-core* Nazis were also separated from the general prison population; however, that hadn't stopped communication lines from being set up and spies from being born in every barrack house.

The officers were kept in separate barracks with four men to an apartment, and apart from when they were on parade, they had little to do with the rank and file. They also were able to issue orders to their *rats* and conduct bullying campaigns that went on daily behind closed doors. It was a fine balancing act for those who only wanted to serve their time and then go home when the war ended.

Wilmot despaired at times, for he was more afraid of his fellow German prisoners, especially those in the Afrika Korps who had been captured early in the war during Germany's greatest military successes, than he was of his American guards. Since his arrival, he'd seen these men lead work stoppages and intimidate other prisoners who didn't toe the line. He despised the troublemakers who made life as a prisoner even more intolerable than the word suggested.

"I'm looking forward to the celebration," Wilmot lied, "but I'm not going to ask the men to stay up half the night when they have work to go to early in the morning, and you shouldn't either."

"We're doing this, Willie, whether you want to or not, so wipe your higher-than-mighty face away and put some enthusiasm in it."

Wilmot shrugged. "Very well, I'll drink the beer and sing songs of the Fatherland, but you can lead the prayers and make the speeches, and then at 2300, I'm calling for lights out."

Half an hour later, Wilmot stood next to Jürgen and faced the men, who were in formational lines of three and standing to attention. Jürgen inspected the men. Wilmot declined to join him, instead he thought about all the reasons why he should give the pompous prick a good talking to in private.

Jürgen returned to his spot beside Wilmot. This time he towered over the men by standing on a wooden crate. He called for them to stand easy, and then began with a prayer for victory and for the defeat of all enemy countries, especially America.

"We find ourselves prisoners, men," he began, with what was going to be another long, senseless diatribe against the Allies, "but we should never forget our brothers in arms who are still fighting for the Fatherland and our Führer. We must not be friendly towards our guards or fail to make escape plans in our every waking moment. I don't care how much food they give us, or beer, for that matter, and neither should you. The Americans are our enemy. They are our *enemy!* We are the Afrika Korps, and we serve Germany, not these slavers who are using us to build up their economy. Do not listen to their lies, men. Do not read their propaganda. We are winning the war, not losing it, as they would lead us to believe. Are we stupid? No, we are not! We are duty-bound to make our captors' lives as miserable as possible and I will come down hard on any man who sees it differently…"

And he carried on and on with a boring, repetitive speech that sounded as though it were coming from an SS officer's parrot rather than someone with a mind of his own. To his irritation, Jürgen failed to uplift many of the men who were barely listening and instead looking longingly at the bottles of beer.

He finally finished with, "… and a happy birthday to our glorious leader, Adolf Hitler – Heil Hitler – Heil Hitler!"

"Heil Hitler! Heil Hitler!" the men echoed Jürgen, and on they went … until somewhere in the main body of men, a voice shouted, "Fuck Hitler!"

Jürgen raised his arm in the air and silenced the men with his fisted hand.

Wilmot braced himself for what was to come. Thinking, mouthing, or whispering expletives against the Führer was not uncommon, but shouting them for all to hear was unforgivable; at least, according to some quarters.

"Who said that?" Jürgen demanded, now walking toward the men. "Who said it?"

"Leave it, Jürgen. It was a joke. Whoever said it won't do it again. Isn't that right?" Wilmot prompted the men.

"A joke? Who jokes about fucking the Führer, eh?"

"It was Günter. He said it," Egon giggled, clearly having no idea the shit storm his words would incur.

Jürgen spun around to Wilmot. "See that? Günter's one of your men. This is what happens when you don't keep them in line. You're useless, Vogel."

The men, still standing in formation, parted to make a clear aisle for Jürgen to get through. When he reached Günter, he said, "This is treason."

Günter, standing with his hands on his hips and his chin tilted upwards in defiance, eyeballed Jürgen and said, "And this is ridiculous. It's bad enough we're thousands of kilometres from home, never mind having to remind ourselves about the idiot who put us here. Do you think he's worrying about us lot? No, Stabfeldwebel Weiner, he's not giving us a second thought. He's getting on with his war ... taking over countries, losing others, and getting more and more men killed every day. I'm sick of hearing about him. Our war is over, and I say we should be glad we're here, drink the damn beer, and forget about it..."

"That's enough, Günter," Wilmot said, joining the men.

"I'm only saying what many of us are thinking, Willie," Günter retorted.

"Take him," Jürgen ordered.

Wilmot was pushed aside as one of Jürgen's goons pinned Günter's arms behind his back.

"Get your hands off me," Günter spat at another man who was pulling him along by his shirt collar.

"Unhand him," Wilmot barked.

"Take him to the showers. I think we need to wash his mouth out with soap," Jürgen shouted.

Wilmot followed Jürgen, pushing his way through men who sought to block his path, but as he reached his fellow staff sergeant, two men grabbed him and twisted his arms behind his back, rendering him immobile.

Furious, Wilmot searched the faces of the men he had fought with in North Africa. Their eyes, frozen with fear, stared back at him, and not one made a move to help Günter.

"This is wrong. Don't stand for this. Come on, you know this isn't right," Wilmot appealed to them whilst still being restrained.

Egon, who looked confused by the whole affair, ran after Günter but was blocked before he got anywhere near him.

"Don't you touch a hair on his head, Jürgen!" Wilmot shouted when Günter's men lifted their hands to Egon.

"Anyone else who tries to defend this traitor will be punished," Jürgen shouted back to the men from the shower room door. Then, he went inside and shut the door behind him.

Wilmot, panting with rage, shrugged off the two men holding him. He glared at them, then looked at the door and made his move.

# Chapter Forty-Six

Three of Jürgen's men blocked the entrance to the shower room door, but Wilmot was too incensed to back down and blazed, "Get away from the door. That's an order!"

The two men who had been restraining Wilmot earlier also joined those who backed Jürgen. They stood in front of the door, their arms folded across their chests and their eyes threatening Wilmot and the men who gathered with him. Wilmot panicked. This was now a face-off. He was either going into an almighty fistfight or leaving Günter in the hands of fanatics, and if he allowed the latter to happen, he would lose any respect and power he had left with the men in the hut.

He turned to the men he had fought and bled with, and seeing his anger reflected in their faces, he said, "I wouldn't leave any one of you with Jürgen and his thugs. We must help him, or this will not end with Günter."

"We're with you, Willie," Egon said, having already forgotten that he had started the altercation by naming Günter.

"I'm ready when you are, Willie," said a man with his fists already in a strike position.

"We're with you, Willie," a few more men echoed.

At first, Jürgen and his faithful followers had shouted and cursed at Günter, but the noises now seeping under the shower room door were much more sinister. Günter's groans and muffled screams, coupled with the sound of men's exertions as they kicked and punched and smashed something against the mirror, were clearly part of a frenzied physical attack that might not stop until Günter was dead.

"Get out of my way," Wilmot ordered the men at the door one last time.

"Fuck off," came the reply.

When the massive fight began, Jürgen and Wilmot's men came out of their previously neutral stance to support their respective staff sergeants. Ten men retreated to the other end of the room, shaking their heads in disgust, but the other thirty-five or so let out their pent-up frustrations in a violent, unforgiving hand to hand battle.

A fist smashed into Wilmot's nose. Blood poured from both nostrils, but his rage drove him onwards towards the door where Egon and three others were tackling Jürgen's guards to the ground. On his way through, he caught more fists to his face. Someone pulled his hair while another crazy bugger jumped on his back and straddled his hips as though he wanted a piggy-back ride. Livid, Wilmot lashed out at Germany, Hitler, and for all his lost comrades until eventually he was blinded by fury and kicked the shower room door in.

"Enough!" he screamed.

Jürgen and his four henchmen stood over an unconscious Günter curled into a ball at their feet.

"We were finished here anyway," Jürgen sniggered at Wilmot, then casually washed his bloody hands in a sink.

In the main room, the men had calmed down. While a few were still exchanging blows, most saw that the fight was over and were now more interested to see what their two staff sergeants were going to do to each other.

Jürgen stepped over Günter's body as though it were trash on the floor and walked out of the shower room with his lapdogs following behind him.

Wilmot got on his knees, rolled Günter onto his back, and gasped at the almost unrecognisable bloodied face. The areas around both his cheekbones were already swollen to twice their normal size and jutted like hills beneath his eyes with pink, puffy eyelids almost the size of table tennis balls. His jaw was disfigured, broken, and a narrow bone protruded through the thin layer of skin on the bridge of his nose.

Under Günter's shirt, swelling and bright-red patches spread across his abdomen to his ribs, and his right hand looked like a red balloon.

"You will pay for this, Weiner!" Wilmot yelled into the main room.

Wilmot's men entered the shower room, their faces cut and battered from fighting.

"Help me get him to the hospital," Wilmot uttered, "and if anyone out there tries to stop us, kick the shit out of them again, and that includes Stabfeldwebel Weiner."

Ten minutes later, Wilmot left the shower room. He was followed by nine men, six of whom were carrying Günter on a blanket used as a makeshift stretcher. Aware that Günter may have broken bones or have internal injuries, the men were careful not to jostle him about. Two held the head of the blanket, two the middle, and the other two took the weight of Günter's legs. And behind them, another three men protected their rear.

Jürgen sat on the end of his bed holding court with his men who were already getting into the two crates of beer, which was not nearly enough for all the men in the hut. Their boisterous laughter sickened Wilmot, and he glared at Jürgen as he passed him.

"Remember the code, Willie," Jürgen called out, then he tapped the side of his nose with his index finger. "It will be very bad for you if you don't." He returned to his beer and laughed with the twenty or so men he had under his thumb.

Wilmot threw a filthy look at the men who had remained neutral. Although they had replaced their bunks to their original positions and were sitting or lying on their beds shamefaced, they had done nothing to stop the assault or to rebuke Jürgen. He wouldn't forget their faces.

"We won't get far before the guards stop us, and when they do, I'll do the talking," Wilmot told the men he was leading to the door.

"Egon, you say nothing, understand? You got us into this mess in the first place," one of the men hissed.

Wilmot's outstretched hand gripped the door handle, but then he yanked back his arm as the door was flung open to admit American soldiers.

"Line up at your bunks – now!" an American sergeant ordered.

Wilmot eyed the sergeant and the three soldiers with rifles coming in behind him. Then a furious-looking American officer entered, shouting, "Stand where you are!"

"We have an injured man here, Sergeant," Wilmot said in perfect English to his American counterpart.

The American sergeant pushed his way past the crowded doorway, took one look at Günter and was quick to react. "Telephone for an ambulance, immediately. Tell the hospital staff they have someone coming in," he ordered one of the soldiers.

Wilmot ordered his men to lay Günter on the nearest bottom bunk as gently as they could. "Line up, as the lieutenant said," the sergeant ordered the Germans.

"What happened here?" the officer asked Wilmot.

"He…"

"*Es war ein Versehen* – accident!" Jürgen shouted, hurrying to Wilmot's side. "I am the senior staff sergeant of this hut, and I will tell you what happened. Günter was sitting on another man's shoulders trying to fix a light bulb, and he fell off. He hit his face against the corner of a bunk. Isn't that right, Feldwebel Vogel?" Jürgen didn't speak a word of English, and his German words came out with abnormal rapidity.

*He's panicking,* Wilmot thought, throwing him a look of disgust. No one in their right mind was going to believe this was an accident. Most of the men involved had taken blows and bore the visible signs of a fight, as did he with his own bloodied nose.

After the American sergeant had translated Jürgen's feeble lie, the American lieutenant spoke to Wilmot, "Well? Are you going to insult me with the same lie?"

Wilmot measured his words carefully. He suspected that regardless of what he said, no action would be taken anytime soon. The Americans seemed to want to take a non-interference posture. There were very few American soldiers on the base who spoke German – he presumed the men who did were away fighting, codebreaking, or interpreting – because of this, the guards focused on the supervising German officers and NCOs who were tasked with maintaining strict discipline. It worked well, to a point. He and Jürgen woke their own men, marched them to and from meals, and made sure they were prepared for work on time. Their routines successfully recreated the feel of military discipline – most if the time – on this occasion, however, that discipline had disintegrated into anarchy.

"I wasn't here when it happened, sir. When I arrived ten minutes ago, Günter was already on the floor," Wilmot lied smoothly.

"An accident? Well, we'll see about that," Lieutenant Grafton scoffed, as he stared at Wilmot's swollen nose. Then he looked at Jürgen who was standing to attention, apparently unaware that his knuckles were cut and reddened.

The lieutenant went to the door and spoke quietly with his sergeant. Wilmot, overhearing the hurried discussion, got ready for a hut inspection during which, he knew from experience, every drawer and locker would be emptied and every bunk space disturbed.

Grafton addressed Wilmot and Jürgen, shifting his blazing eyes from one to the other, as he said, "You two get your men ready for inspection. I will –"

Grafton was cut off as one of his men reported the ambulance arriving at the main gates. A few minutes later the vehicle pulled up outside the hut and, a minute after that, two stretcher bearers entered the hut.

Günter was now semi-conscious and moaning through his swollen lips.

"Please be careful with him. I think his ribs and a hand are broken," Wilmot said, showing the American medics to the bunk where Günter lay.

"That's enough from you. See to your men and let mine do their job," Lieutenant Grafton warned Wilmot.

After Günter had been removed to the ambulance, Grafton called Wilmot back. Jürgen followed Wilmot, looking flustered, as if he were afraid of not being on top of the situation.

"My translator is off duty in ten minutes. Will you work with me, Staff Sergeant Vogel?"

"Yes, sir, whatever you need."

"What did he say?" Jürgen asked Wilmot.

"He said you're a fucking arsehole who needs to be shagged by a goat," Wilmot replied in rapid German.

Grafton walked down the first line of men on the left-hand side, turned at the top, then began to walk slowly down the other row. The men, holding their heads high and refusing to look at the American, were tight-lipped. Wilmot followed behind Grafton, who seemed to be in more of a hurry as he got closer to the end. *The man is out of his depth,* Wilmot thought. He would either hand over this incident to a higher rank or get down to the crux of it by starting to interrogate prisoners in a long, drawn-out procedure that would last throughout the night and halfway into the following morning. He didn't appear to want to question anyone; at least, not at this juncture.

"Make an unholy mess in here," Grafton ordered his men.

The American soldiers who had remained at the hut's door, opened it and then stood aside as Grafton prepared to leave, but when he reached it, he turned again to Jürgen and Wilmot.

"Staff Sergeant Vogel, you will come with me. I know how this will play out. If I question these men, they will all deny knowing how one of their own has been damn near killed. I suspect most of the men in here were involved in one way or another, but I'll be damned if I'm going to waste my time listening to the lies your men will throw at me."

Grafton paused to study Jürgen, who was standing next to Wilmot with innocent round eyes. He grunted, shifting his eyes back to Wilmot. "Tell Staff Sergeant Weiner to assist my men and maintain order here. This hut is on lockdown until further notice." Then he addressed two of his own men. "Make sure you find the beer. Take it all."

Wilmot, a lousy liar at the best of times, sucked in his breath.

"You think this is the first hut we've been called to tonight?" Grafton asked. "We know all about your celebrations for your Führer. You can also translate that to Staff Sergeant Weiner."

After Wilmot had translated word for word to Jürgen, he was marched out of the hut.

Behind him, he heard rattling crates of beer bottles being uncovered.

# Chapter Forty-Seven

Wilmot sat outside the camp's administration offices, dismayed to see that the camp's commander, Colonel Jacobs, had been called in because of numerous disturbances throughout the camp that evening.

Apart from Wilmot, fifteen other staff sergeants from various huts and a Hauptmann he'd never seen before had also been ordered to the administration building. The men were silent, looking like schoolchildren reporting to the headmaster's office for punishment, and even the Hauptmann kept his mouth clamped shut.

To calm himself, Wilmot turned his thoughts to Dottie. He was hoping she was not on duty at the hospital tonight after all. When they had become close enough to have heart-to-heart conversations, she'd told him that she had been afraid of the German prisoners during her first weeks at the camp's hospital. She'd explained that there were around nine hundred American soldiers based at Concordia and over four thousand German prisoners. She didn't know how many civilians worked there but estimated the number to be around two hundred. Her brothers and their friends had warned her that Germans were evil and because they far outnumbered the guards, could easily overpower the Americans, take the place as their own, and kill all the civilians living near the camp.

Wilmot had assured her that the German inmates wouldn't do such a thing. 'We have nowhere to run to, and most of us are happy to be out of the war,' he'd said, wildly exaggerating his fellow inmates' positive feelings about their incarcerations. What would she think when she found out that there had been celebrations for Adolf Hitler's birthday and that Günter had been beaten because he refused to join the party?

Grafton called the Hauptmann into the office and shut the door behind them. Ten minutes later, the lieutenant peeked his head out the commander's door and snapped, "Get in here, all of you."

Colonel Jacobs sat behind his desk with a furious scowl on his usually pleasant face. He had offered a seat to the Hauptmann but ordered the Stabfeldwebels and Feldwebels to line up before him.

*The colonel is a decent man,* Wilmot thought, standing to attention in the front row. He was not an authoritarian, and he kept a low profile compared to the Russian commanders who made a point of holding prisoner inspections every day so they could spit in the faces of their starving, dejected captives. Jacobs, a man in his fifties, often rode into the camp on his horse whilst leading another, which he would hand over to the German commander, General von Aust. Then off they'd go together on their daily ride into the countryside. It was all extremely civilised.

The colonel's appearance was as colourless as his character. He was of medium build and height with a weather-beaten face that sported a heavy white moustache, which evidently tickled his nostrils as his nose twitched when he spoke. His mop of grey hair painted a sharp contrast to the spikey razor cuts that the German officers preferred, and his uniform shirt was creased and sporting a coffee stain next to its fourth button. Tonight, he looked as openly hostile as

Lieutenant Grafton, who was sitting at a typewriter that took up most of his desk.

The lieutenant raised his eyes and asked, "How many of you understand English?"

"Who speaks English here?" the Hauptmann translated to the Feldwebels.

"I do, and I read and write equally as well in both languages, sir," Wilmot got out first.

"I also ... a small piece," another man said in stilted English.

"That's it? No one else?"

Colonel Jacobs, observing from his desk's black leather armchair, studied Wilmot, who looked like a clown with a red bubble nose and a swollen eyelid turning purple.

"Staff Sergeant Vogel, you will translate for the colonel, you hear?" Grafton said. "But do not speak until you are told to. Do not interrupt him, you hear?"

"Yes, sir, I hear," Wilmot said, amused at how frequently Americans asked the question, *you hear?*

Colonel Jacobs let out a heavy sigh. "I'm at a loss here, gentlemen, and by that, I mean I have lost my faith in you," Jacobs lamented, as he eyed the staff sergeants and captain. "Now, I don't know how many of you men organised or encouraged your little celebration tonight, but I damn well know you and the other sergeants in your huts did nothing to stop it."

Jacobs shook his head, tutting as he went down the list of hut numbers whose occupants had held the illicit parties. "I have given you men and others of similar rank an almost-free rein to maintain discipline in this camp, and you've spat in my face. You're treated well. You get a damn sight more food to eat than our American soldiers serving in Europe. You have jobs outside the camp that are neither tough nor stressful on the body or mind, and your wages are the same as those of an American private in our armed forces. In other words, you get the same money as American boys who are away fighting and dying for this great country."

The Hauptmann uttered, "If I may say, Colonel…"

"No. You damn well may say nothin' about nothin', Captain. I didn't say this was a discussion."

A couple of staff sergeants sniggered. Even if they didn't understand a word that was being said, it was apparent their Hauptmann had just been rebuked.

Jacobs glared at the men who had laughed. "What more do you want? We've given you a library with thousands of books to read. We let you have our American newspapers. Hell, we even allow you to publish your own, mostly uncensored paper. You have theatrical and musical groups and can watch movies three times a week, not to mention the honour system that allows you men to go outside the camp, to the restaurant in town. Your living conditions are comfortable, and we take real good care of your medical concerns. Damn it, you're all having a better war here than the people in your own damn country!"

Wilmot agreed with most of Jacob's litany. He'd heard men in his hut remark that unlike here, they didn't have hot water in their tenement buildings in Germany, nor had they eaten meat with such frequency. But he supposed none of that mattered when men were hell-bent on keeping Adolf Hitler on his pedestal and viewing the Americans as the enemy.

"Trust goes both ways," Jacobs continued, "and you've lost mine. There will be consequences, men."

Jacobs swivelled his chair around to face Grafton who'd been continuously taking notes. "I want these staff sergeants to be transferred out of the huts they're in. I don't care which barrack house you move them to, just make sure they're in their new accommodation by tomorrow night."

Wilmot was worried, but he was not stupid enough to protest in front of his fellow Germans. Men in his hut needed him, even those who were yet to realise it.

Jacobs stood, walked around to the front of his desk and rose to full height. "Because of your blatant disregard for the rules, every German prisoner in the camp will lose privileges for the next three weeks. Apart from those, you will also cook your own food and perform all kitchen duties. No town passes will be issued for the foreseeable future, and beer coupons will be rescinded – and I'm just gettin' started."

The Hauptmann rose and joined Jacobs.

"Salute the colonel," the Hauptman ordered.

Wilmot saluted, as did his peers, apart from two men at the end who taunted Jacobs with their outstretched arms and straightened hands.

*"Heil, mein Führer!"* one man said, while the other shouted, *"Sieg Heil!"*

Colonel Jacobs studied both men for a long, disquieting moment. "Lieutenant, make a note that these two gentlemen be transferred to Camp Alva at Major Scott's earliest convenience."

Wilmot, who had not translated the colonel's words, watched in fascinated horror as the two soldiers swaggered out of the colonel's office, congratulating each other on their cleverness.

\*\*\*\*\*\*

Using Lieutenant Grafton's typed notes, Wilmot translated the colonel's lecture to the Germans. Most of the men had been furious to learn they'd been ordered to change their living situations. Each of them had built their power base over time and were not open to starting anew in a hut where another staff sergeant might have solidified his position.

Wilmot had quickly deduced that the men he was speaking to were hardliners, as were many of his peers in the camp. As he spoke, their eyes had sparkled with resentment, as though they thought his words were coming directly from his own mind. He became anxious they might paint him as being anti-Hitler, and when he was heckled by one of the men, he'd blurted, "Don't shoot the messenger. I don't like this any more than you do." Watched by Lieutenant Grafton and the Hauptmann whose name he still didn't know, he let out a sigh of relief when he finished speaking, and the men were dismissed to pass on the message to the soldiers of their respective huts.

"Everything the colonel said tonight will be written in German by tomorrow morning, so don't you guys even think about changing the story to one more to your liking," Grafton warned the men via Wilmot as they were leaving.

The Hauptmann left first, looking disgusted. He'd been a spectator after the colonel had told him it wouldn't be right to use an officer to translate to his men. Officers were above that, in Jacob's opinion, which was also a face-saving gesture for the captain, since Wilmot's English was significantly more articulate. When the Feldwebels left, they looked unrepentant and angry, not at the loss of privileges, but for being told that it was wrong to celebrate the German dictator – the colonel's title for Hitler – and to remember him in speeches … period.

"Well, Sergeant Vogel, were you for the party or against?" Grafton asked Wilmot when they were alone.

"Sir, you shouldn't have asked me to stay behind. The men who have just left here will think I'm a collaborator. And you shouldn't be asking me that question."

"You've taken a beating for something. I want to know why," Grafton parried.

Wilmot, trying to find an advantage for himself, responded with an exaggerated sigh. "Between you and me, I am in the anti-Hitler camp, as are many of the men in my hut. Problem is, if you move me out, you will leave these other men at the mercy of Staff Sergeant Weiner who seems to be devoted to Hitler. I need to stay to protect the most vulnerable … those who have been badly wounded in battle and can't properly defend themselves mentally or physically. Why don't you help me out and move Staff Sergeant Weiner instead of me? I think you'll find that is a more sensible arrangement for both of us."

"Did Staff Sergeant Weiner beat the Schütze we took to the hospital?"

"I didn't say that, sir."

After translating the English written version of the colonel's conclusions into German, Wilmot went to the hospital. He got an update on Günter's condition but was denied access to see him. It was 0005, and the order for lights out was already in place as part of the collective punishment.

As he reached the hut, he decided to wake the men an hour earlier than usual in the morning to share the bad news that they were not only cooking their own breakfasts, but they were also cleaning the kitchen after themselves. While they were complaining about that, he would tell them about all the other privileges they had lost because of a few zealots. He'd had enough tonight and didn't want to get into another altercation. He wanted his bed.

Wilmot waved away the men who were still awake, tread softly to Jürgen's bed and gave him a rough shake. "Come with me," he hissed when Jürgen opened his eyes.

Jürgen sat up and stared groggily at Wilmot. "Why?"

"Because you are not going to want the other men to hear what I have to say to you."

Jürgen got up, cursing under his breath but following Wilmot who was heading into the shower rooms.

Wilmot looked at the floor. "At least you had the decency to wipe away Günter's blood," he said.

"Fuck you, Vogel. What did the Americans say?"

"A few things. I'll inform you and the men in the morning."

"Why did you wake me up if you're not going to tell me now? I should have gone to the administration office, not you." Jürgen leant in until his face was only centimetres from Wilmot's. "I have seniority here."

"You *did* have seniority here. You're moving out of this hut tomorrow and going to 34."

For the first time, Jürgen looked apprehensive. "Who said that?"

"Colonel Jacobs."

"I won't go. Those are my men in the bunks out there."

"Not anymore. I tried to see Günter at the hospital on the way back to the hut but was told to return tomorrow. He's in a serious condition thanks to you and your men, and he hasn't opened his eyes yet. They're afraid he might have fallen into a coma."

Jürgen swallowed uncomfortably and looked at the wooden floor. "Did you tell them it was me?"

"No, and I won't. But they will find out eventually, and when they do, I won't lie for you. Do you even realise what a stupid bastard you've been?"

"He cursed the Führer. No one in this hut does that to my face."

"Well, you won't have to worry about the men in this hut anymore. You'll be gone from here as soon as you get back from the farm tomorrow."

Wilmot paused, but Jürgen seemed to have run out of bravado and rocked backwards and forwards on heels to toes without saying a word.

"Look, Jürgen, take some advice from me. I don't care who you take your orders from, and I don't give a shit about your love for Hitler, but from now on, keep your thoughts to yourself…"

"Or what?"

"Or I will knock you and your teeth into next week if I see you as much as unnerve a man in this hut – nod if you understand."

Jürgen faced Wilmot, his eyes spitting hatred. "You're an arrogant prick, Vogel. The men are with me."

Wilmot scoffed, "And the people who are running this place will be with me. How do you think that will work out for us?"

"What's that supposed to mean?"

This time, Wilmot moved in closer to threaten Jürgen. "I have a weapon none of your men can match…"

"What's that?"

"Language. I speak perfect English. It's amazing what information a man can get across when he knows how to articulate his words. I will use my *perfect* English to bury you and your fellow Hitler lovers and protect the men you target. I will become great friends with the Americans."

Now, Jürgen sneered, "What goes on in this camp is much bigger than you and me, Vogel. Do you think our loyal officers are going to allow you to tell tales on the men under their command? You're a fool. They will come for you next. You wait and see."

Wilmot pushed Jürgen out of his way, but then he turned at the door. The trick with Jürgen was never to give him the last word. "Wake up call will be at 0500. The men will be cooking and cleaning before heading out to work, and you'll be packing. I suggest you get some sleep. You've got a busy day tomorrow."

# Chapter Forty-Eight

## Max Vogel

*North of the Loire River,*
*Maine-et-Loire, France*
*July 1944*

Max rested his head against the aircraft's fuselage wall and began to breathe deeply – in … out – to the count of ten. With one eye open, he stared at the men sitting on the floor opposite him. The Sussex Plan, devised a year earlier by British Intelligence Services and General de Gaulle's *Bureau Central de Renseignement et d'Action,* was a go. Like him, his team of three officers, a radio operator, and an observer had gone through several months of hard training at Prae Wood House, located near St-Albans and some forty kilometres from London. And only a day earlier, they had completed their course at Ringway Parachute School near Manchester. Unlike Max, however, they were French volunteers, untested in combat or in jumping out of an aircraft whilst surrounded by flak from German anti-aircraft guns.

The man sitting directly opposite Max was in distress; sweating, panting, and showing the classic signs of panic. Hugo, the youngest member of the team, had been chosen at the last minute after an original member became ill with stomach flu. Max, now questioning his selection, got up, staggered against the turbulence to Hugo, crouched down next to him, and shouted, "Can you hear me, Hugo?"

Hugo nodded, but his pupils remained dilated.

"Listen to me. We're the lucky ones. You know why?"

Hugo shook his head.

"Because we didn't do this on the day of the Normandy landings when hundreds of planes were in the sky. This is a quiet night, and the odds of us getting shot down are slim to none. Do you hear me?"

Hugo nodded again.

It was almost impossible to hold a conversation because of the deafening noise of the aircraft's engine and the turbulence that rattled everything on board. *Probably just as well,* Max thought. Hugo didn't need to know that between 1 April and 6 June, the day of the Normandy invasion, the British and American strategic air forces had deployed more than eleven thousand Allied planes to fill the smoke-filled grey skies. Everything from P-51 Mustangs, P-47 Thunderbolts, Supermarine Spitfires to Hawker Hurricanes and AK47 Dakotas had pummelled the French ground with almost two hundred thousand tons of bombs. They had cut off German supplies and reinforcements, the French railway hubs and road networks, as well as German airfields, radar installations, military bases, and coastal artillery batteries. But the pilots and their aircraft had paid a hell of a price for their bravery with over two thousand aircraft lost in the preliminary attacks.

"Hugo, if your fear puts this team's lives in danger after we land, I will kill you myself. Do you understand what I am saying, Lieutenant?"

"Yes, Major. I am fine. No problem!" Hugo shouted, looking horrified at the idea of not making the jump.

"Can I count on you?"

"Yes, Major. I am good!" Hugo answered with two thumbs up.

The aircraft fell a few hundred feet then shuddered, making Max's insides tremble and his own fear rise to the surface. *I shouldn't be here,* he thought. Because of his face-to-face meeting with Admiral Canaris in Paris the previous year, his Rolf Fischer and Mirror covers were burnt. At first, he'd been distraught; he'd questioned his identity and purpose: *who am I without Fischer and Mirror?* But then he had dared to hope that he would spend the remainder of the war at Bletchley Park or MI6 Headquarters in London, and the Canaris meeting had seemed like a blessing.

The last seven months had been a gift, Max acknowledged. He'd grown used to his twice-monthly visits with Judith and spending time with his parents. He and Judith had even managed a belated three-day honeymoon to Scotland, where they had stayed with Hannah and Frank. For the first time since the wretched war had started, he had woken up in friendly territory day after day, week after week, month after month, and it had been glorious.

He hadn't initially been earmarked for this job. British Intelligence agents had trained the French volunteers for the Sussex Plan, and they had decided that only French nationals were to execute the operations. Heller, being Heller, however, had pushed for Max to be included because no one on this team spoke a word of German. "It's time you got back into the field, Max. Get your hands dirty before they become too soft to hold a gun," Heller had said when imparting the news.

"Major. Five minutes," the co-pilot informed Max.

Max nodded, gave the man the thumbs up, and then shouted to the five men, "Listen up!"

When he had the attention of the Frenchmen, he spread five fingers, indicating the minutes to go until the jump. Then he lurched to his feet and raised his hands like an orchestra conductor, to signal to his men that it was time to prepare. Under severe air turbulence and the vibrational impact of German ordinance exploding like bursts of white light on the aircraft's path, the men clung with one hand to the overhead wire where they had hooked their parachute cords and stepped unsteadily in single file to the open hatch.

At the hatch, Max turned to the men and pointed with his index finger to his parachute; this gesture indicating that each person should check the working order of the harness and pack of the person in front of them.

The aircraft juddered and bounced again. Max, dangerously close to the open hatch, flinched when a plane in the distance caught fire and nosedived towards the ground.

The air campaign had succeeded in breaking all the bridges across the Seine and Loire rivers, and by achieving that goal, the Allies had isolated the invasion zone from the rest of France. But every day since that momentous Normandy invasion, the Germans had been relentless in their determination to bring British and American planes down, and this July night was no different than any other. Pilots consistently met a hell-in-the-sky scenario not long after clearing the English coastline, but they continued to fly through it until they landed safely back in England unless their planes were brought down in flames or they parachuted out over the English Channel or France. He turned. Hugo was directly behind him, looking as calm as could be expected of any man about to jump into enemy territory.

Max said his usual silent prayer. He, like the other parachutists, was scared out of his wits and desperate to get off the aircraft, but he was also afraid of what was going to meet him on the ground.

He saw the signal to go, raised his hand to his men in a line behind him, and counted down from three to jump...

******

After the team's successful landings, the six men assembled at the rendezvous location; a grassy clearing at the edge of the woods that bordered the Loire River's northern embankment.

"Bury the chutes in the undergrowth. We still don't know if we're behind or facing enemy lines. I don't want to leave any sign of our arrival," Max instructed when all members of the team were present.

Inside the treeline, the men checked their luggage for damage. They had jumped heavily laden with clothes, documents, and other equipment strapped onto them. The radio operator alone carried one Mark 7 British transmitter and receiver, plus an emergency set, one emergency Willard battery, three sulphuric acid bottles, and one hand charger. Each man had a .32 calibre pistol, fifty bullets, one commando knife, one pen for throwing teargas, and two type 69 grenades. They were wearing French-made civilian clothing and had other socks, undershorts, shirts and trousers in their bags. They also had their falsified French identity documents in their jacket pockets, a first aid kit, and cyanide tablets.

Max, going through the same checks as his men, reassured himself once again that his pistol was fully loaded and then transferred his spare bullets to his pockets. He took his documents from their clear polyethylene sleeve and went through them for the umpteenth time. As French citizens in German-occupied France, they had to have all identity papers up to date and at hand should they be stopped at a checkpoint. Thus, he not only carried the essentials – identity card, ration card, clothing coupons, demobilisation papers, census certificate, and employment attestation – he also had a driver's licence and enough French francs to keep him going for a month.

He looked up from what he was doing and asked Jules, the radio operator, "Any damage?"

"No, all good here, Max," Jules replied.

Max checked the time on his Swiss wristwatch. They had been there for fifteen minutes, and the Resistance and *Pathfinders* had not arrived yet. He was concerned; they should have lit the landing beacons at the coordinates before he and his men had even jumped or, at the very least, been in position.

According to the information received just before the team had left England, there were no significant numbers of Germans in this area; however, Max had also been informed that the situation in Normandy was fluid. Ten minutes before getting on the aircraft, the point was pushed home when he and his men were told to belay their previous orders and follow a modified plan that had been hastily put together using almost-real-time intelligence in the field.

The German retreat following D-Day was much faster than anticipated, and MI6 were worried that agents being dropped into France would find themselves chasing an enemy on the run instead of being well behind German lines as intended. In the new orders, they were asked to land in a place well ahead of the enemy withdrawal which risked them being encircled by Axis forces but also gave them more real-time information.

Max unfolded his map and drew his finger along the route they were planning to eventually take in a vehicle supplied by the Pathfinders. These French Resistance men and women were dedicated to the Sussex Plan. Their duties were numerous and included some of the most dangerous missions of the war to date. They prepared safe houses, located drop sites for the agents to be parachuted into, and received and dispatched the agents once on the ground. They also had the task of reporting on German activities as well as confirming arrests and executions of Sussex agents.

Max called over Hugo, the team's observer. The man showed no sign of his previous anxiety and was looking more like his old self; the soldier who had displayed tremendous mental and physical strength on the course for one so very young.

"Hugo, the Castle of La Roche-Mailly should be about five hundred metres from our position on the far side of this coppice. Take Milo with you. Check for German activity in or around the castle and on the embankment." Max folded the map and added sarcastically, "And while you're at it, look out for the Resistance. I think they might have lost their way."

A few minutes later, three flashes from a battery torch came from within a thicket to Max's left. Max flashed twice, signifying he had recognised the Resistance signal, then he waited for them to appear.

******

Hugo and Milo returned with four Resistance fighters; three men and a woman.

"We met them halfway to the castle," Hugo reported. "They know what's going on there, so I thought we should get back here to report."

The French Resistance leader shook Max's hand. "I'm Cesar. Sorry we weren't here to meet you," he said in French. "We saw a lot of movement in this area earlier." Then he took the time to introduce the woman and two other men with him before imparting the bad news. "The Germans arrived at the castle about an hour before you came down. We think they might be going up to join the German Seventh Army reserves."

"Or to Paris," one of Cesar's men suggested.

"The Seventh is in Normandy … over three hundred kilometres from here. That's a bit far from their forward positions, is it not?" Max queried.

"It is, but the Seventh are being hit hard. They're being pushed back through the *Bocage* – the hedge growth countryside is treacherous – and they are haemorrhaging men. Our spies in Normandy estimate they've lost at least a hundred thousand."

"How close were your men?" Max asked.

"They captured two officers and extracted some decent information. Five of the Seventh's generals were killed last month, and they lost their current commander a few days ago."

"General Dollmann is dead? That *is* news. Who took over?" Max asked.

Cesar sat on a log. It was a balmy night without a breeze. It was also humid, and Max's skin was moist with sweat. Milo and Hugo were excited about being back in their homeland and were asking the other Resistance men and woman questions about their hometowns. Max sat beside Cesar and gestured for his men to listen.

"The Seventh is still under the overall command of Field Marshal Rommel's Army Group B. Apparently, he asked for more mechanised divisions but was denied."

Milo, a French Captain and member of Max's team, asked, "If they're moving up to Normandy, what sort of numbers have the Germans left here?"

"Their numbers are low. They've left military police units in most of the towns with no more than a unit or platoon of soldiers to patrol the area. The Resistance is in a position now to fight back. Our numbers have grown, and we're no longer afraid to take the Boches on in the open … if we must."

Max was already planning his first transmission to Allied Command, via Operation Ultra Command at Bletchley Park. His team's job was to provide the Allies with firm information on the German army, its order of battle, troop movements, and the location of its V1 – Doodlebug –and V2 – Rocket – flying bombs' installation and launch pads. This intelligence would allow Allied Headquarters to make informed decisions on the concentrations of troops and materials, including the Panzer divisions and their supply depots, and how and where to bomb German convoys. They might as well begin now with this new information about the castle.

"How many Germans did you see at the castle? What are they hauling?" Max asked Cesar.

"About a hundred or so men. Their officers arrived in Kübelwagens, and about five minutes later, supply vehicles, six open trucks with about fifteen to twenty men in each, and a truck towing a 75-210 mm rocket launcher also went in."

Max looked at the other Sussex team members. He outranked them and was their leader, but this was a French operation, and he had decided from the outset not to throw his weight around. "We should hang around and see which way they head. We may as well start with this intel," he suggested.

Jules, the radio operator, concurred. "This is good news. I say we capitalise on it. I'm sure the Royal Air Force will be happy to bomb the shit out of a nice juicy convoy…"

"Not while they're at the castle," Cesar said, looking horrified. "We would like to keep our historical sites if you don't mind."

Max responded, "You and your people should leave the area."

"We plan to head back to Maine-et-Loire. The Germans have a Gestapo sub-station there. We intend to get rid of it."

Cesar handed Max the keys to an old Citroen van. "It is parked inside a burnt-out weapons factory about a kilometre southeast of here. It has German registration plates. We found it abandoned and broken, and we fixed it for you. Most of the Boches stationed in the Vendôme area moved north to the coast in the middle of June, and they took every vehicle that still had wheels with them. Sorry; the van was the only vehicle big enough for your needs." Cesar gestured to the young woman who was leaning against a tree looking as though she were born with the rifle in her hand. "Marie will take you to it."

"Thank you," Max said.

Cesar handed Max a piece of paper. "I set up two safe houses in the area. Memorise the maps and addresses. The

Resistance have taken over them, and they know you are coming."

"Good," said Max, glancing at the directions on the map.

"God willing, you will be successful, but if you get into trouble, go to our friends. Do not remain in the open. The military police are based in Vendôme, but they are constantly patrolling the Loir-et-Cher area. They found and executed two German deserters last week. They're even more vicious now than they were before the invasion, and they've been given more authority since the local German units moved out."

"Got it," Max responded, shaking the Frenchman's hand. "Good luck to you all."

"And you," Cesar said.

*Jana Petken*

# Chapter Forty-Nine

*Loir-et-Cher,*
*Centre-Val de Loire region, France.*
*9 July 1944*

At 0300, Max drove the van across the Lavardin Bridge at
Loir-et-Cher. Supported by arched stone pillars, the gothic
bridge was only one of the many ancient landmarks in the
Loire region. If it were not for the rumbling aircraft in the
black sky, bombs that exploded in the distance, and destroyed
buildings that the Germans had deliberately burnt to quell
French resistance, one could almost forget the horrors of war
that were raging in Northern France.

One of the things Max hated most about the war, apart
from the death and misery it brought, was man's total
disregard for historical landmarks. This was not the first time
he had been to this region. His family had once spent a week
in the historical province of Anjou, straddling the lower Loire
River.

He and Paul had been enthralled by a castle they had
visited. Their imagination had run riot, and every footstep
they took had been a homage to the medieval knights who had
gone before them. Wilmot, a child at the time, had been bored
and crying to go home. Paul had tried to stir some history into
the spoilt brat, as Willie was at that time, by saying, 'Imagine
you are walking in the footsteps of kings and knights and
horses dressed in armour and fair ladies with hair to their
backsides.' Willie had replied, 'All I see are old stones and

grass and parts of walls that are no longer walls. I want ice cream.'

Max allowed himself a satisfied sigh. Willie was safe. After much ado, their father had found out that his youngest son was in Kansas, in America. It had taken months to get the name of the camp because the Americans were struggling to cope with the influx of a quarter of a million Axis prisoners from North Africa. However, at the end of April, the American military authorities dealing with POWs had finally given the family the answers they were looking for, and the family's letter writing to Wilmot began in earnest.

Milo, sitting in the back of the van, cracked a joke. Good-natured conversations with his French colleagues kept Max's spirits high. The past four days had been tough. The men had separated into three teams of two during the day and had met up every night to transmit the specifics of what they had seen, including today's sighting of another German convoy towing heavy weaponry and heading north.

The men had also reported on their ongoing efforts to find the location of the V1 flying bomb, and the V2 rockets' bunkers or launch pads. British and American intelligence branches were convinced they were situated in Northern France, and both countries deemed them an ongoing threat. In a meeting with the heads of British Intelligence, two days before his departure to France, Max had suggested that if there were a bunker protecting the flying bombs, it would most likely be deep in a forest. He was convinced now that his team were not going to find it in the Loire area, and trusting his gut, had informed Allied Command via the Ultra team at Bletchley that he was travelling north the following day, hoping to get through to the forested areas in the Calais department. It seemed that their quiet time in the beautiful, albeit partly destroyed Loire valley was over.

"How far to the safe house, Jules?" Max asked.

Jules, sitting next to Max in the front passenger seat, shone his shaded torch on the map on his knees to confirm their location. "About two kilometres from here on the road that bypasses Vendôme."

"*Dieu,* I'll be glad of a bed tonight," Milo yawned from the back of the van. "The last four days and nights have played havoc on my bony arse."

"I'll be happy for a glass of wine and a floor," Hugo piped up. "Who wants to go to bed in this heat? No, Milo, what you need is a cold, stone floor."

At one time, there had been a glass panel separating the front and back of the van, but the Resistance had removed it so that the team could communicate with each other. Max, half listening to Milo's complaints about the insects that had crawled over him at his observation spot that day, was also thinking about the safe house; a farmhouse that had been badly damaged during the German invasion four years earlier. According to the woman who had taken them to the van upon their arrival, it was now a substantial Resistance operation's base, situated only two kilometres from the *Feldgendarmerie* – the German military police station.

With only a kilometre to go, Max gasped, then slammed on the brakes. The men and luggage in the back rolled about and thumped against the floor and walls of the van as it screeched to a halt in a diagonal position on the road.

"*Merde,* Max," Jules grumbled as he righted himself.

Max turned off the engine, "Germans. Get your sidearms ready. We're either going to talk our way out of this or kill them."

"How many?" Milo asked.

"Ram them," Hugo said from the back.

The van's dimmed lights picked up the approaching men, but they were shining even brighter torches in Max's eyes, making it impossible to count how many Germans were coming at them and from seeing the road ahead.

"I see four," Jules eventually said.

Max's eyes grew accustomed to the glare, and as the black figures holding the torches reached the front of the van, he also counted four Germans; two with rifles slung over their shoulders.

In those pivotal seconds between the Germans being at the bonnet and getting to the van's front windows, Max noted their dishevelled state, the absence of army issue rucksacks, helmets or caps, a bandage that was wrapped around one of the men's arms, and the expression of surprise on their faces. He switched off the van's lights, deducing they were not patrolling but deserting their army.

"*Geh raus – get out!* We need this transport." The soldier either didn't care if the Frenchmen in the van understood German or believed his brash tone would translate for him.

Max gave the man a blank stare.

"Get out – now!" the soldier barked, this time waving a pistol.

"I fixed this van," Max began in French but then switched to stilted German. "It was abandoned ... broken. The Feldgendarmerie say to me ... you fix for us. I have Ausweis

Pass. I take now to Vendôme. If not take … military police angry."

Max hoped the soldiers would think twice about confiscating a vehicle earmarked for the military police. The Resistance had warned the team that the duties of the Wehrmacht Feldgendarmerie ranged from straightforward traffic and population control to the suppression and executions of people they deemed deserving of death. The French had been monitoring the Feldgendarmerie role in this area since the German combat units moved forward and out of the region and had noted an uptake in executions.

Without warning, the soldier opened the door, pulled Max out of the vehicle by the arm, frogmarched him around the front to the passenger side, and threw him against the van.

Jules joined Max a moment later, about the same time as the back door was thrown open.

"Out – out!" a soldier yelled at the back of the van.

Max raised himself to full height and clasped his hands on his head as the second soldier ordered with a gesture. He didn't see, but rather heard, the scuffle going on at the back. He and Jules were being held at gunpoint by one soldier training his semi-automatic Gewehr 43 rifle. Another German was holding a pistol and shining his torch into their eyes.

The other four team members appeared, stumbling as two soldiers pushed them towards Max and Jules. One of the Germans tugged Hugo's shirt. The latter shrugged it off and got a swipe across the head for his cheek.

"I *no* not these men," Max blurted out to take attention away from Hugo. "I pick them on this road … I *no* not them."

"Shut up," came the response.

"I want to see what they've got in their baggage," one of the soldiers who had brought the Frenchmen from the back, said.

Two soldiers went back to the van doors and began throwing bags onto the road. Max was not surprised that the Germans weren't inspecting identity documents or asking where the four men who'd been in the back were going. The deserters were not thinking like soldiers. They looked panicked, exhausted, and seemed to only want to take the vehicle.

Max imagined escape scenarios in his head while hoping the Frenchmen were doing the same. He pictured his hand going inside his jacket and reaching for his pistol, which was tucked into his waistband at his side, but no matter how many times he played with the scene, he was shot as soon as he lowered his hands…

"I found a radio transmitter," a soldier called out from the roadside near the back of the van.

Max's hopes of escape crumpled when the two Germans who had been inspecting the luggage returned. Furious, they showed their companions the grenades, then followed that critical discovery with the British-registered first aid kit and cyanide pills.

"They're spies," one of the soldiers snapped.

"I don't care who they are. I say we kill them all and get out of here." He turned his pistol on Milo and Gabriel, shooting both Frenchmen in their heads in quick succession.

"Stop – stop!" Max shouted in German.

"Are you a spy, eh? Well, are you, French pig?" the same soldier demanded to know of Max.

Max shut his eyes, waiting for the bullet. Instead, he was pulled out of the line and punched in the stomach. He doubled over, gasping for breath, as a rifle butt thumped the back of his head. He dropped like a stone to his knees, dazed and unable to fend off new kicks and punches to his face and body. When he rolled into the foetal position, he tried to use his hands to shield his face, but now at least two deranged Germans were kicking or thumping him with their rifle butts, and every part of him was vulnerable. In excruciating pain, and not losing consciousness quickly enough for his liking, he wished for a bullet to end him.

As Max lay facing a field high with sunflowers at the other side of the road, he heard the beginnings of a scuffle going on at the van. His beating halted abruptly. Men were shouting, groaning, and swearing in both French and German behind him. He rolled over, unable to rise even to his knees. The torches were on the ground, and apart from their soft rays highlighting the van's immediate area, it was pitch black.

Pistol shots cracked out. The grunts and other sounds of struggle ceased, then a rifle's incessant firing made hearing anything else, indeed even his own thoughts, impossible. Max's forehead and crown were bleeding. Blood dripped into his left eye. He was in agony, dizzy, but lucid enough to go for the pistol that was tucked into his trousers' waistband. *I'm going to die with my gun in my hand.* That thought gave him a modicum of satisfaction as he raised his torso centimetres off the ground and blindly fired shot after shot at the two silhouetted figures spraying the bodies lying on the ground with bullets.

The first bullet struck Max in the shoulder from close range. A second hit him in an area near his hip. His head smacked against the hot ground, but he made another supreme effort to rise again when a rifle began firing along the road in the direction the van had been heading. Still unable to move, Max twisted his head to his right side and through nauseating pain caught a glimpse of blue and white flashes from the muzzle of the weapon as it discharged. Lethargically, he raised his arm with his pistol shaking in his weakened hand, aimed at the flashes, and fired his gun until the rifle grew silent and he had spent his ammunition.

Again, Max sank onto the warm asphalt wet with his blood. An airy sob leaked from his parted lips. The pain was intense, but it paled in comparison to his broken heart. He was losing his dream of a lifetime with Judith, of children, and an England at peace – yes, his dreams were fading; his world was becoming darker … and now thoughts of war and love were draining … draining away.

# Chapter Fifty

Hugo ran in the darkness with rifle fire pushing him on. Bullets whizzed past his ears, but one caught him in the back of the arm, making him stumble and fall. He got up and stumbled on until he heard the echo of a second weapon competing with the rifle. Then, about two hundred metres from the vehicle, the firing finally stopped.

Tripping again, Hugo fell off the roadway and tumbled down a grassy embankment while trying to cradle his wounded arm with his free hand. In the field ripe with the scent of sunflowers, he took the time to settle his breathing. Then he got up, and crouching, made his way back towards the van, his gun now in one hand and the other arm limp at his side. He didn't expect to find any survivors, but someone had silenced the rifle fire, and that someone, assuming it was one of his team members, might still be alive. He had to check.

He halted before reaching the front of the van to listen for signs of life – he heard his own breathing and the sound of crickets – then advanced in a stooped position into the road, his gun primed and ready to fire at the slightest movement. No German torches shone now, and unable to see much, he opened the front passenger door and palmed around the seat and floor area, searching for Jules' torch. He found it on the floor, picked it up, and switched it on.

Hugo had not spotted the German lying a metre in front of the van when he'd approached. Now with the torch lit, he surmised by the body's position that this was the man who had been trying to pick him off with the rifle. The soldier had three gunshots to his back, and his fingers were still curled around his rifle's trigger. Assuming he was dead but taking no chances, Hugo kicked the body. Getting no reaction, he got on one knee and felt for a pulse; finding none, he picked up the rifle and moved on to the other side of the van.

He retched as his torchlight's beam broke on the pile of bodies. Two Germans were lying face down with their heads and torsos partly covering Jules and Marc underneath them. Milo and Gabriel, who had been executed before the fightback even began, lay a few metres past the van. As well as single gunshot wounds to their heads, their bodies were also stained with blood. *Theirs – blood from other men – what did it matter now?*

Hugo stifled a sob and moved his eyes back to Jules and Marc, the two colleagues and friends he had lived and trained with for months. It was clear from the abundant amount of blood on their backs and around their bodies that the German bastards lying half-atop the Frenchmen were dead.

The torch beam enhanced the gory mess; blood looked brighter, thicker, almost like a blanket covering the men in places. He pulled the first German away from the van using his uninjured hand. He felt sick with pain but refused to give up on his team members until he had checked their pulses and heartbeats. Miracles did occasionally happen.

Unable to move the other German's head and shoulders off Marc, he got on his knees and crawled over the man.

*"Merde,"* Hugo uttered. Marc, the French captain who had won a medal of honour, had been shot in the face. His nose was gone, his mouth a gaping, bloody hole without lips.

Hugo moved on to Jules and reverently closed his friend's wide eyes. Jules had a two-year-old daughter. Her photograph was inside his sock, and though it was against orders to carry pictures of family on one's person, he wouldn't go anywhere without it.

As Hugo's shock subsided, sharper and more rational thought returned. He gasped, spun around and shone his light towards the far side of the road, all the way to the grassy verge until he saw the last body.

Hugo finally began to cry, breaking down when he saw the state of Max. If he had a pin, he wouldn't find any place to stick it on Max's face that was not bright red with blood, lacerations, or swollen tissue. The major's usually expressive visage was barely recognisable.

In despair, Hugo sank to his knees, following protocol by feeling for the pulse in Max's neck. Nothing – but then … a feathery vibration under his fingers.

Getting away from the area as quickly as possible was the priority now, but he still had to drag Max to the back of the van and then get him into it and administer first-aid dressing packs to control his bleeding. He had no real expectations of saving the major, not after seeing the two gunshot wounds and the beating he had taken. He'd probably be dead by the time he'd been dragged across ground that was filled in with loose gravel in places, nonetheless, he had to try to save him.

Hugo grimaced at the pain shooting up and down his own wounded arm, but despite the agony, he bent down to grip Max's wrists. The bones were intact, and he could still use the limb to help manhandle Max into the vehicle.

\*\*\*\*\*\*

With tremendous effort, Hugo got the unconscious Max hoisted into the back of the van. He made sure he had the first aid kit but left everything else at the scene. His worries about the German military police becoming aware of the gun battle had grown, and he was beginning to panic. He was only a kilometre from the town and the same distance to the safe house, but he had the added worry that the van might be too badly damaged to drive. Its passenger side was pitted with bullet holes, and gasoline and oil were leaking onto the ground beneath the vehicle.

Hugo got into the driver's seat and went for the ignition. "*Merde. Non!*" He thumped the steering wheel as he faced another setback. *Where were the fucking keys?*

He stared out the window at a black void. His eyes watered with frustration, and although he couldn't admit defeat, Hugo dreaded having to get out again to search for the keys on the ground or in the pockets of dead men. He squinted again at the road ahead, certain he'd heard the faint rumble of a vehicle's engine – silence – he was hearing things.

Moments later, an undistinguishable number of men approached the front of the van. Hugo heard their soft footsteps crunch the gravel. His instincts kicked in and although he saw nothing, he raised his hands and clasped them behind his head.

A blinding beam of light hit his face.

A man holding the torch appeared at the window. He was accompanied by a dozen men armed with rifles. One man carried a sub-machine gun, another, its tripod on his shoulder, but whilst they looked like soldiers, they were dressed in civilian clothing, with most wearing the typical black beret signifying they were possibly Frenchmen.

*"Merci ... merci, Dieu."* Hugo let out a long sigh of relief as he finally recognised Cesar from the Resistance. "As you can see, we met with an ambush. Those on the roadside are all dead, but Max is wounded in the back. He's not looking good."

While he couldn't see anything, Hugo heard the laboured rumbling of an old vehicle. A Resistance fighter flashed his torch in the direction of the noise, and instantly the lights of a Renault farm tractor switched on.

Hugo got out of the van and watched the tractor and the rickety-looking trailer attached to its tow hitch do a five-point turn to face the direction whence it came. Cesar was already organising his men; some to form a perimeter and others to deal with Max. The van's back doors were opened, and two men went in to get to the unconscious British major, as Cesar called him.

Hugo's emotions surfaced, as his shock subsided. The Resistance were going through the carnage at the side of the van, sorting through what he couldn't. *Thank God for small mercies.* Without orders, they silently set to work clearing the area, their faces as blank as the eyes of the dead, their voices muted with respect for the fallen.

As the men carried Max to the trailer, Hugo explained to Cesar, "We got ambushed by German deserters. How did you know it was us out here?"

"We heard the gun battle from the farmhouse and came to investigate. We suspected it might be your team in trouble. You were due to arrive sometime tonight." Cesar observed the dead bodies being loaded into the van and added, "We would have come out regardless. We've been building up our forces and getting ready for a fight. I've got more than thirty men at the farm."

Within minutes, the area was cleared, apart from the van that remained in the same position minus its keys. The dead bodies were piled high in the back of the vehicle, and most of the Resistance fighters were now congregating by the farm tractor.

Hugo got into the front passenger seat. Cesar started the tractor engine and pulled away. Four of his men were on the back attending to Max whilst others, on foot, were protecting the tractor by keeping pace beside and behind it as it drove slowly and carefully along the road.

Hugo started at a *whump* noise and turned sharply to look behind him. A soft bang was followed by a rush of flames ignited by the leaking gasoline and oil now engulfing the van. Lit up by the fire, two men were running along the road towards them and their trailer. He twisted his body and blazed at Cesar, "You've just woken up the Feldgendarmerie and every Wehrmacht soldier in town!"

"I know."

"Then why…?"

"You have questions. I have questions," Cesar replied, turning off the road and entering a field. "But we will have to save them." He glanced at Hugo. "Follow my instructions. Trust me."

Cesar pulled up at a bomb-damaged farmhouse, long since devoid of animals or crops. He turned off the engine and said, "We're finally fighting back. You'll see."

The men got Max off the trailer and straight into a car accompanied by a man whom Hugo presumed was a doctor.

"Go with Thierry. He will look after the British major," Cesar said.

"What are you going to do?"

"We're going to draw the Germans here and then blow them to smithereens along with the remains of this house. Go now."

As Hugo reached the car, he saw at least thirty men around the house. He got in, wondering if his team's demise had been the catalyst for what looked like preparations for a battle. Men were setting explosive devices around the building's façade and at strategic locations outside. Others were unloading the old trailer that had brought them here, and spotters were disappearing into the field. He pulled the car door closed, and as it sped off, he heard Max groaning in the back seat. "He's still alive," he said, daring to believe it.

Thierry, the man in the back seat who was putting pressure on both sides of Max's shoulder wound with linen cloths, said, "*Oui,* but only because the bullets went straight through him."

"Will he make it?"

Thierry shrugged noncommittedly. "If I can get him to my colleague in the next few minutes … maybe."

Ten minutes later, the car pulled up to a house that sat a few metres from the river. Outside was a plaque saying *Docteur Descoteaux.*

******

It was 0400, only an hour since the Sussex team had encountered the Germans, and four of them were dead.

Hugo watched as Thierry and another doctor removed Max's jacket then cut off his cotton shirt and started cutting away his trousers.

"How long has he been unconscious?" the older of the doctors asked Hugo.

"I don't know. Maybe around forty-five minutes ... when the fight ended." It seemed to Hugo that hours had gone by since he and his friends had been joking in the back of the van. "He saved my life. A German was firing at my back as I ran along the road, and then he was shot dead. From where he was lying, Max must have killed him before he passed out – my God..."

"What is it?" Thierry prompted.

"It's just hit me that it is probably true. Max was unconscious when I found him, but his pistol was still in his hand. I don't know how he managed it, but I am standing here because of him."

As if hearing his name, Max's eyelids fluttered, then settled shut again.

Thierry said, "Let me treat your arm. *Mon père* – Henri – will see to your friend."

"I will try, but I'm not hopeful," Henri responded without looking up from his patient.

In another room, surgical and medical equipment sat in complete disarray, looking as though it had recently been brought in and dropped there. Thierry ordered Hugo to sit. "Don't move," he said, as he shone his bright Anglepoise lamp on Hugo's wound site and began to examine the extent of the damage. He lifted his head, taking in Hugo's bloodless, greyish, waxy complexion and pain-filled eyes, then he gestured to a table full of medical supplies. "I've got to make sure this bullet is out. Luckily for you, we ambushed a supply convoy a few days ago, and for the first time in weeks, I have morphine."

"Thank God. I'm not good with pain," Hugo said.

An hour later, Hugo stirred from his morphine-induced stupor, still on the doctor's table. The Anglepoise lamp was turned off, but cosy oil lamps sat on an adjacent table. The blackout curtains on the window were closed, and Thierry was sitting on a stool beside him.

"Ah, you are properly awake now?" the young doctor asked.

"Max ... the major?" Hugo responded, his question a hoarse whisper.

"He lost a lot of blood and is still fighting for his life. According to my father, he will either die before morning or live with a badly damaged hip. We were fortunate to have a donor who is the same blood type as your major, and so we gave him a person-to-person blood transfusion."

"His other injuries, Doctor?"

"You may call me Thierry – *oui,* he took some heavy blows to his head, and he is still unconscious..."

"Still?"

"He could have bleeding or swelling in the brain, in which case, his life will be in God's hands."

Hugo, whilst trying to digest that news, was also thinking about what had happened at the farm. "Were the Resistance successful?"

"Ah, that I do not know. We will learn soon enough. If Cesar and his men succeed, we will remain here. If they fail, we will run for our lives, and your major will die. It is as simple as that."

Hugo was groggy, his mouth was dry, and his arm was beginning to ache. He tried to sit up.

"No, stay where you are." A jug of water sat on a low wooden table. The doctor filled a tumbler and handed it to Hugo. "Drink this, then you must tell me what happened tonight to cause the death of eight people … or nine, if our British friend here doesn't make it."

"The Germans appeared from nowhere. The van's lights were dimmed, and we couldn't see more than a few metres of road at a time. They shone torches directly at us. The major stopped, cut the engine, and then everything got messy. They lined us up against the van, then they found our radio…" Hugo gulped down most of the water, then cleared his throat as the horror on the road came flooding back to him. "A German soldier dragged the major to the other side of the road and began to kick him. Another soldier joined him … they seemed so intent on hurting Max that they took their eyes off the rest of us, and then we … we pounced, without signals or planning, on the other two Germans who were guarding us. One had a rifle, the other a pistol. It was pitch-black apart from the one torch that was shining on us … that fell at some point."

Hugo felt a lump of grief swelling the back of his throat. He gulped, "We tried to disarm the soldiers, but we – and them, I suppose – could hardly see past the end of our arms, never mind what or who we were hitting. We outnumbered the bastards … I think Jules even managed to get to his pistol and take a shot." Hugo squeezed his eyes shut as guilt flooded him. "When the rifle fire began, I was already on the ground and being stood on and kicked by God knows who. I did what I could to get up, but I couldn't move and had to roll under the van – I didn't see what happened after that. I hid like a damn coward until the firing stopped a while later."

As he wiped his tears away, his self-disgust grew. "Everyone was bunched together, and when the torch was kicked away, it must have been impossible … we couldn't see a damn thing! I got to the far side of the van and started to run in the direction of the safe house. I didn't see the German – *le porc* – I didn't think anyone was left alive. He fired his rifle, hitting me in the arm, then he stopped shooting … but when he fell silent, I heard the pistol discharging … damn it. It's blurred like a bad dream."

"Take your time."

"Afterwards, I heard nothing but my own breathing … that's when I went back to see if anyone else was alive, and when I found Max."

Hugo finally looked at Thierry, tears rolling down his cheeks unabated. "We tried to take them on. We fought back." He covered his face with his hands as another wave of grief shrouded him. "I can't believe this. It was all going so well."

Thierry shook his head, "*Oui* – I suppose it always does until everything turns to shit."

# Chapter Fifty-One

## Paul Vogel

*Bielański Forest, near Warsaw, Poland*
*31 July 1944*

Paul and Amelia packed up their meagre possessions, both suspecting this would be the last time they would wake up in the wooden shack they had called home. Paul studied Amelia's downturned head as she rolled up their fur blanket. *How many times had they made love on it, slept in each other's arms, used its warmth on the coldest of winter nights?* The bittersweet memories filled his eyes with tears and blocked his throat with regret.

"It's time, Amelia. We should go to Romek before he moves out," Paul uttered, sensing her sadness.

She raised her bright eyes to him, and in them, he saw his own fear reflected. He had no comfort to give her but love and inflated optimism that wouldn't fool her. "Dearest, this could be our final battle. If we succeed, and we will, we will finally be free to imagine a future together. We must believe this," he urged her.

"I know, but I'm worried we'll be separated, and I won't know where to find you in the madness," she responded, wrapping her arms around his waist and nestling her head against his chest. "I'm scared, Paul."

He tilted her chin. "I will protect you. I will always find you," he said, kissing her hard on the lips.

Over six hundred Polish insurgents with weapons and equipment had amassed in one of the densest areas of Bielański Forest, near Warsaw. Paul had witnessed the build-up during the night. At first, a trickle of people had arrived, but then whole platoons coming from the eastern front at the old Polish border appeared with injured men. Whilst treating the wounded, Paul had learnt that these Home Army detachments had been fighting for weeks; harassing the Wehrmacht forces' rear and cooperating with Soviet forces, which had on 13 July crossed into Poland.

Paul and Amelia found Romek and Kurt deep in conversation with three Poles, all of whom Paul knew from the many missions he had participated in the last few months. He greeted Wójcik, young Bogdan, and Kacper, then he set his and Amelia's rucksacks on the ground.

"What's the latest news?" he asked Romek.

"Sit, both of you," Romek said, looking distracted.

The five men went back to discussing Warsaw locations on a map, but Wójcik managed a good-natured wink at Amelia. The Pole, who had led the operation to assassinate Manfred Krüger, had taken a leap of faith and allowed Paul to go on missions, treat wounded men in the field, and work and train with highly skilled Jewish surgeons under the most appalling circumstances. Thanks to Wójcik, Paul had become a competent doctor with surgical experience.

Amelia waved to a woman she had come to know well and left the men to join her friend. Paul sat on a log, and whilst Romek spoke of strategies and locations, he cast his eyes around the area. The camp, now bursting at the seams with men and women wearing a mishmash of uniforms put together using both Polish army castoffs and civilian clothing, was remarkably orderly. Most of those congregated carried rifles either slung over their shoulders or casually held. Some had buckled grenade belts around their waist, were carrying flame throwers on their backs, or were armed only with the pistols tucked into their trousers. Regardless of age or sex, all wore the same indomitable expressions of determination on their war-weary but resolute faces.

The logs Paul and the other men sat on were strategically placed around a campfire. This group of people had spent many nights together drinking rotten coffee or homemade vodka and eating whatever they had managed to forage that day; and on some days, they ate nothing at all. They had sung songs, Paul had read his poetry aloud, Romek had told his silly Polish jokes, which at times made no sense to Paul or Kurt, but they had laughed anyway, and emotional reunions had taken place between comrades. Here in this spot, they had planned operations, rejoiced in their victories, and lamented their defeats. This had been Paul's world for almost a year, and today it would end for a future of unknowns.

"... but don't go any further than here. Even if you see a breakthrough, you must hold until the other two battalions arrive to back you up," Romek was insisting to Bogdan, the tall, lanky fellow who hardly ever removed his flat cap or trouser braces unless it was to show someone the scar next to his penis.

Jolted back to the present, Paul asked hesitantly, "When are we moving out?"

"General Bór-Komorowski and Colonel Chruściel have ordered the full mobilisation of the Polish Home Army. The offensive will begin at 1700. This is it, Paul."

"It's been confirmed, then? We're really going to take Warsaw?" Paul asked, unhappy with the slight tremble in his voice.

Wójcik's humorous eyes sparkled. "I like your optimism, Lekarz Paul. Yes, we are going to *take* Warsaw. It's as simple as that."

Kurt, wearing a deep frown as he often did when worried, said, "It is not simple at all. I'm not happy about the timing. We were supposed to start the uprising at dawn and take the Germans by surprise."

Bogdan concurred. "It's ridiculous to ask Warsaw's civilian population to go through today pretending they know nothing about the uprising. And what if the Germans decide to round-up people, as they did yesterday?"

"What's going on?" Paul asked, still not up to speed on the ongoing mobilisation plans.

Romek answered. "Four days ago, the governor of the Warsaw District called for one hundred thousand Polish men and women to report for work as part of his plan to construct various fortifications around the city. The people of Warsaw declined the invitation, and their refusal has opened them up to reprisals. If the Germans make mass arrests today, it will diminish our ability to mobilise. Kurt and Bogdan are right … we should be starting the uprising at dawn with the Soviets coming in at our backs."

"Where are the Soviet forces now?" Paul asked Romek, who had just returned from a meeting in Warsaw with Home Army commanders.

"Their armoured units reached Warsaw's eastern suburbs two days ago. The Germans counterattacked with two Panzer Corps, but the Soviets have held," Romek answered.

Bogdan glared at the ashes in the campfire and declared, "They say they will come to our aid, but I think they will watch and wait in their positions and then try to take the city when we've thrown the Germans out. No one in their right mind should believe a word from that Stalin's mouth. They're a deceitful lot."

Romek shook his head. "You're wrong, Bogdan. I was in Warsaw and heard that radio station based in Moscow – *Kosciuszko,* it's called – emit an appeal. They were asking the people of Warsaw to fight the Germans. They said a Polish Army, trained in the Soviet Union, was preparing to enter Polish territory to help us. Do you think these Poles will betray us?"

"If they're under Soviet command, they will do as their Russian masters order them to do. You seem to forget the massacre in Katyn forest, Romek. The Russian NKVD, their Secret Police, killed those Polish officers. I know it. You mark my words, the truth of it will come out one day."

"Cut it out, Bogdan. This sort of talk is not helpful," Wójcik said, narrowing his eyes in warning.

"He's right," Kurt joined in. "We should be focusing on how we're going to wipe out the Hitlerite vermin from Warsaw today instead of second-guessing the Russians."

Bogdan insisted, "I'm telling you the Soviets want Warsaw for themselves…"

"And that's precisely why *we* must take the city before the Soviet-backed Polish Committee of National Liberation can assume control," Romek finally snapped.

Bogdan rose to his feet, rifle slung over his shoulder and a metal flask in his hand. "You don't want to hear what I have to say, so I will leave you to your optimism. My unit is moving out. We're going to get into the city early to take up our positions. Good luck, all of you," he flung over his shoulder as he walked away in a huff.

Wójcik and Kacper, who had said very little during the discussion, also stood.

"We'll meet you back here in thirty minutes. Be ready to move," Wójcik said, picking up his gear.

Romek, Kurt, and Paul remained behind. Paul, studying Romek, noted the deep lines in his furrowed forehead and said, "You're worried, Romek. We all are, but what's bothering you the most?"

"You know me too well, Paul," Romek responded with a deep sigh. "Half these men have not been to Warsaw in years. Apart from the shock of seeing the destruction of the city's buildings and infrastructure, they will confront a German army. There are over eleven thousand troops stationed at the city's garrison alone, including Waffen-SS volunteers, and they have been preparing for an attack for months."

Romek spread his arms, gesturing to the mass of Poles getting ready to depart the forest and head to the city. "They don't have the full picture. Their commanders have skimmed over the full extent of German defences, but I've seen the hundreds of concrete bunkers and barbed wire lines protecting the buildings and areas occupied by the Wehrmacht. They've got army units made up of Schutzpolizei and Waffen-SS, and auxiliary detachments of the rail guard, factory guard, ethnic Germans and paramilitary units stationed on both banks of the Vistula and in the city. You heard the singing last night, the victory cries, the belief that we will throw the Germans out within days? I worry this is not going to be the short, successful offensive the men are hoping for."

"Should we postpone the uprising?" Kurt asked Romek.

"No. We had to make a decision ... either initiate the uprising now in this difficult political situation where we risk a lack of Soviet support, or face Soviet propaganda describing the Home Army as impotent or worse, Nazi collaborators. Our commanders feel that if Poland is liberated by the Red Army, the Allies will ignore our London-based Polish government in the aftermath of the war, whenever that may be. Bogdan was right on everything he said. We can't trust the Soviets, but we cannot back down either..."

Romek hesitated, as though dreading his next words. He stared at Paul, finally saying, "If the Soviets don't come to our aid, I don't believe we will take the city."

Paul, as a doctor first and foremost, very rarely sat in on strategy meetings. He did as he was ordered, went where his unit went, and usually didn't know about missions until the last minute. This was different, however. This was not a stealth-like mission to hijack German supply lorries or weapons on convoys and trains; this was going to be an open battle with Poland's capital being the prize. Romek should be nervous but also optimistic. It seemed, however, that he was neither.

Kurt, also concerned, said, "You've met with our Allies in London, Romek. You know the way they think better than any man here. Will they help us?"

Romek shrugged, "My government-in-exile have been trying diplomacy to gain support from the Western Allies, but the British and Americans say they will not act without Soviet approval. Royal Air Force flights have been dropping Polish personnel trained in Britain … money and supplies, but in answer to your question … no, I think we will have to stand alone."

"Then that's what we'll do," Paul said with blazing optimism.

Romek straightened his stooped shoulders. "No more talk of defeat. You two and Amelia will be with me. Wójcik's unit will also join us. We will be positioned in Area I, in the *Warszawa-Śródmieście* … that's the city centre and Old Town. Paul, after we take it, you and Amelia will be based with the medical teams in the Wola district."

Romek leant in closer to Paul and Kurt, who were sitting opposite him. "From now on, the two of you will speak only Polish. I know you, and Bogdan, Wójcik and Kacper know you, but thousands of Poles will be out for German blood, so don't get yourselves shot for speaking German and being mistaken for spies. Paul, you can tell the medical team you're working with that you are a German Jew, but no more." Romek bent down, picked up a pile of clothing, and handed it to Paul. "It will be confusing in the streets. Wear this Polish army jacket along with the medical armband. All doctors, Red Cross, and medical teams will be wearing the armbands."

Romek seemed to relax. He lit a cigarette and sighed as he blew out the smoke. "No more talking or planning. No more hiding in forests for weeks and months. Now, we fight together. Now we take our capital back, and we're going to do it with over forty thousand men in our first strike force."

Kurt smiled. "If I had a drink, I'd drink to that."

# *Chapter Fifty-Two*

## The Warsaw Uprising

*5 August, Warsaw, Poland*

"Get out!" Kurt's loud, guttural order startled the doctors and patients in the basement, which was already noisy with the unceasing cries and moans of the wounded. Paul, who was treating a man's open fracture of the tibia bone in his shin, whipped his hand away from the wound, turned, and blazed at Kurt, "There are over sixty patients in here, Kurt…"

"You must evacuate now, Paul. Right now."

This was the third basement Paul and his team had been forced to leave in a hurry. The medics had learnt the drill and standing orders that should not be broken; patients too ill to walk were to be left behind. Paul cursed under his breath and threw a sheet over his patient's open wound revealing the shattered bone, muscle and tissue. "I'm sorry," he said, in a subdued voice.

"Kill me, Doctor. I don't want the Germans to finish me off…"

"Move, now!" Kurt's booming shout alarmed Paul again.

Paul glanced around the long, narrow basement. The walking wounded were already being ushered up the stairs by the Red Cross volunteers. The two other doctors working with him began to refill their medical bags and boxes with sterilised surgical instruments, medicines, drugs and anaesthetics, surgical equipment, bandages, and anything else they could get their hands on. Nothing was to be left behind for the enemy or wasted on those who were probably going to die at the hands of the Germans.

Women, including Amelia, left their traumatised patients begging for merciful deaths and followed the evacuees and Kurt's men, who were carrying the physicians' precious equipment out. Paul stiffened his back and hardened his expression. He had discussed this scenario with the other doctors and had timidly suggested that they should find a way to give the dying mercy before the Germans got to them. He was, however, overruled on the two occasions he'd brought the subject up.

"I'm sorry, I have nothing to give you. God bless you," he said to the young man he'd been trying to save.

Paul, the last man to leave the basement, met Kurt at the building's exit. Bullets were flying in both directions, forcing the men to stay put in the doorway. Paul shoved aside thoughts of the wounded downstairs being executed when the Germans came upon them, and instead, focused on Kurt. It had been a week since the two men had spoken together, and Kurt was showing signs of battle fatigue.

"Kurt, your head is bleeding."

"Forget it, Paul. Three German attack groups are advancing westward along Wolska Street. That's only two streets from here. They've got *Einsatzgruppen,* SS death squads, police, and Wehrmacht troops going house to house, room to room, shooting every person they find, regardless of age or gender. I'm sick with the smell of dead bodies, blood, shit, and burning flesh. They're burning bodies inside the buildings and out in the streets. It's a slaughter. The men in our battalion are trying to hold them back so we can evacuate this district up to our main communication lines on Jerusalem Avenue. We're going to regroup before they wipe out our pockets of resistance – if we can get out of this doorway."

"Where did the people from the basement go?" Paul asked, in a calm voice that belied his fear.

"My men are leading them to our lines. I'm taking you to Romek."

Finally, a lull in the firing. "Stay close, Paul," Kurt said, then made a run for it.

Whilst in the basement, Paul had heard the bomb blasts, the racket of sub-machine gun fire, the incessant whistling of shells dropping from the dreaded German *Stuka Junkers 87* bombers, and the terrible rumble of concrete buildings crashing down. But what he'd heard a floor underground had been like a whisper compared to the deafening turbulence of war in the street.

The two men crouched as they ran behind a barricade that stretched the width of Górczewska Street. Halfway across, a German tank shell blew apart much of the protective wall. Paul and Kurt flew backwards in the blast wave, then thudded against the ground. Most of the Poles who had been manning the barricade were either dead or in the same state as Paul and Kurt, lying on the ground some metres from the blockade.

Paul, winded, deaf, and confused, observed obscure figures and shapes doing a strangely slow jig. He rolled over and tried to rise to his knees…

Kurt, swaying as he tugged Paul's arm, mouthed, "Get up, Paul. Stand up."

Unsteady on his feet, Paul followed Kurt's lips moving again; this time mouthing, "Run." The ground vibrated. Paul turned his head and gasped as the tank's gun turret, barrel, and then its body, in an almost vertical position, breached the blockade and crushed the remaining household furniture, planks of wood, stoves, sinks, and everything else that had been used to build it.

"Run ... can you run, Paul?" Kurt shouted, pulling a stunned Paul behind him.

When they reached the junction of a street five hundred metres from the destroyed barricade, the men halted. Paul bent double to catch his breath. At some point during the frantic dash to safety, he had regained his senses and much of his hearing, but now he was in pain. He gingerly touched the bleeding gash on the back of his head with his fingers. It wasn't a shrapnel wound; he had banged it on the ground when he'd fallen from what had seemed like a great height. But it was still dripping blood. In shock and shivering as if he were being hit by a blast of arctic air, he stayed in his bent over position to try to settle his nerves.

"Romek's over there," Kurt eventually said, gesturing to a building on the other side of the street.

Paul zigzagged through the crowd of Polish fighters behind Kurt. The men had sub-machine guns, ammunition crates with grenades, garden hose flamethrowers, mortars plus boxes full of bullets on a truck.

"Gifts from the Germans," Kurt said, following Paul's gaze.

Paul raised his eyes to the rooftops where men were manning sub-machine guns trained down the length of Jerusalem Avenue. Paul wondered how many other transport vehicles and weapons the Poles had managed to acquire. Being under-equipped, the Home Army's policy was to scavenge for every bullet, flask of water, or piece of bread from dead, captured, or wounded Germans as they went through the city's streets. He'd seen Poles fighting with rocks and stones, knives and hammers.

Having come to, Paul observed his surroundings more clearly. A hundred or more Poles were crowded into this narrow street stinking of gun powder, cordite, and diesel fumes. Some were helping load injured men and equipment onto a second German truck while other insurgents sat against a partly destroyed building taking a breather. Pushing through his recent trauma, Paul caught up with Kurt and said, "I think you were right about the retreat."

"I didn't say it was a retreat," Kurt snapped back and then apologised in the same breath. "Sorry, Paul. That tank shook me. It was too damn close."

"It's good to see we have trucks," Paul said, changing the subject.

"Thanks to our earlier gains, we've got transport in a lot of districts. We haven't met our objectives yet, but we've done well. We took a major German arsenal, the main post office, the power station, and the skyscraper, Prudential Building. We have most of the Old Town and the city centre. Come on, we'll find coffee and Romek. He'll know more about the current situation than I do."

In the basement of a partly destroyed building that they would have been forbidden to enter in peacetime, Paul and Kurt found Romek, Wójcik, and other commanders. They were in deep conversation in what had once been a storeroom connected to the main space where medical teams were treating the wounded.

"It's good to see you, Paul," Romek said.

Paul responded, "You, too … you as well, Wójcik. I'll go make myself useful."

Back in the main basement area, Paul saw Amelia and the rest of his medical team, who were already organising the wounded for another evacuation. Paul waved to Amelia, his relief at seeing her in his wide, cheesy grin. She rushed to him, concern on her face as she examined his head wound.

He kissed her, then said, "I'm all right. Go back to work."

Paul's eyes swept the room. Numerous injured patients lay on the floor being treated by men and women wearing their Red Cross armbands. His eyes caught a man bending over an injured woman and he smiled again. Despite the dire situation, he couldn't remember the last time he'd felt this much pleasure.

"Anatol," he uttered softly as he reached his old friend.

Anatol craned his neck, his exhausted face brightening when he saw Paul, "My God, Paul, I hoped I'd see your ugly face."

"Can I help here?"

"No," Anatol said, helping his patient to her feet. "We're clearing out. You can see to the wounded evacuees upstairs, and I'll join you in a few minutes."

When Paul returned to the storeroom, Romek, Kurt and Wójcik were in the middle of a heated debate about decisions that had been made by the Polish commanders. He glanced around the tiny space but hovered in the doorway while a radio operator was speaking to someone on the other end of the line. Activity in the main room heightened. Soldiers had arrived and were helping the last of the injured up the stairs while the doctors were gathering everything they could carry.

"Paul, I'm taking a few volunteers to join Zośka and Wacek's battalions. The scouts are going to try to take what's left of the ghetto. Do you want to come?" Romek asked.

"Yes."

"Good. If we succeed, we'll use the area as one of our main communication links between the Resistance fighting in Wola and those defending Old Town. You will set up a medical station there."

Paul took advantage of the five-minute break before the last of the units were due to move out of the area and sat with Amelia against the ruined building's wall, holding her hand and stroking her fingers. She was brave, efficient, and never cringed at the horrors or lost her calm. Even now, as German tanks closed in and the murderous machine-guns rattled from surrounding rooftops, she maintained her unruffled demeanour.

Anatol appeared. He got down beside Paul and ran his fingers through his sweat-soaked hair. "Paul, you're a sight for my sore eyes."

"And you mine. Have you been here since the day the uprising began?"

Anatol nodded. "I lost my battalion on the second day. I've been in that basement for days. Six of us treating hundreds of wounded."

"Where is Vanda?" Paul asked.

Anatol's jaws tightened. He bit the inside of his lip and stared at the ground. "I lost my Vanda. She was killed two months ago."

"My God ... no, Anatol, I —"

"It's taken a while for me to come to terms with her loss, but I'm getting through it," Anatol interrupted Paul. "She went looking for food with her mother and sister. They were on a tram when the SS boarded it. They ordered the passengers off, and when the Poles began to leave, the Germans counted out the first fifty people. Vanda and her mother were numbers forty-seven and forty-eight. I know this because Nadia, my sister-in-law, told me she was standing some way behind Vanda, and that she would have been number fifty-four. She watched Vanda and their mother being marched to the wall of a damaged building, then being pushed against it and shot. Fifty people chosen at random and wiped out." Anatol stifled a sob. "Paul, my Vanda was murdered because of where she stood on a tram. Does that make any fucking sense to you?"

Paul's face drained. Amelia, also listening, stifled a sob as Anatol broke down in tears.

"I don't know what to say, my friend, except to give you my condolences, which are probably of no comfort to you," Paul eventually said.

Anatol sniffed. "It's been two months, but sometimes I wake up and can't believe I will never see her again." He wiped his nose with a handkerchief. "We weren't even supposed to be in the city that day. We had been with the Resistance for months, but Vanda begged me to take her into the city centre to see her family. We knew about the executions going on. Every time the Home Army struck a convoy and killed a German soldier, the SS took their revenge with a hundred Polish lives. I made her promise not to leave her mother's house – damn it, Paul, she promised she wouldn't."

Kurt appeared. Anatol stood, and the two men hugged.

"I wish we had more time together, Anatol, but I need Paul," Kurt said.

"Where do I go now?" Anatol asked.

"Get on the last truck with Amelia. What's left of us are retreating to the forest to regroup. Paul and I will meet you there tonight."

Paul kissed Amelia goodbye, then said, "I'll see you soon, my love."

# Chapter Fifty-Three

Romek and his assault group, including Kurt, Wójcik, and Paul, rendezvoused with the *Zośka* scouting battalion in the newly formed armour platoon of the Home Army's Radosław Group. In possession of a German tank and one armoured car, they advanced on the Gęsiówka concentration camp, situated inside the ruins of the old ghetto. Its three-metre walls were still heavily defended, and German snipers were reported to be atop a few buildings in the street leading to the main gates.

One of two Panther tanks that had been captured by Polish insurgents on 2 August began the assault on the camp with its main gun firing on the wall. Romek's volunteers, along with the Scouts – both men and women under the command of Ryszard Białous and Eugeniusz Stasiecki – began firing at the enemy blockade. Thus far, no anti-tank guns had fired on the now Polish-owned tank, and this, along with the foot soldiers' success at taking out the German defenders at the barricade, spurred the platoons to advance at a run until the tank finally blew the gates wide open, and the men stormed inside.

For ninety minutes, the two sides fought a battle for control of the camp, and before the end, most of the German *Sicherheitsdienst* – SD security guards, were either killed or captured, although some had fled towards the nearby German-held Pawiak Prison.

Paul tended to the wounded Scouts, determined to treat the German guards who were injured only after he had tried to save Polish lives. Two of the Poles had been killed upon entering the camp, and another three had non-life-threatening wounds. Buoyant in victory, he treated the men with minor first aid, and then, as ordered, sent them off in the armoured car to the forest to receive proper treatment from the battalion doctors.

As Paul was laying out the two young Polish Scouts who had died only minutes after the platoon had smashed through the gates, he saw Wójcik approaching.

"Two dead," Paul reported.

Wójcik removed his cap and gazed solemnly at the teenage boys. He cleared his throat and said, "Leave them for the moment, Paul. There's something you should see at the subcamp."

"What about the wounded Germans?"

"Fuck them. After I show you what we found, you won't want to help them."

Unhappy about leaving groaning Germans lying on the ground, Paul buckled his medical rucksack and reluctantly followed Wójcik. He had come to realise that he didn't hate Germans; he hated the Nazi war machine that had conjured monsters from previously mild-mannered men.

Paul brought himself up short and gasped as he neared the front entrance to a building.

Before him, hundreds of men and women wearing the typical striped inmate uniforms crowded around the Polish resistance fighters. The sight of the emaciated men and women, on their knees trying to kiss the feet of their liberators, heightened the Scouts' already palpable emotions.

Many of the prisoners collapsed on the ground with relief, but most swayed weakly in silence.

Paul, a man accustomed to seeing starved, downtrodden Jews, tried desperately to keep his tears at bay. Romek's eyes flooded. Kurt, the toughest man Paul knew, was trembling as he gave what water he had to some of the prisoners.

Ryszard Białous, one of the platoon's commanders, asked the confused Jews, "Where are you all from?"

A young man answered in broken Polish, his voice breaking on a sob. "We are not from Poland. We were expecting death today … we thought we were going to die … thank you. Thank you."

Paul caught the German accent as he helped the prisoner who had spoken to a window ledge. The lad, about seventeen, looked pained as his skeletal frame with only a fine layer of skin covering his bones pressed into the hard concrete.

"*Danke schön,*" the boy said. "I am Mordche Buchsbaum, from Munich."

"I will translate," Romek told Białous, the commander.

"Very well, ask him where his fellow inmates are from, how many of them are here, how long they have been here … what happened after the ghetto closed … and ask him how they managed to avert deportation."

Romek asked the first question, but then the man continued uninterrupted as he surged ahead with the whole story.

"There are three hundred and forty-eight of us. We are mostly Jews from Czechoslovakia, France, Greece … Hungary … Belgium, and a few of us left over from a larger German contingent. At the end of July, the SD Guards began to evacuate this part of the camp. They were sending us to Dachau. Many of the inmates were too weak to march. The Germans shot about four hundred of them."

Paul sucked in his breath and swallowed painfully as Romek translated what had been said to the Poles.

Mordche continued, "The Germans marched off about four ... maybe over four thousand prisoners. We don't know if they ever reached Germany or another camp in Poland."

"Why were you left behind?" Romek asked.

"The guards you killed retained us as labourers. They planned to rebuild parts of this camp and extend Pawiak Prison next door. They were going to use them as a concentration camp complex. When the fighting began in the city five days ago, the guards took some prisoners and strung them up, and they executed others by firing squad this morning."

"We will try to get you to safety now," Romek said, on behalf of the Polish commanders.

"There are no safe places for us," the boy snapped despite his frailty. "Put weapons in our hands. We will give you a Jewish battalion, ready to fight."

\*\*\*\*\*\*

*Warsaw, Poland, end of August 1944*

From the middle to the end of August, pitched battles raged around Warsaw's Old Town and nearby Bankowy Square. Paul, who was now stationed in a damaged hospital – recently dive-bombed by Stuka ZXC aircraft, despite being clearly marked – was working tirelessly alongside Anatol, Amelia, Red Cross helpers, and three Jewish doctors who'd been in hiding for years. Tremendous casualties were being inflicted by German bombers that struck the city every forty minutes.

'Do not surrender,' a woman had warned Paul that morning. 'The Wehrmacht and SS are not accepting prisoners.

They are shooting everyone they see, even those with white flags and their hands clasped at the back of their heads.'

Romek and Kurt appeared. Paul had not spoken to them for over a week and was, as always, relieved to see them looking comparatively healthy. He handed his patient over to Amelia and joined the two men.

"If we sustain one more attack in here, we will have to evacuate," said Paul after hugging Romek and Kurt. "How much time do we have?"

Romek said, "Wójcik has been hit. He's outside. Come with us. We'll talk on the way."

Paul collected his rucksack with his personal and first aid items. When they got to the street, he rushed towards Wójcik, lying on the ground. *He's dead,* Paul thought, without even examining him. He had suffered at least four bullets in his torso and was lying in a pool of blood.

"We tried to get him all the way to you, but he was in agony, and we couldn't get him up the stairs," Romek said in a broken voice.

For Romek and Kurt's sake, Paul went to Wójcik and felt for a pulse. His stethoscope was hanging around his neck, so he also listened to his heart. He looked up at the men's hopeful faces and shook his head. "I'm sorry. He's gone."

Paul felt sick with sadness for the man who had been his mentor, but his grief was smothered by the shock of seeing his surroundings. He'd not been outside the hospital for days, and although he'd known they were in a dire situation, he hadn't imagined that every building would be virtually destroyed or that dozens of dead bodies would be strewn throughout the street.

Two of Romek's men carried Wójcik off to some temporary resting place. Paul watched solemnly, then returned his attention to Romek. "He was a good man. By the looks of it, you've been having a tough time out here. What's the latest news from command headquarters?"

"The Germans are attacking, and we are counter-attacking all over the city. They're throwing their heavy artillery and tactical bombers at us, and we don't have the anti-aircraft artillery we need to defend ourselves. We're surrounded, Paul, and the only way we're going to get out of Old Town and get to the city centre is if we use the sewers. We will begin evacuating civilians and the wounded tonight. One of our battalions will stage diversionary attacks to keep the Germans busy as we go into the tunnels." Then Romek warned Paul, "Only those who can walk unaided can go. Those who cannot…"

"I know … I know the drill by now, Romek. They will be left behind."

"We do have good news," Kurt said, inhaling deeply from the cigarette shaking in his blood-stained fingers. "The Soviets have attacked the 4th SS Panzer Corps east of Warsaw, and the Germans have been forced to retreat into Praga. It's a major setback for them."

"Does this mean the Soviets have finally decided to help us?" Paul asked, hope rising.

Romek sniggered. "No. They are helping themselves. We've been trying to get them on the radio for days, and they won't answer our calls. They won't even cooperate with us to get supplies into the city. We will not be doing a supply run today or tomorrow."

The patients and medical teams had not eaten since the previous day, and even then, it had been a meal of *spit soup*, thus called because it was made from ground barley that hadn't been husked, and consequently, the husks had to be spat out. For almost the entire month, Warsaw's citizens had lived mostly on barley from the Polish-held *Haberbusch i Schiele* brewery complex on Ceglana Street. Every day, up to several thousand people organised into cargo teams, reported to the brewery for bags of barley, and then distributed them in the city centre. With the heavy fighting, no one was now baking bread in their cellars, or running with water buckets to thirsty fighters, nor even to the medical stations where it was desperately needed.

Paul was dismayed by the breakdown in the supply chain. The people in the hospital were not only being bombed from the air but were also being starved to death, and worse, deprived of potable water. It was an untenable situation, and unlike at the beginning of the uprising, there was now a shortage of safe zones to escape to.

Paul aired his thoughts, "Well, it looks like it's over for this hospital. We can function for a couple of days without food, but we haven't had water delivered for two days."

"Most of the water conduits are either out of order or filled with corpses, Paul," Kurt said.

"The main water pumping station is still in German hands, but our authorities have ordered all janitors to supervise the construction of water wells in the backyards of every house still standing," Romek added.

*That won't help the hospital's situation,* Paul thought.

******

At 2300, Paul and Amelia began their long journey through the murky waters of Warsaw's sewers, right under German positions. They, along with over a hundred people from the hospital and houses surrounding it, had been instructed to follow the Home Army soldiers until they were told to ascend to street level. No one was permitted to stop, loiter, or turn back, for if the orderly line, going through what was a very narrow tunnel, were disrupted, a pile-up could ensue and endanger lives.

Romek and Kurt's fighting units led the group, intending to get to the city centre before the German strike force overwhelmed the Poles who were already there and trying to hold it. The Germans had received reinforcements and were crushing the Polish Home Army with superior weaponry and concentrated numbers, and, although no one was thinking about giving up the fight, some Poles were calling this *the final stand.*

As they advanced under the Warsaw Streets, Paul and Amelia were positioned halfway along, right in the middle of the crowded pack. For six hours, Paul saw nothing but a woman's backside in front of him. The air was rancid and hot. People cried with exhaustion and despair as they lumbered under the weight of their belongings, and all too often he heard splashing sewage water, as someone stumbled and fell into it neck deep.

Their fear was tangible. Every now and again the Germans threw grenades and gas canisters into the manholes at street level, to put a stop to the fleeing civilians and block the sewers with piles of dead bodies. Regardless of stench, danger, and universal terror, the sick, old, young, and fit struggled to reach the manhole at the end of their journey.

"Keep going. You're holding everyone else up," Paul snapped at the middle-aged woman in front of him. She had stopped numerous times to face the wall and cry for her lost children, but Paul, who had for the last hour been patiently urging her to keep moving, finally lost his temper. "Move now, or I'll put you over my shoulder and carry you. I've had enough of your complaining."

She turned, glaring at him through eyes that were red and raw from sewer fumes. "I'm going blind, I tell you. I can't go on. I want to go back!"

The long line of people behind Paul, including Amelia, tried to continue, but their passage was blocked by the woman's determined stance and her feet planted firmly on the ground.

"Get your hands off me," she told Paul when he pushed her for the second time. "I will not walk another centimetre. If we don't die in here, we'll die when we get out. The Germans will be waiting for us. I want to turn around. Get out of my way. You're not even Polish!"

Paul slapped the woman's face. "Shut up and keep moving."

"No, I can't … I can't do this. The smell … the shit in the water, the darkness. I can't. I would rather die!"

"Move!" someone shouted behind Paul.

"What's the hold-up?" another voice yelled from further down the line.

Pushed violently, Amelia was shunted into Paul's back. Paul, in turn, shoved the woman causing the danger. The shouting became louder as more people began to lose their nerve. Men were cursing, women were weeping, and within moments, Paul expected an onslaught of mass hysteria to disrupt the hard fought for, steady pace.

"Paul, do something!" Amelia begged, as she tripped and fell into the filthy water.

Again, Paul tried to push the Polish woman forward.

"No!" the woman screamed, then with calm, shuffling baby steps, she turned a semi-circle to face Paul. They locked eyes, and in those seconds that seemed to stretch to minutes in Paul's mind, she raised a knife to her own throat, slicing across it with one long circular movement.

"My God!" Paul gasped, as the woman's carotid artery burst, and blood spewed over his shocked face.

Blinded, Paul wiped the blood from his eyes, looked down at the lifeless body at his feet, then pushed it under the water. "Amelia, walk over her. We must go forward," he said, trying to keep his voice calm. Then he shouted down the line, "Watch your feet. There is an obstacle in your path!"

Is this what he had become? he thought as he started moving again. He had just described a dead woman as an obstacle. Too wrapped up in his own desperate situation to notice the knife or the moment she had slit her own throat, he had failed to halt the suicide of a despairing woman, grieving for her lost children?

Two hours later, Paul peeked his head over the drain hole onto the street and found himself just forty-five metres from the advancing Germans. After he had pulled Amelia up, he helped several others get out until his position was unsustainable, and he and Amelia were forced to run under a cacophony of weapons fire blasting their ears.

Paul gripped Amelia's hand and sprinted with her towards the Poles who were preparing to defend the area. Halfway across the street, however, German SS troops advanced en masse and shot people still trying to climb out of the manhole.

"Run!" Paul screamed at Amelia above the noise.

"This way!"

Paul heard Kurt's booming voice and stormed towards it until the impact of a bullet hitting him in the back of his shoulder took the legs from him.

In agony, and face down on the ground with his arm raised and hand still clutching Amelia's, Paul couldn't breathe, think or move. He gasped as he lost Amelia's hand, and in its place, he felt rougher hands dragging him across the street.

Like a pliant doll, he was pulled to his feet and pushed into a line. Amelia stood next to him, and he clutched her hand again as he met her bright, terror-filled eyes. German soldiers swarmed the street, and he now saw the full line-up of six Polish fighters and civilians.

SS men armed with pistols faced the captives. Dazed, Paul cast his eyes to the sky. It wasn't peaceful or blue but crowded with Stukas and dark with gathering rainclouds. He blocked out the terror overwhelming him and flicked his eyes to Amelia. Her beautiful face, dirty with sewer water and streaked with tears, was all he wanted to see. When the man at the far end of the line was shot, Paul squeezed Amelia's hand tighter and continued to hold her loving gaze until she faced front. He had fought his war and his conscience with equal passion. He had loved Amelia, and she had loved him back. He was a father; he had enjoyed a brief but rich life.

"I love you, my darling," he said, as the bullet slammed between her eyes.

\*\*\*\*\*\*

"No – no!" Kurt screamed.

Kurt, Bogdan, and Romek crouched behind a destroyed Renault car. Cut off from their battalion's main units and without enough ammunition to defend or strike back at the advancing Germans, they watched helplessly as the SS shot and killed every man and woman in the line-up, including Paul and Amelia.

Distraught and gripped with a rage that consumed him, Kurt screamed obscenities at the Germans in his mother tongue. He started to rise with his rifle raised, his irrational determination to kill every SS soldier involved in Paul's execution unwavering until Romek and Bogdan pulled him down, pinned him to the ground and clamped his mouth shut with their hands.

Seconds later, Polish reinforcements blasted their way along the street using flamethrowers and grenades, rifles and handguns, stones, and whatever other projectiles they had found along the way. Hundreds came into the open whilst other fighters took up positions on buildings' upper floors with sub-machine guns.

Enmeshed in grief and shock, but free of Romek and Bogdan, Kurt lurched to his feet and started running towards Paul's dead body. The fighting intensified further, with most of the Polish soldiers using remnants of previous barricades and bodies for cover as they fought to clear the Germans from the street.

Kurt, thrown to the ground beside a dead German, picked up a Mauser rifle and fired from a lying position using the corpse as cover base. Launched from behind his position, a mortar flew over his head, exploding on the German line and killing the Wehrmacht and SS soldiers beginning to flee. Taking advantage of the smoke-filled air and confusion, Kurt and the Poles moved forward again, shooting mercilessly at the enemy, who had finally lost control of the street.

Eventually, Kurt reached Paul and Amelia's bodies. He dropped to his knees and fingered Paul's neck where the pulse should be. He knew he wouldn't find one. The bullet hole in Paul's forehead was vivid, and the bullet had gone all the way through and out the back of his skull. Cursing, weeping, and furious as reality sank in, Kurt thumped his fist against the hard, unyielding ground and let loose his rage with a torrent of expletives.

A barrage of sub-machine gun fire, some twenty metres behind Kurt, shot over his head and hit the German soldiers who were trying to counterattack. Flat on the ground, he raised his eyes to Paul, who looked strangely peaceful in the mayhem. His eyes were closed, his mouth set in a soft line as if he had prepared mentally for the shot that had killed him.

Kurt rose and re-joined the fight, during which he spent every bullet from every weapon he had picked up in the street. The area was now clear of German soldiers, but they had left plenty of corpses in their wake. He picked up Paul's rucksack and threw it over his shoulder. Poles were taking advantage of their gains, and as more arrived, they moved forward to chase the Germans further and further from the city centre. He picked up another German rifle and joined the fray. He would return for Paul and Amelia's bodies when the Germans were pushed all the way back. He would not leave his only family in the street…

******

That night, Kurt and Romek sat behind the walls of a burnt-out building on the Western suburbs. As planned, the two men had returned for Paul and Amelia's bodies; however, when they got there, the Polish dead had already been moved. They had no idea where the remains had been taken.

Kurt carried Paul's belongings to a more secluded spot. He didn't want to speak to anyone, not even to Romek or Anatol, who were both visibly upset by Paul and Amelia's deaths. When he was alone, Kurt slipped his hand into the green rucksack and found photographs of Erika, the daughter Paul had never met, socks, undershorts, a shirt, medical and surgical instruments, bandages, one vial of morphine, a photograph of Amelia, taken weeks earlier by a Polish journalist documenting the uprising for the Home Army, and another of Laura and Dieter, which he must have been carrying with him since the war began. Finally, Kurt's fingers stroked Paul's leather-bound journal. In it were poems that Paul had written whilst being surrounded by the dead, the dying, and deafening gunfire that sometimes destroyed all rational thought.

When he flicked to the last page with writing on it, Kurt noted the date. It was significant; a record of Paul's final thoughts. *Would Paul want me to see what had been in his heart two days ago? Or was this an invasion of privacy?* Kurt pondered the question for only a moment. He wanted ... no ... he needed to read his friend's final words. Paul wouldn't mind.

*28 August 1944*

*The licentious character of man still shocks me, even after years of witnessing its cruelty. Today, Amelia asked me why we fought so very hard when our deaths at the hands of the Germans were inevitable. She was terribly depressed by seeing the numerous corpses of women and children outside the hospital this morning, and I had no idea how to lift her spirits. I realise now that I should have been more committed to an answer, but at the time, I too was utterly dejected and could find nothing suitable to say to her.*

*Why do we fight? she had asked me for a second time.*

*In retrospect, I should have said that in our hopelessness, we have taken a futile and desperate step that will probably end badly, but what of that? Our bellies are empty, our hearts are in our boots. We are tired and hungry. We have no choice.*

*It seems to me that some mystifying force has fused our emotions and borne us aloft, even knowing that with tremulous wings, we shall be brought down to earth again with an almighty thud, but what of that? Optimism and faith are what drive us.*

*I should have told her that we fight today so that tomorrow men can be free to love whomever they choose, worship whatever Godly presence sustains them through their darkest days, and walk untethered by religious labels, badges, or racial stigma. We fight so we can wake one day to a brighter dawn.*

*I should have told her that it is now, in these hellish times, that I have learnt the true meaning of Polish pride and recklessly brave rebellion – I should have told her all this and more!*

# Chapter Fifty-Four

## Dieter Vogel

*London 4 September 1944*

Heller lifted the telephone off the cradle, covered the mouthpiece with his hand, and said to Dieter, "Give me a second, will you? This is important."

As Heller spoke on the telephone to someone called *Tony,* Dieter gazed out of the office window. He hadn't been told the reason for this unscheduled meeting yet. He had a pile of work concerning Operation Ultra still to get through at Bletchley Park. He and his team were still involved with Obelisk, who had left Cairo for the not-so-nice French battlegrounds, and his section was also overseeing an ongoing operation taking place in Holland. It was not a good day to be ordered to drop everything and get to London.

The sky was grey today. According to the meteorologists, it was going to be a cooler-than-normal September with above-average rainfall. *Ach, well, rain, shine, sleet or snow, it is all the same to me,* Dieter thought, with one ear on Heller's telephone conversation.

"...you've no idea how grateful I am, Tony – yes, of course, I will. I owe you dinner – and I'm looking forward to seeing you as well – yes, I will have all the paperwork ready. Goodbye for now." Then Heller hung up.

"It's not often I hear you grovelling like that. You must be asking a huge favour, Jonathan?" Dieter teased, raising an eyebrow.

"I know. I prefer being the one who is owed the favour." Heller went into his drawer, brought out a file, and pushed it across the desk to Dieter. "I have a mission for you."

"I'm a bit long in the tooth for missions, am I not?" Dieter laughed at the joke.

"Yes, but I have a feeling you will like this one. I want you to represent me at a meeting in Paris with Jacques Chaban-Delmas, from the National Council of the Resistance, and Colonel Henri Rol-Tanguy, from the Communist-led FFI. You are leaving this afternoon. This is your brief on the meeting."

Dieter's rod-straight back tensed in the chair as stirrings of excitement washed over him. He took the file and asked, "You could send one of your own men from here. What specifically are you after from this meeting?"

Heller tittered. "Yes, there's more to it than what's written in that file, Dieter, and you have an uncanny knack of reading between the lines. I'll get to why I chose you in a moment. General de Gaulle is uneasy about the Communist partisans gaining political strength, and if he's worried, then we should be, too. The last thing we need in France is upheaval in the new government."

"Have we not done enough for the French? I would have thought this was the one thing they could sort out for themselves." Dieter sniggered to himself. He had yet to forgive the Vichy government's armistice with Germany and their part in sending Jews to their deaths. "Sorry, Jonathan … you were saying?"

"When the German commander, General von Choltitz, arranged the truce through the offices of the Swedish Consul-General, he travelled from his headquarters at the Hôtel Meurice to the Montparnasse train station, the headquarters of General Leclerc. He and Leclerc signed a surrender, but Chaban-Dalmas and Rol-Tanguy, the communist leaders of the FFI, were also present, and they suggested that Rol-Tanguy should also sign the surrender document. To cut a long story short, Leclerc dictated a new version and put the name of the FFI leader ahead of his own, and when De Gaulle arrived in Paris two hours later and saw the surrender, he was furious about the communists getting their names in at the top. What is said in this meeting is vitally important, Dieter. I need you to extract as much information as you can from the communists without giving in to their demands regarding intelligence sharing. Understood?"

"I understand. You think they might use it against the new government." Dieter drew his eyebrows in thoughtfully. "Why are you not going? It's not like you to miss an opportunity to get out of the office."

"I'm off somewhere else for a few days – need to know basis, so don't ask."

Dieter raised his hand and chuckled. "Far be it for me to interrogate you, boss," he said playfully. "I must admit, I'm looking forward to finally coming out of the shadows. The dead Dieter Vogel rises again. It's quite thrilling."

Heller handed Dieter an official-looking document with his and Stuart Menzies' signatures on it. Dieter began to read it, and from deep inside his chest, a rasping sob escaped him. He drew in a deep breath and unapologetically wiped his eyes. "Laura is going to be ecstatic, not to mention how Judith will feel. I know we've spoken about this, Jonathan, but you can't imagine the worry we've all been going through."

"I understand, Dieter. That's why we're authorising you to bring your boy home. We would have gone for him sooner had he been fit enough to travel."

Dieter lit a cigarette with a Zippo lighter that shook in his fingers. "To be honest, I was half expecting to meet him off a hospital ship in Southampton."

"No. Max went to France as my agent, and I am determined to bring him back on one of my planes. I should never have sent him on that damn Sussex mission." Heller's eyes were full of sympathy. "You and Laura must be going through hell, what with having no word of Paul, and knowing Wilmot is across the Atlantic. You need this win."

"How true. We've come to terms with Wilmot's incarceration. Truth be told, I'm happier knowing he's a prisoner of war than thinking of him in Europe with the Wehrmacht. It's Paul we're most worried about. You will keep trying to get news of him, won't you?"

"If I hear anything from Poland, you will be my first phone call."

Dieter nodded and cleared his throat, "Thank you. Now, what else about Max?"

"He's in the 203rd General Hospital unit in the Parisian suburb of Garches. It's an American Army medical establishment. Our doctor is going with you. He has the necessary paperwork to get Max released from there." Heller stared pensively at Dieter. "I want to be clear, Dieter. Paris has been liberated, but the Germans let off a V-1 rocket last night, and it won't be their last. Be careful over there."

******

*Paris, France.*

Max sat up in a bed that had been wheeled out to the shady part of the garden behind the hospital building. He was sore and aching from the waist down, but he'd been in pain for so long he could hardly remember a time when he was pain-free. He'd gone through two surgical procedures that had successfully removed bone fragments from his hip and around his pelvic area, and he felt much better now that they'd been removed. His recovery was going to be long and painful, he knew, but the prodding and probing had been worth it; according to the American surgeon, he was going to be able to walk again, albeit with the aid of two walking sticks for the foreseeable future.

He shifted his eyes from the book he was reading to glance up at the French doors and patio at the building's back entrance. He sucked in his breath. Tears unashamedly sprang from his eyes, and his stomach did an airy dance as he raised his hand and shouted, "Father!"

Dieter looked in Max's direction, said something to the nurse he was with, then strode onto the lawn, his face beaming.

After the two men had hugged and shaken hands, Dieter pulled over a wrought-iron garden chair, sat beside Max's bed, and sniffed with emotion. "I feel happier than I have for months, Son. Your mother and I have been worried sick about you."

"Father, what are you doing in Paris?" Max asked, still trying to calm down.

"I've come to take you home. Doctor Colbert from our section has come with me, and as soon as he speaks to your surgeons and gets their all-clear for you to travel, we will take you to Queen Alexandra's Military Hospital in London for further surgical assessment and to continue your treatment. Afterwards, you will convalesce at home with your wife and mother at your beck and call."

Max grinned, lifted his face to the sun, and let out a long luxurious sigh. "Thank God. I never thought I'd live to see this day. There was a time I wanted to die, and another time I wanted to live but thought I *would* die. Thank you, Father."

"Thank the people who saved you and be proud of the fortitude you have shown. Will you tell me about the night it happened, Son?"

"Yes, but you go first. How is my Judith? How's the family? Any news from Paul and Wilmot, and what about Frank? Is he still in Scotland?"

For a while, Dieter got Max up to speed with what was going on with the Vogels. They had received letters from Wilmot, which had raised Laura's spirits no end, but they hadn't heard a word from Paul since the Warsaw uprising began on 31 July. Frank was in France, somewhere, and Hannah was beside herself with worry.

Like his parents, Max was most concerned about Paul's situation, but his emotions were all over the place with the news he was going back to Britain, and he didn't know where to begin his story.

"Tell me, Son, what happened to you and your team?" Dieter asked, taking the decision about where to start out of Max's hands.

Even thinking about the Sussex mission evoked tumultuous emotions in Max. At times, he shook so badly he could hardly hold a cup. When he was handed over to the Americans, he had claimed his mission was top secret, thus avoiding having to speak of it. He would face a long, in-depth debriefing upon his return to London. He was prepared for it, but he dreaded having to relive the events that had almost obliterated his team and left him lying in a bed counting the minutes until his next morphine syrette would be delivered.

He accepted a cigarette from his father, his fingers trembling as he took it. After he'd lit it, he wiggled his backside to a better angle in his bed to find a more comfortable spot. "Papa, please don't ask me to go into the details with you. I can't ... I don't want to. The most important thing about that night is that one of my men, and the Resistance fighters who came to our aid, saved my life. I don't remember much about the days after I was wounded, and even the event itself is blurred because I was beaten before the first shots were fired. To be honest, I don't even know who fired first. The Germans had rifles; we had pistols. It was as dark as hell, and according to Hugo – the Frenchman who came back for me – I killed three of the Germans. I don't remember doing that, either."

"I take it the scar on your forehead is from the beating you took?"

"Yes ... probably ... at least, it wasn't there before that night. When I came around in the town of Villiers-sur-Loire a few days after the ambush, the doctor told me he had removed some bullet and bone fragments from my hip. In fact, he operated on me while the Resistance was battling to take the nearby town of Vendôme from the German military police and the two platoons that had remained there after the bulk of their forces went up to Normandy."

Dieter nodded, "We received reports on that night, Son. We heard that the Resistance had taken the town back."

"I imagine the Germans were too busy trying to defend Normandy to take much notice of what was happening in the Loire area. I was there for weeks, and they didn't return to recapture it."

As Max spoke, survivor's guilt reared its ugly head. Instead of this being a proud moment where he could tout his survival against massive odds, he felt like a piece of shit … as though he had cheated death at the expense of others. "I let everyone down, Father. I lost four good men, the mission was a bust, and I will not now be able to finish this war. That's what kills me the most … I can't contribute to the end."

Dieter didn't respond. Even when Max began to cry, he did nothing to fill the otherwise silent void. Max was grateful to his father for not asking more questions. His papa had come for him, and he couldn't be happier, but whenever he reflected on his failed mission, he wanted to crawl under a rock and be left alone to grieve for the men who had died on his watch.

During the silence that followed, Max shifted again. He could remain in the same position for limited amounts of time. He coughed to clear his throat and continued, "Sorry. The doctors warned me I might suffer mood swings with the anaesthetic." He grunted and added, "Not that I need drugs to feel my damn guilt."

"Stop it, Son," Dieter now responded harshly. "You are a hero, and I couldn't be prouder of you. You were in Poland on the day this wretched war started, and you've kept going ever since. Yes, you lost men in the Loire, but you survived with two bullets in you. And don't think I don't know that you saved your man, Hugo – you took out the German who was going after –"

"I don't remember!" Max blurted angrily.

"It doesn't matter if you recall doing it or not. The fact is, you did do it. That man is alive today because of your bravery, and he knows it. Never feel guilty for surviving, Max, because every time you think like that, you insult those who didn't make it."

Max's blinked away his tears, but the emotions he'd tried to lock down in a dark corner of his mind resurfaced with his father's kindly pat on his arm, and it was a much younger-sounding Max Vogel who spoke next. "I wanted to see this through, Papa. I wanted to finish this war and march into Berlin to arrest the bastards who committed genocide. We're going to win, and I wanted to … ach, never mind … my war is finished."

As he looked down his body at the plaster of Paris cast wrapped around his waist and down to his knee to immobilise and hold straight the affected side, he griped, "I look like a damn Egyptian mummy with only a window cut out at the front and back to let me pee and shit through. I'm a bloody cripple."

"Nonsense. You're a very lucky man, that's what you are. I saw your medical records before coming into the garden. You had an open wound with hip socket and pelvic damage, and an infection that could have turned gangrenous. I was talking to Doctor Colbert – whom I mentioned has come to sign you out – he told me about a pioneering American surgeon from Columbia Hospital in Columbia, South Carolina. Doctor Moore is his name, and he has already performed a hip replacement surgery using metal. Such operations haven't been regulated or conducted on the general public yet … that could take some years … but it's a start. You *will* recover from this, Max. You haven't lost a limb or your life, so I won't hear any more self-pity coming from you, all right?"

Max nodded. His father's brash German candour woke him up. "Okay, no more self-pity from me." He even managed to smile.

"Now, why don't you think about the beautiful wife and family you're going home to? Judith and your mother will be at the hospital to meet us when we arrive, and they are both determined to visit you every day until you are discharged."

Max's depression shrivelled at the news he might one day be able to walk freely again with a new metal hip. It seemed like a miraculous innovation to him, as if it were far too good to be true. For the first time, he also admitted that his biggest worry was not how *he* would feel about his loss of mobility, but how Judith would take to his condition. Her sister had been wheelchair-bound, and Judith had sacrificed her youth to care for Hilde. *Would she regret marrying a man she would now have to look after for possibly years and maybe push around in a damn chair for much of the time?*

"This is good news," Max said, trying to cheer up for his father's sake. "I imagine there will be a queue of ex-soldiers waiting for this medical breakthrough. It will give hope to thousands…"

"Then let it give you hope, Max."

Max's lips spread in a genuine smile. His father was like a breath of fresh air that had wafted in to brighten his gloom. He let out a contented sigh. "I'm going home to my Judith."

586

"Yes, you are. She's very excited to see you. The minute I telephoned her with the news, she wanted to meet me in London and accompany me to Paris."

"She is marvellous, isn't she – how are things going here?" Max asked.

"Going as well as can be expected, but with all the post-conflict ingredients of revenge and political ruses to dirty the transition." Dieter looked covertly around him. Soldiers were lounging on deckchairs, sitting in wheelchairs, or like Max, lying in wheeled-out beds. Pretty nurses were showering attention on the sick and wounded, and a couple of women were serving tea on the terrace. "Not a bad place to recuperate in," he muttered to himself.

He turned back to Max and pulled his chair closer. "Between you and me, there's some nasty business going on in Paris. Charles de Gaulle puffed out his chest and came up with the myth that its citizens had freed Paris, with help from the Free French Army. He failed to mention the other components of that army, from Poland, Germany, and Hungary, Spanish anarchists who'd escaped Franco's new Spain, the North African Arabs and Berbers and Senegalese. The Americans were narked they didn't get a mention either. Without their logistical aid, the insurrection would have ended in failure."

Dieter shook his head in anger. "Yesterday, I watched a crowd of men grabbing women off the street and shaving their heads for sleeping with German soldiers. At my meeting this morning, I was informed that the government have set up a military tribunal for people who collaborated with the German army and police, and they have a separate judicial tribunal for economic and political collaborators. They've arrested almost ten thousand French citizens thus far, and in the Seine department, two tribunals sentenced almost six hundred collaborators to death."

"Did they follow through with the death sentences?" Max asked.

"Oh, yes. I don't have exact numbers, but about a hundred or so have already been hanged."

"I'm guessing there's a lot of people trying to get out of France for cosying up to the German occupiers."

"Exactly right," replied Dieter, "but those who have escaped justice have been condemned in absentia. I'd like to see them come back and face justice."

"How did the Resistance do in the battle for the city?"

"They were hit hard. They lost around a thousand men. The communists are claiming they lost more men than any other faction, and of course, they've let it be known that they fought the hardest."

Max's mind shot to Florent Duguay. Despite Romek's warning that the British were not to act against Klara's murderer, Max had hoped to deal with the swine before leaving France. *That idea is up the spout now,* he supposed.

Dieter waved Doctor Colbert over.

Max shook Colbert's hand. "It's good to see you. Thanks for coming, Mathew. Well, what's the verdict?" he asked.

"You have permission to get on the plane, but you will go straight to your hospital bed. You're looking at two months in Queen Alexandra's in London, or maybe even The Royal Orthopaedic, Max."

Somehow, Max was not despondent. He was, he admitted, desperate to touch ground in England, hold Judith in his arms, and kiss his mother. Optimism had sprouted since his father had appeared. This was his victory.

# *Chapter Fifty-Five*

## Wilmot Vogel

*Camp Concordia, Kansas,*
*United States of America*
*September 1944*

"More potatoes, Willie? You're as scrawny as a bantam chicken's leg," Mrs Barrett said, as she did most days to Wilmot.

"Very kind of you, Mrs Barrett," Wilmot said, grinning at Dottie sitting across from him at the dinner table. For the last two days, she had graced him with her presence at the farm. Home because of a severe head cold, she had taken advantage of the time they were able to spend together whilst trying not to be conspicuous.

She had told him earlier that week, 'My father likes you, Willie, but you're a German. He will never allow us to be together. I know he'll be furious if he thinks I'm cavorting with you.'

Her words had stung, but he could understand her father's posture. 'Every stolen kiss is a gift, Dottie. I won't do anything to jeopardise what we have together,' he had assured her.

"Lovely lunch as always, Mrs Barrett. I think we might have put on ten kilos each since we've been in Kansas,"

Wilmot said on behalf of the other three prisoners who couldn't speak English.

It never ceased to amaze Willie that the Barrett family opened their kitchen door to him and his fellow prisoners every day and invited them to a sit-down meal at their table. After their lunchtime break, their bellies were so full they found it hard to continue to work, and often they laid down their tools by mid-afternoon.

One of the other prisoners tried to talk to Mr and Mrs Barrett about his home in Bavaria but failed miserably to make himself understood.

Willie continued to eye Dottie. They had been together the previous day in one of the fields still tall with wheat. He had kissed her hard on the lips for only the second time, and she had liked it. It had only been a five-minute dalliance, during which she had been sheepish, but in that field, he had made her a promise.

He hadn't planned it or even thought about it before yesterday, but the moment their lips had locked, he'd realised she was the woman he wanted to marry. 'When this is all over, and they send me home to Germany, I will feel like half a man with no soul. Will you let me come back to you? You're the woman for me, Dottie. I knew it the first moment I laid eyes on you.'

And she had replied, 'Yes, Willie, do come back for me.'

"Wilmot … Wilmot, will you help us out here? What's Peter saying?" Mr Barrett was asking.

Wilmot reluctantly drew his eyes from Dottie and turned them to Peter, his fellow prisoner. "What is it you're trying to say?" he asked, gritting his teeth. Instead of relaxing, he spent almost every lunchtime translating for his fellow Germans.

"Ask them if they have ever been to Bavaria?" Peter said.

"Bloody stupid question," Wilmot muttered in German. "Peter wants to know if you have been to Germany?" he asked the Barretts.

"No. I almost got there. I fought in France during the Great War. That was a hell of a thing," Mr Barrett answered.

And that was the end of that conversation.

After lunch, the men thanked Mrs Barrett and rose from the table. Wilmot, reluctant to leave Dottie behind, offered to help with the dishes.

"No, that's women's work," Mr Barrett said. "Stay here with me awhile, Willie."

After the three other prisoners left, Wilmot dutifully sat again and braced for the rollicking he was about to get for eyeing Dottie over the lunch table; however, the conversation went in a completely different direction.

"I like talking to you, Willie. I should say it's because you're the only German here that speaks English – why, you speak it better than me, you know – but truth is, you seem less *German* than the other men I've had a-workin' here."

Wilmot let out a silly, nervous chuckle, still convinced he was going to get a telling-off, or worse, be ordered not to set foot on the farm again.

"You get treated well by us Americans, don't you, Willie?"

"Yes, sir. I can't complain about our treatment at all. Trust me, I've seen worse."

"Hmm. You know, newspaper coverage of our prisoner camps is limited … for a damn good reason, mind you."

"I see," Wilmot responded, wondering where this was going.

"Now, I reckon you boys deserve to serve out your time in peace, but I heard tell of a group of men in one of our towns fixing to make trouble for your boys at the camp. I like you, Son. You're misguided, I suppose, in your belief in that Hitler fella, but I see you're a good man, far as I can tell."

"Thank you, sir."

"I ain't got no problem with taking you boys on here at the farm, but the damn unions are up in arms about you stealin' American jobs. They reckon we should follow the War Manpower Commission's rules that require union participation in worker recruitment…"

"Pardon me for interrupting, sir, but I assumed the reason for us labouring in your fields is because there is a shortage of American workers?"

"Sure, on account of them fighting your country and them pesky Japs in the Pacific. That's precisely my point, but the labour unions don't see it that way. They'd rather we all went hungry than pay you boys a dime for getting our wheat and corn off the fields and into the stores. Don't get me wrong. Most of us folks living near the camp accept you prisoners, but the newspapers are telling a story of people sending letters to the government every week demanding you all be killed."

"Oh."

"I think it's the damn casualty lists printed by those fool journalists that encourages hostile sentiments against you boys, but the way I see it, if we treat you according to the Geneva Convention, it makes sense that you Germans will treat our American boys just as well, should they be taken prisoner. Am I right?"

Wilmot took a slug of his cold tea to conceal his somewhat sceptical reaction to Mr Barrett's assumption. He wasn't at all certain the SS would look after American or British prisoners as well as the Americans seemed to do the inmates at Concordia. That thought appalled him.

"I would like to think my country would treat your Americans in the same way as you behave towards us," he said, in a tone he hoped was convincing.

"Yes, well, I just wanted to warn you to expect some crazy-assed fools a-comin' to protest outside the camp's gates about your presence. I asked for an extra guard for the truck, startin' tomorrow, just in case there's any trouble."

Wilmot, not fazed at all by the threat of a few protesters, thanked Barrett for his concern and rose from the table.

"Sit. I ain't finished with you yet," Barrett grunted, as his long, fat fingers clasped around Wilmot's forearm and tugged him back down.

Wilmot clenched his jaw. *This is it.*

"Don't think I ain't seen you makin' eyes at my Dottie, Willie. A little bird told me you kissed my girl in one of my wheat fields. Is that right?"

"Sir, I…"

"Sir, nothin'. I see the way she looks at you. She's smitten, and I ain't goin' to let you break my little girl's heart with no ideas about you promisin' her some sort of future when there ain't one. You hear me, boy?"

Wilmot, shocked by the change in Mr Barrett's tone, uttered, "I would never hurt her. I love your daughter."

"Love?" Mr Barret said, with a surprising chuckle. "You can't love her. You don't even know her."

"With respect, I think I do. I made her a horse." Wilmot clamped his mouth shut. He sounded like a halfwit.

"Dottie, get in here!" Barrett shouted into the kitchen.

Dottie appeared, drying her hands on her apron, her eyes looking at the floor. "Yes, Papa?"

"Wilmot here has admitted to having affections for you. What do you say about that?"

Mrs Barret came into the dining room behind her daughter. "What's going on here?"

"Your daughter has been cavorting with a German prisoner of war, that's what's goin' on."

"Dottie?" Mrs Barrett demanded.

"I'm not carrying on with him, I swear, Papa. We love each other, and we want to be together. That's not the same as cavortin'. When the war is over, Wilmot will be shipped back to Germany, but then he'll come straight back for me. Tell them, Willie."

"Dottie's correct, sir. That's exactly what I will do," Wilmot said, growing in confidence after hearing Dottie's words.

Barrett looked strangely apologetic as he shook his head in dismay. "I can't be havin' this. If my neighbours get a whiff of this nonsense, I'll never hear the end of it. Now, I'm not sayin' you're the only German to be a-likin' one of our fine American girls, but I can't let it stand. I got enough trouble from the damn unions up my ass for hiring you boys, never mind those that hate you for killin' their sons and brothers in the war. That's why I had the conversation with you, Wilmot. I'm sorry, but you need to be looking for a new farm to work on. You're finished here." He flicked his eyes to Dottie. "I don't want you seeing or speaking to Willie in the camp hospital. You hear me, girl?"

Dottie's face crumpled. "Yes, Papa."

"Get to your room. I'll be havin' words with you later."

Dejected, Wilmot watched Dottie leave without a glance in his direction. "I give you my word, nothing untoward has ever gone on between us, sir. Please, let me continue here at the farm?" he begged.

"Oh, come on, dear," Mrs Barrett finally joined the fray. "They aren't doing any harm. They're young and in love."

"You knew about this?" Barrett demanded.

"A deaf, one-eyed squirrel would know about this, George. It's been almost a year. What do you think happens when two young people feel attraction for each other? Or are you too old to remember what it's like to fall in love? Hmm? Has it been that long since Central Park?"

Barrett's face reddened with embarrassment, but he still shook his head. "Nope. Sorry, I ain't havin' it," he reiterated. "I can't stop my Dottie from seeing you in the camp, though I wish you'd respect my wishes on that, but I won't have no flirtin' going on at my table or anywhere else on my land. When you finish work today, you won't be coming back no more, Willie."

\*\*\*\*\*\*

Wilmot was in a foul mood on the drive back to the camp. He looked at the three Germans in the back of the truck with him, his eyes boring into their guilty faces. "Which one of you three numbskulls ratted me out for kissing Dottie?" he demanded.

No response.

"One of you told on me. I will get it out of you, eventually, so tell me now before I make every minute of your waking lives hell."

Peter, sharing glances with the other two prisoners, coughed it up. "I told Mr Barrett you were canoodling with Dottie when you should have been working. It's not fair. Why should we take the extra workload when you're enjoying yourself?"

Wilmot, who had to try every day to curb his frustrations and his infamous temper, bit his lip and focused on the passing scenery. Smashing his fist into Peter's face would only bring him more trouble, and he was already being stalked by a group of Nazi-lovers in the camp. He didn't have much to do with Jürgen nowadays, but the man still held a grudge for losing his power base in Hut 64. Twice on his way back to the barracks, Wilmot had been confronted by a group of men. They hadn't threatened him, but their offhanded, snarky remarks and veiled threats were clear indications he was being targeted. Satisfying as it would be to smash in a face or two, he couldn't afford that degree of trouble.

The truck slowed down as it took a tight corner at the end of Concordia's Main Street. The guard and driver inside the truck's cabin were probably yapping and would be blind to what was going on behind them as the vehicle went around the bend in the road. Wilmot, glared at the three men in turn and spat, "Say one word now, and I'll come down hard on you for the rest of your damn lives," and then with one impulsive jump, he was over the side of the truck and walking towards a bar twenty metres back.

He sat on a bar stool with a pint of cold beer in his hand, no money in his pocket, and no reasonable excuse in his mind for what was going to be called by the military police his *escape attempt*. He didn't give a shit about being arrested and marched back to camp. Living there was going to be hell without the hope of progressing with Dottie. He'd have all privileges revoked. He'd be confined to barracks, and he'd lose the daily allowance he counted on for his material comforts. *So what? What was the worst thing that could happen now when the worst had already occurred?*

The barman stared, his dislike of Wilmot etched in his face, but not enough to deny him service. *Fuck him, too. I'm not the first German to walk into this bar.* Men on the camp commander's honour's system were permitted to go into town without a guard. Wilmot raised his pint glass and said, "Cheers," as the barman began wiping down the counter with a wet cloth.

Fifteen minutes later, two American military policemen entered the bar. "Staff Sergeant Vogel, I presume," one of the men said, his voice laced with dry sarcasm.

Wilmot grinned cheekily, stood, clasped his hands together on his crown, and said, "Could you pay the barman for me, boys? I don't seem to have any money on me."

Upon his arrival at the camp, Wilmot was taken straight to a holding cell. As he waited for something to happen, he pondered on a variety of possible punishments. *I was an idiot,* he finally admitted. He didn't want to be confined to barracks or have his daily allowance taken from him.

The two military policemen sat at a desk drinking coffee in the hallway outside the row of cells. Wilmot looked through the bars and asked, "Can I have a cigarette, please?"

"No. Shut up," came the terse response from the giant of a man who had roughly thrown him into the back of the truck outside the bar in town.

A few hours later, the two guards flanked Wilmot and marched him to the administration offices. His earlier bravado had left him. His head had been heavy with the beer and he'd fallen asleep. Now, with a clearer mind, he felt the full weight of his actions and wondered if or when he would ever learn to curb his impulsive tendencies. "You know I wasn't trying to escape, right?" he said to the guards.

"We don't care what you were trying to do. You're not our problem anymore," one of the guards snapped.

Still mulling over *that* statement, Wilmot entered the commander's office and was met by not only Commander Jacobs and Captain Grafton but also two men dressed in civilian suits.

"You've given us a merry dance, Staff Sergeant Vogel. You picked a fine day to pull your stunt, that's for sure," Commander Jacobs told Wilmot.

Wilmot, feeling like a small child in a room full of adults, glanced surreptitiously at the two civilian-dressed men who were silently studying him. Something about their well-dressed, humourless presence worried him. "I apologise, sir. Call it reckless, disrespectful, a momentary blunder … something that will never happen again. I am genuinely ashamed," Wilmot responded, his plea for leniency heartfelt.

Jacobs gestured to his two guests and said in a somewhat-bored voice, "You're no longer our concern, Vogel. You'll be taken to your hut to pick up your gear, and then these two fine English gentlemen are going to escort you to Washington."

Wilmot's jaw tightened. Shocked, he flicked his eyes to each of the Englishmen.

Ignoring Wilmot, Captain Grafton pulled a document from his typewriter and stood with it in his hand. "I just need your signature, sir, and you're all set," he said to one of the visitors. Then he addressed Wilmot's guards, "Take him to 64."

# Chapter Fifty-Six

*Washington DC, United States of America*
*26 September 1944*

After they had finished their hurried lunch, Jonathan Heller and his American intelligence counterpart, Colonel Tony Cancio, wrapped up their final meeting. Heller had arrived in Washington DC two days after President Roosevelt's return to the American capital from the Second Quebec Conference in Quebec, Canada. Prime Minister Churchill had gone back to London, and Heller had been ordered to travel to Washington to attend a series of Intelligence Services meetings, which usually took place after bilateral war conferences between Britain and America. Heller was ready to go home. It had been a long, arduous trip, but unlike previous conferences, it had also been upbeat and full of optimism.

"Well, Tony, that's the eleventh wartime meeting of President Roosevelt and Prime Minister Churchill over. All in all, I think it went rather well."

The American intelligence section chief gave Heller a sardonic smile. "The meetings between our two leaders always go well until questions are raised by our respective governments. I wonder how often the agreements made between Churchill and Roosevelt over brandy and cigars are altered in the cold halls of power in London and Washington."

"Hmm, you have a point, but unlike previous conferences, this one began with good news. Call me overly optimistic, but I see the end of this war."

Tony sipped the last of his coffee and set the cup on the saucer. "If only *Adolf* would give up now, instead of fighting on because of his damn pride. His immediate surrender could save thousands of lives."

"I think we both know he won't capitulate, which means you and I will probably meet again." Heller grinned crookedly. "Lucky us, eh? We might even be able to get in a game of cricket."

"Baseball," Tony corrected automatically.

Heller chuckled, then checked the time on his wristwatch. "I should make a move. I'll be in the air in four hours. Thanks again for all you've done for me, Tony. I know it was a big favour."

"I'll never let you forget it, Jonathan." Tony grinned. "Your boy's waiting downstairs. The paperwork's done, and he's all yours. I know you said it was a special favour for an important asset of yours, but there must be more to it. Before you leave, tell me again why you've gone to all this trouble for a German staff sergeant?"

Heller was reluctant to go into too much detail about Wilmot Vogel, even with Tony. He'd come up with the idea of getting the boy back across the Atlantic when his orders to attend the Quebec conference with the Prime Minister had been confirmed. It had been a difficult procedure, but Heller had counted on the goodwill he had generated with the American military intelligence agencies to see it through … as well as the personal goodwill between himself and Tony Cancio.

"I did it because of the sacrifices Wilmot's father and brother have made in their service to His Majesty's government. I saw this as payback for the hardships they've both endured. You see, Tony, when Wilmot eventually gets sent back to Germany, he'll have no one to welcome him because his family is exiled in Britain."

Tony tittered. "You feel sorry for him?"

"No. I have no sympathies for Wilmot, but I do for his father and mother who gave up everything they had to serve Britain. It's a long story, and I will tell you about it one day. Can we leave it at that?"

"We can. I'm glad you came to me with this. Despite what some quarters think, we Intel' buffs should help each other out. You have a safe trip home, Jon."

Heller entered Wilmot's holding room and then closed the door softly behind him. The first thing he noticed about the young man standing in front of the window was his black hair, Mediterranean looks, and dark, almost-black, unafraid eyes staring back at him. He had nothing of Max or Paul in him. He didn't look anything like Dieter, either, but Laura – *ah, yes* – Heller was in no doubt that this was Laura Vogel's youngest son.

"Hello, Wilmot. I see you got here none the worse for wear. Let's sit and have a chat, shall we?"

Without taking his eyes off Heller, Wilmot sat in one of the two chairs at a desk devoid of office materials or any other adornments. He remained silent, suspicious, and with an excess of pride in his defiant chin thrust.

"Let me take these off for you," Heller said, gesturing with a key to Wilmot's handcuffs.

When they had been removed, Heller sat in the chair behind the desk. His eyes had been drawn to Wilmot's black puckered scar travelling across his cheek from his nostril to his ear, and now he noticed other scars on the boy's forehead, above his right eyebrow, and another slicing into his top lip. "That's a nasty gash you've got there. How did you get it?" he asked, gesturing to the most prominent scar.

"It's a battle scar. The Western Desert was a dangerous place."

"Quite."

"Who are you? What do you want from me?" Wilmot asked, in a clipped tone.

"My name is Jonathan Heller, and I don't want anything from you."

Wilmot raised a sceptical eyebrow. "Then why did I sit on a train for four days with two Englishmen who said no more than a handful of words to me the whole journey? Am I in trouble … that is, in even more in trouble than being a prisoner of war?"

Again, Heller compared Wilmot to Max. He had his older brother's self-assuredness that came to the fore when he was in the presence of high-ranking government officials. But this Vogel also had a hardness in his face for one so young; as if he were desensitised to the horrors he had witnessed. According to Laura, Wilmot was smarter than the twins, but he'd been a bad student at school since his only ambition had been to serve in the military. She had also admitted that he was the rebel of the family.

"Wilmot, I work for the British Civil Service with your brother Max," Heller began.

Wilmot flinched, but his suspicious eyes pooled at the mention of Max's name.

*The boy is sensitive after all,* Heller noted. "Max and I are friends."

"I see."

Heller, having completed his initial observations of Wilmot, decided to get to the crux of the matter; not softly, softly, as he had intended, but go in hard and get it over with. This conversation was going to be difficult for the young man to comprehend, Heller surmised, and equally as challenging for him to explain. "I know your family very well, Wilmot, apart from Paul, whom I have not yet met in person. The Vogels mean a great deal to me, and to this end, I have arranged for you to be transferred to a prisoner of war camp in North London, England."

A flash of disappointment crossed Wilmot's eyes, leaving Heller perplexed.

"Is this not good news?"

"Why would you do that for me?"

Heller sat forward in his chair. "I am doing it for your family ... for your mother and father."

"My father is dead."

"No, Wilmot. Your father is alive. He is in England with your mother and sister."

"No!" Wilmot thumped his fist on the desk and began to rise.

"Sit down," Heller warned him.

Wilmot's wild eyes held Heller's gaze as he slumped into the chair. "My father died in an air raid in Berlin in 1940. What sick game are you playing?"

"It's no game. Your father is alive and well and working for the British government." Heller pulled a photograph from his pocket. It showed Max, Judith, Dieter, Laura, and himself. He pushed it across the desk to Wilmot. "This was taken at Max's wedding a few months ago. See here ... that's his bride, Judith. She's a German Jew. Your father saved her by getting her out of Germany, and afterwards, he staged his own death and went to London where he has been ever since."

Wilmot seemed reluctant to look at the photograph.

"I understand this must be hard for you to take in, but it is the truth. Dieter Vogel is alive, and you are going to see both of your parents very soon. Look at it, Wilmot," Heller urged.

Wilmot began to cry. His stooped shoulders heaved with heart-wrenching sobs, and his fingers shook as he finally handled the picture. For a moment, he looked engrossed in the family images staring back at him, but then he raised his eyes to Heller and uttered, "I can't believe this … yes, I believe you, but it's … it is a shock to learn that my father is a traitor to our country."

"Your father is a hero." Heller cleared his throat, surprised at his own heightened emotions. "I understand how difficult this must be for you. I practised the different ways I would inform you about Dieter, but I realise now there is no way to tell you other than coming straight out with it. Your father hates the Nazi Party and despises your Führer. He is a loyal and trusted asset of the British Intelligence Service, and he has been for quite some years."

Wilmot sniffed, wiped his eyes with the back of his hand, then spat, "He is an abomination; that's what my father is! I liked him better when I thought he was dead. Send me back to Camp Concordia."

Heller rose. Taken aback by Wilmot's animosity and the arrogance of his demand, he now questioned his doltish idea to surprise the Vogels with the gift of their long-lost son. "I'm afraid that is no longer an option, Wilmot. I have already signed the papers. You are now in the custody of the British authorities. In three hours, we will get on a seaplane and start our long journey to England. I suggest you get used to the idea, and whilst you are at it, drop your foul attitude. You might not agree with what he did, but Dieter Vogel is your father, and you're fortunate to have him."

Heller paused, as Wilmot fished out a packet of cigarettes from the top pocket of his poorly fitting tweed jacket. Someone at Camp Concordia had done a poor job dressing the boy for his journey to Washington. He felt his sympathy for Wilmot return. The boy was in shock, not only with the news about Dieter, but probably because he had spent four days on trains with two British intelligence officers who had been ordered not to tell him squat.

"Do you mind?" Wilmot asked, waving the cigarette. "Your men took my matches off me."

Heller lit Wilmot's cigarette and said, "I'll get someone to bring you coffee and a sandwich…"

"Before you go … how is the war going? Are we winning in Europe?"

Angered once again by Wilmot's hostile tone and the question, Heller snapped, "No, the Allies are winning. We, Great Britain, America, Canada, and our other allies are sweeping across France and into Belgium and Holland. The American Third Army is driving east along with units of the Seventh Army pushing north, and General Eisenhower, now in charge of this theatre, has an unbroken front from Holland to the Mediterranean. We have most of Italy, and Paris has been liberated. The Russians are pushing your forces out of the Soviet Union and the Baltic states and are now in Poland. American troops have entered Germany in force at three points – yes, that's right, we are in Germany. We're hoping to get your Führer's agreement for a total and unconditional surrender by Christmas." Heller sneered. "This is not classified information, Wilmot. You can tell your fellow Nazi lovers all about it when you get to your new camp in England."

Wilmot's gaze was unflinching. "That will please Max."

"It should please everyone. It should please *you*. You don't want to spend years in a prison camp, do you?"

Unable to hide his resentment, Wilmot grunted. "I want victory for Germany, Mr Heller. We have lost too many good men to lay down our weapons and surrender to the Allies. I think you are being over-ambitious in your estimate of what Germany and the Führer will do."

*He's a straight talker, I'll give him that,* Heller thought, and he decided to drop the subject before he admitted he didn't like the youngest Vogel. "Max was wounded in France. He should be in a hospital in Britain by now."

At last, concern replaced Wilmot's surly expression. "Will he be all right?"

"Yes – eventually – it was a serious injury." Heller went to the door and opened it. "Getting you to Britain is a good thing, Wilmot. You'll see,"

\*\*\*\*\*\*

*London, England*
*29 September 1944*

The British soldier opened the three metre-by-three metre cell door and gestured with his thumb for Wilmot to get up off the floor. "Right, we have a change of scenery for you, Staff Sergeant. Come with us; you've got visitors."

After handcuffing Wilmot's wrists, two British soldiers escorted him along a corridor and up the stairs. Wilmot was both dreading and excited about seeing his family; he presumed they were the visitors the Englishman, Heller, had promised him the previous day. His heart cried out for his mother, but it also thumped with an anger he couldn't still.

'Do not bring that traitor to see me,' he had demanded of a shocked Heller. 'My father was dead to me, and he still is.'

He regretted the harsh words now, as he regretted many of his previous temper tantrums. He did want to see his father, but only because he needed to tell him what he thought of him to his face, and then, hopefully, rebuild their relationship down the road. He loved his papa, but all he'd thought about on his long, thirty-hour flight across the Atlantic Ocean on the Yankee Clipper seaplane, and since then in his cell, was how he could possibly forgive his father's betrayal and at the same time remain loyal to Germany. The two didn't go hand in hand.

"In you go," the British soldier said, poking Wilmot in the back as he stood in an open doorway.

Wilmot entered the sparsely furnished room with the customary desk and chairs as its centrepiece. *Another room,* he thought. *More forms to fill out, and more tedious questions to answer.* He was annoyed with the British. He was a Wehrmacht NCO, but they hadn't allowed him to wear his uniform. 'Isn't that against the rules of the Geneva Convention?' he had asked Heller.

"Take a seat," the soldier ordered, then he had given Wilmot a meaningful glare as he removed the handcuffs and left the room, closing the door behind him.

Wilmot let out a dejected sigh and slumped angrily into the hard chair. *What the hell am I doing here when I should be working in Mr Barrett's fields, or sitting at his kitchen table eating Mrs Barrett's waffles with syrup whilst gazing at my love, Dottie?* Thank God, he'd had the foresight to pen a note for Dottie and leave it with Egon. It had read:

*I have been sent away, but I will return for you, my darling, Dottie. Do not forget me or think I have abandoned you. You will see me one day soon, and we will marry. Promise me you will wait.*

Egon had been devastated. He had cried at the news, but Wilmot had been more concerned at the time about his friend forgetting to pass Dottie the note at the camp hospital…

The door opened. Wilmot stood, turned, and came face to face with his mother. She looked older; grey peppering her black hair, wrinkles around her eyes, her loving smile, tremulous and hesitant. His Mama, wrapped in a black coat, looking like a vulnerable little bird, gasping at the sight of his scarred, disfigured face.

"My darling boy," she said, rushing into his arms. "My baby … my Wilmot … my son!"

He pushed her gently away to look at her at arm's length. He was crying, but the hot tears streaming unabated down his face felt wonderful and real, as his emotions, smothered for years, surged and almost overwhelmed him.

Laura helped an overawed Wilmot to the chair, pulled over another one, and sat so close to her son, their knees brushed together. "Please don't cry, Willie. I'm here … I'm here," she sobbed, cupping his wet face in her hands.

Wilmot whispered through his wracking sobs, "*Mutti*, I never thought I would see you again. Even when I got your letters in America, I didn't dare to think about us being together like this. I've missed you. I've wanted to tell you about all the terrible things I have done, and all the horrors I have seen … and the things that were done to me. Mutti, do you hate me for serving Germany?"

"Oh, Son, no … no, of course, I don't."

As they hugged again, Wilmot realised he had not planned to ask that last question. *Why should he be in any way apologetic for supporting the Third Reich when he had grown up in a house with a father who had been a loyal Nazi Party financial donor?* He pulled away again, still overwhelmed with joy, but now also being nagged by a more malevolent inner voice.

"I know about my father being alive. You were wrong to lie to me."

"Wilmot…"

"Please, don't speak – don't defend Father or yourself…"

"She has nothing to defend. If you want to get angry, Son, you will do it with me. Leave your mother out of this."

Wilmot turned sharply in the chair, saw Dieter standing in the doorway, then turned back to Laura. "I can't…"

"Yes, you can, and you will," Laura said decisively, standing. "I will come back after you and your father talk." She bent down, kissed Wilmot's forehead, and then gazed at his face. "My darling, darling beautiful boy," she sobbed again.

After Laura had left, Wilmot glared at Dieter, who sat in a chair on the other side of the desk. Every bone in his body wanted him to get up, kiss his father's cheek and shake his hand, but bitterness and the memory of his staggering grief on the Russian Front when he'd received Kriminaldirektor Biermann's letter announcing that Dieter Vogel had been killed in a bomb attack, still haunted him.

"Mr Heller told me you didn't want to see me," Dieter eventually said, breaking the silence.

"That's right, so why are you here?"

Dieter flinched as if he'd been slapped across the face. He coughed, then recovered to say, "I will speak, Wilmot, and if you don't like what I have to say, I will leave. Is that okay?"

Wilmot was breathless. Unable to handle the emotional turmoil, he begged, "Please go."

"No, not until I explain my reasons to you."

Wilmot felt a tightness in his chest. He took in a long breath, then let it out. "Father, please, leave me. This is too much for me. I am a prisoner of war, and I shouldn't be getting special treatment from the British, who are my enemy. I don't want it."

Dieter's eyes filled up with hurt, but again he recovered. He sniffed, then smoothed down his moustache with his fingers; the thick white line across his top lip was the remnant of the beard he had finally shaved off that morning. Then with his eyes glued to Wilmot's face, he began his story, timidly at first, but becoming more passionate as he went through the years leading to the present.

"… I don't regret any of it, Son. Had I thought we could have unseated Hitler by democratic means, I would have stayed to fight him, but we both know he is a dictator who has never respected the rights of others' political ideals, race, or religion."

Wilmot swallowed painfully. He was shocked, even though he had long suspected the Führer's crimes against the peoples of Europe. He was saddened by his father's accounts of gas being fabricated in German and Polish factories, of special chambers with ovens in which Jews and other ethnic races were burnt after being gassed to death. He was disturbed by his father's calculations on the numbers of death camps being built to house and kill citizens across the continent. He was also disgusted by his portrayal of Kriminaldirektor Biermann, who had been nothing but kind to him.

His fellow prisoners in Kansas had whispered about atrocities and racial cleansing going on in Poland; about Jews and Christians disappearing by the thousands. Wehrmacht soldiers who had recently arrived in Kansas from France had also mentioned the deportations of hundreds of thousands of Jews. Some had gone as far as to suggest they were being exterminated. But since Günter's beating in Hut 64, Wilmot had steered clear of all discussions on the state of the war now being fought against the Allies on European soil; instead, he had poured his energy into helping Günter regain fitness, protecting Egon's back from bullies, and being creative in the Hobby Hall to impress his sweet Dottie. This talk was unbearable, yet his father went on and on…

"… we have proof, Son. The Polish Resistance had a man inside a camp called Auschwitz. He witnessed with his own eyes what I have described to you. Of course, none of it is public knowledge…"

Wilmot's head was exploding. He glared at Dieter with eyes narrowed with pain. "That's enough! Please, no more, Papa – no more of this talk. You are a traitor; that's the truth you're skirting with all this nonsense about slaughters and racial cleansing. You are the criminal, not the Third Reich!"

Dieter looked at his son levelly, man-to-man, and Wilmot felt his stomach knot. When his father spoke, his voice was almost unbearably soft. "I would so much rather be a traitor, my Son, than an accomplice to genocide. *That* is the truth."

An hour later, Dieter, Laura and Heller discussed Wilmot's future in a pub opposite the prison where Wilmot was being held. Dieter had not made a breakthrough with Wilmot, but Laura had assured her husband that despite the anger and hurt, their little boy was still the loving son he had always been.

"My son hates me. I'm not certain he will ever forgive me, Laura," Dieter said.

"He needs time, Dieter. When I went back in, he was weeping. My love, you mustn't be hard on him or yourself. Learning you were alive and working for the enemy must have been a terrible shock for him," Laura responded, giving his hand an affectionate squeeze.

"He'll have time to come to terms with it where he's going," Heller said.

"Will we be able to visit him?" Laura asked.

"No, I'm sorry, Laura, but this is as far as I can take this. You won't be able to visit him or deliver packages or notes by hand. He must not be seen to have ties to England or to receive any privileges other than those that are given to his fellow prisoners."

"Jonathan is right, dear. We don't want the hardcore Nazi prisoners to pick on him." Dieter downed the whisky he'd ordered to settle his nerves. "What happens now, Jonathan?"

"His destination should remain secret, and I count on you that it will." Heller's eyes bored into Laura.

"Of course. Who am I going to tell?"

"Hannah and Judith mustn't know."

"Oh," Laura's face fell. "I promise, I won't say a word."

"He's being transported to Winter Quarter Camp, in Ascot, Berkshire. Your son is clever. He asked me what his cover story will be when he suddenly arrives at a camp full of suspicious Germans. He knows what to say, and he knows how to behave." Heller smiled at the Vogels whose faces were strained with concern. "He's a decent man. He'll get through this, and you will too. Hold on to this thought … when the war ends and he's released, you can both meet him at the camp's gates and take him home. Be patient, Laura."

Laura, who had started crying again, clutched Heller's hand. "Knowing he's in England will help *us* get through this too. I don't know how to thank you, Jonathan. You really are a godsend to my family."

# *Epilogue*

# *I*

*Mauthausen-Gusen Concentration Camp,
Austria, 5 May 1945*

Kurt opened his eyes from a restless nap and stared up at the wooden ceiling above his bunk. *Today. It must be today,* he thought. He rolled onto his side and dry-heaved over the edge of the bed, then groaned with stomach pains as he turned again to lie on his back. It was past dawn. A brilliant white light was shining through the glassless, barred window, breaking on the side of his face. The sun was up, but he wasn't going anywhere: no work in the quarry, no roll call, no possible death at the hands of the SS for no other reason than he was still breathing and was in the wrong place at the wrong time. It had been an astonishing three days, during which the lives and futures of the inmates had been turned on their heads, and the seemingly omnipotent SS and Gestapo guards had run for the hills in fear.

Kurt twisted his head to the right. Romek, lying in the same bunk, was as still as a dead man, his lips parted, his face serene – but he was breathing. Nothing, not even the brutish Kapos had managed to end Romek Gabula.

The young man lying on Romek's right-hand side was unequivocally dead and probably had been for hours; rigour mortis had set in, and he was as stiff as the wooden board they lay on. His caved-in face with harshly protruding cheekbone ridges made his eyes look as though they had been pushed into deep hollows. His dropped jaw and gaping mouth revealed bare gums and a swollen black tongue, and old facial scars were black against his whitish-grey, waxy skin. Bogdan, his long-time Polish friend, had fought hard in Warsaw and was a hero to his people. How undeserving he was of this cruel, undignified end which left him the equal of every other corpse in the camp.

Kurt shook Romek a second time. "Come on, Romek, wake up. Romek, I must tell you about last night."

"Shut up, Kurt. I will not move from here until someone with proper authority arrives. Everyone has gone mad, and I'm not dying now in a chaos of our own making."

Kurt pulled out his winning card. "The SS guards have left and so has Commandant Ziereis. Most of the Austrian police have also gone. We're hunting for Kapos. Don't you want revenge?"

Romek checked Bogdan's pulse, then pushed his corpse off the bed. "*Psiakrew* – damn it, Bogdan." With a heavy heart, he rolled onto his side to face Kurt. "It's really happening?" His emaciated face brightened with the possibility of liberation.

"Yes. The *Volksstrum* militia and the Vienna firemen they brought in have left, too. Guess where I was three hours ago?"

Romek groaned, "No riddles, please."

"I went to the kitchens. Prisoners were swarming all over it, looking for food. A fight broke out, and people were stabbed with carving knives. I managed to get this."

Kurt, who had been hiding the unopened tin of sardines in his baggy inmate trousers, whipped it out like magic. "When you feel well enough to get up, we'll go look for something to open it with."

"I see you got yourself a shirt at last," Romek croaked, his lips turning up in a slight smile.

"And I also brought one for you," Kurt said, pulling it out from under his thigh. Men were like gluttons, rigging themselves out with four or five shirts and two or three pairs of trousers. "After we left the kitchens, I followed the crowd to the *Kommandantur's* offices. I shouldn't have gone there. Another fight started over some tins of food hidden in Ziereis' desk drawers. They destroyed the place..."

Kurt stopped talking and studied Romek. His friend's skin was pasty, and his breathing was laboured. He looked worse than he had the previous day. "You're right, Romek. You stay where you are ... no sense in both of us going out there. If there's food and water, I will find it and bring it back. Don't you dare die on me."

"I'll try not to," Romek said, a strange quiescence in his voice as he stared again at Bogdan.

Kurt was worried sick, both literally and figuratively. About three hundred prisoners were dying from typhus every day. Since January, Jews who had been in the death camps in and around Poland had been arriving in their thousands from *death marches,* as those who had walked the hundreds of miles called them. According to recently arrived Jews, thousands of people had died on the road or were shot because they couldn't keep up on the gruelling march. More had died than arrived, one man stated poetically.

Kurt didn't know how many prisoners were now in the camp; by some accounts, maybe fifty ... sixty thousand. For the first time since arriving at Mauthausen, he had spoken to

Hungarian Jews who had been sent directly from Auschwitz to the Mauthausen subcamp of Gusen to work in the munition's factories.

*Was Romek dying of typhus?* Kurt wondered, glancing at his friend whose eyes were now closed. God, he hoped not. The camp was rife with disease, lacking in clothing, shoes and linens, and not a loaf of bread was to be found anywhere. The subcamps, Gusen I and II, were filled beyond human limits. There were as many as five sick men to a narrow camp bunk, and it wouldn't surprise him if Romek had caught the disease through head lice from the recently arrived men whose heads had not yet been shaved. If help did not come today, the dead would pile up, and Romek would be amongst them.

Deciding it was time to move, Kurt rolled again, using every muscle as he laboriously swung his scrawny legs over the edge of the bed. Since being deported from Warsaw at the end of the uprising, he had lost almost a third his body weight. He could lie on the bunk with Romek to wait for an Allied army to liberate the camp, but he was also afraid he'd die if he didn't keep his mind occupied and his body moving. He hid the tin of sardines in the folds of Romek's oversized shirt; it would be safe there while he searched for an opener. Then, without shoes, Kurt went to join the prisoners who had organised resistance operations.

By 1000 hours, news that a group of prisoners had sabotaged the factories came back to Kurt and the men he was with. In the mayhem of the last three days, the transportation system had broken down. A few men decided to take their chances and flee the camp on foot, but Kurt was against that idea. Dangers lurked outside the fences; he'd pointed out to fellow Germans wanting to leave.

'SS soldiers are probably still in the vicinity. And where do you think you're going to find food, medical help, or clothing for the nights that are still cold? The Americans or British will be here soon. They will find this place, eventually.' But they left, regardless of him cautioning them to wait for the Allies, rumoured to be in Austria.

Along with another fifteen men, Kurt made his way to Block 6 where it was reported that a group of German scum and Kapos were taking refuge. The prisoners, armed with sticks, rocks from the quarry, and their wooden-soled shoes were weak with hunger; nonetheless, between them, they managed to knock down the hut's door and enter.

Inside, Kapos, who had a week earlier beaten inmates with batons for not transporting rocks up the one hundred and eighty-six steps from the quarry floor to the main camp quickly enough, cowered with block bosses and room chiefs. These men, who had over the years been complicit in the murders of tens of thousands of prisoners of numerous nationalities, were now on their knees begging to be spared with a hundred pathetic excuses on their tongues. "They made me do it – I didn't want to help them – I was a prisoner, like you." On and on they gave their contemptible apologies for the torture and death they had caused.

The Kapos and other collaborators were now going to die, and in the most horrific ways imaginable, Kurt thought, as he watched them being marched out of the hut. He wasn't willing to participate, but such was the depth of his pent-up anger that he was looking forward to watching them die.

In the roll-call yard, Kurt observed the last Kapo brute, discovered in Block 7, being hauled into the centre of an enraged circle of prisoners where his fellow murderers were already on their knees. Only one man stood, his arrogance mirrored in his upwardly tilting chin and in his angry, hooded eyes.

"They are going to suffer before they die … the way they have made our comrades suffer and die for years!" a bag-of-bones prisoner shouted.

What the inmates lacked in weapons, they more than made up for in numbers and rage. Kurt was shunted and knocked down as people pushed past him to get to their prey. Pure rage sat on the faces of every man in the yard. Those too weak to kick or punch were consoled by fitter men who pounced on the collaborators with wooden sabots on their feet or in their hands. Kurt, enthralled by the abuse, held his breath as the men floored their victims, and then began stomping on their faces and stomachs until their guts came spilling out and their heads were flattened into shapeless masses of flesh and tissue.

*Do I feel better after seeing that?* Kurt pondered on his way back to the hut. *No. We are all monsters.*

After seeing to Romek and finally getting him to share the sardines, Kurt went to the gates to wait for a miracle, a disaster; something extraordinary to happen. At 1300, his patience was rewarded when American trucks carrying about twenty soldiers broke through the trees.

Beside Kurt, dead bodies were piled up, ready for burial or burning. More bodies were piled high on handcarts. One could not escape the dead, for they were everywhere; either visible in the flesh or with their residual stench permeating the huts and in every corner of the camp. The Americans, with their stars-and-stripes flags fluttering on short white poles on the sides of their trucks, were going to be shocked, but Kurt couldn't care less about their horrified reaction to the genocide in Mauthausen-Gusen Concentration Camp. They should have reacted at least a year earlier when their government had been informed of the slaughters.

Metres from the main gates, Kurt surged forward with a crowd of Spanish inmates. They were surrounding an M8 Greyhound armoured car, and euphorically yelling, "Anti-Fascists salute the liberating forces!" and "Viva España!" Kurt laughed, their joy contaminating him as robustly as the many diseases in the camp.

Kurt got on well with the Spanish Republicans who had fought against General Francisco Franco's Fascist forces in the Spanish Civil War. Most of them had escaped to France when the Republicans lost the war, but they were interned by the French, and later, when the Germans defeated France in 1940, they had been incarcerated as political prisoners because of their hatred for the Nazis and Fascists. They were boisterous by nature, and despite their lack of strength, they out-shouted and out-sang all the other prisoners combined.

"You are happy, my friend?" Kurt cried, his eyes smarting with emotion.

"I am, Kurt. They are *nuestros salvadores* – our saviours!" the small, skinny Spaniard wept.

The sounds of celebration increased, but Kurt, spent emotionally and physically, was now on his knees. A hand touched his bare shoulder, and he recoiled from habit. He looked up at an American soldier holding out a flask to him.

"Drink … you want drink?" the young American asked with eyes full of sympathy.

"Thank you," Kurt replied in English, as he took the flask full of water and put it to his lips.

When he'd drunk a small amount, for that was all he could manage before becoming breathless, he handed it back to the American and asked, "Will you help my friend? He is in a hut not far from here. He needs water now. Please?"

The sergeant replied, "Sure, I'll help you. Your English is pretty good. Will you help us translate?"

"Yes, Sergeant. And will you help me get to a British intelligence unit? I work … I was an agent for the British government, as was my friend in the hut."

Shock crossed the American's face. "Gee, you've been dealt a hard hand. I'll talk to my captain about that." Then he nodded. "Okay, how about this … you get through to your fellow prisoners for us, and we'll get you to your buddies at the nearest British Company Headquarters?"

\*\*\*\*\*\*

Three days after the camp was liberated, Kurt and Romek, now dressed in the civilian clothes the Americans had provided to them, lay on mattresses in the yard. The two men had been starved for months, but they were in better condition than many of the inmates who had been incarcerated for years or those who had been marched to death. Prisoners were still dying in front of the Americans, who were doing all they could to help the inmates. Kurt supposed a starving person must get to a certain point where no amount of food, water, or medicine could resuscitate his body.

The American 11th Armoured Division brought in medical teams to treat the casualties, cooks to prepare calorie-rich food for the starved inmates, and engineers to clear the hundreds of corpses from the main camp. They also brought in Austrian civilians from neighbouring towns, who were being tasked with digging mass graves at the far side of the football field and quarry.

The American doctor gave Romek good news. The Pole had a severe stomach infection that would probably have killed him in days without the antibiotics he was now receiving, but he did not have typhus.

In the yard, Kurt and Romek lay on mattresses like kings, sunning themselves while eating crusts of bread and boiled potatoes in their skins. Upon his arrival, an American doctor had been furious to see soldiers handing out full loaves of bread to the inmates. Kurt, who had fought his way to the supply truck, had been horrified to see the food disappear moments after the truck's long-awaited arrival. In hindsight, however, after seeing many prisoners die just after they had eaten, Kurt agreed with the doctor's assertion; overfeeding prisoners whose stomachs had shrunk to the size of peas was more damaging than not giving them food at all.

As soon as he learnt he might live, Romek began mapping his future.

Kurt wanted to return to Germany, and as he chewed his crust, he said to Romek, "I am going to look for the Vogels. The American captain has promised to help me get to Berlin in due course. Will you come with me, Romek? I told the sergeant you were also working for the British. You don't want to return to Poland, do you?"

Romek took tiny bites of his potato, as instructed by an American corpsman. He swallowed painfully, then answered Kurt's question. "Poland is not an option whilst the Russians are there, but neither is Germany. I think I will eventually use my past collaboration with MI6 to get to England, but first, I have unfinished business in Paris."

Kurt raised a sceptical eyebrow. "You're not talking about the communist Duguay, are you?"

"Yes. If he still lives, I'm going to kill him, and if he's dead, I will piss and spit on his grave."

"Maybe you should let it go and begin afresh, Romek. Trust me, I watched the Kapos die, and their deaths didn't appease my anger. Making a good life for yourself … that's the way forward."

"There is no way forward while that scum Duguay still breathes."

"Okay, you know yourself best," Kurt said, popping the last crumbs of crust into his mouth.

"Why are you determined to go to Germany? I don't know why you want to go back there after everything those people did to you."

"I'm going to look for the Vogels."

"But they're in England."

"I know, but I can get to them through the British in Berlin. Why do you think I told the Americans about my connection to British Intelligence? Do you think they are going to give train and boat tickets and a new house to every inmate in this place? Anyway, I know Max and Dieter, and I'll bet you my boots they will turn up in Berlin to see what's going on."

"Max will take Paul's death hard," Romek said.

"I know." Kurt's voice was husky with emotion. "They are my family, Romek, and I must tell them how their son died – ach, I wish Paul could be here with us, and go home to Berlin with me – I'm so damn proud of that man."

*Berlin, Germany*
*5 June 1945*

Dieter and Max sat in the back seat of the British-registered Austin 10HP staff car being used by representatives of the British Intelligence Services. Dieter studied Max's profile. He had not spoken a word since leaving their headquarters in the British sector of *Ortsteil Zehlendon,* now more commonly known as the Green Zone. Not even the sight of British Union flags flying from tall white poles on every street corner and British soldiers marching in files of three in a spectacle of power on Berlin's streets had moved his son.

Dieter erred on the side of patience. He would not press Max into conversation or ask him how he felt; his grief was obvious. A light had gone out and cast a dark shadow over his face as if half the brightness in his soul had dulled. Max, a deeply private man by nature, had refused to talk about Paul and had, instead, plunged into work and the mission at hand. Not even Judith could get through the wall of silence he had erected.

As the British army driver took them west through Berlin's rubble-filled streets, Dieter swallowed his own grief and stoically stared through his tears out of the window. It had been a monumental morning; excitement still coursed through him, but that feeling was accompanied by dark, contradictory emotions: regret, sadness, bitterness; but then also the sensation that a renewal was coming, one in which his country of birth would slip into a more tolerant and peaceful age. His Paul was dead. The Vogel's opulent home in Berlin was irreparably damaged, his factories in both Berlin and Dresden were flattened, his holiday home by the river destroyed, his money in Germany lost; yet, somewhere in this mess, loomed a brighter future.

He glanced again at Max, and this time, the latter returned his gaze.

"Tell me about this morning, Father? Keep my mind off what we are about to do," Max said.

"I was not involved, of course. I didn't even get into the room, but I did manage to catch sight of the four leaders when they arrived at Niebergall Street in Wendenschloss. The Russian, Marshal Zhukov got there first – I presume because he had based his headquarters there. I thought he was going to fall over with the weight of his numerous Soviet medals. Eisenhower arrived second for the United States, our Montgomery with his oversized entourage got there a few minutes later, and he was followed by Jean de Lattre de Tassigny for France."

"Do you think the declaration will hold firm with all four countries?" Max asked, his face drained of colour, his eyes encircled by sorrow-induced, dark rings.

"It must. We cannot afford to upset each other, not whilst military forces are still armed to the teeth in Europe."

"I agree," Max said, "although I worry about Russia. Churchill has never warmed to the Soviets. He calls the Bolsheviks *crocodiles*. He's never trusted them. I think if there's going to be trouble, it will start with Stalin making moves to annex more land than he's been given."

"That is a possibility, but Winston Churchill will not always be in power to make the hard decisions for Britain. Heller accompanied Anthony Eden to Checkers Court earlier this year and told me afterwards that Churchill was worried about what will lie between the white snows of Russia and the white cliffs of Dover after the war ends."

Max mused, "I hope Churchill remains as Prime Minister to temper the notion of further conflict with a cool head. He doesn't dislike all Soviets. He stills feels a twinge of pity for Tsar Nicholas II, and he's praised certain Russian individuals in the past, like Savinkov and Maisky."

"I agree, but the reality is if the high commands of the Anti-Hitler Coalition who signed the declaration this morning don't stick to the accords laid down by the Allied Control Council, we may well be facing a new war with the East sooner rather than later."

The car arrived at its destination, signalling the second intelligence car behind it to also stop. "Are you ready for your last undercover job for a while, Max?" Dieter asked his son.

"This is something I will never be ready for. Let's get it over with, Father."

Dieter nodded. "Remember, don't speak unless you must. The more you say, the more chance there will be for Biermann to uncover you, and I will not allow that man to have the satisfaction of knowing Paul is … no longer with us."

A woman opened the front door. She stared at Dieter, then gasped as her hand shot to her throat. *"Mein Gott* – you are alive!"

Dieter, not in the mood to give explanations about his resurrection to Freddie's neighbour, Frau Mayer, asked, "Is Herr Biermann home?" He was also not inclined to call Freddie *Herr Kriminaldirektor. He is a murdering swine, that is all.*

Frau Mayer, ignoring the question, shot Max a contemptuous glare. "*You've* come back, too, Paul … after running away from your duty?"

"Is he home?" Max snapped, with less patience than his father had displayed.

She nodded, and despite Max's earlier worries that he and Dieter might not be invited in, she opened the door and led them to the living room.

Biermann sat in his armchair, looking frail, sickly, and timeworn. Erika, now two years and three months old, stood between his legs with her little arms resting on each of her grandfather's knees.

"No. No … it can't be?" Biermann stuttered, transfixed on the two visitors.

"Yes, Freddie, it can. Why are you so shocked? Didn't you always believe I was alive?" Dieter questioned.

Biermann flicked his eyes from a satisfied-looking Dieter to Max, and then back to Dieter, as if not knowing where to begin unravelling the knot of surprise.

Max stared at his niece, his eyes watering with emotion. Erika, with her golden curls and sky-blue eyes, had Paul's blood running through her. She was family. She was all he had left of the twin brother he'd adored. He sniffed awkwardly and realised that enacting this scenario was much more emotional in reality than it had been in his mind when he rehearsed it. He lifted his eyes to Biermann, who painted a perfect picture of an old, decrepit man, dressed in his pyjamas, dressing gown and slippers, with his hair greasy and sticking to his head, his mouth agape and his tiny round mobile pupils shifting nervously from one visitor to the other.

"I was sorry to hear about Valentina and Frau Biermann. Please accept my condolences. I am here to take my daughter home with me," Max said.

"How dare you! Take Erika upstairs, Frau Mayer," Biermann said hurriedly.

Max, leaning heavily on his walking stick, shot Frau Mayer a warning look not to move, then he hobbled a couple of steps towards the armchair. Erika was becoming upset. Her little plump lips were trembling, and she was cowering into Biermann, who had placed possessive arms around her. For Erika's sake, Max relented. "Frau Mayer, you may take my child upstairs. I don't want my little girl upset any more than you do."

"Frau Mayer, take her, now!" Biermann demanded, as though he thought he should stamp his authority on the matter.

Max waited until the neighbour had left with the baby before addressing Biermann. "Erika will be in my arms when my father and I leave here. I am her father, and I have the custody papers with me. Please, do not make this harder than it already is for all of us."

Dieter sat on the couch. Max, however, remained on his feet, for at times, sitting was more bother than it was worth.

"Well, here we are, Freddie. You and I sitting here like old times, chatting with each other like the best of friends. A lot has happened since the last time we did this, eh?" Dieter said, with a wry smile.

"You are no friend of mine, Dieter Vogel. Get out, both of you. I will not have two traitors in my house."

Max, although desperate to defend Paul's honour, reminded himself that the more words he uttered, the greater chance there was of Biermann discovering that he wasn't speaking to Paul. Meanwhile, Dieter shrugged off the insult.

"I may be a traitor to some, but I am a hero to others," Dieter replied through narrowed eyes that did nothing to conceal their contempt for their host. "You, Freddie are scum, and when you die, you will be remembered as a mass murderer, an abomination to all of mankind. Oh, I'm not innocent, but when I lay my head down at night, I don't hear the screams of the women and children dying in agony on my orders. I don't feel the perverse pleasure of seeing their bodies being incinerated in ovens – I can live with my deeds – can you say the same?"

"I did my duty to the Führer and the Fatherland. I am proud of my service to my country." Biermann threw Max a sneering glare of reprisal. "Look at you. I was right about you all along. You're no patriot. What sort of man abandons his army, his country, his wife, his daughter? I will fight you for custody of Erika. No court will give her to a deserter, especially not a crippled one. It's comforting to see God has punished you in some small way, although I would have preferred to have been informed of your death."

Dieter chuckled with genuine amusement sparkling in his eyes.

"Does the state of your crippled son amuse you, Dieter?" Biermann asked, raising an eyebrow.

"No, not at all. What I find comical is that you still think there are German courts. Let me tell you what happened this morning. Representatives of the four Allied States signed the declaration of the defeat of Fascist Germany. Adolf Hitler's successor, Karl Dönitz, tried to establish a civil government, but the Allies found that notion unacceptable. As a result of the gross criminal abuses of Nazism and in the circumstances of complete defeat, Germany now has no government or central administration – in essence, the vacated civil authority in Germany has been assumed as a condominium of the four Allied Representative Powers on behalf of the Allied Governments. There are no German courts, Freddie, no men in power who will do you favours, no one to whom you can kowtow or bluster or grovel to. No Gestapo to use as your personal resource for blackmail and coercion and bullying. My granddaughter will go with her father to England, and you will never see her again. This is fact."

Max, remaining silent, watched Biermann's face play a melody of expressions, as he tangled with both sorrow and rage. *Were Paul here, he would feel a modicum of pity for his father-in-law.* He would see the affection Erika had for her grandfather, and perhaps he'd even allow Biermann access to the child. *But Paul is not here,* Max thought, and he had no such qualms about ripping Erika from Biermann's arms and seeing the evil bastard suffer.

"Shall we go, Father?" Max said, breaking the long, tense silence.

Dieter smiled at his son. "Why don't you go outside for a bit of fresh air? I would like a word with Freddie in private."

"I despise you, Vogel, and I hate Paul for the coward he is," Biermann spat, as soon as Max had left. "I loathe your youngest son, Wilmot, too. He's a self-pitying whiner who thinks he has suffered more than anyone else. Cried like a baby when he was here. 'oh, poor me, no one knows what I went through.' Damn sissy. You can't possibly be proud of any of your sons."

"Oh, but I am, Freddie. Paul is wounded, but he will recover. Max is going to receive a medal for valour, and Wilmot will be returned to us from a prisoner-of-war camp within months. We receive letters from him every week. He plans to go back to America. My boy is in love. Isn't that wonderful?" Dieter's voice broke, but he quickly recovered. "My sons have fought well ... all of them. You, on the other hand, have proved yourself to be a monster who needs to be put down."

"I don't give a damn what you think of me! I did what I was ordered to do. I didn't shirk my responsibilities." Biermann leant forward in his chair. "You hypocrite. You felt the same way about the Jews as I did. You were all for the racial cleansing programmes, Dieter. I was not the one who facilitated the gas production ... that was you, in *your* factory. You know, I reported you to the SS and Gestapo. I told them you were a traitor and probably still alive, and they believed me, I know they did. You should not have returned to Berlin. Someone in the Reich will shoot you for the dog you are."

Biermann was sweating, and his lips were turning blue. Pity crossed Dieter's eyes, but it was gone in a flash. Rising from the couch, he said, "You really don't know what's going on, do you? You are a deluded old fool. Face reality, Freddie ... your glorious leader has blown his brains out. There is no Reich, no Himmler, Göring, Goebbels or Bormann – they're all defeated, incarcerated, powerless, or dead – already dusty words in the annals of history." Without another word, Dieter left the room.

Two British military policemen entered the living room seconds after Dieter left. They were followed by a British intelligence officer, dressed in a captain's army uniform. Sweeping his eyes over Biermann, he said in fluent German, "My name is Captain Duncan Anderson. Fredrich Biermann, I am arresting you for the crimes of mass murder and abuse of human rights, committed in the city of Łódź, Poland..."

"Get out of my house. Get out! You have no authority here," Biermann spluttered.

Anderson continued, "Abiding by the tenets of the Allied Governments' Declaration on German Atrocities in Occupied Europe, which states that those who planned, carried out, or otherwise participated in mass murder and other war crimes will be hunted to the uttermost ends of the earth in order that justice may be done, I order you to come with me." He nodded to his men. "Handcuff him."

"This is ridiculous," Biermann said, recoiling in his chair with a look of horror. "I am a servant of Germany! I am not a criminal. I did my duty – take your damn hands off me!"

Breathless, Biermann was unable to fight off the hands gripping his wrists and locking the handcuffs on him before pulling him out of the chair. He swayed on his feet like a drunk. "You will regret this."

"Get him out of here," Anderson said.

Being held up by his arms, Biermann looked around his living room with panicked eyes "I have to organise my belongings. I can't ... no, I can't leave my house like this! May I at least put on my uniform and say goodbye to my granddaughter?"

"We will see to your uniform," Captain Anderson said, without mentioning the child.

"This is outrageous. I demand a lawyer," Biermann panted as he was half-carried to the front door.

Frau Mayer stood on the top landing in the hallway, stunned realisation and fear in her eyes. Biermann shouted over his shoulder, "This is a misunderstanding. I'll be back soon."

Outside, the two British military cars were parked one behind the other. Biermann shaking with the weakness of body and mind, lost his legs from under him when he saw Kurt holding the back-passenger door of the second car open.

"No – no. This can't be!" Biermann, losing all semblance of dignity, froze in front of Kurt at the car door, panting for air like a heat-stricken dog. Unable to shift his ogling eyes from Kurt's face, he spat, "How are you still alive, Sommer?"

Kurt, looking thin and wan smirked, "Ach, call it fate … luck, destiny … the chance to do this. Get in the car, Herr Biermann. Mind your head."

When Biermann was pushed into the back-passenger seat, Dieter approached Kurt's car. "Wait a moment, please," he told the driver. Then he got into the car beside Biermann.

"You and I will never meet again, Freddie," Dieter said, with no hint of regret. "You will be tried with all the other criminals, and you will hang for your crimes."

"I will not. I was a German policeman. I did nothing wrong."

"Yes, that's right. You were *just* a policeman, not an important government figure at all, which means you will spend considerable time in a prison cell whilst awaiting trial. Perhaps you will even appreciate the luxury in which you will be held, compared to … the Łódź ghetto? Ach, look on the bright side, with a bit of luck, your heart will give out before you reach the scaffold."

"Go to hell, Dieter," Biermann muttered.

Dieter began to leave but turned back to Biermann with one foot already out of the car. "I almost forgot. My man, Kurt, mentioned you were interested in the whereabouts of my valuable artworks?"

Biermann stared at Dieter, as though hypnotised by his voice.

"Yes? No? Whatever. They were collected undamaged yesterday from under the floorboards of a hut in the Grunewald forest where I hid them in 1940," Dieter said. "They are in the hands of the British authorities now. I thought you would like to know."

******

Late that afternoon, Dieter, Kurt, Max, and baby Erika arrived at the Vogel's damaged house. Dieter got out of the car and looked at the one side of his home that still had a roof and walls. The Vogels would never live there again. It, like all other ties to their previous lives in Germany, including Dieter's sister and brother-in-law who had been killed during an Allied bombing raid, had been destroyed.

Laura and Judith hurried down the driveway, now devoid of the ornamental wrought-iron gates. Dieter, leaving the car first with Erika, beamed at Laura as he handed the baby to her.

"Meet your granddaughter," he said.

Erika, understandably traumatised by the brusque changes in her life, stopped crying and studied Laura curiously. Laura beamed at her in turn.

Judith took Max's arm, and Kurt followed behind as the family went inside.

Two hours later, the Vogels prepared to say goodbye to their old home. Laura and Judith had managed to salvage a few possessions that held sentimental value. The house had been looted, but no one had seemed interested in old photographs or the copper teapot that Laura's grandmother had given her years earlier. The teapot had been Laura's prized possession; the last thing her granny had ever given her before her death, and she had been delighted to find it still there.

Judith sat on the cushions of the broken couch with Erika in her arms, while outside, Dieter and Kurt packed the car with the family's bags. The little girl was comparatively calm and tolerant of the strangers who were cuddling and pawing her. She giggled at Judith, who was pulling funny faces.

*"Sappt!"* Erika demanded, mispronouncing the German word for juice. Then she quirked her head thoughtfully and added, *"Bitte schön?"*

All three Vogels jumped to fulfil her request.

Max, once again leaning against the living room wall, observed how easily Judith had slipped into a motherly role. "Are you certain this is what you want, darling?"

"Yes, my love. It is also what Paul would want. He will always be Erika's father, and Valentina was her mother, but we will be good parents to this little angel. I've never been as certain of anything, except my love for you. She will be our daughter, Max, and I couldn't be happier about it."

Laura, who had been at the living room window watching Dieter at the car, dried her eyes and went outside to join him.

"Are we ready to leave?" she asked Dieter.

"Yes, I'm ready."

Laura stared at Kurt, her eyes pooling with sorrow. "Kurt, you and I have not always seen eye to eye, but I can't thank you enough for looking after my Paul and for telling us about what a good, brave man he was at the end."

"I'm sorry we've not had the time for me to tell you everything that happened to him, but one day, I will write to you about his years in Poland, Frau Vogel." Kurt, who had been at the house upon the Vogel's arrival in Berlin two days earlier, glanced at Dieter, and then shifted his eyes back to Laura. "There is one thing I want to say. I don't know if it will bring you comfort, but you should know that Paul was in love with a wonderful woman. Her name was Amelia, and when they died, they were holding each other's hands. No one can be truly happy in war, but he was fulfilled with her at his side."

Kurt then surprised a tearful Laura by pulling Paul's journal from his inside pocket. He had removed the most intimate accounts in it; those parts he felt should remain with Paul. "He loved to write poetry and record his thoughts in this notebook. I know he would want you to have it. It will explain what was in his heart much more than I ever could."

Laura took it and held it close to her heart. "Thank you for this, Kurt. It means a great deal to me. Are you packed?"

"Me? Why?" Kurt frowned with confusion.

"You're coming to England with us, silly man! And I don't want to hear you calling me Frau Vogel again … I am Laura from now on. You are family, and we have plenty of rooms in our house in Kent. Dieter told me you wanted to make your way to England when you got security clearance, but we couldn't bear to leave you behind, so Dieter and Heller rushed through the paperwork with the British authorities. It's all been decided. I'm going to feed you up, Kurt Sommer, and I won't take no for an answer. That man! I can't believe he didn't tell you."

As Laura held Kurt in a warm hug, Dieter looked on and chuckled to himself. Finally, his Laura had softened towards Kurt. He had his old friend back, two of his sons were safe, and he was looking forward to spoiling his grandchildren.

All would be well for the Vogels.

Hi, dear readers.

I hope you enjoyed the German Half-Bloods Trilogy. If you did, please leave a comment on Amazon.
Until the next book, coming in 2020.

### About Jana Petken

Jana Petken is a bestselling historical fiction novelist. She served in the British Royal Navy and during her service studied Naval Law and History.
After the Navy, she worked for British Airways and turned to writing after an accident on board an aircraft forced her to retire prematurely.
She is critically acclaimed as a gritty, hard-hitting author who produces bold, colourful characters and riveting storylines, and she has won numerous major international awards for her works.

### Contact Jana Petken

Website: http://janapetkenauthor.com/

Blog: http://janapetkenauthor.com/blog/
Facebook: https://www.facebook.com/AuthorJanaPetken/
Twitter: https://twitter.com/AuthoJana
Pinterest: https://es.pinterest.com/janpetken/
Youtube: https://www.youtube.com/watch?v=gmrLECGgP8I
Goodreads:
https://www.youtube.com/watch?v=gmrLECGgP8I

Email: petkenj@gmail.com

## Other titles available from Jana Petken:

Multi Award Winning #1Bestseller, **The Guardian of Secrets**
Screenplay, **The Guardian of Secrets**
#1 Bestselling Series: **The Mercy Carver Series:**
Award-Winning Bestseller **Dark Shadows**
Award-Winning Bestseller **Blood Moon**
Multi-Award-Winning #1Bestseller, **The Errant Flock**
Award-Winning Bestseller, **The Scattered Flock**
Award Winning, **Flock, The Gathering of The Damned**
Multi-Award-Winning #1Bestseller, **Swearing Allegiance**
Multi Award Winning, #1 Bestseller, **The German Half-Bloods**
**#1Bestseller The Vogels: On All Fronts**
**Before The Brightest Dawn**

Audio Books

**The Guardian of Secrets,** in association with Tantor Media
**Swearing Allegiance, The Mercy Carver Series, The Flock Trilogy.**
**The German Half-Bloods.**
in association with Cherry-Hill Audio Publishing

69815437R00385

Made in the USA
Middletown, DE
22 September 2019